INSIDE DOPE

Paul Thomas was born in the United Kingdom and grew up in New Zealand. He graduated from the University of Auckland and subsequently worked in journalism and public relations in Auckland, London, Toulouse and Sydney. He has written several books on sport. *Inside Dope*, his first novel, was joint winner of the 1996 Ned Kelly Award for best Australian crime novel. His second, *Dirty Laundry* is also available in Vista.

Also by Paul Thomas in Vista

DIRTY LAUNDRY

PAUL THOMAS

INSIDE DOPE

VISTA

First published in Australia 1995
by Mandarin

This Vista edition published 1998
Vista is an imprint of the Cassell Group
Wellington House, 125 Strand, London WC2R 0BB

A catalogue record for this book is
available from the British Library.

ISBN 0 575 60394 1

Printed and bound in Great Britain by
Caledonian International Book Manufacturing Ltd, Glasgow

98 99   10 9 8 7 6 5 4 3 2 1

To Jeni, and to my mother and father.

Acknowledgements

The author would like to thank Penquin Books Ltd for permission to reproduce material from *Money: Whence It Came, Where It Went* (pp. 116–17) by John Kenneth Galbraith (second edition by Penguin Books Ltd 1995, first published in the UK by André Deutsch, copyright © John Kenneth Galbraith, 1975, 1977).

I want to thank Jacqui Porter and Neil Porter for their invaluable help. Thanks are also due to Steve Barter, Alan Everton, Murray Williams and S.K. Witcher.

Prologue

On a soft, overcast night in October 1983, a 38-foot yacht skimmed down the section of Coromandel Peninsula's east coast which faces Great Mercury Island on a 15-knot breeze from the north-west. Shortly before 3 a.m. it hove to off the long sweep of white-gold sand which is Otama Beach.

Running Dog was owned by a charter company operating from the Rushcutters Bay marina in inner east Sydney. Ostensibly, it had been chartered to cruise the Whitsundays; however, after clearing Sydney Heads six days earlier, the crew had turned *Running Dog* right rather than left and set sail for New Zealand. The crew consisted of the Dawes brothers, Bruce and Ron, a pair of minor and slightly disreputable identities in Sydney boating circles. Their fee for lying to the charter company, sailing *Running Dog* across the Tasman and back, and maintaining an attitude of total incuriosity towards the whole exercise, was A$10,000 which more than doubled their joint earnings for the year to that point.

Having to carry out their assignment on a 'no-questions-asked' basis didn't unduly bother the Dawes brothers: Ron's intellectual curiosity hardly extended beyond marine engines and weather patterns; Bruce, who was more worldly, didn't need to ask what it was all in aid of because he already knew. There was only one reason why anyone would pay ten grand for a clandestine boat ride to New Zealand and that was drugs. He assumed that the drugs in question were in the large plastic Esky which their client, who called himself John Brown, hadn't let out of his sight since they'd motored out of the marina.

Ron Dawes dropped the mainsail and the yacht rolled lazily on the gentle swell. Only the occasional slap of the sea against the hull and the rhythmic murmur of little waves licking at the sand 100 metres away disturbed the hush which falls on an empty stretch of coast in the dead of night. No lights shone.

'This is it, Mr Brown,' said Bruce Dawes. 'You want me to give the signal?'

Brown nodded. Dawes stood up in the cockpit and pointed a heavy torch at the shore. He flicked the beam on and off three times, waited a few seconds, then repeated the signal. An answering signal – two flashes, pause, one flash – came from the beach.

Brown gave Bruce Dawes a quick, nervous grin. 'Sweet as a rat,' he said. 'I'll just grab my stuff from down below.'

'Drop the pick, Ron,' said his brother. 'Nice and quiet.'

Five minutes later Bruce Dawes called down to Brown in the cabin that the pick-up boat was approaching.

'Righto,' he replied. 'You and Ron better hop down here. This bloke's a bit shy.'

Brown came up on deck. He wore a bulky black anorak and carried the Esky in one hand and a nylon sports bag in the other. He put the bag down and leant over the rail to shine the torch on the aluminium dinghy which was drawing up alongside the yacht. He didn't like what he saw.

'Who the fuck might you be?' said Brown, biting off the words angrily.

The man in the dinghy, who was burly and dark with a Zapata moustache which threatened to overgrow the lower half of his face, held up a hand to shield his eyes from the torch beam.

'No names till you're off there, eh?' he said. 'You Know Who sent me.'

'Where the hell did he get to?' said Brown. 'He was meant to be here.'

'Come on, mate. Since when did you catch him up to this sort of caper – buggering around in the tide at this hour of night?'

Brown stared down at the man in the dinghy for a few seconds then let out an exasperated lungful of air. He dropped the sports bag into the dinghy and called down to the Dawes brothers: 'Thanks for the ride, fellas. Safe trip home.'

Brown, whose real name was Dale Varty, climbed over the rail and lowered himself into the dinghy. He sat in the stern facing the other man, so close that their knees touched. When they'd pulled clear of the yacht, the oarsman introduced himself.

'Grills is the name, Al Grills. I do stuff for Spurdle.'

'Pleased to meet you, I'm sure,' said Varty sourly. 'Nice of Spurdle to warn me I'd be collected by someone I don't know from a bar of soap.'

'Shit, you know what he's like about security.' Grills nodded at the Esky between Varty's knees. 'In there is it?'

'Could be.'

Grills chuckled. 'You're as cagey as he is.'

When they were a few metres from the shore, Grills shipped the oars. 'Now you just sit tight, Varty. Wouldn't want you to get your tootsies wet.'

He stepped carefully into the sea which came up to his knees and pulled the dinghy to the shore. Varty threw his sports bag onto the beach and climbed out over the prow. He helped Grills drag the dinghy a little way up the beach.

'What do we do with this?' asked Varty, indicating the dinghy.

'What do you bloody think?' demanded Grills. 'We take it with us. I've got a trailer on the car. Stick your stuff in there and we'll carry it.'

They carried the dinghy up the beach, through some low dunes and up a track past a few obviously unoccupied beach houses clustered in a small hollow to the shingle road where Grills' car was parked. Varty was getting the Esky out of the dinghy when Grills walked around from the other side of the car and said, 'Oh by the way, Spurdle jacked up a little welcome home surprise for you.'

Varty turned around. Grills was grinning mirthlessly and pointing a sawn-off .22 rifle at him.

'What is this – you trying to ratfuck me?' said Varty, his voice shaking with alarm. 'Spurdle and me had a deal.'

Grills, still grinning, raised his eyebrows. 'If I was in your shoes, pal, getting ratfucked would be the least of my worries.' He nodded at the Esky. 'Open it.'

Varty released the clasps and removed the lid.

'Back off,' commanded Grills.

Varty stepped back a few paces. Grills came forward and peered into the Esky. Evidently he liked what he saw because he straightened up nodding with satisfaction. He was still nodding when a figure materialised out of the darkness and slammed him over the head with a shovel. It was a savage blow, so savage that it wouldn't have added to Varty's bewilderment if Grills had been driven into the ground like a tent peg. Instead he crumpled like a crushed beer can as the sharp, bony clang of metal on skull echoed faintly in the stillness.

The newcomer was tall and wide-shouldered. He wore a long navy-blue raincoat, gloves, jeans and a turtle-neck pullover and had a stocking over his head. He put down the shovel, picked up the rifle and, with his other hand, reached into the Esky and brought out a sealed plastic bag tightly packed with white powder.

'How much crank we got here?' he asked.

It was a voice from the right side of the tracks; Varty was sure he'd never heard it before. 'Ten kilos,' he said.

The man whistled briefly, dropped the bag back in the Esky, snapped the lid on, and put the Esky on the back seat of Grills' car.

'My car's half a mile back up the road,' he said to Varty. 'I'll leave this one there for you.'

He climbed in behind the steering wheel.

'Jesus Christ, hang on a sec,' said Varty, running around to the driver's side. 'Who the hell are you?'

The man in the stocking mask wound down the window. 'Under the circumstances,' he said, 'I'd say I'm your guardian angel – especially seeing my instructions were to let him finish you off before I grabbed the stuff.'

'Instructions? Who from?'

The newcomer laughed, a rich, deep, pleasant sound. 'I think that better remain my little secret. See you.'

'What about him?' asked Varty, jerking his head towards Grills, who lay in an awkward heap.

'My sentiments exactly,' said the man in the stocking mask. Then he started Grills' car and drove away.

For a few minutes Varty puzzled over the mystery man's identity and how he'd been able to crash a party that was meant to be the best-kept secret since D-Day. How many people knew he was coming into Otama tonight with a cargo of cocaine? Obviously that cunt Spurdle but why would he want to pull some sort of triple-cross? His off-sider Grills, lying there with a caved-in scone? Safe to assume he wasn't in on plan C. The Dawes brothers in a manner of speaking but they didn't find out Otama was the rendezvous point until a couple of hours ago. That's the lot.

Eventually Varty decided that figuring it out would take a lot more time than he could afford just then and turned his mind to more pressing matters. It was a good thing, he thought, that he knew this part of the Coromandel like the back of his hand. It was an even better thing that just before he'd got off the yacht, he'd taken the plastic bags containing the ten kilos of pure cocaine out of the Esky and taped them to his body. When the mystery man discovered that all he'd scored was a shitload of high-grade Australian icing sugar, when Grills came to, and when Spurdle found out he'd been shafted, things were going to get too hairy for comfort. He had to hide the dope somewhere and then disappear, just get lost.

As it happened, Varty needn't have worried about what Grills would do when he regained consciousness because he never did.

One

It was an awful scream, even by Asian prison standards. The fact that it was so quiet in the cell at the time made it all the more unnerving.

The only sounds were the rustle of magazine pages being turned, the German humming softly to himself as he listened to his Walkman, the occasional moan from the Cambodian who had a large, ugly and, judging by the smell, possibly gangrenous wound on his right ankle, caused by the leg irons he wore as punishment for having seriously bucked prison discipline although no one in the cell seemed to know exactly how, and the quiet murmur of conversation coming from the corner furthest from the open toilet, where Duane Ricketts was playing Scrabble with one of the Nigerians.

As usual he was being trounced. Ricketts seldom won at Scrabble against any of the Nigerians and never against his opponent on this occasion, Augustine Adeyemi, the acknowledged leader of the seven Nigerian nationals incarcerated in the Bombat Drug Rehabilitation Centre which is located on the outskirts of Bangkok.

The name is entirely misleading since there is no rehabilitation involved in doing time in Bombat. It is simply a place where men found guilty of drug offences, usually of a minor nature, are sent to serve their sentences and, for all the authorities care, rot, as the Cambodian with the leg irons seemed to be doing.

At any given time there will be approximately 2,000 prisoners in Bombat, which comprises five compounds, each compound having a building containing up to 20 cells. This particular cell was on the first floor of Building 4 and was notable for the mix of nationalities it contained. Apart from

Thais, there were Cambodians, Australians, New Zealanders, a Dutchman, a German, an American and a Singaporean. And of course the Nigerians.

The presence of so many Nigerians in a Thai jail had come as a surprise to Ricketts. With undisguised pride Adeyemi had informed him that Nigerians were the world's best and most active drug smugglers, a status which had been officially bestowed in a recent report on international drug trafficking issued by the US State Department.

Bombat is a short-stay prison. Most of the inmates have been sentenced to terms of up to two years or are awaiting trial on charges which carry sentences of that duration when – rather than if – they are found guilty. There were exceptions: Dale Varty, like Ricketts a New Zealander, was nearing completion of a ten-year term and had been transferred to Bombat to await release. Adeyemi owed his presence in Bombat to the fact that when he was stopped by Customs agents at Bangkok International Airport carrying, as he put it, 'enough number one China White to put Switzerland to sleep', he'd also had ten thousand American dollars in his money belt. At Adeyemi's suggestion, the two Customs agents had split the money, taken the heroin, which no doubt found its way back into circulation within 24 hours, and replaced it with a small plastic bag containing two dozen marijuana seeds. As a result, Adeyemi had been sentenced to nine months in Bombat as opposed to 20 years or even life – which really amount to the same thing – in an even grimmer institution.

Ricketts called Adeyemi 'Jumbo' after a cricket bat he'd once had. The bat was a Stuart Surridge Jumbo, 3 lb 2 oz of finest English willow. When he'd got used to the extra weight, Ricketts relished the power the bat gave his strokes. At Keith Hay Park one summery Saturday afternoon he'd played a hook shot which struck the square-leg umpire on the left knee, shattering his kneecap. The ball had then cannoned off to the long-on boundary with scarcely diminished velocity. Ricketts had grown to love that bat.

Like most of the Nigerians, Adeyemi talked a great deal about – and sometimes to – his penis. Generally these monologues dwelt on his member's size, beauty and capacity to gratify the opposite sex. Now and again, he'd expand on this theme to muse on the white race's shortcomings in the penis department and what a pity it was that prejudice, culture and circumstance so often conspired to keep apart black men and white women, who, he believed, had much to offer one another. Jumbo's penis and his deep attachment to it reminded Ricketts of his bat, hence the nickname. Adeyemi thought it had something to do with elephants.

Ricketts got on well with the Nigerians. He didn't moan incessantly like most of the other First Worlders – as far as the Nigerians were concerned, spending time in prisons such as Bombat was just an occupational hazard – and he took his humiliations at Scrabble philosophically. Early on he'd got into their good books by teaching them a song he'd learned at intermediate school. To the tune of 'Funiculi, Funicula' the song went:

> Last night I had the urge for masturbation
> And it was strong, and it was strong;
> I took my penis in my right hand –
> What a prong, what a prong;
> I switched it to my left hand
> And pulled it long, and pulled it long.
> Whack it, smack it, bash it against the wall;
> Pinch it, punch it, anything at all:
> Because it's long, because it's strong,
> Because it's twice the length of me!
> Forty pounds of penis hanging down between my knees.

The song delighted the Nigerians, none of whom, as Ricketts had reluctantly but unavoidably observed, could be accused of singing it under false pretences. It immediately became part of the program for their nightly choral sessions. Sometimes they would be faithful to the traditional arrangement and perform it rousingly, in the style of a Gilbert and Sullivan chorus; other nights, perhaps when homesickness weighed upon them, it would be transformed almost beyond recognition into a quiet and rather mournful African chant.

As well as being the best-hung inmate in Bombat prison, Jumbo was the leading Scrabble player. This was no surprise to Ricketts who estimated that Jumbo spent approximately one-third of his waking hours playing the game, one-third studying the dictionary to find new words, and the balance talking about – or to – his penis.

At 4 o'clock that afternoon the prisoners, as was customary, had been allowed to escape the heat and humidity of the compound and return to the marginally less oppressive environment of their cells. The Nigerians were very well organised, having Thai bank accounts which they could access from prison to buy in supplies. As a result, they ate well by Bombat standards: prison fare, eaten only by those prisoners who couldn't afford to feed themselves, was two helpings of brown rice with fish heads a day. That lunchtime for instance Jumbo had cooked a remarkably tasty chicken and rice dish on the charcoal cooker in the compound, which Ricketts, on account of his honorary Nigerian status, had been invited to share. Thus when Jumbo suggested a game of Scrabble on their return to the cell, Ricketts was in no position to decline, even though yet another drubbing was about the last thing he felt like. They'd spread out their cardboard mattresses and made themselves as comfortable as possible on the stone floor.

After they'd traded monosyllables, Ricketts added 'oze' to a 'd' to make 'doze'. With 'z' being a ten-pointer and a triple-letter-score on the 'e', this was worth 16 points and represented a steady, even promising, start by his standards; usually when he drew high-scoring but uncommon letters like 'z' and 'x', he could never find a way to use them.

Jumbo's response was devastating: he added an 'r' to 'doze' making 'dozer' then, doubling up on the 'r' and using a blank for the second 'x', laid 'xeroxed' down the right-hand column. It began on a triple-word-score square and the second 'x' fell on a double-letter-score square.

'That's a brand name,' protested Ricketts. 'You can't use that.'

Jumbo shook his huge head. 'Oh no, man,' he said serenely. 'That's a fine word.'

He reached for his *Concise Oxford Dictionary*, opened it, coughed politely, and began to read: 'Xerox: reproduce by a certain process of xerography.' He snapped the dictionary shut. 'Now then.' He counted his score. 'Your word's worth 15 to me, 'xeroxed' is 22 times three equals 66, then add 50 for using all the letters – that's … 131. Extremely bloody good.'

A few turns later Jumbo built 'adipocere' and leant back with his head tilted to one side, admiring his handiwork. Noticing Ricketts' bleak expression, he grinned massively and said: 'Hey boss, you like that one?'

'Come on, Jumbo,' whined Ricketts half-heartedly. 'What the fuck sort of word is that?'

'Man, you've got to learn to trust folks,' said Jumbo with a satisfied smile. He reached for his dictionary again. 'Where are we? Okay, "adipocere: greyish fatty or soapy substance generated in dead bodies subjected to moisture".'

Ricketts grimaced. 'Useful word for a lifeguard.'

'I've been storing that little fellow up for weeks. Thought I'd never get to ...'

It was right then that they heard the scream. It came from the stairwell through the open door on the far side of the cell. After three weeks of sharing a ten-square-metre cell with 38 men, some of whom, perhaps as a result of habitual drug-taking or maybe because they were born that way, undoubtedly weren't altogether sane, Ricketts had got used to hearing strange, even disturbing, noises, particularly in the night. The scream was different: raw, shrill, agonised.

Whatever anyone in the cell was doing – leaning against a wall daydreaming of home, red meat and clean sheets, lying on the concrete floor hoping to doze off and wake up a year later, flicking through a dog-eared magazine or playing Scrabble – they stopped doing it.

'Holy Christ,' said Ricketts. 'What was that?'

Jumbo leaned back and shrugged. 'Probably just another little yellow monkey getting his lumps. It's your go.'

For the Thai prisoners, being beaten by the guards for such transgressions as not bowing low enough when walking past a guard or not grovelling sufficiently when speaking to one was part of Bombat routine. The beatings usually consisted of a truncheon drumroll on the skull, followed by a stomping, with a top-to-toe thrashing with a long stick to finish off. If he knew what was good for him, the victim would then thank the guard profusely for his time and trouble. The Nigerians, who appeared to despise all Thais, found these performances mildly entertaining and occasionally signalled their appreciation with a polite round of applause.

Ricketts shook his head. 'That wasn't a Thai getting worked over; one thing about the little buggers, they take their medicine without a peep.' He stood up. 'I'm going to have a look.'

Jumbo tut-tutted. 'Duane man, it's not your problem.'

Ricketts made his way across the cell, stepping carefully over and around his cellmates, who followed his progress with mute interest. He went through the doorway to the stairwell and looked up the steps which led to an identical cell on the next level. Halfway up the steps, wearing his trademark abbreviated cut-off Levis and striking a dramatic pose, was the Thai ladyboy who called himself Brandi.

The transvestite looked down at Ricketts wide-eyed, one hand pressed to his mouth, then back up to the landing above. Ricketts went up past him taking the steps two at a time. Dale Varty, the 53-year-old narcotics entrepreneur, was slumped on the landing, his face screwed up in pain. He was bleeding hard from the stomach. Standing over Varty with a knife in his hand as if trying to decide where to make the next incision was a Thai prisoner whose name Ricketts didn't know.

Brandi and the Thai with the blade were known around the compound as an item. Ricketts had heard talk that if one was that way inclined or perhaps just horny in a broad-minded sort of a way, Brandi was open to offers. The fine print was that the boyfriend wasn't too keen on Brandi taking his love to town nor was he someone who, if you'd upset him, it was smart to turn your back on. Given the talk and the scene which confronted him, Ricketts guessed that the stabbing was sex-related. The fact that Varty's shorts were around his ankles also tended to support that theory.

*

Ricketts said, 'Jesus, Dale ...'

The Thai shouted belligerently and inched forward, jabbing the air with his blood-streaked blade. It looked to Ricketts like the blade had started life as a pretty harmless piece of cutlery and, through hard work and application, grown up to be a fair imitation of a boning knife. It also looked to Ricketts as if the Thai had decided that he might as well be hung for spiking two blue-eyed foreign devils as one.

Ricketts took a step back and held up his hands in a let's-not-do-anything-hasty gesture. When the Thai stopped advancing, Ricketts pointed down at Varty.

'He's in a bad way,' he said earnestly. 'He needs a doctor.'

The Thai's flat eyes flickered to Varty. He spat copiously, missing Varty's left ear by no more than three centimetres, and muttered something which Ricketts interpreted as Thai for 'stiff shit'. Then he scuttled past Ricketts, heading downstairs. As he did so, Ricketts flicked out a foot to clip his heel. The Thai bounced three times on his way to the lower floor where he slid to a halt in a flurry of arms and legs at the feet of a guard who'd come to investigate. The guard proceeded to lay into him with his truncheon, presumably for failing to prostrate himself satisfactorily.

'Get a doctor,' Ricketts yelled. 'There's a man here's been stabbed.'

The guard gave the prisoner a final fierce backhander then started up the steps. He looked enquiringly at the ladyboy who was still emoting silently halfway up the stairway. On the landing he stared impassively down at Varty who lay on his back clutching his stomach. Blood was leaking between his fingers and running onto his bare thighs. The guard sat on his haunches and with surprising gentleness moved Varty's hands and inspected the damage. Having completed his inspection, he stood up, nodded curtly at Ricketts, skipped down the stairs, and led the Thai prisoner away by the hair.

Ricketts knelt beside Varty.

'Christ mate, what happened?'

Varty closed his eyes. 'What a way to go,' he croaked. 'Knifed in mid-blowjob by a jealous slope fag. The ladyboy's been waving her tongue at me ever since I got here. Well shit, there was nothing like that in the other joint so I figured why not? When I thought the boyfriend was asleep, I offered her a packet of Marlboros for a BJ. We came up here and were getting along like a house on fire when the little cunt crept up and stuck me. Didn't even get my rocks off.' He sighed heavily. 'Fuck, it's been that long, when the mutton gun went off, it would've been like a flock of seagulls flying backwards out my arse.'

Varty released a short, bitter chuckle which ended as a groan. 'Talk about a fucking loser – you know I was getting out next week?'

'You'll be right, mate,' said Ricketts. 'They'll fix you up. You'll be on the plane home before you know it.'

Varty's head lolled back. He tilted it up again with a grunt of effort and focused blearily on Ricketts. 'Come on, pal. He carved me like a Sunday joint. Besides, imagine the fucking bugs'd be on that knife.' As if to validate his diagnosis, Varty hiccupped gently and a little wave of blood surged over his bottom lip and down his chin.

Varty spat weakly and grasped Ricketts by the wrist. 'Listen, mate, if I don't make it, I want you to do me a favour. Will you do that? There'd be something in it for you.'

'You name it, Dale.'

'You're out of here any day now, aren't you?'

'If that dickhead from the embassy gets his act together.'

'You heading back to Auckland?'

Ricketts nodded.

Varty breathed laboriously and closed his eyes. As they waited for help to arrive, he told Ricketts his story. It took five painful minutes. Twice Ricketts urged him to save his strength but he carried on. When he'd finished, he made Ricketts recite his instructions to confirm that he'd got it all. Then he passed out. A minute later the guards arrived with a stretcher and a chubby little civilian Ricketts assumed was the prison doctor.

After they'd taken Varty away, Ricketts noticed Brandi the ladyboy was still hanging around.

'What do you want?' snapped Ricketts.

'My cigarettes,' said the ladyboy with a toss of his head. 'He owe me. You his friend, you give me.'

Ricketts brushed past him. 'You should give up,' he said. 'It's unladylike.'

Dale Varty's analysis of his predicament proved accurate in all respects and he died far from peacefully at 11.42 the following morning.

Two

Jason Maltby, the administration officer at the New Zealand embassy in Bangkok, sat in the back seat of the embassy Honda Accord and made a mental note to look up an encyclopaedia to find out who invented air-conditioning.

Whoever it was, thought Maltby, he – it would almost certainly turn out to be a he – hadn't been given his due, not by a long shot. To the diplomat's way of thinking, the inventor of air-conditioning was a towering figure in scientific history, up there with Newton, Edison and Pasteur.

Maltby had come to Bangkok having previously served his nation in London, Brussels and Canberra. After two months in the Thai capital, he'd concluded that his masters in Wellington could hardly have selected a less agreeable posting for someone of his physiology and temperament if they'd tried. Possibly Cairo; probably Equatorial Macheteland whose ruler kept a freezer stocked with especially fattened piccaninnies and where every second person from the archbishop down had AIDS. But that was about it.

Maltby's distinguishing features began and ended with his overactive sweat glands. When he'd worked in Wellington, it'd been a standing joke amongst his colleagues in the Foreign Affairs Department that he could break out in a sweat walking along Lambton Quay in the middle of winter into the teeth of a southerly howling straight off the polar ice-cap. In steamy Bangkok he had only to stray briefly from an air-conditioned environment for dark sweat stains to appear on his trousers. After 15 minutes in the open air, one continuous stain would run from his crotch, between his legs and up the seam marking the conjunction of his buttocks, proclaiming to the world, Maltby felt, that here was a hopeless incontinent.

And whereas in his previous postings he'd dealt with matters of some substance, all he ever seemed to do in Bangkok was traipse after reprobates who'd got themselves into trouble over drugs. Today, for example, he was on his way out to Bombat prison, which given Bangkok's more or less permanent traffic jam meant spending at least two hours staring at the back of his chauffeur's misshapen head, to finalise Duane Ricketts' release and to try to establish what on earth had happened to Dale Varty. That morning the embassy had received a garbled message from the prison to the effect that Varty had been involved in some sort of fracas and was in rather a bad way.

Maltby hoped Varty was all right. For a career criminal, he thought, Varty wasn't a bad sort; quite an engaging character in his own way. Which was more than one could say for Ricketts: he was about as engaging as a rat in a kindergarten. It wouldn't have come as much of a surprise to hear that he'd got himself sliced up in a brawl – or sliced someone else up.

Maltby remembered his first meeting with Ricketts. The police message had informed him that New Zealand passport holder Duane Kenneth Ricketts, 38, had been arrested on a possession charge. Maltby had expected an ageing-hippie type who'd come up to Thailand to get stoned for a few months, bum around, live cheap, sleep on the beach: feckless, clueless, probably crapping himself at the prospect of a couple of years in a Thai jail and pathetically grateful for a friendly face.

With the benefit of hindsight, Maltby doubted that Ricketts had a grateful bone in his body. When he'd been shown into the interview room, Ricketts had looked him over uninterestedly and without even bothering to sit up straight had said, 'You're from the embassy, are you? Bring any cigarettes?'

No panic, no drama, no 'I won't last a week in this place, you've got to get me out of here', no claims of being set up, no horror stories about the police, no complaints about prison food or having to have a shit on an open toilet in front of everyone in the cell.

None of that. Instead, telling Maltby how to do his job: 'Varty tells me you've just arrived. Yeah? Okay, I've talked to a few guys in here and this is how it works: the first time I go to court, it's just to confirm the charge and the plea. I plead guilty, no point doing anything else. The second time they offer me bail – it'll be about fifteen thousand NZ. I put up bail – get onto my lawyer in Auckland, he'll organise it. Soon as they let me go, I jump on the first fucking plane out of this shithole. The cops'll probably play silly buggers over my passport. They're meant to hand it over to you but they'll hang out for a bribe. Well, stuff that – 15 grand's all they're getting out of me. You can jack me up a temporary one to get me home.'

Then he'd tilted his chair back, eyebrows raised as if to say, 'Any questions?'

'Does it occur to you,' Maltby had replied, automatically adopting the patronising demeanour embassy staff employ to quell outbreaks of taxpayer assertiveness, 'that you're asking the New Zealand Government to collude in bail jumping?'

Ricketts had lurched forward, the legs of his chair banging on the wooden floor, and planted his elbows on the small table. His grey eyes looked like frosted-up windows.

'Tell me something,' he'd said slowly. 'How do they treat you, the local cops and the characters who run this place? How'd you describe their attitude?'

Maltby, caught off guard and aware that he was losing the initiative, had shrugged defensively.

'I don't know. Pretty offhand, I suppose.'

'Dead right. That's because we're Kiwis and we don't count. We're pretty much slugfuckers as far as they're concerned. Now if we were Japs … I could've been caught red-handed selling smack from a stall in the lobby of the Oriental Hotel and they'd still've been lining up to French kiss your freckle when you came to see me. If you were from the Japanese embassy, you'd walk in here like you owned the joint, scatter around a few million yen, and I'd walk out with you. But us Kiwis don't have that sort of grunt, do we? So we have to play by their rules. But give me credit for finding out exactly what the rules are. The fact is, it's not against Thai law to leave the country when you're out on bail; they're quite happy for me to piss off. Look at it from their point of view – they get my 15 grand, they get rid of me, and they know I won't come back. I'd say that's pretty cost-effective law enforcement.'

It still annoyed Maltby that Ricketts had been absolutely correct.

*

Before he issued a temporary passport, Maltby needed to know a little more about Ricketts and how he'd wound up in the Bombat Drug Rehabilitation Centre.

According to himself, Ricketts made his living finding people, mostly children, who'd fled the nest and, for one reason or another, broken off communications. When the parents got anxious, which could take anything from seven hours to seven years, they'd go to the cops who'd point out that the preservation of the family unit wasn't their responsibility. Some parents would be steered to Ricketts by cops who knew him or perhaps someone in social welfare he'd dealt with. His clients would give him their kid's last known address and he'd go find them.

A lot of it was looking for 16-year-old girls who'd run away from towns like Opotiki, Thames or Dargaville to have fun in the big smoke. Most of the stories had mundane endings: he'd find the runaway working behind a check-out counter at Foodtown or Woolworths. Getting them home was another matter – usually they decided that living in Auckland, while it wasn't the buzz they'd expected, was still a step up from what they'd left behind – but that wasn't his problem. Sometimes the ending came right out of the parents' darkest nightmares, the ones they didn't even share with each other, and Ricketts would find Leah or Jasmin or Shelley – 'such a pretty girl but she could be, you know, a little wild' – standing on an inner city street corner in high heels and a short skirt, with a packet of condoms and a needle in her handbag.

Ricketts also got referrals through a couple of Auckland lawyers. Now and again these led to Sydney to find daughters who were too busy getting in touch with their creative selves to get in touch with their families; or maybe sons who were pretty sure that Mum and Dad would freak out if they knew their broth of a boy, who'd captained the first XV and been a young Rotarian, now went home at night to a partner with a nipple ring, a tattoo and sideburns like Zorro the Masked Avenger.

Ricketts had arrived in Bangkok on 17 March on the trail of Toby Ellifritt, 21, who'd failed to front up at Auckland University two weeks earlier to continue studying for the distinguished medical career which everyone seemed to think lay ahead of him. Four days later Ricketts had found him sitting on the beach at Phuket smoking marijuana with a startlingly beautiful 19-year-old German girl called Petra. Ellifritt didn't seem surprised or impressed – let alone at all embarrassed – that his parents had sent Ricketts all the way from Auckland. He said he'd decided that medicine was for nerds and he and Petra were going to South America to look at Aztec ruins and stuff. When Ricketts asked him how he was fixed for money, Ellifritt replied that Petra's old man was the twenty-third richest person in western Europe so who gave a fuck about money? Ricketts said give him a few minutes, he'd think of someone.

Ricketts thought about pointing out that one didn't amass the twenty-third largest fortune in western Europe by being a benefactor to every pretty boy one's daughter scooped up for amusement value on her travels. He decided against it on the basis that, if he'd been in Ellifritt's thongs, he would've regarded any such advice as sour grapes. Instead he wished Ellifritt good luck and suggested that if he had a spare moment in between looking at piles of old stones and doing cocaine, he might like to send his parents a postcard from Peru. Ellifritt said he'd think about it.

Ricketts had returned to Bangkok on 22 March, checked into the Capital Hotel in Khao San Road, and made a collect call to Dr Phillip Ellifritt of Arney Road, Remuera. He'd told the doctor that his son was alive and well and would more than likely pitch up on his doorstep in three or four months' time, a sadder but wiser young man. *And possibly a full-race cokehead*, thought Ricketts as he put the phone down.

That evening Ricketts had purchased two heroin cigarettes from a man he'd met in a pool hall in Khao San Road. He'd returned to his hotel, laid down on the bed, and smoked one of the cigarettes. It induced a dreamy, floating sensation, slightly nauseating but on the whole rather pleasant. He assumed he passed out because when he woke up, he was lying on a concrete floor in a cell and someone was trying to steal his watch.

According to the police report, two officers had gone to the Capital Hotel at 11.15 p.m. in response to a call from a housemaid who said she'd discovered the guest in Room

202 unconscious on his bed. She'd been unable to revive him and, suspecting that drugs were involved, had called the police. The officers had found one heroin cigarette in the guest's toilet bag and remains of another in the ashtray beside the bed. They'd taken Ricketts to the Central Bangkok police station and, when he came to just after midnight, placed him under arrest.

Foreign Affairs in Wellington had nothing of interest to contribute to Maltby's file on Ricketts but the New Zealand Police liaison officer in Bangkok certainly did. His routine trawl through the Wanganui computer's database turned up the fact that Ricketts had once been a policeman. It seemed he'd embarked on an alternative career path shortly after being kicked out of the police force.

*

Duane Ricketts was saying goodbye to Jumbo Adeyemi.

'Anything I can do for you on the outside?' he asked the Nigerian.

'Oh no man, everything's just fine. I've only got a couple more months.'

'I might drop you a line one of these days. You got a permanent address?'

Adeyemi rubbed his chin. 'Well, you know, I'm a bit of a nomad, I move around a lot. Best idea, send it to Poste Restante, Stockholm. I'll get it eventually.'

'Stockholm? That's a long way from Mama Africa. How do you handle the cold?'

Adeyemi shrugged. 'I dress like a bear. I have a beautiful fur coat, gloves with fur inside, and a fur hat like a Cossack general. It's true the weather can be very hard but I like Swedish people. Especially the women.' He showed his perfect teeth. 'They are very open-minded – and very white.'

'I guess they don't come much whiter,' agreed Ricketts. 'Listen, Jumbo, maybe you can do me a favour. You've got contacts here in Bangkok, business associates?'

'Oh yes.'

'Let me ask you a question: what do you think happened to me? I mean, how come the cops got onto me?'

'Oh man, that's plain. Whoever you bought your stuff from fingered you. That's how some of the street dealers, these insects, work: they sell to you, then tip off the police. The police catch you with some drugs so you must bribe them to stay out of jail; they confiscate what you bought and sell it back to you or return it to the dealer, who sells it to the next sucker. Really, quite a neat little operation. You spoilt it by being unconscious – you couldn't bribe them so they arrested you.'

Ricketts nodded. 'I figured it was something like that. So that little weasel in the pool hall who sold me the cigarettes, he's cost me 15 grand. That's the bail, that's what it's costing me to get out of here. I mean, shit, apart from my house, that money was pretty much it for me.'

Adeyemi raised his eyebrows in sympathy or perhaps surprise that anyone could get so worked up over such a paltry amount.

'If it was your money down the gurgler,' asked Ricketts, 'what would you do to the fucker who set you up?'

'I would kill him of course – slowly if circumstances permitted. You want my associates to get rid of this cockroach? It can be arranged, no problem. It will be a parting gift to my New Zealand friend.'

'Christ, Jumbo, I don't want him killed ...'

'I have an excellent idea. The gangs in Lagos punish informers by cutting out their tongues. A person without a tongue serves as a warning to others.'

Ricketts nodded thoughtfully. 'Yeah, that seems about right: cruel but fair.'

*

Ricketts and Maltby were in the embassy Accord on their way back into town. Maltby had arranged for Ricketts to overnight in a hotel and catch the 8 o'clock flight to Auckland the next morning.

'This business with Varty,' said Maltby. 'I couldn't get much sense out of the superintendent.'

'What can I tell you?' said Ricketts. 'He went behind the bikeshed with a ladyboy and the ladyboy's steady didn't like it.'

'This ladyboy as you call him – her, it, whatever. He's a transvestite, I take it?'

Ricketts nodded.

'It never occurred to me that Varty was that way inclined.'

'I doubt if it occurred to Varty either,' said Ricketts. 'I think it was more a case that after ten years without it, he would've fucked a pot-plant.'

Maltby took a little time trying to come to terms with that concept. Having failed to do so, he moved the conversation on to less difficult subjects.

'The superintendent was saying you spoke to Varty after he was stabbed. Did he say anything I should know about?'

Ricketts looked straight ahead and cocked a bemused eyebrow. 'Well, I suppose your report should mention that Varty was attacked before he shot his bolt. It's worth having that on the record in case the ladyboy sues the government for his fee – he's still bitching that he never got his cigarettes.'

'Do you have to be facetious about everything?' said Maltby testily. 'The man's dead, for God's sake.'

'Exactly. He doesn't give a shit so why should you? All it was, if you must know, Varty asked me to do something for him back home – family business.'

They sat in silence until Maltby decided to do some needling of his own.

'Now that we've got you out, perhaps you can explain something: what's a supposedly intelligent person like you doing taking heroin? I mean, you should know the harm it does better than most people.'

Ricketts gave Maltby a long, slightly puzzled, slightly amused look.

'Jason, you mean to say you've never thought to yourself "I wouldn't mind trying it just once, just to see what the attraction is?" ' Ricketts turned away and looked out the window. 'No, I don't suppose you have.'

Maltby didn't react to Ricketts' implication. Instead, in as casual a tone as he could achieve, he asked, 'Actually, there was something else I was wondering about: why were you expelled from the police force?'

Ricketts shifted on the car seat and looked hard at Maltby, who willed himself to hold his stare.

'You've been checking up on me, Jason. I suppose that shouldn't surprise me. How come you didn't get the whole story while you were at it?'

Maltby looked away. 'All I saw was the bald fact. I think it said something like "conduct unbecoming for a police officer".'

Ricketts leaned back on the seat. 'I kept a photo, one of a set taken at the home of a guy I'd arrested. I showed it to a few mates and a guy who was hanging around, a friend of a friend, nicked it; he turned out to be a reporter for *Truth* and they ran the photo. The family and the lawyer kicked up a hell of a stink. It made no odds that they'd pinched the photo – as far as everyone was concerned, I'd given it to them. So I was kicked out.'

Sensing that he'd finally found a tender spot, Maltby tried to suppress a smirk. 'That's laconic even by your standards but listen, if you'd rather not talk about it …'

Ricketts smiled back. 'Shit, it doesn't worry me. You want to know the details, fine. Come to think of it, it's probably right up your alley. I was working at Henderson – this'd be 15 years ago now – and we got this call from a woman out near Taupaki who said her boy and a couple of his mates had seen this bloke doing strange things with a horse – farm-yard frolics if you get my drift. Me and another constable talked to these kids and there was no way they were mak-ing it up. The victim – a big black mare – was in a paddock down the road so every now and again we went out there and did a bit of surveillance. A few days day later I'm sit-ting in amongst the trees keeping an eye on Black Beauty and an old bloke, about 60, comes along. He's acting a bit shifty, looking around and that, and he's got a rope in one hand and a beer crate in the other. He tethers the horse, puts the crate down behind her, hops up on it, drops his tweeds and starts rattling away.'

Maltby looked incredulous. 'Good grief. What did the horse do?'

'Yeah, everyone asks that. It sort of looked at the bloke over its shoulder as if to say "Oh Christ, not you again" and just carried on grazing; didn't seem too bothered one way or the other. Anyway, I arrested the poor old bugger. Later we went to his place and' – Ricketts' mouth formed a tight and, to Maltby, rather nasty grin – 'here's the funny part: he had horse photos all over the walls, like pin-ups. He even had bloodstock magazines in the bog. We took a few photos for evidence. The one I kept was of the guy's bedroom – there was a bloody great colour poster of a horse on the wall opposite his bed. The horse was arse-on to the camera – the view from the beer crate, so to speak.'

Three

Jason Maltby sat in his office in the New Zealand embassy in Bangkok staring at the telephone on his desk. He'd turned his attention to the phone after having gazed for some 15 minutes at the cream-painted wall which he found restful but lacking in inspiration, and then, more briefly, at the painting which hung to the left of the door.

To Maltby the painting, a still life of an unremarkable vase surrounded by cylindrical, purplish objects, symbolised everything that was unsatisfactory in his life. He knew that the cylindrical, purplish objects were tamarillos because the artist herself had told him so. The artist was the ambassador's wife, which explained why the painting disfigured Maltby's office instead of being where it belonged – out of sight and out of mind in a storage cupboard, behind the reams of embassy letterhead with the out-of-date telephone number which the ambassador insisted on keeping in case of emergency. Quite what sort of emergency he had in mind was unclear to Maltby; given the paper's coarse texture and sharp edges, he hoped the ambassador hadn't picked up a whisper on the diplomatic circuit that Thailand was about to experience a severe shortage of toilet paper.

Maltby regarded the telephone with as much distaste as he had *Oriental Vase with Fresh Fruit*, which the ambassador's wife had knocked off in a two-hour creative frenzy after a sudden downpour had forced the cancellation of her weekly tennis lesson. He had no particular objection to the phone itself – it worked more often than not and his vigorous cleaning had, he was sure, removed most of the germs left on the mouthpiece by previous users. What disturbed him was the knowledge that he was going to have to pick it up and make a call in the course of which he would entreat, cajole and plead. And, when each of those approaches had failed, as he was pretty sure they would, he was going to have to grovel.

It wasn't the grovelling per se which bothered Maltby. He had, after all, been in the diplomatic service for 15 years and had therefore grovelled for his country on occasions too numerous to recall. He'd also done a fair amount of grovelling in his own cause to ambassadors he'd served under, departmental superiors and junketing politicians. *And a fat lot of good it's done me*, he thought bitterly.

What really bugged Maltby was that the person to whom he was about to grovel was someone he'd known and patronised for almost 25 years. When he was completely honest with himself, Maltby could identify only half a dozen people to whom he could confidently condescend and they included his parents. Any erosion of this little group's membership had unpalatable implications.

Five days previously Bernie Gemmell, a New Zealand Press Association journalist based in Hong Kong, had passed through Bangkok. Gemmell had managed to talk his bureau chief into letting him make a three-week tour of the region to research what would supposedly be a weighty series of features on the Asian economic miracle. Had the bureau chief been less preoccupied with his upcoming job interview with the *Asian Wall Street Journal*, he almost certainly would have vetoed the request on the grounds that the subject had already been done to death by commentators far better equipped for the task than Gemmell.

Gemmell and Maltby had attended Palmerston North Boys High School together in the early 1970s and subsequently kept in regular if not close touch. During Gemmell's brief stay in Bangkok, they'd gone out for a meal and a few beers. Late on in the evening, Maltby had mentioned his recent dealings with Dale Varty, who was about to re-enter society after a ten-year stretch.

Without taking his eyes off the bargirl gyrating on the small stage, Gemmell had replied: 'Oh yeah, and who's Dale Varty when he's not in the clink?'

'Didn't I mention that?' said Maltby, enjoying the moment. 'Dale Varty is probably the last surviving link with the original Mr Asia drug syndicate.'

Having got Gemmell's attention, Maltby told the story hinting, at regular intervals, that there was a direct cause-and-effect relationship between his joining the Bangkok embassy staff and Varty's imminent freedom. When Gemmell began making notes on the back of a coaster, Maltby made him promise not to file a story before 14 April, Varty's release date.

Maltby was thus confronted with an extremely tricky task: he had to explain to Gemmell that events had moved along somewhat since their night on the tiles and that the story as outlined – 'Deft Diplomacy Gets ex-Mr Asia Man out of Asia' – no longer stood up; he then had to persuade Gemmell not to go with the new and rather more sensational version – 'Transvestite Holds Fatal Attraction for ex-Mr Asia Man'. Maltby knew very well that getting Gemmell to hold fire on such a juicy yarn would be difficult; failure, however, brought to mind various appalling scenarios which could be summed up in just two words – Equatorial Macheteland.

Before Maltby began staring vacantly at the wall, he'd been in the ambassador's office briefing him on the sordid circumstances of Dale Varty's demise. As he listened to Maltby's report, the ambassador's pink, bland features had gradually arranged themselves in an expression of pure revulsion.

'My God, that's bloody charming, that is,' he exclaimed when Maltby concluded. 'Look here, Jason, if we do nothing else, let's make absolutely sure the press don't get wind of this. The buggers would have a field day; they'd make it into an international incident and we'd get it in the neck from both sides.'

Up until that moment Maltby hadn't reassessed his beery conversation with Bernie Gemmell in the context of Varty's death. He did so then, in one panic-driven flash of comprehension which triggered a full-body sweatburst: every pore seemed to dilate to the size of a gorilla's nostrils and begin pumping out perspiration like burst water mains. He exited the ambassador's office in a military jog-trot, towelled himself dry in the men's room and returned to his office to don a change of clothes, one of two full sets he always kept in his office cupboard.

Having stiffened himself for the task, Maltby picked up the phone, dialled the number of the NZPA office in Hong Kong, and asked for Gemmell.

'I sorry, sir,' said the receptionist in a sing-song voice. 'Mr Gemmell out of town right now on assignment. He not back till next week.'

'Where can I get hold of him?'

'That not possible. You see, Mr Gemmell travelling in Laos and Vietnam. We don't have contact number for him till he reach Hanoi on Friday.'

'Well, surely he rings in regularly?' demanded Maltby. 'To get his messages and so on?'

The receptionist giggled infuriatingly. 'You never know with Mr Gemmell. Sometime he go away and we don't hear from him for a whole week.'

Maltby choked off a surge of envy. 'Oh, for God's sake,' he snapped. 'Very well, I'll leave a message. If and when he does call in, tell him not to proceed with the Varty story – that's V-A-R-T-Y – until he's talked to me, Jason Maltby, at the New Zealand embassy in Bangkok. It's very important, absolutely imperative. And get a contact number from him.'

'How you spell your name, sir?' asked the receptionist matter-of-factly, as if to say that she'd be the judge of how important it was. Maltby ground his teeth, told her and hung up.

Today was Tuesday; Gemmell had undertaken not to file until Thursday at the earliest. As long as he was arsing around in Laos and Vietnam, he wouldn't be sending anything to New Zealand.

Satisfied that he still had a couple of days up his sleeve, Maltby turned his mind to other matters. The subject had never really crossed his mind but if it had, he would've guessed that his old schoolmate lacked the technological nous to microwave a TV dinner. It certainly would've astonished him to learn that Gemmell never went on the road without his laptop computer and modem.

*

It really wasn't until he felt the exhilarating surge of power lift the Qantas Boeing 747 off the Bangkok airport runway that Duane Ricketts relaxed.

He hadn't slept well the night before even though for the first time in three weeks his bed actually was a bed as opposed to a sheet of cardboard on a cold, concrete floor. Maltby had warned him that the flights out of Bangkok to Australia and New Zealand were chock-a-block for the next month so he was dead lucky to have got a seat on the Qantas flight even though it meant a one-night stopover in Sydney. But if he missed that flight, he could be sitting around for weeks: waitlisted on flights, dragging himself out to the airport at 6 o'clock every morning hoping for no-shows; and all the time running up a hotel bill he couldn't afford. Each day he remained in Thailand would bring his trial date closer, and there was always the possibility of being hauled in and slung back in the slammer on the stroke of a pen of a malicious or simply careless clerk somewhere in the twisted bowels of the Thai legal system.

On top of all that, Ricketts felt it'd be sensible to have several oceans between himself and Thailand when the double dealer from the pool hall informed his pals in the police force, in writing and probably in a shaky hand, that he'd been de-tongued.

So he'd tossed and turned imagining that the alarm wouldn't go off, that the wake-up call wouldn't eventuate, that he'd sink into the mattress' soft embrace and sleep on and on, not waking till around midday, by which time the aircraft he was meant to be aboard would be approaching the west coast of Australia. In the end, he avoided missing the flight by a mere three hours and ten minutes.

As the aircraft climbed to cruising altitude, Ricketts recalled Jumbo Adeyemi's parting words. They were standing in the middle of the compound. Jumbo had briefly interrupted their conversation to swap banter with his fellow Nigerians who were playing a high-spirited game of Scrabble in the shade of the compound wall.

'They're good boys,' said Jumbo turning back to Ricketts, 'but I worry about them sometimes. They make plenty of money, you know, but they spend it all – on cars and women, women and cars. That's all they think about. When I was that age, I was the same except – this is very interesting – me and my friends, we all wanted American cars and European women; now it's the other way round. What does that tell you?'

'Dunno,' said Ricketts. 'Seems a bit rigid either way.'

'You may be right,' said Jumbo gravely. 'One shouldn't be too – what's that word, doctrinaire? – in these matters. Of course, in here I'm always talking about women and this big fellow' – he patted his groin – 'and so on but that's just to pass the time. Out there' – he gestured expansively – 'you must put your mind on the job. I tell you, man, when I became 30, I realised it made no sense, no sense at all, to do all these dangerous things and then see the money disappear. I set myself a goal – to stop taking risks when I reached 40. I began to be more careful, more choosy about the deals, I put money away in long-term deposits where I couldn't get at it, I made some investments, I didn't change my cars and women so much. Now I can stop as I planned.'

Adeyemi lowered his voice as if to reveal a confidence. 'I didn't have to do this run. And for sure, I would've preferred not to get caught but in a way, it's good for business to be here with my boys, good for team spirit. Next time, instead of thinking of me as the boss who sits in his big house counting the money while they're in jail, they'll remember I was here. But that's it; no more.' He draped a heavy arm over Ricketts' shoulders. 'Duane man, it bothers me, the fix you're in. It's no good to be like these boys – drift along, be cool, have a good time, don't worry about tomorrow. You've got to think ahead to when you can't run around anymore. In your situation, definitely, you have to keep an eye out for the big score. Then when you see the chance man, you go and make it, whatever it takes.'

I'll drink to that, thought Ricketts. He hailed a passing hostess. 'I'll have a couple of beers and a double Scotch when you're ready.'

The hostess, an experienced-looking campaigner, eyed him warily. 'This is a long flight, sir. Don't you think you should pace yourself?'

Ricketts shook his head. 'Don't worry about me, I won't give you any trouble. I have those drinks, I'll be out like a light.'

When the hostess moved away, Ricketts turned to his neighbour, a middle-aged woman who now had a slightly trapped look on her face. He smiled pleasantly and said: 'I just got out of jail.'

*

Special agent Harold 'Buddy' Funke of the United States Drug Enforcement Administration sat naked in the wing-back chair in Room 517 of the Royal Thai Hotel in down-town Bangkok thinking to himself, *Goddamn, I love this town.*

There were three immediate reasons for Funke's fondness for the Thai capital. They were draped across the king-sized bed wearing only the exotic lingerie which Funke himself had provided, and in poses which, because none of them were a day over 15, were more artless than lewd.

Agent Funke had joined the DEA in 1981 and spent most of the years since outside the USA. All told he'd worked in nine of the 73 foreign offices maintained by the DEA, which was created by President Nixon and progressively expanded by his successors into a vast global apparatus with a mission to wage war on the international drug trade. As the drug trade has grown, so has the DEA; the question of whether it constitutes a sensible response to the problem has long since ceased to be deemed relevant. Some of Funke's postings had been pleasant but a little on the quiet side – Bridgetown, Nicosia; some had been hair-raising – Asuncion, Port-au-Prince; some hellish – La Paz, Peshawar. None of them, even on presidential pardon days, were a patch on Bangkok.

The thing about Bangkok, as Funke never tired of pointing out, was that if you had greenbacks and the right connections – and outside of the royal family and the top military brass, not too many folks were better connected than a DEA man with some seniority under his belt – you could do whatever you damn well liked. Didn't matter what was your bag, your thing, your kink, no-one gave a fuck. And sure as hell somewhere in old Bangkok, it was for sale. Jesus, the things some guys did! Anywhere else, they'd lock 'em up and throw away the key.

Funke regarded himself as a normal, well-adjusted American. His particular fancy, which he indulged once a fortnight, was to rent a hotel room for the afternoon and send out for a jailbait three-pack from one of the girlie bars along the Patpong Road. Funke believed that a man hadn't lived until he'd been given a body massage by three bouncy, squirming, squealing, well-oiled little yellow-brown dolls. These sessions culminated in the girls arranging themselves side by side across the foot of the bed, sometimes on their backs, sometimes on their knees. As he worked his way back and forth along the line-up, Funke was reminded of a chess master playing several opponents at once, going from board to board making his moves.

Funke stood up, pulled on his boxers, and clapped his hands. 'Okay, kiddos, that's it for today. Uncle Bud's got to get back to work.'

As the girls scrambled off the bed and got dressed, Funke rang his office at the US embassy to check for messages. There was just one: the deputy superintendent at Bombat prison had called. Funke rang Bombat and was put through.

'Pong, Buddy Funke. What's happening?'

'Mr Funke, something happen at the prison I thought you be interested. A prisoner called Dale Varty stabbed in a fight over a ladyboy. He dead now. Before the doctor arrive, ladyboy hear Varty talk to another prisoner about lot of drugs hidden in New Zealand. I thought you want to know, that's all.'

'That's for sure, Pong. Who's the guy Varty told all this to?'

'His name Duane Ricketts, also from New Zealand. He gone now.'

'Say what?'

'Ricketts get bail. Someone from his embassy pick him up from here yesterday afternoon.'

'Shit, if he made bail, he's a gone goose. We won't see him for dust. What about the ladyboy, where's he at?'

'His name Kham Phumkumpol, call himself Brandi. He due for release next month. We very much like to get rid of him now – he cause plenty of trouble.'

'Ain't it always the way? Why don't you just push the little faggot back on the street? Say it's for his own safety or some shit like that.'

'I think maybe you right, Mr Funke. Maybe some of Varty's friends try to get even, huh?'

'They surely could. I was you, I'd just get him out of there. Say, Pong, you can do me one more favour – make a copy of the files on Varty, Ricketts and the ladyboy, okay? I'll see you in Chico's bar, 10 o'clock tonight. You bring the files, I'll bring something for you, pal.'

Funke hung up and sat in the armchair with his elbows on his knees, staring at the carpet. He was so preoccupied that the girls had to say goodbye three times before he responded.

Four

After leaving Bangkok first thing on Wednesday morning and overnighting in Sydney, Ricketts finally arrived in Auckland at 3.20 p.m. on Thursday afternoon. When he presented his passport at the Immigration counter, the official studied it for a moment then turned and nodded to a Customs officer standing behind the row of booths.

The Customs officer came forward and quietly asked Ricketts to accompany him. Ricketts shrugged and picked up his bags. He'd had a going-over from Customs at Sydney airport and was reconciled to getting the treatment again. The officer escorted Ricketts through Immigration to a door marked 'Airport Staff Only' and then down a corridor to a small interview room. The room contained a table, three chairs, and two men in civilian clothes. Ricketts knew one of them, the Maori: he was Detective Sergeant Tito Ihaka of the Auckland CID, 34 or thereabouts and weighing in at around 110 kilograms, a lot less of which was fat than people tended to assume. It was a misconception Ihaka was happy to encourage. The other man was ten years younger, 30 kilograms lighter and many shades paler.

'What's this?' said Ricketts. 'The black-and-white minstrel show?'

Ihaka displayed a broad 'we're all good sports here' smile to which Ricketts attached absolutely no significance. 'Detective Constable Van Roon,' said Ihaka to his companion, 'meet Duane Ricketts, otherwise known as Mister Ed.'

Ricketts dumped his two canvas hold-alls on the table and sat down. 'Can we get this over with, Ihaka?' he asked wearily. 'Do what you like, put on some rubber gloves and grope around up my backside if it gives you a thrill, but please, spare me the horse jokes.'

Ihaka ignored him. 'Would you believe this loser used to be a cop?' he said to Van Roon. They kicked him out because he couldn't be trusted around horses. Guess what he does for a crust these days? Finds runaways. I mean, who the fuck's going to send a smackhead to find their little girl lost?' He shook his head. 'You'd be a hopeless bastard, Ricketts. I suppose you're looking forward to getting the full body search?'

Ricketts looked stonily back at the policeman, saying nothing.

Ihaka nodded to the Customs officer. 'Okay, mate, off you go. I doubt you'll find anything, but; even Mr Ed isn't that dumb.'

As the officer went through his bags, Ihaka asked Ricketts what he'd been doing in Thailand and how he'd managed to get out so quickly. The responses, delivered in a monotone, were models of brevity. Then Ihaka asked about Dale Varty.

'Isn't that a matter for the Thai cops?' said Ricketts. 'I gave them a statement; you want to know what I said, get them to send you a copy.'

'Touchy, aren't we?' said Ihaka. 'We did get a report from our liaison bloke up there. Christ, it's terrible what prison can do to a man, isn't it? How long were you inside for – three weeks? Did you go queer like Varty or just jerk off thinking about Cardigan Bay?'

Ricketts rolled his eyes and went back to staring at the floor.

The Customs officer zipped up Ricketts' bags. 'They're clean,' he said.

Ihaka stood up. 'Right then, we'll leave you lovebirds to it.' He paused in the doorway and said to the Customs officer: 'Mate, just sing out if you get your arm stuck up his ringpiece.'

*

As Funke had expected he would, Kham Phumkumpol *aka* Brandi celebrated his first night out of Bombat by putting on his glad rags and checking in at his old haunt, a Patpong Road bar renowned for its ladyboys. After Brandi sashayed in to a heroine's welcome around 10.30, Funke left the bar and returned to his car which was parked across the street. Settling down for a long wait, Funke leaned back against the headrest and recalled the incident which had changed his whole outlook on life.

At 5 o'clock one hot Friday afternoon in the summer of 1962, Buddy Funke, just turned 18, closed up his father's hardware store on Main Street in the small south-west Texas town of Pecos.

While his family was spending the summer vacation at Corpus Christi on the Gulf of Mexico, Buddy was stuck in Pecos minding the store and earning some money so he could buy himself a car when he went up to college in Austin in the fall. Walking down the street thinking about the swell times he'd have himself at college with his own car, Funke didn't notice the cherry-red convertible until it was right beside him.

'Well, if it ain't Funke the punk,' said Lyle Gorse, braking the convertible to a halt.

It was three years since Funke had laid eyes on Lyle Gorse and he didn't look much different: he'd filled out some but he still wore his hair rock 'n' roll style, long and greasy, kind of teased up on top of his head; he still rolled his shirt-sleeves way up past the elbow to show off his muscles; he still had a cigarette slanting from the corner of his mouth; he still looked like the town bad boy.

Ever since Buddy Funke was old enough to get into trouble, his mother had been warning him that if he didn't watch out, he could end up like Lyle Gorse. Lyle's father was a no-good with a petty crime sheet as long as your arm; he'd run out on Lyle and Mrs Gorse when Lyle was twelve. Then a few years after that, a travelling salesman from Amarillo had come into the diner where Mrs Gorse waitressed. When the salesman finished up his ham and eggs and paid the bill, she'd tossed her apron on the counter and walked out the door with him.

Most people figured Lyle would've gone bad regardless. It just seemed to come naturally to him: he got into fights, he skipped class and when a teacher went round to his house, Lyle pointed a 12-gauge shotgun at him and told him to get the hell off his property. He stole cars to go thrill-riding and got sent to the correctional center in El Paso for six months; there was talk he'd gotten away with worse because he was too smart for the sheriff and his deputies (although, as Buddy's mother was fond of saying, anyone who could put his boots on in the dark would be too smart for the sheriff's department); and he got a girl in the family way. That was always on the cards because the way it went, the more their parents talked about Lyle being no good, the more the boys wanted to be like him and the more the girls just plain wanted him.

What with one thing and another, Pecos eventually got too hot for Lyle Gorse and the day after his seventeenth birthday, he just up and left. There'd been a few sightings of him since then: someone said they'd seen him up in New Mexico, working on the highway; another story had him living in Amarillo with his mother and her second husband, earning his keep pumping gas. Not many folks in Pecos attached much credence to these reports on account of the fact that Lyle hadn't done a day's work in his life. Most people, if they had to pick where he'd got to, would've said the state penitentiary but they didn't really care where it was as long as he stayed there. He hadn't.

'Hey, Lyle,' said Funke. 'Long time no see. Where you been?'

Gorse shrugged. 'Around. Arizona mostly – Silver City, Tucson, Yuma. I like to keep moving.'

Funke nodded. 'So what brings you back to Pecos?'

'What do you think? This is my home town, Buddy boy. Came back to see all my old amigos.'

'Well, shit, Lyle, you can do that and be gone before sundown.'

Gorse grinned. 'You always did have a smart mouth, boy. As a matter of fact, I'm just passing through on my way down south of the border. I've been working my butt off on an oil rig for six weeks straight and I believe I owe it to myself to relax a while, have some fun. Here's an idea – why don't you come along? I'm just going for the weekend; I'll have you back Sunday night. What do you say?'

'What sort of fun you got in mind?' asked Funke warily.

Gorse took a final drag on his cigarette and flicked it away. He draped an arm over the car door and leaned towards Funke. 'I want to catch a donkey show, kid. Guy on the oil well was telling me about donkey shows he'd seen in TJ; says he's heard they have them down in Juarez too.'

'What's a donkey show and where's TJ?'

'TJ is Tijuana, is a greaser town over on the coast, just across the border, one wide-open burg. I aimed to go see for myself when I was in Yuma but something came up. Now a donkey show is what you might call a performance put on by a senorita and her favourite burro.'

Funke looked at him blankly.

'Jesus, kid, do I have to spell it out? The dame gets screwed by the donkey.'

Funke folded his arms. 'Lyle, I'm not sure I want to watch a dame getting screwed by a donkey.'

Gorse took off his dark glasses and stared at Funke. 'Well, there's no accounting for some folks' taste. There's plenty of other stuff to do in Juarez – Christ, you can go to the fucking market if you want, buy your kid sister one of them beanie dolls.' Gorse slammed his hand against the car door. 'Son of a bitch, I just thought of something – you been laid yet? Brother, there's no need to answer that – I can tell from looking at you. All right, that's settled: you come on down to Mexico with old Lyle and we'll get your cherry popped, I guarantee it.'

Although Buddy Funke was one of the brighter teenage boys in Pecos, not even his mother, to whom he bore a close resemblance, would've claimed he was one of the more handsome. He was short and stocky and had a flat face splattered with freckles, eyes that appeared to focus in slightly different directions like maladjusted headlights, and ginger hair which his father insisted he wear in a military crewcut. He was also shy. Funke's homeliness and diffidence meant that although he was as anxious as any of his contemporaries to lose his virginity, the best he'd been able to do was to momentarily mislay it a couple of times. With Lyle Gorse as guide and negotiator, there had to be a good chance of finding a senorita in Juarez who'd be prepared to take it off his hands once and for all.

*

When the two young Texans crossed back into the United States late on the Sunday afternoon, Funke was no longer a virgin. Apart from that, all they had to show for their trip were hangovers and Montezuma's Revenge.

Gorse hadn't found a donkey show. In fact his enquiries had met with undisguised hostility from the locals, who clearly took umbrage at the suggestion that the ladies of Juarez would perform bestial acts for the titillation of visiting gringos. The frustration of missing out on a donkey show combined with the disorienting effect of a steady intake of tequila and Mexican beer at one end and an equally fluid outflow at the other had put Gorse in a mean mood.

Instead of branching left at Sierra Blanca and heading north through Van Horn up to Pecos, Gorse continued south towards Valentine. A few miles past Sierra Blanca, he turned off down a back road.

Funke asked, 'Lyle, where are we going?'

'Down this fucking road, that's where,' snapped Gorse.

They drove on in silence for a few miles until they came to a little general store with a gas pump, stuck out in the middle of nowhere. Gorse swung off the road and pulled up in front of the store. He opened the glove box and took out a revolver. He pulled his shirt out of his jeans, shoved the revolver in the belt and covered it with his shirt.

'What's the gun for, Lyle?' asked Funke nervously.

Gorse lit a cigarette and got out of the car. He planted his hands on the top of the car door and smiled crookedly down at Funke. 'Well, it's like this Bud – I had my heart set on seeing a donkey show but I didn't get to see one; now I got a powerful urge for some double chocolate ripple ice-cream. If they ain't got double chocolate ripple in there, I'll just have to shoot someone, nothing else for it. Stay here.'

For the ninety or so seconds it took Gorse to walk over to the store, mount the steps to the porch, take a long look around, open the screen door and go inside, Funke sat in a trance-like state in the convertible imagining how various people, notably his parents, would react to the news of his arrest for being an accessory to armed hold-up. Then he leapt out of the car and ran to the store. As he pulled open the screen door, he yelled 'Lyle, don't do it …'

It was too late. Gorse was pointing the revolver at a grizzled, middle-aged man in faded blue overalls who stood behind the wooden counter with his hands in the air. The man's name was Bobby Ray Doble and right then he was just about the worst person in south-west Texas to point a gun at.

Six weeks previously Bobby Ray's wife Martha had driven up to Abilene to see her sister. The highway patrol thought she must've fallen asleep at the wheel because just north of Sweetwater, her car had veered across the road into the path of a southbound Greyhound bus. Since Martha's funeral, Bobby Ray had spent a lot of time sitting on his front porch with a bottle of whiskey thinking about the future. Whichever way he looked at it, the future didn't seem worth waiting around for. When the whiskey ran out, he'd go back into the store and reach under the counter to where he kept his army issue Colt .45 automatic. Back in '59, a bunch of bandidos had come across the Rio Grande and held up a store down near Rocks Springs, gunned down a whole family in cold blood; ever since, Bobby Ray had kept the automatic in its holster, taped to the underside of the counter. He'd pull it out and look at it, then put the muzzle to his temple. After a few seconds, he'd put it back in the holster. 'It won't be long now, Martha honey,' he'd say out loud. 'I'm fixing to do it real soon.'

When Funke burst into the store, Gorse turned his head to tell him to get the fuck back in the car. While he was doing that, Bobby Ray Doble reached under the counter and came up with his .45. He shot Gorse just behind his left eye and from where Buddy Funke saw it, it was like a grenade had gone off inside Lyle's mouth.

Doble pointed the gun at Funke, aiming it at the tip of his nose. Funke noticed that the gun was rock steady and that there was nothing in Doble's brown eyes except mild indifference.

'Boy, you live to be a hundred,' said Doble, 'you ain't never going to get luckier than right now.'

Then Bobby Ray Doble put the muzzle of the .45 in his mouth and pulled the trigger.

Funke felt something warm on his leg and looked down to see that he'd wet himself. Later he'd reflect that there was something to be said for having spent most of the morning on the can with the squirts after all.

He drove Gorse's convertible back to El Paso, slept in it that night, sold it on the first car lot he came across the next morning, and took a bus back to Pecos. He spent some of the bus trip thinking about the cars that were now in his price range. Mostly though, he thought about how close he'd come to getting killed. By the time the bus reached Pecos, he'd concluded that seeing as how he was so lucky to be alive, he really ought to do something more exciting with his life than teach high school in south-west Texas.

*

It was almost 2 a.m. when Brandi the ladyboy came out of the bar, turned left and began walking towards the Surawong Road end of Patpong Road. As he started his car, Funke found himself thinking that when some of the ladyboys got all dolled up, it was a hell of a job to pick them from the real thing.

Funke eased his car up alongside the ladyboy and wound his window down. He flashed his ID and told Brandi to get into the car, then drove three blocks towards the Chitladda Palace, turned down a little side street, pulled in to the kerb and turned off the headlights.

Brandi got the wrong idea. He darted his tongue between red lips and leaned towards Funke smiling coyly.

'You want that I ...'

'Hold your horses, missy,' said Funke. 'This is police business, not sweet-time. No offence intended – this town's full of imitations but you beat the shit out of any fake Rolex. Truth to tell, there've been times in this old boy's life when I'd have been happier than a nigger with new shoes to let you play with my johnson. Could be I'd be partial to a helping now, weren't for the fact that just yesterday I was sucked and fucked every which way by three – count 'em, three – of the prettiest little gals this side of Chiang Mai and the plain fact is, I'm plumb out of poke. All I want from you is to tell me what went down at Bombat the other day when citizen Varty went to Jesus.'

Brandi pouted and shifted away to lean against the car door. 'I told them ten times at the prison. This Varty, he say he pay me for a suck, okay? We go up the stairs but Samran find us. He crazy jealous, push me away, then – I don't know what happen – Varty scream and fall down and I see blood ...'

'You're one hell of a witness, missy, but we'll let that fine body of men, the Bangkok police, worry about that side of it. What I want to know is what you heard Varty tell his friend Duane Ricketts.'

'He talk about he used to be in drug syndicate – sound like he call it Asia but that make no sense, huh? He say they move some cocaine from Australia to New Zealand by boat – talking about years ago, right? – and hide it somewhere. It still there.'

'He say how much?'

'Plenty – he say worth millions of dollars.'

'Okay, this is the important part. Where's the coke at?'

'I didn't hear. By this time his voice get real quiet. The guy Ricketts he like bent over so his ear right by Varty's mouth. I not hearing much what he say, okay?'

'He must've said where, there must've been a name?'

Brandi sighed. 'Maybe, I don't know. If he say name of a place, I don't understand. Now I told you all I hear, huh?'

Funke shook his head. 'No way that's all. Like the guy's going out slow, he's not telling Ricketts all this to give his tongue exercise; he had a reason. So what did he tell Ricketts to do?'

Brandi nodded. 'Okay, I think he want Ricketts to find the coke but he also talk about his daughter. He tell Ricketts go see her. You want to drive me home now?'

'That's it, absolutely everything? You haven't left anything out, maybe because it didn't make sense to you? I mean, he didn't talk about a map showing where the coke was stashed, anything like that? He didn't mention anyone apart from the daughter?'

Brandi shook his head. 'I told you, I miss some of what he say. Only other thing I hear – he say someone killed when he bring the cocaine to New Zealand. Don't ask who, okay?'

'Well now, there's a coincidence,' said Funke. He reached under his seat and brought out an automatic pistol. 'Will you look at this little beauty – Beretta 9 millimetre. Took it off a mule we whacked up in the Triangle last year. Feels so good, could've been custom-made for me. It's a real shame I have to lose it.'

Brandi pressed back against the door and looked at Funke with big, scared eyes.

'That's your cue, sugar,' prompted Funke with a thin smile. 'You're supposed to ask why is it, if I'm so all-fired attached to this piece, I'm going to throw it away?'

'Why you do that?' said Brandi in a barely audible whisper.

Funke reached across to open the glovebox and take out a silencer which he screwed onto the Beretta. 'Well, now, after I've used it to pop you, it wouldn't be too smart to hang on to it, would it?'

'Please, no,' beseeched Brandi. 'I do nothing ...'

'What's your problem?' said Funke. 'Don't all you zippy-heads believe in reincarnation? You come back with a pussy, I'd have done you a favour, ain't that so?'

When Brandi grabbed the door handle, Funke shot him first in the chest and then in the head as he'd been taught when he'd joined the CIA out of college back in 1967: first shot to the body, the big target, to stop and disable; second shot to the head to make stone-cold sure of it. Taking people out like this was called 'wet stuff' in company parlance, although some of the older guys at CIA headquarters in Langley, Virginia, claimed 'wet stuff' was actually a translation from the Russian of the KGB slang for any activity which involved spilling blood.

Five

At 10 a.m. local time on Thursday, 14 April, Bernie Gemmell, the foreign correspondent, entered the Boomerang Bar in downtown Vientiane. He got a cold San Miguel beer and commandeered a corner table on which he arranged the contents of his large leather satchel. He lit a cigarette, sipped his beer, and discreetly studied the dozen or so other men in the bar, only two of whom were Asian.

Although few would have suspected it, Gemmell possessed a romantic streak. In his slightly overheated imagination, a seedy, dimly lit bar in the capital of Laos was the milieu of the undercover world, the world behind the headlines, and as such the habitat of adventurers, gun-runners, agents, double agents, and mercenaries killing time until the next war by reminiscing, over their beers and vodka chasers, about comrades who didn't survive the last one. Therefore he examined the other patrons in the expectation that they'd be exotic, sinister, and probably bound for damnation. After a few minutes' careful inspection he decided that they mostly looked like sheetmetal salesmen from Stoke-on-Trent or Milwaukee or Gdansk or Wollongong. So much for the mysterious East, he thought. Gemmell finished his beer, opened up his laptop computer, and studied the notes he'd made of his recent conversation with the diplomat, Jason Maltby.

Gemmell's enthusiasm for the Dale Varty story had waned since he'd left Bangkok. Now, as he stared at the laptop's screen, he asked himself who really gave a toss about some middle-aged sleazebag getting out of a Thai jail? Dale Who? Had anyone ever heard of him? The Mr Asia syndicate was past tense, practically ancient history. And compared with the likes of the Colombian cartels, they were small-time, almost quaint: a bunch of low-rent hoods who had their 15 minutes of media attention and then took to murdering each other. Eventually Gemmell decided that seeing he'd come up with absolutely nothing new or insightful to say about the Asian economic miracle in two and a half weeks of gallivanting around the region at his employers' considerable expense, it would be prudent to file a Varty story, however modest.

He began to write:

From Bernie Gemmell, NZPA correspondent
Bangkok, 14 April
New Zealander Dale Varty is nothing if not a survivor.
The 53-year-old Varty, a veteran of the notorious Mr Asia drug syndicate, will be released today from the Bombat Drug Rehabilitation Centre in Bangkok after serving a ten-year sentence for drug trafficking.

Officials from the New Zealand Embassy here who have been in contact with Varty confirm that he is in reasonable physical shape and good spirits.

The fact that he has come through such an ordeal – Thailand's prison system is notoriously hard on Westerners – should not come as a surprise: Varty was, after all, a member of the Mr Asia syndicate and lived to tell the tale. Many of the Mr Asia team met violent fates, usually at the hands of fellow syndicate members, when the organisation fell into internecine conflict in the late 1970s.

Fortunately, the collapse of the Mr Asia syndicate was as swift and comprehensive as its rise was spectacular and bloody.

The August 1983 death – ironically of a heart attack suffered in an English jail – of the syndicate's boss Terry Clark, or Alexander James Sinclair as he was also known, completed the disintegration of one of Australasia's most successful, albeit shortlived, and murderous criminal enterprises.

Varty, an Aucklander, was never a senior figure in the syndicate. Originally one of the syndicate's go-betweens with distributors in Sydney and Auckland, he eventually rose to become a buyer, sourcing product from South-East Asia.

After the syndicate's collapse, Varty came to Thailand intending to tap his contacts here to put together a major deal on his own behalf. However the plan came to grief in March 1984 when he was arrested by Thai police on the resort island of Phuket on drug trafficking and conspiracy charges.

Since his arrival in Thailand three months ago, Jason Maltby, administrative officer at the New Zealand embassy, has energetically promoted Varty's cause and personally handled negotiations with the Thai authorities to finalise his release. Although Maltby maintains a diplomatic silence over the nature of the negotiations, it can be safely assumed they were not straightforward: Thai authorities sometimes seem to delight in spinning out the release of Western prisoners and are past masters at creating obstacles where none seemed to exist.

Maltby told this correspondent that he had been impressed by Varty's resilience and his determination to leave his criminal past behind him.

'Mr Varty's come through this remarkably well,' said Maltby. 'He possesses that famous Kiwi adaptability and he's remained positive by focusing on getting back to Auckland and starting a new life.'

That's all it's worth, thought Gemmell as he gave it a swift read. It gives the papers a hook for a 'Mr Asia Revisited' feature if they've got a hole to fill. Maltby should be happy; it makes him sound like Henry Kissinger.

He walked over to the bar.

'Can I use your phone?' he asked the barman, a 45-year-old Western Australian called Len with a beer belly like an inflated spinnaker and a nose with a radioactive glow and strange, pitted extensions as if it was in the throes of reproducing itself, amoeba-like. 'I want to make a collect call to New Zealand.'

Len folded his arms across his chest. 'You bet your pimply arse it'll be collect. You a Kiwi?'

Gemmell nodded.

'You hear about this Kiwi joker walking down George Street in Sydney with a sheep under each arm?' asked Len. 'Cop car pulls up and this cop says, "You a shearer?" "Get your own," says the Kiwi, "I'm going to root 'em both myself." '

'I don't get it,' said Gemmell, cutting off Len's guffaws.

*

Jason Maltby's telephone ran hot on Friday morning. His first call was from DEA special agent Harold 'Buddy' Funke.

'Jason, I understand you handled the file on one of your nationals been doing time here, a perpetrator by the name of Dale Varty, now deceased?'

'That's correct but ...'

'Look, I'm real sorry to be hassling you with this, but you know what us Americanos are like – no such thing as something that's none of our business, right? Leastways, that's surely how my outfit operates. You might not believe this but among the fun things we get to do is file reports on any what you might call untoward event involving known narcotics traffickers happens to take place on our piece of dirt. You read where I'm coming from? Now I know this ruction with your Mr Varty happened in the joint and all, but I'm obliged to report on it just the same.'

'Yes, I see,' said Maltby. 'How can I be of assistance?'

'Well, Jason, it embarrasses me all to hell to waste your time with such a chickenshit matter but our procedures require me to include Varty's last known address in his home country. Don't ask me why – just more crap they can feed into their computer I guess. Now the local uniforms have a

Phuket address – must've been where he was hanging out when they arrested him – so I figure if anyone can help me close off this sucker of a report, it's the good people at the New Zealand embassy.'

'Well, I'm not sure that we can, as a matter of fact. You see, Varty was domiciled in Australia – Sydney to be exact – before he came to Thailand.'

'That was downright inconsiderate of him. You have a next-of-kin for this asshole? Worst comes to the worst, I can go with a NOK address. I mean, who the hell in DC's going to know different?'

'Just a moment. Let me get his file.'

Maltby collected Varty's file and returned to the phone. Not quite a next of kin, I'm afraid. All I have here is his ex-wife.'

'Better than nothing I guess. What's her story?'

'Her name's Rayleen Crouch. The address we have is 108 Crimea Avenue, Grey Lynn, Auckland.'

Funke repeated the address back to Maltby, then said: 'Ex-wife, huh? He have any kids?'

'I seem to remember there was a daughter but there's nothing on her in the file. If you really feel you need her details, I suppose I could try Wellington, but the department might baulk at her name going into your computer ...'

'Can't say I'd blame them if they did. No, that's fine; you've solved my little problem. I'm much obliged to you, sir.'

'Any time.'

Funke hung up. *No wonder so many folks believe Elvis is still alive,* he thought. *Some people will believe just about any goddamn thing.*

*

Maltby's second call that morning also concerned Dale Varty. The caller was Amanda Hayhoe, a reporter from Television New Zealand.

'Mr Maltby, I work for a current affairs program called 'Sixty Minutes'. We might be interested in doing a story on Dale Varty. I was wondering if he'd left Thailand yet and if not, where could we get hold of him?'

Jesus, what? 'Dale Varty,' stammered Maltby. 'What do you know about him?'

'Absolutely stuff-all apart from what's in this morning's *Herald* about him getting out of jail,' said Hayhoe breezily. 'We just thought he might have a good yarn to tell.'

Varty felt a huge bead of sweat slide down his right temple like a snail. *That idiot Gemmell must've sent a story to New Zealand. How the bloody hell did he manage that?* This line of thought was interrupted by a voice bellowing at him to get off the phone and out of the embassy to somewhere he couldn't be contacted. It took him two or three seconds to realise the voice was coming from inside his head.

'Look, Ms Hayhoe, I'll have to call you back on this …'

'I'm confused – I mean, what's the problem here?' asked Hayhoe. Her tone had cooled from pleasant to neutral with a hint of 'don't fuck with me, I work for television'. 'After all, you are quoted in the story.'

'Quoted?' whimpered Maltby, standing up to unstick his trousers which felt like they were glued to his buttocks. 'Saying what?'

'Oh, just how Varty's come through it all intact and whatnot. You should be pleased with the story; it makes you sound … well, as if you're on top of things up there.'

Maltby closed his eyes and squeezed his slippery forehead. This was disastrous; he had to stall her, buy himself some time to think.

'Ms Hayhoe, would you mind very much faxing me a copy of the story,' said Maltby, calling on his reserves of self-control. 'I really think I should see it before I say anything. I'll call you back as soon as I've read it.'

Maltby's third call came through while he was reading the faxed copy of the story which had appeared in the *New Zealand Herald*.

He snatched up the phone. 'Suan, what's the matter with you?' he barked. 'I told you only five minutes ago I'm not taking any calls for the time being.'

'I sorry, Mr Maltby but this gentleman say he have a message to call you urgently. It's Mr Bernie Gemmell – he ringing from Hanoi.'

Six

Amanda Hayhoe was not the only person in Auckland to be intrigued by the single column NZPA story about Dale Varty which appeared on page 5 of the *New Zealand Herald* on Friday, 15 April.

Varty's ex-wife Rayleen Crouch came across it while having breakfast in the kitchen of her two-bedroom villa in Grey Lynn. When she spotted the headline, the spoonful of muesli and banana stopped midway through its journey from the Peter Rabbit bowl out of which she'd eaten her morning cereal since her fifth birthday in 1961 to her mouth and remained poised in mid-air as she read the story. When she reached the paragraph quoting the man from the New Zealand embassy in Bangkok about how her former husband intended to start a new life in Auckland, Rayleen Crouch snorted. The snort expressed both surprise and amusement and was sufficiently explosive to cause the spoon to jump in her right hand. A slice of banana fell from the spoon to the bench to her lap to the floor. Crouch's gaze flicked to the slice of banana which rolled like a hoop across the kitchen floor and under the oven. She said 'pisshole', but without putting much feeling into it, and returned her attention to the newspaper.

When she'd read and re-read the story, Crouch ate the now banana-free spoonful of muesli then, chewing doggedly, tipped what remained in the bowl into the sink waste disposal. She rinsed the bowl, put it in the dishwasher, cleaned her teeth in the bathroom, picked up her handbag, and left the house locking the front door behind her. She was so preoccupied that she quite forgot to retrieve the piece of banana from under the oven, which was quite out of character for someone who was tidy to the point of being a self-diagnosed anal retentive.

It was the first weekday morning for eleven months that Crouch had left for work without having done the *Herald* crossword, which usually took her between four and five minutes. Then she'd departed from her routine in response to a frantic phone call from her office informing her that one of her clients – as they are known in the welfare industry – had just walked into the McDonald's in Karangahape Road where, upon being informed that the Egg McMuffin special offer had ended the day before, he'd unbuttoned his shirt and sliced off his left nipple with a razor blade.

*

Another who was riveted by the story was the lawyer Bart Clegg. Clegg read the paper sitting in his leather swivel chair in his office on the eleventh floor of the Trubshaw Trimble building in Queen Street. Like many of Auckland's high-rises, the building was actually owned by Singaporeans; as the lead and most substantial tenant, the law firm in which Clegg was a partner had been granted naming rights.

When Clegg graduated from law school in 1976, he'd joined the Auckland Legal Co-operative, a group of young lawyers whose political stances ranged across most variations of left-wingery from Maoist to sandal-wearing Utopian. Clegg himself was an anarcho-syndicalist for 50 weeks of the year; the other two, he went skiing at Mount Ruapehu. The Co-operative's self-appointed mission was to stand up for the poor and downtrodden and to defend the civil liberties of put-upon minorities; the members regarded policemen as stooges of the system at best, corrupt neo-fascist thugs at worst, and the legal establishment as a mutual support group of money-grubbing fat cats.

Like many zealots, Clegg was so attached to his opinions that he took them everywhere, rather like modern parents who take their babies to restaurants and dinner parties.
One Friday night he had too much to drink in the University Club and began ranting about the bench. A stout, middle-aged man waiting at the bar briskly suggested that he
was talking rot. Clegg, ignoring his friends' tugs on his
sleeve, eyed the interjector up and down, thrust his red-
dened face forward so that their noses were almost touch-
ing, and demanded in a grating snarl, 'Who asked you, you
fat lard? And what the fucking hell would you know about
it anyway?'

The middle-aged gentleman turned a deep crimson colour
which very nearly matched the dry red wine in Clegg's glass
and stalked from the room. Clegg turned to his companions
with a triumphant beam, expecting plaudits for seeing off a
class enemy with such pungent efficiency. Instead of praise,
however, he was given the news that the man he'd just pub-
licly and gratuitously insulted was widely tipped to be the
next chief justice.

Clegg awoke the next morning with a hangover and an
unsettling feeling that his rudeness to Justice Gibbon was a
more serious matter than he'd been prepared to acknowledge the previous evening. By mid-afternoon unease had
become gnawing anxiety. He wrote a letter of apology to
Gibbon which he hand-delivered to the judge's secretary. The
letter impressed Gibbon, who'd thought that in his 30-year
legal career he'd seen the parameters of self-abasement extended about as far as they could go. Clegg, though, had
pushed the envelope, as test pilots say. Gibbon decided to
grant Clegg's request to be permitted to elaborate on the written apology in person.

It was a deflated Bart Clegg who entered Justice Gibbon's
chambers at midday the following day. He cleared his throat

nervously and began the speech that he'd worked on until 3 o'clock that morning. Gibbon listened for 45 seconds then interrupted.

'That'll do,' he said. 'You've made your point. I've been apologised to by some of the biggest crawlers in the business but you lose nothing in comparison. Sit down.'

Clegg did as he was told.

Gibbon studied him in silence for a few seconds. The judge's eyes were black and a little bloodshot and to Clegg they looked as cold and indifferent as those of a cat toying with a bird with a broken wing.

'Why did you take up the law, Mr Clegg?'

Clegg swallowed. 'Well, I suppose I wanted to serve the cause of justice and help those who, you know, don't get a fair shake from the system – the poor, Polynesians, gays …' His voice trailed off.

'Hmmm … and would it be true to say that you believe most people in the profession don't give a damn about justice, they just want to make a lot of money?'

'Well, I'm not sure I'd put it as bluntly …'

'Come on, man, yes or no?'

'Yes, I guess.'

'Of course they bloody well do. Let me tell you something, Mr Clegg, you're hardly the first young lawyer to think that way. Nine out of ten drop all that nonsense and come to see the law as a job pure and simple, a meal ticket, a way of making quite a good living. Now, on the basis of our brief and disagreeable acquaintance, I'm quite confident you have neither the character nor the intellect to achieve anything remotely useful as an idealist. If you want to be a crusader, that's entirely up to you, but in 20 years' time, you'll be in a miserable little practice in a miserable little office handling pathetic clients; no-one will take the slightest notice of you except the media, who'll ring you up whenever they need an inflammatory quote. Every quote you give them will only serve to make you even more of an object of derision to the rest of the profession. My advice to you therefore is to stop posturing and try to make yourself into a half-decent lawyer. If you manage to make some money along the way, then the chances are you'll have been of assistance to at least some of your clients. Now I have some matters to attend to before luncheon.'

Clegg rose. 'Thank you, sir. I really appreciate your advice.'

Clegg had his hand on the door knob when Gibbon spoke again. 'Oh, two more things. Go easy on the grog; you can't handle it. Secondly, if at some stage in the future you're faced with the prospect of appearing in my court and are wondering how you'll be treated' – here Gibbon smiled for the first time but it was a private smile which contained no comfort for Clegg – 'then be advised that I'm not disposed to let bygones be bygones. My philosophy is that forgiveness is for clergymen; judges are society's instruments for taking the revenge that we deny the individual. So if you're ever unwise enough to appear before me, I'll take great pleasure in humiliating you.'

Clegg took Justice Gibbon's advice. He quit the co-operative and joined a medium-sized downtown firm. He'd been a jack of all trades for a few years, then specialised in conveyancing and property law. Now, even after a divorce, he was quite comfortably off and sufficiently secure in the Trubshaw Trimble hierarchy to scarcely bother trying to conceal the fact that he was sleeping with his secretary.

He'd steered well clear of Justice Gibbon's courts too. In fact, he'd only encountered Gibbon once since that audience in chambers. It was at the Northern Club. Turning away from the urinal, he found himself looking straight into Gibbon's black eyes. The shock caused him to snag several pubic hairs in his zip. The judge was greyer, stouter, more florid and his unblinking stare was, if anything, chillier.

'Clegg, isn't it?'

'Yes, Your Honour.'

Gibbon looked him up and down, rather as Clegg had done to him in the University Club 13 years earlier.

'You look moderately prosperous, Mr Clegg. Who are you with?'

'Trubshaw Trimble.'

Gibbon grunted enigmatically.

'And what do you do at TT?'

'Property mainly.'

The judge nodded with satisfaction, as if the information legitimised a deeply-held prejudice. 'Haven't had you in my court, Mr Clegg. You obviously took my advice.'

Clegg ventured a quick smile. 'Yes I did – to the letter.'

Gibbon's eyes narrowed suspiciously. 'You a member here?'

'Oh no, I'm here as a guest.'

'Thank the Lord for that. Now if you don't mind clearing off, I prefer to urinate in private.'

A year later ill-health forced Gibbon to retire from the bench. According to legal gossip, the judge had never been quite the same since being passed over for the position of chief justice. The fact that he drank a bottle of Famous Grouse Scotch whisky every day was also thought to have contributed to his decline. To mark Gibbon's retirement, Clegg sent him a bottle of Wilson's New Zealand whiskey and a 500 gram block of lard. Anonymously of course.

When Clegg finished the story in the *Herald,* he leaned back in his leather swivel chair and thought about his connection with Dale Varty, for whom he'd acted in the late '70s and early '80s. Seeing that the connection involved an unsolved murder, Clegg thought about it very carefully.

*

Bryce Spurdle, the semi-retired investor, read about Dale Varty in what he'd come to regard as his Auckland office, the Sierra café in Jervois Road.

Spurdle lived in a sprawling mock-Tudor monstrosity on 25 hectares near Albany, no more than 20 minutes' drive – outside rush hours – from downtown Auckland. Several mornings a week he'd get into one of his three cars and drive down the motorway, across the harbour bridge and up Shelly Beach Road to Jervois Road. Then, if the weather permitted, he'd sit at one of the Sierra's pavement tables with a cappuccino, the *Herald*, and his mobile phone. He'd use the phone to ring his stockbroker, his young wife to make sure she was out of bed, and his mates to organise a round of golf or a lunch.

There'd been a time when Spurdle and Varty were best friends. They'd grown up together in Ponsonby in the 1940s and '50s; in those days, people who lived in the eastern suburbs regarded Ponsonby as the closest thing in Auckland to a slum and wouldn't have been seen there in an advanced state of decomposition. For that reason it tickled Spurdle to sit outside at the Sierra and watch the svelte women pull up in their 3-series BMWs, having come all the way from Paratai Drive for a cup of coffee.

Varty's father was a seaman and rarely at home. Spurdle's father, Bevan, went off to war in 1941 with regular features and good health; he came back with a compacted nose, breathing difficulties and a booze habit. He collected the mangled nose and the associated breathing difficulties when he walked into a bar in Port Said, Egypt, during an all-in brawl. Roughly speaking, the brawl was between Australian and British infantrymen; the Antipodeans had set upon their allies because they were Poms, physically smaller and numerically fewer, a combination which tended to have the same galvanising effect on Australian servicemen out on the tear as red rags on bulls. Unfortunately for the Australians, these particular Poms turned out to be Welshmen, farmers from the Brecon Beacons and the Black Mountains and coal miners from little pit villages in the Rhondda Valley. Not only did the Welshmen seem impervious to pain, they also fought like rabid weasels, displaying no respect for the etiquette of the intra-alliance Saturday night knuckle.

Bevan Spurdle entered the bar shortly after one of the Australians had retired from the fray having had a forearm chewed, a tooth knocked out and his scrotum almost wrenched off its mooring by a goblin-like creature half his size and probably twice his age. Lurking by the doorway sick with pain and burning with humiliation, the Australian lashed out at the first person to cross his path. The king-hit, a whistling uppercut, landed flush on the tip of Spurdle's nose, driving the nose bone up into his forehead and reducing the nose itself to smears of blood, gristle and mucus across his cheekbones, like warpaint on a Comanche brave.

A year later Spurdle and half a dozen others from his unit were coerced into unloading a supply ship in the port of Alexandria. The exercise, which was largely unsupervised, took several days and was almost completed when they discovered several barrels of 100 proof Navy rum in the depths of the ship's hold. After three days of hard labour in the North African heat, the working party felt it had earned a dip or two. They ended up drinking solidly for the rest of the day. Bevan passed out and remained in a state of suspended animation for 60 hours. He was one of the lucky ones; two of his comrades had literally drunk themselves to death. It should've been a textbook case of aversion therapy; in fact, it had the opposite effect on Spurdle, who took to the bottle with increasing single-mindedness.

With one father often absent and the other often befuddled, young Spurdle and Varty were less constrained by parental control than most of their contemporaries. They roamed the streets in search of excitement and soon discovered that larceny was as much fun as anything and more rewarding than most. They learned that because some people liked to pray by themselves instead of or in addition to attending services, churches had collection boxes into which the solitary worshippers could drop their offerings. The boxes were usually left unlocked so Varty and Spurdle would sneak in and rifle them during their lunchbreaks. Varty always wanted to flog the lot but Spurdle, who even then was more astute in financial matters, would insist that they took no more than half. That way, he pointed out, the priests wouldn't realise the collection money was being pilfered; they'd just think that pickings in Ponsonby were getting even slimmer.

The young thieves also learned that people who were old enough to get the old-age pension were often lax about locking back doors and bolting windows; they tended to be set in their ways, so they kept their savings in the same drawer or jar or under the same sofa cushion. And they were absent-minded, so if you just skimmed off a note, chances were they'd assume they'd spent it or lost it, that is if they missed it at all.

After school Varty and Spurdle would catch a bus to somewhere like Newmarket or Remuera, where the shops were better stocked and the shopkeepers didn't know them and were so used to kids who behaved themselves that you could just about nick stuff right off the counter under their noses. They shoplifted comics, toys, sweets, even things they didn't need or want and ended up chucking away. They stole chocolate bars by the score; they'd get the bus back to Ponsonby with their schoolbags crammed with the big two-shilling blocks, go down to their den under the Varty house, and scoff till they made themselves sick. Next day, they'd take the leftover bars to school and trade them to girls who'd pull their knickers down behind the toilets. That was worth plain chocolate, your Dairy Milk; the girls who were game for a fiddle got Chocolate Crunch, the one with hokey-pokey, or Caramello.

Varty probably would've done it just for the hell of it but Spurdle was driven by an urge to accumulate. He'd seen the boys from King's Prep School dragging their elegant mothers into Storkline, the big toy shop in Newmarket, and just pointing at what they wanted; he'd stared in wonder through the bus window at the enormous houses along Remuera Road. By the time he was 14, Bryce Spurdle had made up his mind that he was going to be rich.

Spurdle got rich in three phases. In the '60s he worked in the music business, managing bands and promoting concerts. By the early '70s, drugs had become part of the music scene; once Spurdle got over his amazement at the sort of money musicians and their hangers-on were prepared to part with for a little bag of what was meant to be marijuana but could've been clippings off his front lawn for all half of them knew, he set out to meet the demand. By the time the '80s rolled around, he was one of Auckland's leading drug-dealers and a millionaire.

But it wasn't all plain sailing: a guy Spurdle funded into a deal got caught with a briefcase full of acid and went to jail for the rest of the century. Another time, his man got himself killed and the product in question, a swag of high-grade cocaine which was going to catapult him into the big league, vanished into thin air. Then the stockmarket went crazy. It didn't take Spurdle long to figure out that playing the market was an easier and less risky way to make money than dealing drugs. By 1987 he'd parlayed $1 million of drug money into $10 million, give or take a few thousand, virtually all of which was invested in the stockmarket.

It never occurred to Spurdle that the party wouldn't go on forever. He often used to wonder why everybody didn't jump into the market and make themselves some serious money. Not that he particularly gave a shit; if some people were too dumb to see what stuck out like a big dog's dick or didn't have the nerve to get into the action, fuck 'em – they deserved to be poor.

On his way out to the airport one day in late August 1987, Spurdle dropped in to see his broker. He'd got sick of winter so he was off to Hawaii for a couple of weeks. Wanting something to read on the plane, he spotted a paperback called *Money* on the broker's bookshelf. Seeing money was the be-all and end-all of his existence, Spurdle borrowed the book, despite the broker's warning that it probably wasn't his cup of tea.

The broker was right. Spurdle had assumed that the author, John Kenneth Galbraith, would share his uncomplicated attitude towards money and was looking forward to picking up some shrewd tips on wealth enhancement. Instead what he got was a lot of egghead blather about economic theories and all this historical crap about things that happened in Europe and America fucking centuries ago.

Spurdle flicked disgustedly through the rest of the book; it didn't seem to get any better. He was about to give up and watch the in-flight movie, *Wall Street*, even though he'd seen it three times and hated the ending, when his eye fell on the following passage:

Speculation occurs when people buy assets, always with the support of some rationalising doctrine, because they expect their prices to rise. That expectation and the resulting action then serve to confirm expectation. Presently the reality is not what the asset in question – the land or commodity or stock or investment company – will earn in the future. Rather, it is only that enough people are expecting the speculative object to advance in price to make it advance in price and thus attract yet more people to yet further fulfil expectations of yet further increases.

This process has a pristine simplicity; it can last only so long as prices are rising reliably. If anything serious interrupts the price advance, the expectations by which the advance is sustained are lost or anyhow endangered. All who are holding for a further rise – all but the gullible and egregiously optimistic of which there is invariably a considerable supply – then seek to get out. Whatever the pace of the preceding build-up, whether slow or rapid, the resulting fall is always abrupt. Thus the likeness to the ripsaw blade or the breaking surf. So did speculation and therewith economic expansion come to an end in all of the panic years from 1819 to 1929.

Spurdle wasn't sure if he entirely got J.K. Galbraith's drift but the passage made him feel slightly queasy nonetheless. He knew very little history but he was aware of the significance of 1929: that was the year of the Wall Street crash which led to the Great Depression. His mother had often talked about the depression; Jesus Christ, people lived on turnips for five years. What Galbraith reckoned had happened in the run-up to 1929 sounded uncomfortably like what had been going on in New Zealand for the past couple of years.

Spurdle flicked on, looking for more on the Wall Street crash. On page 220 his eye was caught by a reference to one Irving Fisher, whom Galbraith described as 'the most versatile and, by a wide margin, the most interesting of American economists'. Fisher's economic theories were double-Dutch to Spurdle but there was one thing about the inventor of the price index which he had no problem getting his mind around; in fact, the shocking clarity of it caused him to begin hyperventilating and prompted solicitous attention from an air hostess: Fisher lost between $8 million and $10 million on the stockmarket in the aftermath of the 1929 crash.

It was the figure of $10 million that set Spurdle off. If Fisher had dropped a couple of mill, he mightn't have taken that much notice. But $10 million? *Fuck me dead, that's exactly what I'm worth. And if Fisher, who was obviously Captain Cock when it came to economics and finance and that, could fuck up big-time, where does that leave me?*

Spurdle rang his broker from Honolulu and ordered him to sell his entire share portfolio. When his broker tried to talk him out of it, Spurdle asked him if he'd actually read John Kenneth Galbraith's *Money*.

'Oh I started it but I didn't get far. I told you it was dry balls.'

'So you didn't get to the bit about Irving Fisher?'

'Irving who?

'Irving Fisher. He was a hot-shot economist, a real fucking brainbox, who sucked the pineapple in the Wall Street crash. If you'd heard of him, I might listen to you but seeing you haven't, just pipe down and sell my fucking shares – every last one of the bastards.'

Thanks to J.K. Galbraith and Irving Fisher, Spurdle sat out the October 1987 stockmarket crash and was now even richer. However, it was the nature of the beast that no matter how rich he got, it wouldn't be rich enough.

So Bryce Spurdle sat out on the pavement at the Sierra café sipping his second cappuccino, nibbling on a blueberry muffin, and thinking about Dale Varty and money. *That was Dale's big problem*, he thought; *he never really understood money, never grasped that money wasn't just the main game, it was the only game. Personal stuff didn't enter into it – you couldn't afford to let it get in the way. Christ, just because I pulled that number on him down at Coromandel didn't mean I'd gone off him; it was just the smart thing to do.*

But Varty had turned the tables on Al Grills, something Spurdle wouldn't have picked in a hundred years. And he'd taken it personally all right; by Christ he had. Two nights after the rendezvous at Otama, Spurdle's bedside phone rang at 3 o'clock in the morning. He'd checked the time and picked up the phone on the sixth ring.

'Who the hell is this?'

There was a few seconds' silence. Spurdle started to repeat the question when Varty interrupted him.

'It's me.'

'Dale, where the hell are you, mate? I've been waiting to hear from you. Jesus, what happened the other night?'

'You can knock that shit off,' said Varty in a flat, hostile voice Spurdle hadn't heard before. 'Grills told me all about it. "Spurdle's jacked up a little welcome home surprise for you" was what he told me.'

'I don't get it. What are you talking about?'

'You know fucking well. You lined up that bastard to get rid of me.'

'Dale, just listen to me for a minute. Grills must've decided to go solo. He would've made out I had something to do with it just to rub it in. That'd be the sort of shithouse ...'

'You'll have to do better than that, arsehole. Grills was just the hired help; it was your idea all right. You set me up, you fucking cunt. This call is just to tell you that I know what you did and that one of these days, I'm going to get you for it. When I do, I'll cut your nuts off and feed them to you, you poxy piece of filth.'

*

Spurdle was getting up to pay the bill when his mobile rang.

'Bryce Spurdle.'

'Mr Spurdle, this is Leith Grills – Al's brother.'

'How'd you get hold of this number?'

'I rang your place and the woman who answered the phone gave it to me. That okay?'

Spurdle sighed and shook his head. 'Yeah. What can I do for you?'

'You seen the paper?'

'You mean about Varty coming back? What about it?'

'That fucker killed my brother, Mr Spurdle. Al was working for you at the time. I reckon we owe it to Al to pay Varty back.'

Owe it to Al? What was this moron talking about? Spurdle glanced around. The only other people at the pavement tables were two overdressed women trying to talk over each other; they wouldn't have taken any notice if he'd recited all 20 verses of *The Captain of the Lugger* at the top of his voice. Spurdle hardly knew Leith Grills; he vaguely remembered him as a bigger, uglier and denser version of his dead older brother – and, by all accounts, even more of a headcase. *I could do with someone like that right now*, he thought.

'Well, Leith, I reckon Al understood that risks were part of the job,' said Spurdle in a low voice. 'Went with the territory, you know what I mean? Anyway, let's not worry about that. Fuck Varty – the bastard promised he'd come back and get me too. Listen, why don't you come out to my place tomorrow, say around lunchtime? We can have a bite to eat and a few beers and talk about this.'

After he'd got off the phone, Spurdle went back to thinking about Dale Varty and the deal that went sour. Varty had obviously gotten away with the ten kilos of cocaine; there was no way he'd taken it with him when he skedaddled out of the country and he obviously hadn't been back to collect it since then. Spurdle knew the local drug scene well enough to be sure the cocaine had never found its way onto the market. Christ, you couldn't have missed it, not that much top-shelf snort, even if it'd been drip-fed. Where all that led was that the coke was still wherever Varty had hidden it.

It wasn't the first time that Spurdle had thought about the cocaine but without any sort of line on its whereabouts, it had never been worth pursuing. Now the only person who knew where the treasure was buried was coming back.

Because Spurdle was a cautious man, he didn't use his mobile phone to make the call. Instead he drove around till he found a public phone box. He rang the chemistry department at the university and asked to speak to someone who was an expert on narcotics. He was put through to a Dr Wong.

'Dr Wong, my name's Bevan Jones. I'm a journalist at the *Sunday News* and I'm working on a story about drugs. I was wondering if you could tell me how long drugs last for? I mean, do they have like, a use-by date?'

'Which drugs are we talking about?'

'Let's say cocaine.'

'In solution cocaine has a ten-year half-life, that's to say after ten years, it retains 50 per cent of its potency. In powder form it could last considerably longer. Of course, that's the laboratory answer if you like; in practice, all sorts of factors could cause it to degenerate much more quickly.'

Spurdle didn't like the sound of that. 'Like what?'

'Well, is it pure? Is it bulk raw material? Is it moisture-free? Is it away from the light? What temperature is it being stored at? You see, the higher the temperature, the quicker it degrades.'

Spurdle thought swiftly: *if there's one thing Varty knows about, it's dope; he would've done it dead right.*

'Let's say it's pure and it's been stored properly.'

'In that case, the best answer I can give you is that I don't really know how long it would last because very little research has been done in that area. Certainly ten years but who knows beyond that? If it's completely airtight and kept at a low temperature, it could quite conceivably remain potent for 20 years. Again in theory the potency would reduce at a rate of ten per cent over five years but if it was pure to start with, it would still be extremely potent.'

In the phone box Spurdle grinned broadly. 'Thanks, doc. You've been a big help.'

'Tell me something,' said Dr Wong. 'Did a big drug story break today? The reason I ask is you're the second journalist who's rung this morning asking that question.'

Seven

After the Customs officer had finished going where no man had gone before, Duane Ricketts got dressed, picked up his bags and walked somewhat gingerly out of the terminal. To save money, he got a mini-bus rather than a taxi. Because he was the last passenger on board and because the mini-buses operate on a first-on, first-off basis, the trip lasted a little over an hour and a quarter which is how long it takes to get from the airport to Mt Roskill if you go via One Tree Hill, Ellerslie, Mt Eden and Balmoral. Ricketts whiled away the time thinking about what he'd do with the $10 he'd saved.

Ricketts' house was a moderately ugly, white-painted wooden bungalow with a garage, a shed, front and back lawns bordered with sparsely planted flowerbeds, a washing line and a vegetable garden in which he'd once tried to grow potatoes, capsicums and lettuces but now just weeded a few times a year for the exercise. He was pleased and mildly surprised to find that his seven-year-old Toyota Corolla was still in the garage and the house hadn't been broken into. The letterbox contained a few bills, leaflets advertising everything from bulk meat to three different types of manure, and an invitation to be present at the Second Coming, which apparently would take place a few doors down the street ten days hence. Ricketts, who didn't believe in anything much, let alone God, found the notion that the Lord Jesus would choose Mt Roskill as the venue for his comeback a little far-fetched.

Mt Roskill has a well-deserved reputation for religious zaniness. Ricketts sometimes amused himself at the supermarket by advising shoppers not to go overboard on toilet paper because he had it on good authority that the end of the world was nigh. Now and again a shopper would nod solemnly, say something like, 'Gosh, so it is; it'd slipped my mind', and put a few rolls back on the shelf. When people told Ricketts that Mt Roskill had no redeeming features, he'd reply that that was what made it affordable. He'd also point out that it was one of the few, if not only, parts of Auckland where you could get a three-bedroom house for under 150 grand within five minutes' drive of two reasonable golf courses.

After he'd had a shower, Ricketts weighed himself on the bathroom scales. He was 74 kg, almost a stone underweight in the old measurement. He looked in the mirror; the face that looked back at him was only half-familiar. His eyes had sunk deep into their sockets; there were lines which hadn't been there a month ago etched into his cheeks and his dark hair seemed faded and lifeless, like a cheap wig. *Maybe you should go along to the Second Coming*, he thought, *you'd blend right in with the mad and the marginal.* Instead he decided to go and see his sister down on the farm.

Ricketts' sister Shirley and her husband Lloyd had a dairy farm on the Hauraki Plains, not far from Paeroa. Ricketts got there just after ten the next morning, having rung ahead. Shirley took one look at him and said: 'Jesus, Duane, what've you been up to this time?'

He started to tell her about his adventures in Thailand but she interrupted saying they had all day to gasbag, right now the main thing was to get some food into him, he looked like he hadn't had a decent feed since Christmas dinner. Then she cooked him bacon, sausages, eggs, fried tomatoes and mushrooms which, apart from the mushrooms, was exactly what Ricketts had expected. Lunch, three hours later, was cold leg of lamb and salad followed by bread and cheese. That evening they had roast beef, potatoes, kumara, carrots and beans, with homemade apple pie and ice-cream for dessert. By the time the kids went to bed, Ricketts was two shots into his bottle of duty-free Remy Martin and starting to feel like a new man.

Ricketts had intended to stay the weekend at Shirley and Lloyd's. He'd thought the rehabilitation process would take at least that long and had contemplated putting in a few hours' work around the farm to reactivate muscles and get that country air through the lungs. In the end though, he decided to head back to town on Saturday. He had two reasons for cutting short his stay: the first was that when, following Varty's instructions, he'd rung the lawyer Bart Clegg, Clegg had said they'd have to meet on Sunday; he had a case in Wellington starting Monday morning that would probably go all week. The second was Ricketts' feeling that he was beginning to outstay his welcome.

He'd started to get the feeling just after he'd confessed, halfway through his third cognac, that 'to be absolutely honest, it was heroin I got done for, not marijuana'. At breakfast the next morning Shirley carried on as if she thought the moment she turned her back, he'd be sprinkling some mind-rotting addictive substance on the kids' Cornflakes. And from Lloyd's reaction when Ricketts offered to give him a hand, there was obviously no way he was going to allow a dope-sucking degenerate in the same paddock as his Friesians.

On Saturday morning, just before noon, Ricketts stopped to buy fruit and vegetables at a roadside stall at the foot of the Bombay Hills. The place was busy, so while he waited to pay, he flicked through a copy of that morning's *Herald* which was lying on the counter; it was the first time he'd looked at a newspaper since he'd got back. He wasn't really concentrating so it was a fluke he even noticed the story which was little more than a filler tucked away at the foot of an inside page. The two-deck headline said, 'Mr Asia Man's Mystery Death', and the story went:

Mystery surrounds the death in Bangkok of former Mr Asia drug syndicate member Dale Varty.

Yesterday the New Zealand Press Association reported that the 53-year-old New Zealander was about to be released from a Thai jail after serving a 10-year sentence for drug trafficking.

However Thai authorities subsequently informed the New Zealand embassy in Bangkok that Varty had died of unspecified causes shortly before he was due to be released. The authorities said Varty had been taken ill suddenly in Bangkok's Bombat Drug Rehabilitation Centre and died a short time later in the prison clinic. The embassy is now seeking information on the exact circumstances and cause of death.

What the hell's all that about? wondered Ricketts. By the time he'd paid for his fruit and vegetables, he'd concluded – correctly – that it was about people covering their arses.

*

Rayleen Crouch slept in on Saturdays so she didn't get around to reading the paper until mid-morning. After she'd made a cup of tea and heated up a croissant, she took her breakfast and the paper back to the bedroom and opened the curtains to let in the autumn sun. She was sitting on the bed in her dressing-gown propped up on two pillows when she learned that her former husband's old life was the only one he was going to have.

The news caused mixed emotions. The previous afternoon she'd spent a frustrating hour and a half trying to get hold of her daughter, Electra, who didn't look at a newspaper from one year to the next, to let her know that her father was coming back to Auckland. Electra, who was 18, had moved out of her mother's house a couple of months earlier after a row. Crouch couldn't remember whether the row had been over Electra's new nosering, new boyfriend or new rock band; seeing she'd disapproved of all of them, it was just a question of which one she'd criticised first. In fact it was the band they'd argued about: Electra was the founder member and lead singer of The Homo Dwarves, and Crouch, who held a range of progressive views, felt strongly that to call the band one politically incorrect name was bad enough but two was verging on shameful.

Ever since Electra was 14 she'd been threatening to leave home – she'd actually done it a few times although only for a day or two – so Crouch hadn't taken much notice when she'd packed her bag and stormed out. This time though, she seemed to be serious. Her mother assumed it meant she'd found herself a sugar daddy or else The Homo Dwarves were hot.

Electra rang in now and again to confirm she was still in one piece. Each time Crouch assured her she was welcome to come home whenever she wanted to; each time Electra replied that she'd bear it in mind but she felt it was doing her some good standing on her own two feet for a while. And each time, on hearing those words, Crouch, who was enjoying having some space, uttered a silent prayer of thanks.

Because Electra was rather vague about exactly where and with whom she was living, her mother had been unable to track her down the day before. Under the circumstances, thought Crouch, it was just as well.

*

Leith Grills hadn't read the paper before leaving home. That didn't really matter because when the front door of the Spurdle residence opened and he saw Jody Spurdle standing there pointing her extraordinary breasts at him, his mind went completely blank as it tended to do at moments of sensory overload.

Bryce Spurdle was sitting at the bar in his den-cum-snooker room having his first beer of the day and reading the racing pages when his wife ushered in their guest. Spurdle looked up. The first thing he noticed was that Jody had on a new gym outfit; in keeping with tradition, it exposed even more of her body than its predecessor. The second thing he noticed was that Leith Grills wasn't looking at him; instead he was staring at Jody's breasts, which were partly encased in a white sports bra, with the glassy, disbelieving expression of a man who's just run over his foot with the lawnmower.

Grills certainly wasn't the first man to ogle Spurdle's wife in his presence; none of the others, though, had been anywhere near as brazen about it. Spurdle noted Grills' slack jaw, his fixed, dull gaze, and the thick, black, continuous strip of eyebrow which seemed to wriggle across his low forehead and the bridge of his blunt nose like a tropical caterpillar. Having done so, he decided that expecting social graces from Grills was as unrealistic as expecting a sheep to play the guitar solo from 'Layla'.

'I'm off to the gym, hon,' said Jody. 'See you later.' She looked briefly and dubiously at Grills and told him, with patent insincerity, 'Nice to've met you.'

Grills lifted his empty dark eyes from her chest to her face and attempted a polite half-smile. Jody, who was used to men looking at her with longing and worse, left the room thinking that Grills' lewd, vacant grimace was one of the most horrible sights she'd ever seen.

'Fucking hell, Mr Spurdle,' said Grills after Jody had closed the door behind her. 'If you don't mind me saying so, your wife – she's a knockout.'

'You noticed, did you?' said Spurdle dryly.

'Shit, you couldn't help it. Tell you what, you're a lucky bloke …'

'Yeah, so I've been told. I tried to get hold of you this morning, to tell you not to bother coming over. Varty's dead.'

He handed the paper to Grills who read the story, mouthing the words.

'It doesn't make sense, Mr Spurdle. Yesterday the paper said he was coming back here.'

'Well, what it said was he was going to come back when he got out of jail. He must've picked up some fucking disease at the last minute and croaked on it. You'd think he'd have been immune after that long, wouldn't you? Anyway, that's him fucked. Bit of a bummer really. You know that dope he ripped off Al? I'm bloody sure it's still sitting there, wherever he hid it. I was hoping we could persuade him to let us in on the secret.'

Grills thought about it for a while. 'He must've told some bastard.'

Spurdle shook his head. 'Doubt it. He didn't trust a soul, Dale.'

'Didn't he have a wife? A fair-looking piece if I remember right – not in your missus' class but not too foul all the same. You reckon he might've told her?'

'Rayleen? No – she'd be the last person he'd tell. The reason they split in the first place was him pushing drugs, then they had a real shitfight over the kid. By the time it all went down, they were history.'

*

Jody Spurdle had been deliberately vague when she'd told her husband that she was going to the gym since she was actually a member of three gyms – one in Mairangi Bay, one in Shore

City, Takapuna, and one over in the city. She found that having a choice of gyms as well as outfits provided that element of variety which helped her keep to her exercise routine.

Another benefit of belonging to three gyms was that it made it harder for Bryce to keep tabs on her, which was useful when, as was the case that Saturday afternoon, she used going to the gym as a cover for seeing her lover. He was a fitness instructor and part-time model named Troy Goatley who rented a waterfront house in Belmont for $300 a week. Jody contributed $100 of that out of her allowance so that Troy didn't need to have a flatmate; having someone else around the place would've inhibited their relationship and the gymnastic and vocal sex of which it almost exclusively consisted.

After Goatley and Mrs Spurdle had had sex, which involved a lot of changing of positions, sometimes for technical reasons and sometimes so that they could get a better view of themselves in the full-length wardrobe mirrors, Troy went to the kitchen to make a restorative drink. When he returned to the bedroom Jody was lying on her back, an arm behind her head, staring at the ceiling.

'You're looking serious, babe. Got something on your mind?'

'You know that cop who comes into the gym, the one who told you Bryce used to be involved in drugs?'

'Wayne? What about him?'

'Could you ask him if he's ever heard of a guy called Leith Grills?'

'Leith Grills? Yeah, sure. Who's he?'

'This really creepy guy who came out to see Bryce today. He looks like a real hood.'

'You think Bryce might be going back into the drug business?'

Jody rolled onto her side. 'Even if he was ever in it – and we've only got that Wayne's word for it – why would he want to do that now? No, it's just this guy Grills; he gave me the screaming shits – he looked at me as if he was like, trying to memorise every detail about me. Coming over here I suddenly thought, Christ, maybe Bryce's hired him to check up on me. I don't know, maybe I'm getting paranoid; it's just there's been a couple of things lately made me wonder if he suspects something. The other night, right, I walked into the bedroom and found him going through the washing basket. My gym gear was in there but I hadn't been to the gym. I was here all afternoon.'

She looked at Goatley expectantly; he looked back blankly. 'I don't get it, babe. So what?'

'When I've done a workout, my gear's real sweaty, okay?' said Jody impatiently. 'Sometimes it's like, sopping wet. So if he touched it when he was rummaging in the washing basket, don't you think he might've wondered how come it was dry?'

Goatley shrugged his meaty shoulders. 'So if it wasn't sweaty, why'd you put it in the basket in the first place?'

'Oh gee, thanks, professor,' said Jody sarcastically. 'I just thought it was safer seeing he'd seen me walk out of the house in it. He doesn't make a habit of going through the washing basket, believe it or not.'

'You don't have to bite my head off,' said Goatley with a wounded air. 'I just wondered, that's all. You ask him what he was looking for?'

'Course I did. He said he thought he'd left some money in a shirt pocket. He didn't find any.'

'Well, did he say anything about your gym gear?'

Jody rolled onto her back, swung her long, golden-brown legs to the floor and stood up. 'If he had've, I probably wouldn't be here, would I? I told you, I could be getting paranoid but this guy today freaked me out. Just do me a favour, okay, and ask that cop about him?'

'I said I'd do it, didn't I?' said Goatley a little sullenly as it dawned on him that the matinee wasn't going to have an encore. 'In fact I'll do it this arvo. Got nothing better to do.'

*

Everton Sloan III, the youngest and brightest of the CIA officers attached to the US embassy in Bangkok, was sitting at his desk trying to catch up on his paperwork when the embassy chief of staff burst into his office.

'You seen that fucking Funke?' he demanded.

Sloan, who knew that his Ivy League appearance and mannerisms annoyed the chief of staff more than most people, slowly removed his horn-rimmed glasses.

'Buddy?' He shook his head. 'Haven't set eyes on him for a couple of days. I seem to recall him muttering something about going up country. Why? Is there a problem?'

The chief of staff slumped into the chair in front of Sloan's desk. 'You'd think I'd know better than to come in here on a Saturday, wouldn't you? The goddamn phone rings, you answer it, and you're stuck with someone else's fucking problem.'

'Anything I can do?'

The chief of staff gave Sloan a sharp look. If anyone else in the embassy asked a question like that, he'd automatically assume they were being sarcastic; either that or they'd have some outrageous favour in return up their sleeves. Sloan was his usual boyish and apparently guileless self. The chief of staff had learned long ago not to judge a book by its cover. Besides, he kept hearing how Sloan was as smart as a whip and already earmarked for stardom by the big dicks at Langley.

'You mean it?' he asked suspiciously.

Sloan held out his hands, palms upwards. 'I'm just doing paperwork – nothing that won't keep.'

'Well, I'd sure appreciate it, Ev. I promised Milly I'd be home by one. We're having a cookout and guess who's on chef duty.'

Sloan smiled pleasantly. 'Well, seeing as how I'm not invited, who better than I to pick up the ball?'

The chief of staff grinned weakly. 'Hey Ev, it's one of those family things – kids everywhere. You'd be bored shitless. But listen, if you get though by three or so, come on over by all means.'

Sloan's smile broadened slightly. 'We'll see. Now what've we got here?'

'Okay. The other night a transvestite was found shot dead down by the Chitladda Palace. So fucking what, right? Well, it turns out he should've been in the slam instead of peddling his ass on Patpong; he'd been in Bombat, wasn't due out for another month. The call I took, it's the superintendent at Bombat and he's pissed off; his deputy's telling him it was Funke's idea to turn this character loose early. Now the transvestite's family's making waves and everyone's running around looking for someone else to blame. Shit, you know how it goes.'

Sloan nodded. 'You got any details?'

The chief of staff handed him a piece of paper containing a list of names and phone numbers. 'Phumkumpol, that's the dead fag. The name below that is the cop handling the case and the bottom one is the deputy superintendent.'

'Leave it with me,' said Sloan. 'I'll check it out.'

The chief of staff stood up beaming. 'I owe you one, pal.'

Sloan put his glasses back on. 'Rest assured, I'll think of something.'

Eight

Although Everton Sloan III was philosophically and temperamentally inclined towards pessimism, he didn't expect the brouhaha over the murdered transvestite to amount to much: a 24-hour wonder, he reckoned, if that.

The way Sloan figured it, if Funke really had leaned on the deputy superintendent of Bombat to spring the transvestite, he was probably just doing an informer a favour. Either that or he'd had a use for him, maybe as a stooge, witting or unwitting, in some kind of entrapment operation. It hadn't gone entirely to plan – such ploys seldom did – and Phumkumpol had been dispatched to the great sex-change clinic in the sky. That was an extremely bad break for him but the Thais would be pissing against the Hoover Dam if they tried to make an issue of it. Funke was, after all, a badge-carrying agent of the US of A engaged in the war against the forces of darkness. It was a war which was short on rules but long on collateral damage. That was a fact of life and the superintendent of Bombat could either like it or he could eat it raw.

It took four phone calls to persuade Everton Sloan III that the situation was somewhat more complicated than he'd imagined.

The first call was to a contact in the Bangkok police to get the basic facts about the victim and the circumstances of his demise. The contact rang back half an hour later with the information that Kham Phumkumpol *aka* Brandi had been in Bombat on a two-bit marijuana charge, probably as a result of getting caught up in some kind of police shakedown. He had no known links to the drug gangs, big or small. The murder had taken place in the early hours of Thursday morning, shortly after Brandi left the ladyboy hang-out on Patpong Road. That indicated it might have been transactional in origin; on the other hand, he'd been blown away in a no-nonsense, even professional, fashion which tended to undermine the theory that Brandi was shot because he'd over-charged or under-performed.

Next Sloan rang the deputy superintendent at Bombat.

'I understand,' said Sloan, 'that it was special agent Funke's idea to release Mr Phumkumpol early?'

'Right. Mr Funke, he tell me to let Brandi go because he cause so much trouble,' answered the deputy superintendent in the agitated tone of a prison administrator who's seen the future and it largely involves washing out latrines. 'Also he could be in danger here – maybe some guys want to get him for what happened.'

After a pause to admire the deputy superintendent's ability to utter that last sentence without a trace of irony in his voice, Sloan asked: 'What did happen?'

The deputy superintendent told Sloan about Brandi's role in Dale Varty's stabbing, concluding, 'Ladyboys, they make trouble all the time, but this one, he the worst, for sure.'

'As a matter of interest, how did agent Funke get to hear about this incident?'

'Mr Funke, he DEA, okay? So when Brandi tell me how he hear the New Zealand guys talking about their drugs, I say to myself "you got to call Mr Funke".'

Whoa, thought Sloan. *New Zealanders? Drugs? Run that by me again.*

The deputy superintendent told Sloan that Varty, the one who was stabbed by Brandi's boyfriend, had told Duane Ricketts, the one who'd got bail and been driven away from the prison by someone from his embassy, about a stash of drugs hidden in New Zealand. While Sloan was trying to make sense of it all, the deputy superintendent asked the question he'd been wanting to ask since the start of the conversation: 'Why you not talk to Mr Funke? He explain everything.'

'Agent Funke's not around right now. He's out of town somewhere.'

'Maybe he gone to New Zealand, huh? Find the drugs. That his job, right?' The superintendent's voice dropped to a near whisper. 'For sure he very interested in this. I know because he ask me for copies of files – for Brandi, Varty and Ricketts. I not meant to do that but hey, we on the same side, right? We have to help each other.'

Sloan hung up and stared thoughtfully at the ceiling for a minute or two. Then he rang the New Zealand embassy and asked to speak to the official who'd collected Ricketts from Bombat. The call was put through to Jason Maltby who was tidying his desk prior to taking a fortnight's leave in New Zealand – at the ambassador's suggestion.

Sloan introduced himself and asked Maltby if he could confirm that Ricketts had returned to New Zealand.

'I believe he has. Put it this way, he was booked on a flight to Auckland last Tuesday and we haven't seen or heard from him since. You'd be aware of course that it's not against Thai law for someone to leave the country when they're on bail?'

'Is that right? Frankly, over here we don't lie awake nights worrying about what is or isn't against Thai law...'

'Don't tell me you've got to do a report as well? Good grief, you people must be in constant danger of being buried alive under an avalanche of paper.'

'Excuse me?'

'Just the other day I had a colleague of yours – one of the anti-drug police whatever they're called – on to me, wanting details of Varty's next of kin; said he needed it for a report he was doing. The mind boggles. Rather you than us is all I can say.'

'Would that've been agent Funke?'

'Funke, that's the man. Seemed like a nice chap. What part of the States does he come from with that accent? Somewhere in the Deep South, I imagine.'

'Agent Funke's from Texas – a good ol' boy from the Lone Star state.'

Texas, thought Sloan, *where everything's bigger and better than anywhere else. Including the bullshitters.*

Sloan's fourth and final call was to Funke's condominium. The Filipina maid said Funke had gone away the previous evening. He hadn't said where to or for how long.

Sloan walked down the corridor to Funke's office which he carefully searched. As he'd expected, he didn't find anything which shed light on what Funke was up to. There were a few colour photographs in the top drawer of the desk; they'd been taken at a country club outside Bangkok, the expat American community's favoured R and R locale. One of them showed a grinning Funke making a pistol sign at the camera with his thumb and forefinger.

Sloan's mouth twisted into a sour, ironic smile as he looked at the photo. The blithe confidence with which he'd sallied forth an hour earlier had now dissipated completely. Perversely, he found it almost reassuring that his optimism had proved ill-founded. Like most pessimists, Sloan believed it was safer to expect the worst; that way, life held fewer disappointments.

At 10 o'clock that night Sloan went into the ladyboy bar on Patpong Road. He bought a Heineken and showed the barman the photograph of Buddy Funke in his gunfighter pose. The barman shrugged unhelpfully. Sloan showed the photograph to the other staff and a few of the regulars. One of the regulars, a petite transvestite, was sure Funke had been in the bar only a few nights before, maybe Wednesday or Thursday. The reason the transvestite remembered was that when he'd asked the man in the photo to buy him a drink, he'd told him to go rub his phoney gash up against someone else.

*

At 9.25 the next morning Jody Spurdle was driving back from the bakery in Forrest Hill in her Volkswagen Golf convertible with a Sunday paper, a crusty white loaf for her husband and a mixed grain loaf for herself when the car phone rang. It was her lover Troy Goatley.

'Hey, babe, you were right on the money about that Grills character – he's a bad dude.'

'Why, what's he done?'

'Well, he hasn't killed anyone – not that the cops know of anyway …'

'Troy, Jesus, don't joke about it, all right? Just tell me.'

'He's just a lowlife, that's all. He's been inside a couple of times, once for receiving stolen goods, once for burglary, and he got off some other stuff. How about this though: his brother, who was also a crim, was murdered about ten years ago – beaten to death somewhere down Coromandel. They never caught the killer. Is that spooky or what?'

Over breakfast in the sun room, Jody Spurdle studied her husband for signs that she was under suspicion. There were none. As usual he didn't close his mouth as he chewed so watching him eat was like watching a paisley shirt in a tumble dryer; as usual he made wet, lapping noises of the sort she associated with cats or old ladies with wobbly teeth; as usual he dredged his teacup dry with three or four abrupt slurps, rarely lifted his eyes from the sports section, and made a beeline for the toilet as soon as he'd finished. It was all reassuringly normal.

He was still in the toilet when the phone rang. Jody answered it.

'That you, Mrs Spurdle? Leith Grills here. How're you going today, kicking on?'

Over the sudden pounding of her heart, Jody heard the toilet flush down the corridor.

'I'm okay. You want to speak to Bryce?'

'Yeah, he called here this morning, left a message for me to ring him.'

'I'll just get him...'

'Oh, before you go Mrs Spurdle, let me ask you something. How regular do you go to the gym? Reason I ask, just recently my missus has porked up in a big way and I was thinking she could take a leaf out of your book. Not that she'd look like you if she worked out till kingdom come, but it might stop her turning into a complete blob, eh?'

Jody could hardly believe her ears; her cheeks lit up like a neon sign. She stammered, 'Four or five times a week I guess,' and dropped the phone with a clunk.

She ducked into the bathroom to splash water on her face then walked down to the den to tell her husband, who was setting up balls on the snooker table, that Leith Grills was on the phone. She went back to hang up the phone in the hall. Before she did so, she listened for a few seconds.

'... you know what I said yesterday about the wife?' she heard Bryce say. 'Well, I've had another think about it and I want you to get onto her straightaway. You reckon you can handle that?'

'Just leave it to me,' replied Grills, his voice brimming with anticipation.

Jody replaced the handset shakily, terror leaping from the pit of her stomach like vomit.

*

Varty had told Ricketts to use the lawyer Bart Clegg as a go-between for getting in touch with his daughter. He'd explained that if his ex-wife Rayleen got wind of what was happening, she wouldn't let him get within a bull's roar of Electra. So at 1.35 that afternoon, Ricketts pulled up outside Clegg's house in Ladies Mile, Remuera. He was five minutes late. It was a still, overcast afternoon and the lack of activity in the street suggested the residents were concentrating on Sunday lunch.

Clegg lived in a gracious old white-painted wooden villa, screened off from the street by a towering oak tree in the middle of the front lawn. Ricketts walked up the path and mounted the steps to the veranda. He pressed the doorbell and waited. A minute passed; no-one came to the door. He jabbed the button several times in quick succession but that too failed to draw a response. Ricketts peered in the window into a dining room which contained an expensive-looking table with seating for eight and a matching sideboard on which were arrayed several crystal decanters and a set of goblets. To the left of the house was a single garage with a tilt door which was lowered but not locked. Clegg lifted it up. The garage housed a dark-blue Alfa Romeo 164 but, like the dining room, was devoid of anything resembling a lawyer.

Thinking that Clegg might be round the back of his section pruning his roses or playing in his tree-hut and hadn't heard the doorbell, Ricketts followed the path down the right of the house. Clegg's back yard was even more private, with a two-metre fence and some fine old trees to block prying eyes, not that there was anyone in it to observe.

Steps led up to a wooden deck and the back door. Ricketts stopped at the foot of the steps and listened; he could hear a hissing, bubbling noise. He went up the steps. The noise was coming from a spa pool; no-one was in the spa but it was on full-bore, bubbling away furiously and foaming over the rim onto the deck. On the deck beside the spa pool was a three-quarters empty champagne bottle and a long-stemmed glass.

Ricketts looked in the window; there was nobody in the kitchen. He knocked loudly on the back door and called Clegg's name; still no answer. After a minute or so, he walked over and looked down at the spa. There were a few filmy white patches, like big soapflakes, among the bubbles. Ricketts knelt and scooped one off the froth. He found the switch for the spa and turned it off. It took a couple of minutes for the bubbling to die down and reveal more flakes floating on the surface.

The spa pool was oval, about two metres long and a metre and a half across with an underwater seat protruding from the sides. As the turbulence subsided, Ricketts could make out something large and white jammed under the seat. He craned forward for a closer look.

It took him a few seconds to work out that what he was looking at was a body. It took him a few more seconds to realise that, that being the case, the filmy white substance he'd skimmed off the surface of the pool was more than likely skin.

*

Ricketts didn't waste much time wondering what to do next. He knew he had no choice but to report his grisly find and hope for the best. He could wipe down the doorbell and clear off but the cops would almost certainly get on to him before long. His call to Clegg to set up the meeting might've been logged by the lawyer's secretary; more to the point, Clegg probably put the meeting in his diary. His car had been parked out the front for a quarter of an hour so if he did a runner now and one of the neighbours had happened to notice the car, he'd be in deep shit.

Ricketts went in the back door to the kitchen. He used the phone on the bench to ring Auckland Central police station and ask for Detective Sergeant Ihaka. It was Ihaka's day off.

'Track him down,' Ricketts told the officer who'd taken the call. 'Tell him it's Duane Ricketts and it's important. Get a phone number off him. I'll call back in ten minutes.'

When Ricketts rang back, the officer gave him a number, adding, 'Ihaka said he's really looking forward to hearing from you.'

Ricketts dialled the number and a little girl answered. He asked for Tito Ihaka and heard her holler, 'Uncle Tito, you're wanted on the phone.'

'Ricketts?'

'Uncle Tito – how cute.'

'Let me guess, Ricketts: you want me to sponsor you onto a methadone program?'

'No, that's under control – I held up a chemist this morning.'

'Then what can I do for you?'

'What you can do for me is eat shit and die. What you can do for the people of Auckland, who you're paid to protect and serve, is get your fat arse over to Ladies Mile. There's a death by extremely fucking unnatural causes awaiting your attention.'

'Who?'

'Don't know for sure but if I had to make a wild guess, I'd go for Bart Clegg.'

'Who's he?'

'A lawyer.'

'A lawyer? Dearie me, we can't afford to lose one of them. What happened to him?'

'Under the rather unusual circumstances, I'll have to pass on that.'

'I take it we have a corpse?'

'We sure do.'

'Where?'

'In the spa pool. Been in there for quite a while I'd say – with the juice on. When you pull him out, I reckon he'll be like a great big lump of industrial-strength soap.'

'I can't wait. All right, what's the address?'

Ricketts told him.

'Oh Ricketts, one more thing.'

'Yeah.'

'Did you do it?'

'As a matter of fact, no.'

There was a long silence.

'Don't you believe me?'

Ihaka guffawed explosively. 'What sort of poophead question is that? I can think of a couple of people who I'd put down as incapable of committing a murder but you sure as fuck aren't one of them. And if you did clip someone, this is just the sort of sick but tricky way you'd do it. Plus, of course, you'd have the nerve and the nous to do exactly what you're doing now.'

'You know something, Ihaka?'

'What?'

'That's the nicest thing you've ever said to me.'

Nine

As instructed, Duane Ricketts reported to the Auckland Central police station at 9 a.m. on Monday morning. He was taken up to the eighth floor and shown into a small conference room. A few minutes later Detective Sergeant Tito Ihaka booted the door open and came in. He was dressed in jeans and a T-shirt and carried two plastic cups containing coffee, one of which he plonked down on the table in front of Ricketts.

'It's sewage but it's all there is,' said Ihaka. 'McGrail's on his way.'

Ricketts nodded. He hadn't met Detective Inspector Mc-Grail and wasn't particularly anxious to do so. He'd once heard a cop describe McGrail as having all the warmth and personality of a dead eel. He took a tentative sip of the coffee; it was quite horrible.

He pushed the plastic cup away. 'Christ almighty, how can you drink that shit?'

'It's not easy,' said Ihaka, as if he was giving the question serious consideration. 'We look at it as a challenge. By the way, the weirdos downstairs tell us the thing we pulled out of the spa definitely used to be Bart Clegg.'

'What sort of state was he in?'

'What you were saying about a lump of soap wasn't far wrong. We'll learn fuck-all from the autopsy, you can put the ring around that.'

'Do you know what that soapy stuff on a floater's called?'

Ihaka looked at his watch. 'A corpse joke at ten past nine on Monday morning – that could be a record.'

'It's not a joke – it's called adipocere.'

'Adi-fucking-what?'

'Adipocere. Look it up in the dictionary – it might come in handy next time you play Scrabble.'

The door opened and Detective Inspector Finbar McGrail, ex of the Royal Ulster Constabulary, entered the room. He wore shiny black shoes, sharply creased grey trousers, a glossy, perfectly ironed white shirt with the sleeves carefully rolled above the wrist, and a navy-blue tie with the words '1987 Boston Marathon' in yellow lettering. His face had a pink, freshly shaved tinge and his short dark hair had been combed into place while still damp. Ricketts suspected McGrail trimmed his ear- and nose-hairs every morning, in fact, he would've put money on it.

McGrail had several manila folders under his left arm and a bone-china teacup and saucer in his right hand. He sat down opposite Ricketts, took a sip of tea, and leafed through the contents of one of the folders. Ricketts glanced at Ihaka, who winked at him and leaned back, tilting his chair precariously. Finally, McGrail looked up. He examined Ricketts, wrinkling his nose suspiciously like a health inspector sifting through the innards of a suspect meat pie.

'I see you used to be a police officer, Mr Ricketts,' he said in his Ulster brogue. At the far end of the table Ihaka, trying not to laugh, made an unpleasant, phlegmy noise.

'Yeah. Few years ago now.'

'Hmmm, you've picked up some bad habits since you left the force.'

Ricketts started to ask what the bloody hell his habits had to do with anything when McGrail, raising his voice, interrupted: 'Your movements, please, since you arrived back in the country.'

'I got back on Thursday afternoon and was met at the airport by my faithful manservant Ihaka.' McGrail's thin lips formed a wintry smile. 'Then on Friday morning I went down to my sister's place on the Hauraki Plains – that's sister, brother-in-law and a couple of kids in case you were wondering. I came back on Saturday afternoon and I've been at home since – apart from going to Clegg's.'

'We'll check with your sister's family and you'd better cross your fingers that Clegg died while you were out of town. As you can imagine, establishing time of death isn't a straightforward matter. So what were you doing at his house?'

'I told one of your blokes all this yesterday.'

'Now you're about to tell me.'

Ricketts breathed through his nose long-sufferingly. 'When I was up in Thailand, I came across Dale Varty ...'

'That was in jail, of course?'

'No, in a Buddhist monastery. He asked me to give Clegg a bell when I got home, pass on his regards. I rang Clegg last week to do that and he said come over for a beer on Sunday afternoon. That's what I was doing there.'

'Varty was about to get out of jail himself – why did he need you to get in touch with Clegg?'

'This was after he'd been stabbed. He didn't think he was going to make it.'

McGrail stood up and walked around the table to lean against the wall behind Ricketts who kept looking straight ahead.

'Let's picture the scene,' said McGrail in a 'once upon a time' voice. 'Varty's been stabbed and thinks he's going to die; with what may be his last breath, he asks you to get in touch with Clegg. Obviously he and Clegg were bosom buddies?'

'How the fuck would I know? That's what the guy asked me to do and I did it.'

'Sergeant, you spoke to Clegg's ex-wife last night,' said McGrail. 'Assuming I've managed to decipher your report, she had an idea Varty was a client of Clegg's at one point but didn't think they had a personal relationship to speak of, correct?'

'Got it in one, sir,' said Ihaka brightly.

McGrail put one hand on the back of Ricketts' chair, the other on the desk and brought his face close to Ricketts'. 'Surely you don't expect us to believe that this man's on his last legs and all he can think of is sending a good wish to his ex-lawyer?'

Ricketts turned his head to look at McGrail and said carefully: 'I don't expect you to believe anything.'

McGrail returned to the other side of the table, sat down and resumed looking through his folders. Without looking up, he asked: 'What else did Varty say to you?'

'Nothing. The doctor arrived and they carted him away. That was the last I saw of him.'

McGrail produced another of his quick, cold smiles. For a moment Ricketts thought he saw a glimmer of something approaching amusement in the policeman's eyes.

'I think that'll do for the time being, Mr Ricketts,' said McGrail. As Ricketts stood up, he added: 'Incidentally, why did you insist on dealing with Sergeant Ihaka yesterday?'

Ricketts glanced at Ihaka, then looked back at McGrail. 'Whenever I find a naked corpse in a spa pool, I think of Ihaka. They just seem to go together.'

He paused at the door. 'If you haven't already done it,' he said, 'maybe you should check whether the champagne glass that was by the pool is part of a set. If it is, I bet the set's one short.'

Ihaka went 'Eh?'

Ricketts shrugged. 'Call me a party animal but if I had a spa and a bottle of champagne, I'd probably get someone round to share them – in fact, I thought that was the whole idea. Maybe Clegg had someone round, someone who'd prefer to remain anonymous and so they removed all traces of their visit. But shit, why am I telling you this? You're the experts, right?'

Ricketts smiled to himself as if he found this notion amusing then exited, closing the door behind him. McGrail looked at Ihaka and raised his eyebrows. Unlike Ricketts, Ihaka was in absolutely no doubt that what he could see in the inspector's normally bleak brown eyes was amusement.

'Fuck it,' said Ihaka. 'I should've thought of that.'

McGrail nodded. 'Interesting man, your Mr Ricketts,' he said. 'I wonder what Varty really said to him.'

*

Everton Sloan III's father was a colossally expensive Washington DC lawyer who was sometimes described in the press as a powerbroker or even an *éminence grise*.

These are terms Washington political journalists apply to obviously high-powered but low-profile individuals who from time to time have lunch in expensive restaurants with congressmen, members of cabinet or presidential advisers. It was true, nevertheless, that Everton Sloan II was widely acknowledged to be a smart cookie. Whenever a new administration was taking shape, his name would be bandied about as a contender for a cabinet post or high-level staff job in the White House. It didn't really matter whether the administration was Democrat or Republican, since Sloan wasn't a member of either party; insofar as he held political views, they were of the 'strong defence, safe streets, sound money' variety espoused by most of those who counted on both sides of politics.

However, Sloan had never responded to the various feelers put out to him by recruiters for incoming administrations. Whenever he was accused of playing hard to get or of lacking a sense of civic responsibility, he'd reply that, as a young man, he'd made a vow never to work for anyone who wasn't as smart as he was. Because this remark was always accompanied by a gentle, self-deprecating chuckle, only those who knew Sloan well were aware that he wasn't joking.

Those who knew him well were also aware that there was another reason for his reluctance to work in the White House or for any of its occupants: Everton Sloan II was a snob. The Sloan family had been pillars of the old money, anglophile, East Coast establishment for six generations; in their scheme of things good manners, a familiarity with the higher expressions of English culture, the ability to look well on a horse, and a sound wine cellar were more admirable attributes than the dubious knack of achieving popularity among the little people. Respect was another matter, but then few presidential candidates ever seriously contemplated trying to earn the electorate's respect.

The last president of whom Sloan had wholeheartedly approved was Dwight Eisenhower. Like many New England Episcopalians, he'd been immune to the charisma of the Irish-Catholic Kennedys; his attitude to that ill-starred clan was summed up in the phrase 'I told you so', which he never tired of using.

Of the others, he regarded Lyndon Johnson as a vulgar, arm-twisting fixer; Richard Nixon as capable but mean-spirited and irredeemably common; Gerald Ford as a small-town Rotarian who had somehow blundered into the presidency when people's attention was elsewhere; Jimmy Carter as a cracker who talked about God as if he played rackets with Him, and introduced the offensive practice of holding hands with one's wife in public; and Ronald Reagan, while a pleasant enough fellow, as an actor, a huckster, and, worst of all, a Californian. Sloan and George Bush came from similar backgrounds but Bush failed to measure up on grounds of syntax: as Sloan told his friends, 'I'm too old to learn whatever language George speaks.' The idea of working for Bill Clinton was anathema on more grounds than he cared to enumerate for fear of appearing unpatriotic. Since the 1992 election, Sloan had taken to spending more and more time on his farm in upstate New York, brooding on the future of the republic.

Whatever else he was, Everton Sloan II was exceptionally well-connected. Thus when his only son rang from Bangkok on Sunday evening Thailand time seeking advice, he told him to go and see Theodore Natusch in Singapore.

*

First thing Monday morning Everton Sloan III caught the shuttle down to Singapore; shortly after 9 o'clock he was ushered into Theodore Natusch's office on the thirty-eighth floor of the Westin Plaza building. Natusch came out from behind his desk to shake hands, noting with approval that Sloan still dressed like an East Coast Wasp: dark-grey suit in Prince of Wales check, pale-blue Oxford weave shirt with button-down collar, expensive but understated silk tie and sturdy black brogues. It was completely unsuitable attire for South-East Asia but experience had taught Natusch to distrust men who too readily shed their skin on entering a new environment; in his view it smacked of rootlessness and a lack of fixed allegiances. Natusch himself was dressed for Singapore's enervating climate in a light cotton short-sleeved shirt without a tie, linen trousers and black leather moccasins.

Theodore Natusch was a paunchy six-footer with a round face which crinkled when he smiled, which was a lot of the time, warm hazel eyes and rust-coloured hair worn in a crew-cut, as it had been for nearly all of his 58 years. In 1966 he'd arrived in Saigon to cover the Vietnam war for United Press International. After Nixon's re-election in 1972, when it became crystal clear that America was going to cut and run, he'd resigned from UPI and set himself up as a freelance journalist, based in Tokyo. He spoke Mandarin, Japanese and Vietnamese, he was industrious, and he possessed excellent analytical skills, a limpid prose style, and laughter lines and friendly eyes which encouraged complete strangers to confide in him. It was little wonder therefore that within five years he'd gained a reputation as something of a sage on Asian affairs. What the editors of the many newspapers and magazines in which his articles appeared didn't know was that, as well as being a fine journalist who knew his way around Asia, Theodore Natusch was a CIA agent.

He came close to exposure in 1983 when a disgruntled CIA officer leaked the information to a reporter with one of the American television networks. When the news that Natusch's cover was about to be blown reached the CIA's Deputy Director, Plans (Clandestine Services), he rang a supportive senator who rang Everton Sloan II; Sloan in turn rang the network's major stockholder. They had a 45-minute conversation which on Sloan's side comprised equal parts charm, menace, and legal razzle-dazzle, and on the network bigshot's side opened with bluster and closed with timid gratitude. The story was killed.

In 1986 Natusch quit journalism and moved to Singapore. He opened a public relations consultancy which he proceeded to build into a successful business, largely by exploiting his network of high-level contacts throughout the region, backed up with a little judicious blackmail. When he turned 60 he planned to start looking around for a buyer for the consultancy – he had a figure somewhere between US$5 and US$7.5 million in mind – and, once it was successfully offloaded, to work out the inevitable management contract via modem from a beach house in Bali or possibly Sri Lanka if the political situation there stabilised.

'So how's your father, the great attorney?' asked Natusch as they waited for coffee.

'He seems fine. I'm not sure he finds Washington entirely to his taste these days.'

'I'm surprised anyone does.'

'How long since you saw him?'

'Sad to say I've never actually met him, although we've spoken by phone. He did me a great service once: saved my reputation and quite possibly my skin. Going by what you said when you rang last night, I'm about to have the opportunity to repay a little of that debt.'

'I was hoping to pick your brains and perhaps get some advice.'

'Go ahead.'

'What do you know about Buddy Funke?'

Natusch closed his eyes for a few seconds. 'Texan, joined the company out of college, by reputation a moderately good operative, perhaps a touch erratic. Went over to the DEA, would've been late '70s, early '80s. Lost track of him since then.'

'He's in Bangkok.'

Natusch shifted in his seat. 'Ah. Well, a man with his background in the DEA, you'd expect him to be either out here or in Colombia.'

'Why did he switch?'

As the conversation had become more business-like, the warmth in Natusch's eyes had gradually been replaced by a cool wariness. 'What makes you think it wasn't just a straightforward career decision?' he asked.

'Common sense. Going from the company to the DEA isn't a brilliant career move now, let alone back then.'

Natusch nodded. 'How are you on recent British history?'

'Okay.'

'A rather morbid taste in one so young. In that case you'll have some idea of the state of play in Britain in the mid-70s?

The miners had seen off Heath's government; the Labour Party was back in office but the trade-union bosses were calling the shots and they seemed hell-bent on wrecking the country. The majority of them, in their misguided way, were simply making the most of finally having the upper hand in the class war but we knew some were sleepers and others were taking Moscow's gold. Whatever their motivation, they were getting the job done; the place was going to hell in a handcart. As things went from bad to worse, a few right-wing patriotic organisations sprang up, GB '75 and the rest of them. It was our old friend, the man on horseback syndrome: retired generals announcing their readiness to save the country from the politicians, make the trains run on time, and send Sambo back to Jamaica while they were at it.

'Funke was in the London station which was taking a pretty alarmist view of things. The way they were calling it, Britain was heading down the road to voluntary Finlandisation; it was going to be Yanks Go Home and wave goodbye to all those wonderful listening posts and airbases. Buddy was monitoring the right-wing groups. Well, he was as gung-ho as all hell and he kind of got involved with one of them, a genuine paramilitary outfit headed by an ex-SAS crazy. The long and the short of it was, he offered to help them get their hands on some serious weaponry. The company was doing shady arms deals all over the place, so diverting a shipment wouldn't have been all that difficult.

'I'm sure you can guess the rest. This splendid band of patriots had been thoroughly infiltrated by MI5 and Funke's kind offer got back to Whitehall in the time it takes to make a phone call. The Brits went ballistic. The ambassador was summoned and chewed out; he got on the horn to his golfing buddy in the White House and within 24 hours Funke was out on his ass, cast into the outer darkness.'

Natusch stood up and stretched. He walked around his desk and perched on the edge of it, looking down at Sloan. 'At least, that's what we told the Brits. What really happened was that Funke flew a desk at Langley for a year or so, then got reassigned – to southern Africa, working with the Unita rebels, Jonas Savimbi's motley bunch, in Angola. He wangled some shoulder-launched SAMs for them, the idea being that if they knocked down a couple of planeloads of Cuban troops, Fidel and co. might be less enthusiastic about being Moscow's Gurkhas. In the middle of all this, a Brazilian aircraft manufacturer doing a sales pitch to the Angolans sent an airplane to Luanda on a demonstration visit. The Brazilians invited a couple of ministers and assorted VIPs and their wives on board and took them up for an airborne cocktail party and a little sightseeing.

'For propaganda reasons, the Angolan government decided it'd be a good idea if the plane landed in Huambo: Unita was claiming they had the town blockaded and nothing could get in or out. As propaganda stunts go, it left a lot to be desired. When the airplane was on its final approach into Huambo, Unita blew it out of the sky using a SAM supplied by our mutual acquaintance.

'Whether it was a mistake or whether Unita knew there were ministers on the flight was never really established but all hell broke loose in Washington. No-one was shedding tears over the Angolans – they were commies after all – but the Brazilians were another matter altogether. They were critical to holding the line down south: El Salvador, Nicaragua, Guatemala – you name it, we needed Brazil on side down there. Our proxies shooting down one of their civil airplanes with a Brazilian delegation on board, including members of a couple of the big families, wasn't the way to win friends and influence people. It was deemed to be a major league screw-up and someone had to take the fall. Come in agent Funke, your time is up.'

Natusch refilled Sloan's coffee cup and went back behind his desk. 'Well, that's the history lesson,' he said. 'How about you tell me what Buddy's done now?'

*

Sloan told Natusch briefly and dispassionately about the murder of Brandi the transvestite and what he'd learned through his detective work at the weekend. When he'd finished, the two men looked at one another without speaking for a few seconds. Then Natusch said, 'Let's have it, son. What's your theory?'

'I think Funke killed the transvestite and he's gone down to New Zealand for the drugs. I don't think he's got it in mind to throw them in an incinerator when he finds them.'

'How was the transvestite killed?'

'By the book – two shots at close range, chest and head.'

Natusch raised his eyebrows non-committally. 'Why should Funke do it?'

Sloan shrugged. 'To shut down the connection, make it harder for anyone to pick up the trail. Who knows? Maybe he gets a jolt out of it.'

'Do you know for sure that he's left Thailand?'

'No. Yesterday I got a computer print-out from Thai Immigration of people who'd left the country in the last 48 hours. He wasn't on it but I didn't expect him to be; he would've used a false passport or slipped out on a fishing boat and been dropped off somewhere down the Malay coast. Then he'd make his way to KL or here and catch a plane.'

'I was under the distinct impression this neck of the woods was awash with drugs. Why on earth would he go all the way to New Zealand?'

'Less risk: no-one knows him, there's no DEA presence, no-one looking over his shoulder. Hell, it's about as far off the radar screen as you can get.'

'So how's he going to play it?'

Sloan shrugged again. 'Most likely just go in, do his thing and get out. Anything goes wrong, he'll wave his ID and say he was just doing his job.' Sloan slipped into a fair imitation of a Texan accent: '"See here hoss, I'm a maverick – always have been; the Good Lord willing, always will be. I follow my nose like an old hound dog; I don't give a hoot in hell about jurisdiction and all that bureaucratic crap." Only an idiot would believe it of course but we've got enough of them.'

Natusch ducked his head to acknowledge the performance. 'You seem to have it all figured out,' he said.

'You think I've read it wrong?'

'No, I dare say you're right,' said Natusch smoothly. 'Funke certainly fits the profile of a potential rogue: he's single, amoral, unorthodox, closing in on retirement; given what must've been his aspirations 20 years ago, his career's gone down the toilet. He's operated in places where the corruption's right there, under your nose – that puts ideas in a man's head. As a wise acquaintance of mine once said, he's lived too long in a world with no respect for the laws of God or man. Unfortunately, I find it all too easy to believe he's decided it's time to feather his own nest. I mean, he's hardly the first, is he?'

'Look, Mr Natusch, if I thought there was nothing more to this than Buddy Funke topping up his superannuation, I could probably be persuaded to look the other way. But this is a dangerous man and he's out of control; he's likely to kill anyone who gets in his way. Okay, that might be a drug dealer or a scumbag of one sort or another; on the other hand, it might be a policeman or a civilian who happens to be in the wrong place at the wrong time – or a harmless lost soul like Brandi. He's got to be stopped.'

Surprised and a little nettled by Sloan's sudden and uncharacteristic vehemence, Natusch responded more tartly than he'd intended. 'What are you telling me for? Blow the whistle on him.'

Sloan resumed his air of thoughtful detachment. 'If I did that, following correct procedure, what would happen? Assuming it was taken seriously, by the time it was all checked out, it'd probably be too late. More than likely though, it'd be deep sixed. I can hear them over at the DEA now: "Can you believe this little Yalie fuck, trying to sell Buddy down the river?"'

Natusch sighed. 'Okay, Everton. Tell me what you want me to do.'

Sloan leaned forward. 'How high can you reach at Langley?'

Modesty and pride struggled briefly for squatter's rights to Natusch's face; pride won. He smiled smugly. 'I'm godfather to a certain deputy director's daughter.'

'That's high. Can you tell him what Funke's done and what he's going to do?'

Natusch nodded slowly. 'If that's what you want, I'll do it. Then what?'

Sloan took off his glasses and held them up to the light, then polished them with the back of his tie. He put them back on and looked at the older man with a level gaze.

'Then they'll send a cleaner after him.'

'You know about the cleaners?' asked Natusch, quite unable to keep the incredulity out of his voice.

'Before I went to Bangkok, I did a couple of research projects. They came down from the top and involved pretty major security clearance.'

Natusch studied Sloan with a mixture of surprise, respect and faint embarrassment. *You're going to go a long way son,* he thought. *I wonder how many more terminations you'll initiate before you're through.*

Ten

Special agent Harold 'Buddy' Funke left Bangkok on the evening of Friday, 15 April on a Thai Airways flight to Hong Kong where he treated himself to an overnight stay at the Peninsula Hotel. As Everton Sloan III had suspected, Funke travelled on a false passport, according to which he was Donald Edwin Surface, a native of Oklahoma. Funke had obtained the false passport in Macau six months previously, on the principle that one never knew when it might come in handy.

The false passport was the work of a 78-year-old Portuguese who'd spent much of his adult life labouring under the misapprehension that he was blessed with artistic talent. The considerable bitterness he felt over the art world's total lack of interest in his extensive output was only partially alleviated by the handsome income he earned from forging US passports, mainly for Hong Kong Chinese who wished to reside in the land of the free and the home of the brave.

However, as well as being very bitter, the old forger was also extremely greedy. So on the last Friday of every third month, he'd catch the 8 a.m. jetfoil ferry from Macau to Hong Kong. At some point during the 55-minute voyage, another passenger – it was always someone different – would sit down beside him and surreptitiously slip a fat wad of US$100 notes into his navy-blue British Airways flight bag. The money came from the US Immigration Service, although establishing that would have required a lengthy investigation by people experienced in the workings of the international banking system. In return for his quarterly US$15,000 retainer, the forger would pass the courier an envelope containing the details of the false passports he'd produced during the previous three months.

Although Funke wasn't aware of it, the passport in the name of Donald Edwin Surface had the distinction of being the Portuguese forger's final creation. A few days after the DEA man had picked it up, two hard-muscled young Chinamen burst into the forger's apartment, tied him up, and proceeded to torture him by the crude but effective method of pulling out his teeth with a pair of pliers. After he'd confessed that he routinely betrayed his customers to the American authorities, his assailants yanked out his remaining teeth just for the hell of it, then doused him with several litres of petrol and set fire to him. Mercifully, the old man died of shock within 75 seconds of being set ablaze which gave him just enough time to work out that at least one of his recent customers had been a member of the Triads.

Funke left Hong Kong the next afternoon on a Cathay Pacific flight bound for Los Angeles. When the 747 reached cruising altitude, Funke requested a Scotch and 7-Up and was about to settle back and listen to some country music when the passenger in the next seat sought to strike up a conversation.

'Listening to that accent, I'd say I'm sitting alongside a fellow American,' said his neighbour, extending a pudgy hand. 'Gene Pokorny's the name, coming to you from Bakersfield, California.'

Funke sighed and turned his head to look at Pokorny. He registered blow-dried hair, puffy features, a fixed, beaming smile, a loud tie and a louder tie-pin. *Just my luck,* he thought. *Sat next to a fat fucking salesman all the way across the Pacific.* He placed a lifeless hand in Pokorny's.

'Howdy,' he said without a trace of warmth. 'Donald Surface.'

'Where are you from, Don?'

Funke went back to fiddling with his Walkman. 'Oklahoma.'

'Uh-huh. I'm a computer man myself. What business would you be in?'

Funke slowly looked up at Pokorny. 'Well, since you ask, friend, white slavery's my line of work. I just got through delivering a matching pair of 14-year-old chickees to a middleman in Hong Kong who'll sell 'em to one of them people's tycoons in Shanghai. I'm talking serious dinero.'

Pokorny's professional smile faded. He studied Funke very carefully, as if attempting to count the blackheads on his nose. Funke put down the Walkman and twisted further round in his seat.

'I'll let you into a secret, Gene,' he said, dropping his voice. 'These days, the biggest status symbol in the Third World isn't a chopper or a goddamn big pleasure boat or a private jet; no siree, it's having your very own all-American fuckdoll. No shit, I can't keep up with the demand. Problem is, these niggers – I use the term in the widest sense – all want the same thing: blue eyes, blonde hair, no zits and a hymen. Believe me, Gene, that package doesn't grow on trees. You think the coloureds like to fuck? Well, let me tell you, they ain't got that all to themselves. I had to snatch these little cuties right off the sidewalk as they walked home from bible class.'

Pokorny continued to stare at Funke. Eventually he said, 'Fella, that's a very dangerous sense of humour you got there. I was you, I'd be real careful who I laid that stuff on.'

Funke chuckled and snapped the George Jones tape into his Walkman. 'Had you going for a minute there, didn't I?'

'I guess you're not into conversation right now, huh?'

Funke turned his strange, unaligned gaze on Pokorny again. 'No offence, Gene, but I've just got this feeling in my bones that we look at life from different perspectives.'

*

With the lawyer Bart Clegg no longer available to act as a go-between, all Duane Ricketts had to go on in tracking down Dale Varty's daughter was her Christian name – Electra – and the fact that she was in a punk rock band. He assumed that Varty's ex-wife would've reverted to her maiden name and the daughter would've followed suit. Unfortunately, Varty hadn't got round to sharing that information with him.

After his session with McGrail and Ihaka at the Central police station, Ricketts walked across town and up the hill through Albert Park to the university. The first person he asked was able to tell him where to find Radio BFM, the student radio station.

Radio BFM operated from a scruffy collection of rooms on the second floor of the student union building, which was behind the cafeteria. When Ricketts explained his mission to the receptionist, a plump 20-year-old with a shaved head, she told him, 'Gabby's your best bet.' She walked over to a door off the reception area, knocked quietly, and opened it.

From within came a husky female voice speaking in a conversational tone: '... and that was Tracy Chapman and "Talking 'bout a Revolution". Nice song but did you listen to the lyrics? "Poor people gonna rise and get their share/Poor people gonna rise up and take what's theirs." Course they are Tray, you daft bitch. Just like I'm going to be the next dean of the law school. Coming up next, a track for all you psychos out there – music to cut up the family photo album by. It's from The Doors. Remember their lead singer, Jim Morrison? He thought he was a poet and to prove it, he pulled his knob out and waved it at the crowd. Then he went off to Paris, took loads of drugs, and croaked in the bath. Way to go, Jimbo. As the saying goes, he lived fast, died young and left ... well, as a matter of fact, it wasn't such a good-looking corpse; he was a bit of a fat bastard by the end. And speaking of the end, that's the name of the song. It's an everyday tale of mass murder and incest about a bloke who wants to kill his brother, sister, father and mother; in mommy's case, he wants to play hide the salami before he knocks her off. Weird scenes inside the goldmine indeed.'

The music began. A tall fine-featured young woman wearing a woollen skullcap, jeans and a T-shirt with the message 'Smells Like Teen Vomit' emerged from the studio. She flicked Ricketts an uninterested glance and walked past him over to the coffee machine behind the receptionist's desk.

'This is Gabby,' said the receptionist tripping along in her wake. 'One of our deejays. She might be able to help you.'

Gabby was making herself a cup of coffee. 'I'm trying to get in touch with a girl called Electra,' said Ricketts. 'She's in some kind of punk band.'

'A punk band?' said Gabby. 'How quaint.' She flopped onto a battered couch against the wall. 'Who are you and what do you want her for?'

'My name's Duane Ricketts. I've got a message for her from someone I met overseas.'

'The meaning of life perhaps? A recipe for the perfect date scone?' Gabby took off her woollen cap and scratched her short dirty-blonde hair. She made a noise like a siren and chanted 'Dandruff alert' several times, then tugged her cap back on. 'She a dyke, this chick?'

'Wouldn't have a clue. Why?'

'She a midget?'

Ricketts shook his head in bemusement. 'Look, for all I know, she could have two heads and a hump – I've never set eyes on her.'

Gabby raised her eyebrows. 'Now that'd be a good look. The reason I ask is I seem to remember the chick who fronts The Homo Dwarves calls herself Electra.'

'The Homo Dwarves? That's the name of the band? How would I get hold of her?'

'You could try Jerry Naismith – he promotes a lot of the gigs round town.'

'You got a number for him?'

She pointed with her chin. 'If you can read, it's right there on that socking great poster behind you.'

Ricketts borrowed the receptionist's ballpoint and wrote the number on the back of his hand.

'Thanks for your help. You ever do requests?'

'Sometimes. You want one?'

'How about Tom Petty – "Even the losers get lucky some-times"?'

*

With the 16-hour time difference, Buddy Funke arrived in Los Angeles an hour and a half before he'd left Hong Kong. He bought a ticket on that night's United Airlines flight to Auckland, then checked into an airport hotel and slept solidly for seven hours.

The United flight arrived in Auckland on schedule at 6.25 on Monday morning. Funke entered New Zealand on his other false passport, the one in the name of his boyhood part-ner-in-crime Lyle Gorse, which he'd had for almost 20 years. He caught a taxi into the city and, on the advice of a stew-ardess, checked into the Regis Hotel. After a nap and a long, hot shower, Funke was sitting on the bed towelling his hair when it dawned on him that, for the first time in his adult life, he was unarmed and without immediate access to a firearm.

Weaponry hadn't been an issue for Funke in the past. Whichever godforsaken and hostile corner of the globe he'd found himself, he'd been there in an official capacity;

obtaining a weapon therefore was simply a matter of rendezvousing with the local friendlies or slipping into the embassy.

Funke had a vague idea that New Zealand was like a little outpost of England stuck down at the ass-end of the world. That being the case, they probably shared England's communistic attitude to gun control; in other words, it wouldn't be the sort of place where you could walk into your friendly neighbourhood gunshop a sitting duck and walk out with enough firepower to turn the Dallas Cowboys defensive line into two tons of steak tartare.

A stroll around town later that morning confirmed his fears. There wasn't a gunshop in sight and when Funke raised the subject with a passer-by who had the gimlet eye and vaguely paranoid demeanour of a shooting man, he'd been informed that the first step to obtaining a firearm was to discuss the matter with the police.

Shortly after 10 o'clock that evening, Funke walked out of the Regis and asked the concierge to whistle him up a cab. When a taxi pulled up, Funke checked out the driver. Satisfied by what he saw, he climbed into the back seat. The driver, 61-year-old Stan Mattamore, looked at Funke in his rearview mirror and asked him where he wanted to go.

'How long you been driving a cab?' asked Funke.

'Thirty-odd years, on and off.'

'I guess you must know where the action is in this town, right?'

Mattamore swivelled round. 'You want a root, is that it?'

'You mean, do I want to get laid?'

Mattamore nodded.

'A root, huh? That's a new one on me. Okay amigo, how about you take me to the best root in Auckland.'

Mattamore shrugged. 'I'll take you to a knockshop but whether it's any good or not … from what I hear, you've been to one, you've been to them all.' After a pause he added, 'I'm a married man myself', as if that explained his unfamiliarity with the vice scene.

Mattamore drove Funke to The Pink Wink, a massage parlour in Fort Street. As Funke paid the fare, he asked, 'You folks haven't legalised prostitution, have you? You know, like the Dutch?'

Mattamore stared at him blankly for a few seconds. 'Mate, if you're worrying about getting arrested, believe me, the cops have got better things to do.'

'As long as it's not legal,' said Funke. 'I find that takes the fun out of it.'

He was offered his pick of two young women who stank of cigarettes and paraded for his inspection with the enthusiasm of virginal peasant girls summoned to an audience with the Marquis de Sade. Funke, who surmised from their vacant expressions and waxy skins that they were junkies, decided he'd seen more desirable armadillos. He chose the marginally more alert of the two, who led him upstairs. In the bedroom Funke told the prostitute to sit on the foot of the bed and keep her clothes on. He sat up on the bed with his back against the wall.

'Okay sugar, you can relax,' he said. 'I don't want to screw. Just let me look at you a while.'

The prostitute, who often felt slightly sick when she looked at herself in the mirror, thought this was just about the oddest thing a punter had ever said to her.

'You want me to play with myself?' she offered helpfully. 'Or I could talk dirty – I'm pretty good at that.'

'I'll bet you could come out with stuff that'd make a tugboat captain puke but I'll pass on that, thanks all the same. Tell me this though: that gal downstairs who's kind of organising things – she the manager?'

'Nadia? No, she just like runs the shop.'

'So who's the boss?'

'Guy called Ronnie.'

'He around tonight?'

'Think so. Why?'

'Tell me about Ronnie.'

'What's there to tell? He's a pimp.'

'Is he a tough guy?'

The prostitute thought about it for a few seconds. 'He only hits us if we miss a shift.'

'What a prince. Is he your source?'

Her eyes widened. 'Hey, what the fuck is this …' She stood up and made for the door. 'I'm getting out of here …'

Funke rolled off the bed and intercepted her. 'Don't go making a fuss now sugar or you'll piss me off,' he said calmly. 'I want to talk to the man, that's all, but first I want to know if he's worth talking to. Just tell me yes or no: does he deal?'

The prostitute knew that it was extremely unwise to discuss Ronnie's unlawful business activities with a complete stranger. On the other hand, she was a hell of a lot less scared of Ronnie than she was of this Yank, even though to look at him you'd think he was harmless enough: just another drab little middle-aged bloke losing his hair. Christ though, the way he moved – when she went for the door, he'd come off the bed like a scalded cat. But what really freaked her was the way he looked at her. Not even the pimps who rented her out like a hire car – 'we don't mind if you thrash the shit out of her, just bring her back in one piece' – or the worst sort of customers, the misfits who'd never had a woman reach for them without being paid or frightened, looked at her that way – like she was nothing more than a speck of dirt he'd just noticed under his fingernail. She dropped her eyes and nodded.

'Good,' said Funke. 'Ronnie sounds like my kind of guy. Let's go see him.'

Ronnie Traipse, the manager of The Pink Wink, was in his dirty, pokey office reading a bodybuilding magazine when the prostitute put her head round the door and said a customer wanted to talk to him.

Traipse sat upright and threw the magazine aside. 'Jesus, Leanne,' he said threateningly, 'you didn't fucking fall asleep again, did you?'

Funke slid past Leanne into Traipse's office. 'No sir, she was just dandy. What I want to talk about is a business matter.'

Traipse, who had a big chest, a bigger gut, stupid eyes, and a jaw that harked back to the palaeolithic era, stood up and flexed his shoulders in what was meant to be intimidating fashion. 'Oh yeah?'

Funke nodded to Leanne. 'You run along now, my dear.' He closed the door behind her and took a good, long look at Traipse. *If this boy's not dirty,* he thought, *granddaddy never stepped in buffalo shit.*

'I'm in the market for a pistola,' said Funke. 'A handgun. I thought maybe you could advise me on how I'd go about getting one.'

Traipse squinted at him moronically. 'A gun? What makes you think I could help you get a gun?'

'I just thought you might have the connections,' said Funke with an ingratiating smile. 'A man in your position.'

Traipse sat down. 'What do you want a gun for?'

'Well you see, I come from Texas where we believe very strongly in a man's inalienable right to bear arms. Fact is, I've carried a gun since I was this high and I feel downright uncomfortable without one. So how about it, son – reckon you can rustle me up a piece?'

Traipse scratched his chin. 'Could be. How much you prepared to pay?'

Funke shrugged. 'I'll pay the going rate, whatever it is. Mind, I want a man's weapon, not some itty-bitty purse gun – nothing smaller than a .32. And I want it asap, like tomorrow.'

'Sounds to me like you'd be up for a couple of grand.'

'Holy shit, two thousand dollars? Son, in Vladivostok I could buy me a truckload of plutonium for that sort of money.'

Traipse, who had no idea what Funke was talking about, heaved his shoulders. 'You want a pistol in 24 hours, that's what it'll cost. It's up to you.'

What the hell, thought Funke, *I'm not exactly flush with options*. 'Okay son, this is the deal: you get me a .38 revolver, clean and in prime condition, plus say a couple of dozen rounds, by this time tomorrow night, I'll pay you 2,500 of your dollars. Are we talking turkey?'

Traipse nodded slowly. 'Sounds good. I'll ring around, see what's available. What's your name?'

'Well now, I don't see as there's any need to bring names into it.'

Traipse's eyes took on a stubborn glaze. 'Have to, mate. First question these guys are going to ask is "Who's it for?". They might want to check you out.'

Funke thought about it for a few seconds. 'If that's the way it works, I guess I don't have a choice. I'm called Donald Surface.'

Eleven

On the days when he didn't have a luncheon meeting, Richard Thames, the Deputy Director, Intelligence of the CIA, ate his midday meal alone at the conference table in his large office at the agency's headquarters in Langley, Virginia. These solitary lunches generally consisted of sourdough bread, peppery Italian salami, black olives, a tomato, some cheddar cheese and an apple. He washed his food down with half a litre of the dark Prussian beer for which he'd developed a taste during his seven years in West Berlin.

Thames drank the beer from an old pewter mug which his 22-year-old daughter, who'd always had an acute sense of how to gain entry to her father's good books, had given him for his most recent birthday. Thames' 28 years as a spy – half of it spent in the field, half in Washington – had planed away the outer layers of his personality. At the age of 50 and having attained a level of seniority which allowed him some leeway, Thames had decided to add a dash or two of colour to what had become a study in grey; he began accumulating old and anachronistic objects and incorporating them in his daily routine in the belief that they would make him appear quirky or even mildly eccentric: he told the time by a 60-year-old Rolex, scrawled comments on documents with a fountain pen of similar vintage, played golf in plus-fours, and went for walks with a knobbly wooden walking-stick even though both legs were in reasonable working order. Six months after his birthday, by which time the pewter mug had become part of the Thames persona, his daughter confessed that she'd stolen it from a village pub with a thatched roof somewhere in south-west England, not far from the town with the wonderful Georgian architecture. Thames assumed she meant Bath.

As he drank his beer, Thames thought about his daughter and her troublesome habit of simply commandeering things which took her fancy, the latest of which was her former best friend's fiancé. That train of thought led to her godfather, Theodore Natusch, who'd rung from Singapore the night before to raise the alarm about Buddy Funke. Natusch had repeated word-for-word what he'd been told by Everton Sloan III and when Thames had asked him what he made of it all, he'd replied that Sloan's reputation as a bright young man appeared to be merited.

When he'd finished his lunch, Thames picked up one of the three phones on his desk and asked Leon Rehbein to step into his office. Rehbein worked in the Office of Central Reference in Thames' department. In addition to being a computer wizard, Rehbein was an irredeemable social misfit with a major personal hygiene problem. Thames frequently used him to carry out sensitive and confidential little research projects. He chose him on the basis that Rehbein's interaction with his colleagues was pretty well confined to saying 'hello' in the morning and 'goodnight' in the evening while they in turn seldom, if ever, leaned over his shoulder and asked him what he was working on.

Rehbein knocked and entered. Thames greeted him and pointed him to the chair in front of his desk. The computer wizard was tall and thin and very pale and had frizzy blond hair which he wore in an Art Garfunkel afro. The consensus among his colleagues was that Rehbein looked a lot like Kermit from 'The Muppet Show' but that was as far as the comparison could be taken since, personality-wise, the frog left him for dead.

Even though Rehbein was 32, much of his face and neck was covered with angry red acne which he fingered incessantly when nervous, as he invariably was in Thames' presence. Once Thames had been explaining an assignment to him when he'd prodded a ripe, white-crested crop of boils on the point of his chin a little harder than, presumably, he'd intended. There was an audible popping noise and a trail of pus had splattered across the sheet of crisp, white blotting paper on Thames' desk. Because the memory of that incident still caused him to tremble with nausea and because Rehbein's body odour attacked the senses like nerve gas, Thames had taken the precaution of shifting the visitor's chair a further two metres away from his desk.

'Leon, I've got another little assignment for you,' said Thames forcing himself to smile. 'Needless to say, it's a sensitive matter.'

Rehbein nodded eagerly and clawed at his cheek which caused Thames to flinch and push his chair back a few centimetres.

'I want to locate a man named Harold Funke, usually known as Buddy. He used to be one of us, went over to the DEA about 1980. His details will be on file. He disappeared from Bangkok late last week and we think he's gone to New Zealand. He would've used a false passport so what you'll need to do is get on to the embassy in Wellington and have them send you a list of passport holders who've entered New Zealand since last Friday. Break out the males in the right general age bracket and run them through the computer. I need to know for sure that he's down there and what name he's using.'

*

An hour and a half after Thames had briefed his computer wizard, at 7.30 on Tuesday morning New Zealand time, Buddy Funke checked out of the Regis Hotel. He took a short taxi ride across town to the Hyatt Kingsgate hotel on the corner of Princes Street and Waterloo Quadrant. He paid the driver, got out of the taxi, and entered the hotel by the main entrance. Inside, he sat in an armchair in a corner of the lobby pretending to read the paper for almost half an hour, until he was absolutely satisfied that no-one was taking any notice of him. Then he stood up, picked up his bags, and walked through the lobby and out of the hotel by a side exit which took him onto Princes Street. He walked down Princes Street, turned left into Eden Crescent and walked down the hill till he came to the Crescent Lodge boarding house.

The manageress of Crescent Lodge greeted Funke as if she'd known him all her life which she obviously hadn't, otherwise she wouldn't have called him Mr Williams. That was the name Funke had used when he'd walked in off the street the previous afternoon and booked a room.

*

After five years in the police force, Detective Constable Johan Van Roon had more or less come to terms with the unpleasant aspects of the job. He'd lost count of the number of dead bodies he'd seen, something that not that long ago he wouldn't have thought possible; whenever he thought about them, which he tried to avoid doing, they tended to merge into one asexual, featureless lump of flesh.

The family in Howick were the exceptions. The husband was slumped over the kitchen table, the wife was on the floor in the corridor looking like she'd got tangled up with a propeller, and their twin daughters were tucked up in bed with their throats cut. They were eight years old with blonde hair and blue eyes, just like Van Roon's niece. In fact, put the three of them together, you might've picked them as triplets.

They worked it out that the wife had been in the lounge watching TV when her husband had come up behind her and stabbed her with a short-bladed kitchen knife. After 17 goes at it, he must've decided the knife wasn't really designed for stabbing people to death and gone back to the kitchen to find something better suited to the task. While he was doing that, the wife had started crawling down the corridor towards the bedroom where the twin daughters were asleep. She'd got halfway along the corridor when the husband had come back with a carving knife.

Afterwards, the husband had sat down at the dining room table and written a note of explanation. It was all his wife's fault, he said. She'd announced that at the end of the school term, she was off and taking their daughters with her even though she knew full well that he couldn't face life on his own. Seeing that she didn't deserve to live, and he no longer wanted to, and it would've been unfair on the twins to leave them all alone in the world, the only solution was for them all to die. Then he'd taken just enough sleeping pills to qualify as an attempted suicide. Van Roon's guess was that the husband would be released from the mental hospital around the time his niece brought home her first boyfriend.

Afterwards, Van Roon had had to take some time off work. Detective Sergeant Tito Ihaka had turned up at his flat one afternoon, claiming he'd been in the neighbourhood and decided to drop in for a beer. Seeing Van Roon didn't drink, he'd brought his own. For a while they avoided the subject. Eventually Van Roon had said he thought he was going to be okay, he just never wanted to see anything like it again. Ihaka had looked at him with a sad little smile on his bulldog face and gently pointed out that it didn't really matter a fuck what he saw or didn't see from there on because he was going to keep seeing the little girls and their mother till the day they put him in a box. When, after a

minute or so, Van Roon nodded to indicate that he understood what Ihaka was telling him, the sergeant had punched
him sickeningly hard on the upper arm and told him it was
time to get back to work.

Until that afternoon, Van Roon had basically been shit-
scared of Ihaka. While most of the guys rated the big Maori
as a hell of a cop, Van Roon had also heard him described
as a thug, a slob, a degenerate, a vindictive bastard, and his
own worst enemy; the word around Auckland Central was
that Ihaka had gone as far up the ladder as he was ever going to go because senior officers considered him 'unsound'.
On the basis of his personal experience, Van Roon had been
inclined to believe that all of these opinions, even the con-
tradictory ones, had some validity. Even though Van Roon
now felt something approaching fondness towards Ihaka,
he still dreaded having to pick him up from his place.

For a start, you never quite knew what to expect. Once
Van Roon had turned up at the Sandringham bungalow to
find Ihaka's car in the vegetable garden. Apparently Ihaka had
come up his drive at high speed, failed to negotiate the left-
hand turn into the carport, and just ploughed straight ahead,
across the lawn and into the garden. Another five metres and
he would have parked in his next-door neighbour's back bedroom. Ihaka had blamed it on antibiotics he'd been taking
for a sore throat, claiming they'd affected his night vision.

Another time Van Roon had discovered a blow-up sex doll
in a deck chair on the front porch. The doll had a large cu-
cumber jammed into its mouth slot and a sign around its
neck which said 'I claim this house in the name of Satan'.
Ihaka's explanation was that he was being harassed by God's
door-to-door salespersons.

Secondly, Ihaka lived alone and was as undomesticated
as he was lazy, so his place was always a mess. Whenever
Van Roon called there, Ihaka would try to browbeat him into

doing a week's worth of dishes or a few loads of washing or – horror of horrors – changing his bed. Thirdly, if Ihaka had a hangover, you could bet he'd be in a foul and abusive mood, not that he was Mr Sweetness and Light at the best of times.

It was just after 10.30 a.m. when Van Roon pulled into Ihaka's drive. He got out of his car and went up the steps to the front door. He rang the bell; it got no response. Van Roon sighed. Ihaka was still asleep: that meant he'd been on the piss the night before so it was odds-on he'd be grumpy all day. Van Roon knew that Ihaka never bothered to lock the door when he was at home so he opened it and went in. He found Ihaka stretched out unconscious on his bed, fully clothed. On his chest were the remnants of fish and chips in newspaper wrapping and a fat ginger cat which was nibbling on a piece of fish in batter.

Van Roon shook Ihaka's right foot. After a few seconds Ihaka opened his eyes. He looked at the cat, then at Van Roon, then back at the cat. He said, 'Help yourself, you ginger cunt,' then punched the cat in the face. The left jab knocked the cat, yowling, to the floor. It bounced to its feet and scrambled past Van Roon's ankles out of the bedroom.

Ihaka screwed the newspaper containing what was left of the fish and chips up into a ball, dropped it on the floor, and heaved himself into a sitting position.

'Shagnasty,' he said, rubbing his eyes. 'How'd you be?'

Van Roon, who'd been called far worse names than 'shagnasty' by Ihaka and considered it a hopeful sign, said, 'I'm okay. How's your head?'

'My head?' said Ihaka, feigning puzzlement. 'What about my head? You trying to suggest I got pissed last night, you cheeky little ape?'

Van Roon shook his head. 'Why would I think that?'

'Why indeed?' said Ihaka. He gulped in air and unleashed a thunderous, reverberating burp which filled the room with the odour of beer and takeaways. 'Give us 20 minutes for a shit, shower, shampoo, shave and shoeshine, and I'll be right with you.'

*

An hour later Ihaka and Van Roon and Jody Spurdle were having tea and biscuits in the sunlit living room of a house in one of the short, no-exit streets which run off Hurstmere Road down to Takapuna beach. The house belonged to friends of Jody's. Van Roon was in a jacket and tie, Ihaka in his usual outfit of jeans, sneakers and bomber jacket. Jody wore a low-cut lambswool sweater, a short black skirt, and black stockings with high heel shoes. She sat on a sofa and crossed her legs at intervals of approximately two minutes. At first Ihaka was flattered by this; after a while he realised she was completely unaware that she was doing it.

Jody looked anxiously from one policeman to the other. Ihaka was expressionless; Van Roon smiled encouragingly. She addressed herself to the detective constable: 'As I said on the phone, I know I sound like a drama queen but I think my husband has hired someone to kill me.'

'Because he found out about lover boy?' asked Ihaka with a directness which made Van Roon uncomfortable. For a moment he thought Jody was going to burst into tears. She bit her lip and looked away while Ihaka glanced at Van Roon and made a grotesque face simulating sexual ecstasy. To Van Roon's relief, Jody swiftly composed herself and counter-attacked.

'That makes it okay, does it?' she demanded. 'Like, if a woman's unfaithful, she deserves everything she gets?'

'Shit, no,' said Ihaka, quite unabashed. 'Especially not if they're married to an old weasel like Spurdle.'

Jody started to say something but Ihaka interrupted: 'Listen, why don't you just tell us exactly what makes you think your husband wants you out of the way – right from the word go?'

Surprising herself as much as Ihaka with her matter-of-factness, Jody told them about her affair with Troy Goatley, finding her husband going through the washing basket, the sudden appearance of Leith Grills, and the scrap of overheard phone conversation.

'What did your husband say?' asked Ihaka. 'The exact words.'

'He said, "You know what I said yesterday about the wife? I've had another think about it, I want you to get onto her straightaway. Can you handle that?"'

'Does he normally call you "the wife" when he's talking about you? As opposed to "my wife" or "Jody" or "the war office" or "that bitch"?'

'I don't know, probably not. I guess he'd usually say "Jody".'

'Mrs Spurdle, I don't want you to run away with the idea that we're not taking this seriously but it's not a hell of a lot to go on.'

'What about that creep Grills? I thought he was a well-known criminal?'

'Sure he is but that doesn't prove anything – your husband's been hanging out with ratbags for years. Look, we'll check out Grills, see if we can find out what's going on. In the meantime, I suggest you and the boyfriend give it a rest and let us know if anything else happens.'

On the way back into town, Van Roon asked Ihaka what he thought.

'What I think is that Spurdle would've had her sussed ages ago. She's obviously a bit of a sausage jockey – with a body like that, it'd be a crime against nature if she wasn't – but she's not tricky enough to pull the wool over his eyes. Spurdle's so crooked, he couldn't lie straight in bed. That sort of bloke suspects everyone. If the Mother Superior told him she was just off for a quick crap, he'd follow her to the bog to make sure.'

'So you reckon there's nothing to it?'

'I didn't say that. Spurdle wouldn't have that shithead Grills around for his conversation. He's up to something – the question is, what?'

Twelve

The village of Manacle is situated on the east coast of the Coromandel Peninsula. It was founded in the early 1880s by six married couples who felt that the gold towns of the Thames–Coromandel area were unsuitably volatile environments for growing children. The would-be settlers bypassed a few likely sites on their trek up the peninsula before they reached a little bay just north of Whangapoua Harbour. It was a pretty spot, autumn was approaching and reserves of stamina and stoicism were running low, so they decided that they'd found what they were looking for. Since they couldn't agree on what to call their settlement, they drew straws; naming rights fell to a Cornishman whose father had gone to Davy Jones' locker, along with a smuggled consignment of French brandy, just off a part of the Cornish coast known as Manacle Point.

Nothing of any great interest happened in Manacle during the next 50 years. Then one fine afternoon in March 1938, an Englishman by the name of Errol Swarbrick, who was 18 months into a world tour which didn't have a schedule or an itinerary but was simply proceeding as the spirit took him, rode over the ridge on a dapple-grey mare. Swarbrick got off his horse, stretched his legs, and admired the view: green hills rolled gently down to a golden sand beach which stretched almost half a mile from the point, where he could make out children paddling in the rockpools, to a native bush-covered bluff. After contemplating the scene for a few minutes, he decided that he'd chanced upon the most beautiful, most peaceful place on earth. That would have been a minority view even among Manacle's 175 residents, but being in the minority didn't worry Errol Swarbrick in the least because he was quite odd and very, very rich.

Swarbrick's father, the late Sir Ned, had laboured all his life to build Swarbrick Breweries into the dominant brewing company in the north of England. Having achieved that goal, he'd dropped dead from a massive brain haemorrhage at the Headingley cricket ground in Leeds. England were playing Australia and Sir Ned keeled over shortly after stumps had been drawn on a day in which the visitors had accumulated 455 runs for the loss of one wicket with Don Bradman contributing 271.

Four years earlier, in 1930, Sir Ned had spent a day at Headingley watching England play the Australians and suffered apoplexy brought on by the build-up of seething, impotent rage as the men from Down Under made 458 runs for the loss of three wickets. Bradman's share on that occasion was 309. On the advice of his physicians, Sir Ned had, in the intervening years, abstained from all activities which excited his passions, particularly watching cricket matches involving Yorkshire or England.

Encouraged by the situation after the first day's play of the 1934 Test match – Australia was struggling at 39 for the loss of three wickets in reply to England's first innings of 200 – and in the conviction that lightning on such a scale couldn't possibly strike twice, his physicians had lifted the ban to allow him to attend day two.

While Sir Ned was fond of his only son, he was, in his hard-headed Yorkshire way, well aware that the lad was as daft as a brush and quite incapable of running a whelk stall, let alone a multimillion-pound business. Under the terms of his father's will, Errol became a 20 per cent shareholder in Swarbrick Breweries provided he did not take a seat on the board. In addition to dividend pay-outs, he received an annual income of £20,000; all he was required to do to earn that staggering sum was refrain from setting foot on any company property. The arrangement suited Errol down to the ground since he heartily loathed the north of England and everything connected with it, particularly Swarbrick's Bitter, the company's flagship brand.

Swarbrick camped in Manacle for a few days which did nothing to diminish his enthusiasm for the place. He then travelled to Auckland and paid a visit to the offices of the law firm Prawle Prawle & Mulvany where he outlined his plans to a startled Sefton Prawle KC, the senior partner. Swarbrick instructed Prawle to arrange the purchase of a large block of waterfront land in Manacle and to commission New Zealand's leading architect to design and oversee the construction of a residence along the lines of an English country house, complete with appropriate landscaping, on the property. He would contact his bank in London forthwith to arrange the transfer of £100,000 for the purpose.

A fortnight later Swarbrick boarded a ship bound for California where he intended to rent a house on Malibu Beach, bathe in the Pacific Ocean, assess investment opportunities in the motion picture industry, and have sex with as many female movie stars as possible. His plan of attack was to begin with Mary Astor and work his way through the alphabet till he got to Mae West. Swarbrick believed that every woman had her price, and nothing he'd heard about the prevailing moral code in Tinseltown suggested that screen goddesses were any different. Sefton Prawle went down to the wharf to see him off and inform him that negotiations over the purchase of the section were proceeding satisfactorily. He never saw or heard from Errol Swarbrick again.

Construction of the Swarbrick house was completed in December 1939, three months after the outbreak of the Second World War, at a total cost of £113,000. Prawle didn't hear a peep of complaint from Swarbrick's bankers or the

London solicitors administering his affairs over the fact that the project had gone over budget.

Prawle journeyed to Manacle to inspect the house and surroundings. They were magnificent. The house was an imposing two-storey, 30-room, Edwardian-style mansion with a panelled entrance hall, a large and ornate dining room, a library and a billiards room. The broad veranda, bay windows and upper-floor balconies looked out to Great Mercury Island. Built of kauri and painted white, it had heavy eaves and blocks of timber at the corners to represent stone quoining and a grey slate roof. Its four landscaped acres contained a tennis court, a croquet lawn, a gazebo, a variety of flower gardens, and shaded walks.

Back in Auckland, Prawle wired Swarbrick's solicitors in London to inform them that their client's new residence had been completed, that it was entirely splendid and now only required his presence. In the meantime, he enquired, should he undertake the recruitment of domestic staff? The solicitors wired back to say that Swarbrick had taken himself off to an artists' colony in Mexico for an indefinite stay. They would send funds to cover the upkeep and maintenance of the house and grounds and would appreciate Prawle providing them with a quarterly accounting of disbursements.

Three years passed. Prawle heard nothing from Swarbrick or his solicitors. When the funds in the property maintenance account had all but dwindled away, Prawle wired London again. He received a prompt but barely civil response, the gist of which was that it appeared to have escaped his attention that there was a war on. A few days later he received a follow-up cable advising that money was on its way to restore the property maintenance account to its original balance.

Early in 1945 Swarbrick's solicitors in London received a wire from their client. The cable, sent from San Diego,

California, was the first communication they'd had from him for 20 months. It instructed them to transfer a quarter of a million pounds to his account at the San Diego city branch of the Wells Fargo bank forthwith. They wired back to Swarbrick, care of the San Diego post office, pointing out that their explicit instructions forbade them from releasing more than £500 in a calendar month without written authorisation from Swarbrick himself. Written authorisation duly arrived. Worried by the shakiness of Swarbrick's signature and aghast at the thought of losing the income which flowed from their administration of such a vast amount of money, the solicitors dispatched one of the partners to New York to hire the Pinkerton's Detective Agency to track down their client.

Three weeks later a Pinkerton's operative found Errol Swarbrick in the basement of a house in the Californian coastal town of Carmel. He was existing on a diet of pet food and water provided by his captors, a failed painter and his failed poet girlfriend who'd met Swarbrick a year earlier on the beach at Mazatlan and who were the authors of the recent instructions to his solicitors. Swarbrick weighed seven stone and had a bushy beard and hair down to the small of his back; he was wearing a cowboy hat and boots, leather chaps and a fringed buckskin jacket and told the man from Pinkerton's that he was the legendary gunfighter, Wild Bill Hickock. The Pinkerton's man, who was a Wild West buff, didn't bother to tell Swarbrick that Wild Bill Hickock had been shot dead in the Number Ten saloon in Deadwood, South Dakota, in 1876. Even though the private detective knew a lot more about the Wild West than about mental health, he was pretty sure he could recognise stark, raving insanity when he saw it.

Shortly thereafter the London solicitors instructed Prawle to sell the Manacle mansion to the highest bidder. Prawle did the deal over lunch at his club the day after receiving the instructions, although he didn't advise London until a couple of months later. The buyer was a prominent Auckland businessman, a client and close friend of Prawle's, who'd often waxed lyrical about the mansion, which he admired whenever he sailed past Manacle during his summer holiday cruise. They agreed on a price of £9,500, only £9,000 of which was sent to London. The shortfall was Prawle's cut for not telling anyone else that the property was for sale.

The mansion, which had come to be known as 'Swarbrick's Folly', remained in the businessman's family until 1986 when a newly and enormously rich corporate criminal made his grandson an offer he couldn't refuse. In 1989 the owner went bankrupt and ownership passed to his principal creditor, the Bank of New Zealand. In view of the disparity between the failed entrepreneur's assets and his liabilities, it could be argued that the bank paid close to $40 million for the privilege of owning Swarbrick's Folly.

Swarbrick's Folly was then the focus of six months' frantic activity on the part of a number of real estate agents galvanised by the depressed state of the property market and its effect on their lifestyles. Eventually the mansion was purchased, for the proverbial song, by an Indonesian company which planned to convert it into an exclusive hotel.

*

Fleur Wolfgramm, the manager of Manacle Grange, as the Indonesian hotel company had named Swarbrick's Folly, stared resentfully at the fax she'd just received from Jakarta. It was from her boss, a 29-year-old South African who was the company's sales and marketing director, and it read:

Next week I have to give the board a property by property break-down on how the group is performing. Having just reviewed the figures for the last six months, I'd have absolutely no concerns about my presentation if it wasn't for Manacle Grange which, un-believably, is doing worse than ever. This isn't the outcome we en-visaged when we hired you; in fact, I distinctly remember you expressing complete confidence that MG would be operating prof-itably within six months. Not only hasn't that happened, the oc-cupancy rate has continued to head south.

Fleur, I'd like to know what you propose to do about it. I ac-cept the fact that my arse will be kicked around the boardroom over MG's pathetic performance; my objective is to make sure that's as far as it goes. I'm therefore counting on you to revert, by week's end, with a summary of your planned marketing and pro-motional initiatives to enable me to demonstrate to the board that we're doing more than just shuffling the deckchairs at MG.

Wolfgramm had been around for long enough to know that the fax meant she'd soon be out of a job. The sales and mar-keting director's fallback position, if the board started heavy-ing him, would be to suggest getting rid of her. Even if it didn't come to that, she was on borrowed time. Regardless of what the fax said, she knew for a fact that at least two other prop-erties in the chain were losing money, so in order to keep his CV clean, the sales and marketing director would soon jump before he was pushed. The first thing his replacement would do would be to sack the managers of the non-performing properties: it was much easier than actually analysing the sit-uation and doing something constructive and it would make him or her look tough and decisive, a hands-on, kick-butt troubleshooter. After the new boss had axed a few people, he or she could focus on the things that mattered – like spending their entertainment allowance and flying around the world first class to attend travel exhibitions.

Wolfgramm re-read the fax. *What a little turd*, she thought. She was amazed that he remembered any of her waffle at the job interview; he'd spent the whole time staring at her tits.

A lot of men stared at Fleur Wolfgramm's tits, partly because they were jolly nice tits by any standards and partly because she tended to dress in a manner which made it difficult to ignore them. She was a statuesque 40-year-old brunette with expressive green eyes and a wide, full-lipped mouth which admiring men and envious women alike took as evidence of an ardent, even lascivious temperament. She'd worked in the hospitality industry in New Zealand, Australia and the South Pacific since she was 21, acquiring a modest reputation for professionalism and a stupendous one for her prowess between the sheets. As is often the case with reputations for being good in bed, it was bogus to the extent that most of those whose testimonies had contributed to it weren't in a position to know one way or another. As it happened, Wolfgramm was quite proficient in a range of sexual activities; she was also extremely selective about whom she was prepared to be proficient with.

She'd taken the position at Manacle Grange for two reasons: she'd thought it would be a cushy number and hence an opportunity for recuperation and stocktaking after a frenetic few years involving frequent changes of jobs and addresses, marriage, divorce, and a wealthy fiancé's death of a heart attack a fortnight before their wedding and 18 hours prior to an appointment with his solicitor to discuss changes to his will. Wolfgramm had witnessed her fiancé's death after a fashion: she was sitting on his face at the time.

Secondly, she'd calculated that many of the male guests at Manacle Grange would fit the age/income profile of her ideal second husband. While she was correct in this assumption, there was a major flaw in her logic: unattached plutocrats rarely visited Manacle Grange; generally, the wealthy middle-aged or elderly gentlemen who came to stay there had either wives or companions. These companions, often sharp-witted adventuresses of similar outlook to Wolfgramm herself, could sense the presence of a rival predator the instant they set foot in the hotel.

The Grange had thus failed to live up to its promise. She wouldn't be sorry to leave but would prefer to have something lined up before she did so. That meant buying herself some time; *in other words, girl, extract digit and at least make out you're doing something to bring in a few punters.*

Wolfgramm had an idea. She rang the Tourism Board's Auckland office and asked for the public relations department. She was put through.

'Hi, this is Fleur Wolfgramm at Manacle Grange, down at Coromandel. I'm looking to get some international exposure for the Grange. Would you happen to know if there are any overseas travel writers in the country at the moment?'

*

Duane Ricketts met Jerry Naismith, the rock promoter, at the Atomic Café in Ponsonby Road at 3 o'clock on Tuesday afternoon. Naismith was fortyish trying to look 25, with the mandatory ponytail and mobile phone. They ordered coffees. Ricketts asked if Electra was meeting them there. Naismith said yes, she was, but his evasive expression said otherwise. Ricketts was a little surprised; he'd assumed that to be a rock promoter, you'd have to be a reasonably good liar.

'Does Electra use her old man's surname or her mother's?' asked Ricketts.

'It's Crouch; I wouldn't know whose it is.'

Ricketts nodded. 'And this band of hers – The Homo Dwarves: is that a full-time thing or does she do something else?'

Naismith glanced at his watch. 'There's not a lot of full-time musos in this town. She goes to uni.'

'Oh yeah? What does she study?'

'English. She's right into literature – poetry and that. She reckons it helps her song writing.'

Naismith had been watching the door over Ricketts' shoulder. He raised his eyebrows to greet someone, then stood up.

'Well, I'll leave you guys to it.'

A tall young man, early 20s, wearing jeans, motorcycle boots, a leather waistcoat to show off his tan and biceps, and a few bits of junk around his neck, slid into the seat Naismith had vacated. He had earrings in both ears and his long brown hair was jelled and swept back off his forehead.

Ricketts stirred his coffee and looked up at Naismith. 'Who's your boyfriend?'

The newcomer reached across the table and grabbed Ricketts right hand, bending the thumb back.

'What the fuck did you say ...'

Ricketts was stirring his coffee with his left hand. He took the teaspoon out of the coffee and pressed it down on the back of the newcomer's hand; he swore and jerked his hand back, letting go of Ricketts' thumb.

'Hey, hey, take it easy, guys,' said Naismith in a high, nervous voice. 'This is Jake, Electra's partner. You want to meet Electra, you've got to square it with him first, okay? Right, I'm out of here. Catch you, Jake.'

Ricketts put the teaspoon in the saucer and sipped his coffee. It was very hot. He smiled at Jake who was rubbing the back of his right hand and giving him the dead-eyes look.

'So Jake,' he said. 'You're Electra's social secretary?'

'Fuck you, man. Try something like that again and you'll be fucking sorry.'

'Okay, I get the message: the reason you walk like that is you've got great big balls. Good for you. Now can we get on with it? All I want to do is talk to Electra – for five minutes.'

'Electra doesn't know you and she's pretty sure she doesn't want to know you. That's why you're talking to me. You got a message for her, you give it to me and I might pass it on or I might not.' It was Jake's turn to smile. 'Depends what sort of mood I'm in. Right now it's seriously shitty.'

Ricketts shrugged. 'I met Electra's father up in …'

'Her old man? He's dead.'

'Yeah well, before he was dead, he was alive. That's the way it works, see? I met the guy in Thailand; when he found out I was coming back, he asked me to get a message to his daughter. That's all it is – he asked me to do him a favour and I'm trying to do it. Personally, I don't give a shit if I never set eyes on Electra.'

Jake leaned forward and put his elbows on the table. 'Is that right? Well, take it from me pal, she feels the same way about you. So what's the message?'

Ricketts shook his head wearily and got to his feet. 'It's personal. Look, how about you explain the situation to Electra? If she's interested in hearing what her old man wanted to tell her, she can leave a message with Naismith. If she's not, then to hell with it. I've kept my side of the deal.'

Ricketts headed for the door. Jake followed, talking to his back. 'You know what I think? I think you're full of shit. I think this stuff about a message from her old man is all shit.'

Ricketts stopped and turned to face him. 'So why am I wasting my time trying to get in touch with her?'

Jake's lip curled like a breaking wave. 'You've probably got the hots for her. I bet you saw her at a gig and she gave you a rat-on. You wouldn't be the first jerk-off to come crawling round.'

Ricketts winked at him. 'You're getting warm.'

*

After their meeting with Jody Spurdle, Detective Sergeant Tito Ihaka and Detective Constable Johan Van Roon went over to Remuera where they interviewed some more of the late Bart Clegg's neighbours. They got back to Auckland Central just before 6 p.m. Ihaka had a message to ring Kit Fawcett. It was code. What it meant was: ring Blair Corvine and do it now.

Corvine was an undercover policeman. Paranoia is an un-avoidable by-product of undercover work and Corvine's had reached the stage where he distrusted everyone, police in-cluded; hence the code. Ihaka sometimes got tired of Corvine's elaborate security procedures. When that happened, he'd re-mind himself that if certain people around town did happen to find out that Corvine was a cop, it was odds-on that within 24 hours his body would be discovered floating in the Manukau oxidation ponds; where they'd find his head would be anyone's guess.

The way the code worked was that if Corvine had to leave a message, he'd use the name of an obscure All Black. The degree of urgency depended on what position the All Black had played, working from front row to fullback. So for in-stance, if Corvine called himself Perry Harris, who was a prop, it meant don't bust a gut; a second five, say Phil Gard, meant get your skates on, and a fullback like Fawcett was red alert.

Ihaka found an unoccupied office and rang Corvine.

'Yeah?'

'Kit Fawcett?'

'That's me.'

'Kit, something I always wanted to ask you: you know how when you went on that tour to South Africa, you said you'd score more off the field than on? Well did you?'

'You'd fucking hope so, wouldn't you?'

'What's up?'

'You know Ronnie Traipse, runs that scrub and tug joint The Pink Wink, down in Fort Street?'

'Vaguely. What about him?'

'He put the word out today for a shooter. Apparently he's got a guy prepared to shell out two and a half grand for a .38 revolver.'

Ihaka whistled. 'Someone's keen.'

'You'll love this. The buyer's a Yank tourist called Donald Surface.'

'A tourist? Jesus, you wouldn't want to fuck up his bookings, would you?'

The squad car Ihaka sent to The Pink Wink got there 20 minutes too late. By mid-afternoon Traipse had found someone who could supply the goods; by 4.30 the goods had been delivered. Funke called just after five to check what was happening and was told the item was ready for collection. By the time the police, flak jackets and all, got there, the gun had gone and so had the mysterious Mr Surface.

Thirteen

Duane Ricketts had never met a writer, at least not that he knew of, so after he got out of the shower on Wednesday morning, he stood around in his old dressing-gown getting cold and trying to decide what to wear. Eventually he settled on a woolly jumper, old corduroy pants and brown suede shoes with rubber soles, the sort his father used to call 'brothel creepers'; not that Tom Ricketts would've known where to find a brothel, let alone what to wear to one. He had some fruit and cereal then got a couple of second-hand paperbacks from the bookcase and wrapped them in brown paper. On the way down Dominion Road towards the city, he stopped at the Mt Eden post office to buy stamps. He parked in the Victoria Street car-park and walked up through Albert Park to the university. It was 9.45 a.m.

He asked a group of students where English lectures were held. They said they thought some of them anyway were in the big lecture theatres on the basement floor of the library building and pointed the way. A crowd of students was milling around in the basement-floor corridor, obviously waiting for a 10 o'clock lecture. Ricketts went up to a young woman wearing jeans and a man-size blue shirt who was leaning against the wall by herself, reading a book.

'Excuse me, is there an English lecture in here at 10 o'clock?'

'Sure is – Shakespearean tragedy.'

'Who's the lecturer?'

'Davenport.'

'Is Davenport he or she?'

The student seemed amused. 'There are people round here – Dr Daniel Davenport, for instance – who think he's the sexiest male since Lord Byron.'

Ricketts raised his eyebrows. 'What do you think?'

'Well, Byron died in 1824. Call me sceptical but I find it hard to believe that Davenport's the best your gender could do in 170 years.'

Ricketts agreed that, when you looked at it like that, it did seem unlikely. He asked her where the English Department's administrative offices were and was told the fifth floor.

Ricketts waited till five past ten, then took a lift to the fifth floor. He went through a set of glass doors with a sign saying 'English Department Administration'. A middle-aged woman was sitting behind a reception desk working at a computer terminal. She looked up at Ricketts and offered to help him.

'Is Dr Davenport about?' he asked.

'I think Dr Davenport's lecturing at the moment. I'll just check.' She punched a key.

Ricketts clicked his fingers. 'Course he is – Wednesday mornings, he's got Shakespearean tragedy.'

The receptionist was peering at the screen. 'That's right, Stage Two.' She looked up at Ricketts. 'If you'd like to come back in an hour or so ...'

Ricketts grimaced and glanced at his watch. 'Look, I'm in a bit of a rush – perhaps you can help me. I'm Phillip Quayle, the writer ...' He paused; the receptionist met his expectant look with a blank stare. Ricketts cleared his throat and continued: 'Anyway, I'm a friend of Dan Davenport's. A while ago he introduced me to a student here, Electra Crouch. I promised I'd send her a couple of my books' – he put the parcel on the reception desk – 'but wouldn't you know it, I've gone and lost her address. You couldn't give it to me, could you, so I can get this lot off to her? They've been sitting around for two weeks, all wrapped up ready to go. I've even got the stamps, look.'

'Well ...' The receptionist hesitated. 'Under the circumstances I suppose it would be all right.' She hit the keyboard a few times. 'What was that surname again?'

'Crouch. Electra Crouch.'

'Here we are.' She passed Ricketts a pen. 'Flat 3, 13 Datchet Terrace, Westmere.'

Ricketts wrote the address on the parcel and thanked the receptionist. As he headed for the glass doors, she reminded him that there was a post office on campus.

*

At 6.10 on Tuesday evening Washington time, Leon Rehbein rang his boss Richard Thames to say that he'd made some progress on the Funke assignment. Although Rehbein spoke in his usual nasal drone, Thames knew that the computer wizard had struck pay-dirt; he wouldn't have rung him otherwise. He told Rehbein to come straight up.

Although the prospect of having Rehbein in his office for the second time in as many days caused a fluttering sensation deep in Thames' abdomen, he consoled himself with the thought that no matter how proud of himself Rehbein might be, he'd deliver his report without embellishment or theatrics. Some of Thames' staff could make tailing a seven-foot tall African diplomat in full tribal regalia through Central Park in broad daylight sound like mission impossible.

Rehbein knocked, entered, sat down, briefly consulted his notes, and embarked on his report: 'Sir, from Friday, 15 April to Monday, 18 April inclusive, 137 male US passport holders aged between 40 and 55 entered New Zealand. I ran all of them through the computer and cross-referenced them against Harold Funke. I eliminated a number because of the discrepancy in height and weight; eventually, I narrowed it down to 18 possibilities on the basis of rough phys-

ical resemblance and Southern background. One in particular stood out because the gentleman in question and Funke
have the same place of birth: Pecos, Texas. This party is
named Lyle Gorse; he was born two years before Funke.
From 1973, when Mr Gorse's passport was issued, till now,
it hadn't been used to enter or exit the US. I tapped into the
Texas state police computer in Austin and found that a Lyle
Gorse, born Pecos 1942, was shot dead in the course of a
suspected hold-up in south-west Texas in 1962. I also got
into the computer holding Texas' education records and it
seems that this Lyle Gorse and Funke were at the same high
school in Pecos at the same time. I think it's safe to assume
the Gorse passport is false; my guess is it's one of ours. I
assumed you wouldn't want me to pursue that line.'

'Correct. What you've got there seems pretty conclusive
anyway, Leon. Excellent work.'

'Thank you sir. There is one other thing. The embassy in
Wellington has received an urgent query from the New
Zealand police concerning a man described as an American
and using the name Donald Surface. It seems Surface obtained
a hand gun by way of an illegal transaction. As you may be
aware sir, New Zealand has very strict regulations concerning firearms. This took place in Auckland – which is the gate-
way for most international flights – yesterday, Tuesday their
time. The embassy has checked and no US passport holder
by that name has entered New Zealand in the past two
months. On a hunch I contacted Bangkok.' Rehbein's mud-
coloured eyes warmed and he permitted himself a brief smile;
it was as animated as Thames had ever seen him get. 'A Donald Surface left Bangkok for Hong Kong on a US passport
last Friday night. The next day Surface flew to LA which is
where Lyle Gorse flew out to Auckland from.'

'How many false passports does the son of a bitch have?'
asked Thames.

It was a rhetorical question but Rehbein answered it anyway: 'Probably one more.'

*

Rayleen Crouch wasn't a big drinker. She'd sometimes have a glass or two of white wine when she ate out, or a light beer, which she'd sit on for an hour, when she went for a drink after work. If Crouch's friends and workmates, who regarded her as a borderline teetotaller, had seen the litre bottle of Chivas Regal in the cupboard above the sink, they'd have assumed it was for visitors who wanted or needed a stiff drink; maybe, given that Rayleen kept pretty quiet about her lovelife, she had a man friend with expensive tastes. They would've been taken aback to learn that not only did she drink the Chivas herself but she got through it at the rate of one of those litre bottles every few weeks.

Crouch went to the cupboard above the sink on the nights when the job really got to her. She'd be sitting in the lounge with the TV on but not seeing anything, not hearing anything, just wondering why she was wasting her life running after fuck-ups, losers, loonies and misfits, putting up with unbelievable crap to try to help people who half the time resented you or abused you or tried to stab you in the back – sometimes literally.

On those nights, Crouch would get out the bottle, drop a few ice-cubes in a glass, pour in some Scotch and throw it back. She actually quite liked the taste but that was a bonus; what she was after was that jolt when it hit the stomach and the way the tingles went all the way out to her fingertips. Pour another dollop and do it again. Starting to feel pleasantly light-headed now; no need to gulp, just settle back on the couch and nibble at it. It was as if she'd pulled the plug on the connection between her mind and her emotions, what she'd been thinking about and how it made her feel. Instead of feeling bitter and guilty for feeling bitter all at the same time, she just felt like 'fuck 'em all'.

Rayleen Crouch was a 38-year-old social worker. Over the years her beat had covered psychiatric hospitals, crisis centres, refuges for battered wives, and halfway houses for ex-criminals. These days she mainly worked out of youth hostels, dealing with state wards, abused children, runaways, kids who'd gotten into trouble with the law. She had a sociology degree, a hefty mortgage, a dead ex-husband, a semi-estranged daughter, a sixth of a bottle of premium Scotch whisky, and a portfolio of clients who covered the spectrum from social cripples to sociopaths and included some of the most dedicated, hard-core substance abusers this side of the point of no return. And when she woke up tomorrow morning, nothing much would've changed: she'd feel like shit and the Scotch would be all gone but her clients would be getting ready for another day with their demons.

The ones with genuine psychiatric disorders weren't so bad. Even like now, when she was in one of her fuck 'em all moods, she couldn't blame them. The poor sods couldn't help it. When they were up, when the moon was in a certain phase or whatever the hell it was, they were fine and what's more, they understood what you were trying to do for them and were grateful. But then just when things were going well and they seemed to be making progress, they'd hear a voice from somewhere – maybe from the man in the hardware shop's black Labrador, maybe from the old gumdigger in the painting at the top of the stairs – and it'd set them off again. When that happened, you had to be on your toes because you never knew what was going on behind those shining eyes.

The ones who really got her down were the kids who hated the world and everything in it, most of all themselves.

Even after 15 years as a social worker, Crouch could still be chilled by the sheer force of their self-destructive impulses.

There was one kid who slashed himself with a razor blade when he couldn't score any drugs. They'd take him to hospital to get him patched up and when the nurse's back was turned, he'd steal used alcohol swabs. He'd smuggle the swabs back into the hostel, squeeze the fluid out of them, and inject himself with it.

Her black mood had been triggered by a confrontation with this particular kid that afternoon. He'd asked her to lend him some money. The line he spun was that it was to buy a few car magazines; he was getting really interested in cars and thinking maybe he'd like to be a mechanic.

She'd stared at him and asked, 'Steven, do you really expect me to believe that? This is me you're talking to, not some church group do-gooder.'

Steven, who wouldn't be a bad-looking boy if he stopped doing drugs, ate properly and got a decent haircut, looked at her as if he was going to burst out crying. Instead he said, 'Dried-up old cunt', and spat on her blouse.

Crouch had fought down the urge to slap the little shit till his ears bled. Instead she'd wiped away the spit with a handkerchief and said, as calmly as she could, 'I'd rather be a dried-up old cunt than a pathetic little junkie.'

Then Steven really had burst into tears.

Crouch had been so angry that she'd completely forgotten about the note one of the girls at the hostel had given her, telling her not to read it till she got home. This girl, Merelle, was a tragic case. She'd been sexually abused by her mother's de facto, although the way Merelle preferred to tell it, she'd seduced him. They got her out of there but the damage was done. She went through a phase of offering herself to any adult male who as much as looked sideways at her; lately, she'd got herself together a bit but that side of her, a mix of exhibitionism and self-humiliation, was never far away. Crouch doubted that she'd ever forget the time she and Merelle were at a crowded outdoor café in Parnell; Crouch went inside to get something else to eat and when she came back, Merelle had her dress up around her waist, one leg up on the table, and one hand inside her panties, diddling away.

Crouch was stretched out on the sofa near the bottom of her third Scotch when she remembered Merelle's note. It was kind of sweet the way Merelle had come up to her, all shy, and slipped the note into her bag. Crouch stood up and swayed. She walked a little unsteadily through to the kitchen where she'd left her handbag on the bench, found Merelle's note and unfolded it.

In her surprisingly neat handwriting, Merelle had written: 'Get a life lezzo slut.'

*

Crouch stared at Merelle's note for ten seconds. Then the grim line of her mouth slowly curled into a sour smile. She chuckled. The chuckle became a laugh. She put her head back and hooted with laughter for a full minute. Then she abruptly stopped laughing, said 'Little slag' out loud, screwed up the note and dropped it in the rubbish bin. She was pouring herself a final Scotch when the doorbell rang. She looked at her watch; it was 9.20. *That'll be Electra*, she thought. *About bloody time she put in an appearance.*

She negotiated the corridor with just the single ricochet off the wall. If she'd been sober, she wouldn't have just taken it for granted that it was her daughter at the door and she certainly wouldn't have opened the door without taking the elementary precaution of asking whoever was on the other side of it to identify themselves. But she wasn't sober and she didn't ask; she just opened the door. It was only then that her mental machinery ground into action: *this is not my daughter; this is a large beetle-browed man with a very dark five o'clock shadow and thick, blunt-fingered hands. All the better to strangle you with. Oh Jesus, no.*

Crouch went to slam the door but the man was too quick for her; he flung out his right arm and blocked the door with the heel of his hand then jammed a foot in the doorway.

'Hey,' he said. 'That's not very nice.'

Crouch shoved as hard as she could but the man stepped right up to the door and leaned his shoulder against it. She couldn't budge it.

'Please,' she gasped. 'Go away.'

'Keep your hair on, Rayleen,' said the man in a non-threatening, almost reasonable tone. 'I just want a quiet word.'

He pushed the door open and came inside. Crouch backed away down the corridor.

'Who are you?'

'You mean you don't remember me? Leith Grills? Fair play though, it was a while ago now, not long after you got hitched to Varty. You know that shitrag killed my brother?'

She retreated into the lounge. Grills sauntered in after her and looked around like a house hunter at an open home.

'You've got the place looking nice,' he said, nodding his approval.

'When?'

Grills looked puzzled. 'When what?'

'When did he kill your brother?'

'Nineteen eighty three it was. Varty brought some dope over from Aussie on a boat, I mean millions of bucks' worth. It was a 50–50 deal, him and this other guy. Al, my brother, was working for the other guy. Al went down to Coromandel to meet Varty and got his head bashed in for his trouble.

Varty wanted the lot, see? As a matter of fact, that's what brings me here.'

Crouch had never sobered up faster. 'What's it got to do with me?'

Grills grinned. His eyes gleamed with greed and dumb cunning. 'Varty had to shoot through in a big hurry, right? So he never had a chance to shift the stuff. Well, me and his partner, the bloke he ripped off, want to get our hands on it; trouble is, we don't know where the prick hid it. But we reckon he must've told someone.' Grills' grin disappeared and he moved closer to her. 'Maybe his pretty little wife.'

Crouch, who'd relaxed a fraction and was half-sitting on the arm of the sofa, sprang upright and retreated behind it.

'That's ridiculous,' she exclaimed. 'Varty and I had split up way before that. I didn't see him or speak to him from one year to the next.'

There was a sharp rap on the window of the French doors which opened out to the back yard. A short, stocky middle-aged man stood in the half-light. He smiled and made a little waving gesture.

'Who the fuck's that?' snarled Grills.

'I don't know,' said Crouch starting towards the French doors.

Grills pushed in front of her. 'Get out of it. I'll take care of him.'

The key was in the door. Grills turned it, pushed the doors open, and told the stranger, 'You can shove right off, who-ever you are.'

'Well now,' said the stranger in a lazy American drawl, 'I was sitting in my car across the street there when you sort of barged in without a real big "come on in and set yourself down", far as I could tell. I've been standing out here observing the two of you and I assessed from the lady's demeanour that you ain't exactly a long-lost friend. So maybe you should take your own advice and shove the hell off yourself.'

Grills, flabbergasted, stared down at the American for a few seconds. He began to make a low growling sound then suddenly yanked back his right arm and let fly. The American ducked under the haymaker and counterpunched, snapping off a short right which thudded into Grills' throat as he lunged forward. Grills made a noise like a sink waste disposal unit trying to cope with a bucketful of gravel and clutched his neck. The American slipped his right leg behind Grills' and judo-threw him. Grills went down, hitting the back of his head hard on the floor. He felt something cold and metallic rasp between his teeth and opened his eyes to discover that he had two inches of gun barrel in his mouth.

'Okay, compadre,' said the American who was squatting on his haunches beside him. 'What happens now is either you haul your sorry ass out of here or I pull the trigger and blow whatever's inside your skull all over the little lady's nice, clean floor. Would you care to indicate a preference?' There was a click, a very loud one it seemed to Grills, as the American cocked the revolver.

Grills' eyes bulged in supplication and he gagged on the gun barrel. The American looked up at Crouch and smiled.

'I'm picking he'll go for the tactical retreat. What do you think, ma'am?'

Crouch, utterly bewildered and half-expecting that at any moment she'd awake from this whiskey-induced nightmare with a thundering hangover, responded with a dazed nod.

The American stood up and gave Grills a casual kick in the ribs. 'Scram asshole. Be advised that if we meet again, you won't be getting a vote on the outcome.'

He followed Grills down the corridor, the pistol dangling in his right hand, and watched him get into his car and drive off. Then he slipped the gun into the waistband of his trousers and returned to the lounge. He reached inside his jacket and produced a badge for Crouch's inspection.

'Allow me to introduce myself, ma'am: special agent Buddy Funke of the United States Drug Enforcement Administration at your service. Begging your pardon for crashing the barn-dance, but it seemed like a good idea at the time.'

Fourteen

Tito Ihaka didn't have a telephone beside his bed on principle. He believed that having a phone in your bedroom was
an invitation to people to ring you at all hours of the day or
night, including those normally set aside for sleeping. The
phone beside the bed implied, he felt, not just that you did-
n't mind being rung at ungodly hours, you expected, if not
actually welcomed, it. Ihaka didn't welcome it at all. Among
his friends, ringing Ihaka at the wrong time and for anything less than a matter of life and death – say, for instance,
that a giant meteorite was about to land in his street – was
known as 'Dial-A-Diatribe'.

Thus when the phone rang at 6.27 that Thursday morning, Ihaka didn't curse or groan because he assumed it would
be important. There was a second possibility – that it was a
wrong number – and Ihaka spent the short time it took him
to get out of bed and walk through to the living room considering what he'd say to the caller if that was the case. When
he picked up the phone, he'd progressed no further than a
couple of old stand-bys – leprosy, consumption of animal
droppings – so he was almost relieved when it turned out to
be Detective Inspector Finbar McGrail.

'Sorry about the hour,' said McGrail. 'If it's any consola-
tion, I got a wake-up call too – half an hour ago.'

Pull the other one, it's got warts on it, thought Ihaka who
knew that McGrail got up at 5.30 every morning and went
for a run.

'Not to worry, sir,' said Ihaka. 'I'll catch up on my sleep
at work. What's up?'

'You're on a plane to Wellington leaving in just over an
hour. You'd better get weaving.'

'What about the Clegg briefing? Isn't that this morning?'

'Forget it. You won't miss much.'

'Autopsy a fizzer, eh?'

'Well, it simply confirmed that there's no physical evidence to show that someone drowned him, then jammed him under the seat. The pathologist believes the body had been in the spa for 30 to 40 hours – since Friday night in other words ...'

'That's Ricketts off the hook.'

'Indeed. You saw the body – if there ever were marks indicating the use of force, they're not discernible now. The coroner will bring in an open verdict; he couldn't do otherwise.'

'Pretty fucking weird way to commit suicide, but.'

'Agreed. And quite how the body could get under there if it'd been some sort of accident escapes me, but there we are.'

'What about that missing champagne glass? The cleaning woman says there was a full set when she did the place last Wednesday and the rubbish had already been collected.'

'Interesting but hardly conclusive. The point is that whatever logic and instinct tell us, at the moment we've got no actual physical evidence of foul play, no reports of disturbances, no-one seen coming or going from the scene and no apparent motive; therefore we can't as yet make a watertight case for murder – if you'll pardon the expression. And with all due respect, Sergeant, I don't think anything you might contribute at the briefing will substantially alter that state of affairs.'

'I hear you,' said Ihaka thinking, *Christ, he's in fine fettle this morning*. 'So what's the go in Wellington?'

'You've got a 10.30 meeting at the Beehive, in the Police Minister's office ...'

'That tosser ...'

'Sergeant, can I suggest that for once in your life you just play a straight bat – if for no other reason than self-interest. The American ambassador will be at the meeting, as will a few high-ranking officials from various government departments; I think you'd be wise to proceed on the assumption that these people are unlikely to share your rather unusual sense of humour.'

Ihaka smiled to himself and asked what it was all in aid of.

'It's to do with your man Donald Surface. It seems he's some sort of American agent who's gone off the rails. I dare say the minister and the US Embassy want the thing handled as discreetly as possible.'

'Has Surface got diplomatic immunity?'

'I shouldn't think so. I doubt the Americans would be being this polite if he had.'

'Sir, this is bloody silly. You should be at the meeting, not me – you're far more cut out for this sort of shit.'

'How kind of you to say so, Sergeant,' said McGrail, 'but it's not up to me. As soon as the district commander knew you were in the loop, he was adamant that you should represent us.'

'For Christ's sake, why? Hang on, let me guess: has it got anything to do with the fact that I'm Maori?'

'Oh, I don't think I'd care to speculate on the district commander's thought processes.'

Ihaka's brow furrowed as he picked up the undertone of amusement in his boss's voice. *Where's McGrail coming from?* he wondered; *he's probably hoping I make a goose of myself and the DC ends up getting kicked in the nuts.*

'Well did you warn him about my lack of – what do they call them? – people skills?'

McGrail chuckled drily. 'My word yes, but he's confident that cometh the hour, cometh the man. Your ticket's at the Ansett desk. Enjoy your trip, Sergeant.'

He hung up. Ihaka put the phone down thinking, *this is a hell of a time for McGrail to develop a sense of humour.*

*

At 7.45 that morning, Duane Ricketts parked his seven-year-old Toyota across the road from 13 Datchet Terrace, Westmere. It was a three-storey brick and plaster block which someone with a real estate agent's jaunty attitude towards the unvarnished truth might have described as art deco. The pale pink paintwork was flaking but probably not fast enough to suit the neighbours. Datchet Terrace sloped down towards the harbour; Ricketts guessed that if Flat 3 was on the top floor, Electra and Jake would be able to admire the view down Waitemata Harbour to Hobsonville and Greenhithe, in the unlikely event they ever got bored with admiring themselves.

Shortly before 8.30 a young woman came out of the building and began walking up the hill to the main road. She was quite tall and slim with short, spiky, reddish-brown hair and walked with an eye-catching, loose-limbed sway, swinging her free arm like a sergeant-major on parade. She wore black boots, black leggings, a black denim jacket over a black T-shirt and had a black and purple backpack slung over her left shoulder. Her nosering glinted in the early morning sunshine, which was bright without being warm. Experience had taught Ricketts to be cautious in making assumptions about people's appearances; *on the other hand*, he told himself, *it hasn't taught me how to do the perfect boiled egg.* He got out of his car, locked the door and followed the young woman who was on the opposite footpath.

On the corner where Datchet Terrace met the main road was a little grassed area, about ten square metres, containing a large rubbish bin, a bench and many dog turds of varying chalkiness. When the girl reached it, Ricketts crossed the road. She heard his footsteps and glanced over her shoulder. He said, 'Electra Crouch?'

She looked at him warily. Up close he could see that she had several studs in both ears, huge black eyes like wet stones, a slight pout and flawless pale skin. She was very good looking. *I bet a lot of guys tell her she's beautiful,* thought Ricketts, *and some of them would believe it.* He wondered if she believed it herself.

'Who are you?'

'Duane Ricketts. I saw your father in Thailand.'

'Not you again? Jake says you're a jerk-off.'

'I'm sorry to hear that. I thought he was a wonderful human being.'

'Is that your idea of a joke?' she sneered. Ricketts couldn't quite understand how she managed to sneer and look attractive at the same time.

'He's your boyfriend – you tell me.'

She looked at her watch, a garish, plastic thing the size of a small landmine. 'I've got a bus to catch.'

'Don't worry about that: I can give you a lift – my car's back there.'

'Oh wow,' she said, batting her eyelashes. 'It's been ages since a strange man tried to get me into his car.' She switched from facetiousness to suspicion. 'How'd you find out where I lived?'

'It wasn't very difficult; I make a living out of finding people. Look, I don't know what all the drama's for – I only want to pass on a message from your old man. It'll take five minutes, tops.'

Electra kept the suspicious look in place for a while longer. Then she shrugged and went and sat down on the bench. When Ricketts joined her, she said, 'I haven't seen him since I was seven and he wasn't exactly the model father.'

'Yeah well, I guess old Dale did make a couple of bad moves along the way. It seemed to me that he felt he'd let you down and wanted to make it up to you.'

She was completely unmoved. 'Spare me the soppy stuff. You got something to say, say it.'

Ricketts had known all along that this would be the tricky bit. He'd considered various approaches but none of them, he decided, were going to make it: this girl was too bright to con and too cynical to get sentimental. *When all else fails*, he thought, *try telling the truth*.

'I talked to Dale just before they carted him off to hospital. He told me about a shipment of drugs – cocaine – he brought over from Australia in 1983. He walked straight into trouble: he was double-crossed by his partner, a big-time drug dealer called Bryce Spurdle, someone ended up getting killed, and he had to hide the dope and get out of the country. He said he hid it in a special place, somewhere down at Coromandel he took you when you were a little kid.' Electra's eyes widened. 'What he wanted was for us to find it so you could, you know, benefit from it.'

She frowned. 'Have I got this straight: he wanted me to tell you where this special place is so we could find the coke, sell it, and I get the money – Daddy's parting gift? Sort of like, and to my darling daughter Electra, I leave an absolute shitload of cocaine?'

'Yeah, that's about it.'

'And what's in it for you? Or would you be doing it out of the goodness of your heart, wonderful human being that you are?'

Ricketts detected a hum of suppressed anger beneath the sarcasm. He shifted on the bench, recrossing his legs.

'Well, I think the way Dale saw it, there'd be something in it for me if I, you know, did the work and took the risks.'

Electra took a packet of cigarettes out of her bag and lit one. She leaned back on the bench and stared straight ahead without speaking, sucking in her cheeks with violent drags which burnt the cigarette down a centimetre a time. *Maybe she's taking a while to get used to the idea*, thought Ricketts hopefully; *after all, it's not every day a complete stranger offers to make you a millionaire.*

She stood up. 'Look, I'm really flattered that Dad thought I've got what it takes to carry on the family tradition but I'll have to pass.'

She started to walk away, then stopped. She walked back to Ricketts, now on his feet, and fixed him with a look of sheer loathing. There were tears in the black eyes and her voice was an acid hiss: 'Drugs ripped my family apart and me and my mother are still a bit screwed up because of it. My father's dead because of drugs. The very last thing he did was to send you sliming around trying to suck me into a drug deal. What sort of fucking father does that? And what sort of dreg does that make you?'

Ricketts met her accusing stare for a few more seconds then looked away.

'I'm sorry,' he said. 'It was a bad idea, okay? Don't be too hard on your dad. He was dying, don't forget; he just wanted to do something for you. The thing to remember is that when the time came to think about the people who really mattered to him, he thought of you.'

Large, pear-shaped teardrops swelled from Electra's eyes and slid slowly down her cheeks to the corners of her mouth. Soon there were steady trickles. A drop splashed onto her denim jacket. She reached up with her right hand and with two abrupt movements, wiped the tears off her face with the back of her hand.

Quietly but without the slightest tremor in her voice, she said, 'Fuck the fuck off.'

*

The Minister for Police was shorter and seedier than he appeared on television, which didn't surprise Ihaka; in his experience, most politicians were. He shook hands, coating Ihaka's palm with an oily film, then introduced him to the other participants in the meeting: the US ambassador, a tall, bulky, almost completely bald, almost elderly black man; his chargé d'affaires who, apart from being male, was none of those things; a matching set of bureaucrats, one from the Foreign Affairs Department, the other from the minister's staff; and a woman from the Attorney-General's office who wore tartan and looked disgruntled, as if being there had made her miss her bagpipes lesson. Ihaka was seated next to her at the meeting table.

'I guess the transsexual dwarf couldn't find a park for the wheelchair, eh?' he said to her in a low voice. She pulled a hideous face, which Ihaka interpreted as a glare of disapproval, and transferred her attention to one of the bureaucrats.

The minister sat at the head of the table. He cleared his throat to bring the meeting to order and set off in a squeaky, cartoon-character voice: 'Mr Ambassador, Ms McHarg, gentlemen – thank you for attending at such short notice. I called this meeting because we seem to be confronted with an unusual, if not unique, situation. Mr Ambassador, perhaps I could ask you to start the ball rolling.'

The ambassador bowed his gleaming cranium and opened a manila folder.

'Thank you, Minister,' he said in a double-bass rumble. 'After the Auckland police notified us about this guy Donald Surface procuring a firearm, we put it back to Washington. They tell us his real name is Harold Funke; he's a senior officer in the Drug Enforcement Administration, currently on a posting to Bangkok. Seems he's operating under two aliases, the other being Lyle Gorse. He entered New Zealand on a passport in that name.'

The ambassador's mouth twitched with distaste or perhaps discomfort and he adjusted his tie. *We're about to get to the guts of it*, thought Ihaka.

The ambassador continued. 'Our people in Bangkok and Washington have been on Funke's case since the beginning of the week; their conclusion is that he's come here after a drugs cache. Under the circumstances and given that he has absolutely no jurisdiction here and has made no effort to inform us or the authorities of his presence, we must assume his intentions are criminal.'

The ambassador paused and looked at the minister who smiled, nodded and turned to Ihaka. 'Detective Sergeant, I gather you found no trace of Surface last night?'

Ihaka shook his head. 'He moved out of the Regis Hotel on Tuesday morning and got a taxi over to the Inter-Con but he didn't check in there as Surface or anything else – we went through the guests and none of them matched up. We tried all the main pubs and the car-hire companies and came up empty. We should get that other name circulated right away.'

'It's under control,' said the minister's assistant. 'It was passed to Inspector McGrail earlier this morning.'

'Sergeant, any questions or comments on what we've heard from the ambassador?' asked the minister.

Ihaka didn't try very hard to keep a straight face. 'Well, I think we're on safe ground assuming this bloke's a baddy. Sir, you said your guys had been onto him since Monday – before he went looking for a gun. Why was that?'

'Someone in our Bangkok embassy seems to have had an attack of initiative,' said the ambassador sliding several typed sheets of A4 paper across the table. 'This should explain a few things.'

It was a copy of a report prepared by Everton Sloan III, summarising his investigation. Although not noted for his animation, Ihaka did a double-take worthy of a churchgoer coming across an advert for a dominatrix in the parish magazine when he spotted the names Dale Varty and Duane Ricketts. What really worried him though wasn't anything he read; it was the bits he couldn't read.

He looked up at the ambassador. 'In amongst all the stuff that's been blacked out, would there be anything we – as in the police – ought to know before we go any further?'

The ambassador sighed and flexed his jaw. 'Funke used to be in the CIA,' he said.

'Oh right. What as?'

'He was an operative.' The ambassador gestured vaguely. 'An agent in the field.'

Ihaka looked around with a cheerful but slightly puzzled smile. 'Is that what simple folk like us would call a highly-trained killer?'

The minister intervened. 'Sergeant, the ambassador is well aware of the seriousness of the situation. Indeed, he brought it to our attention.'

Ihaka's smile withered to a thin, cynical line. 'Well, that's fine. Maybe he'd like to make the arrest as well?'

The minister's face fell. The man from Foreign Affairs embarked on a prolonged and, by the sound of it, productive, throat clearance. The ambassador's offsider looked at Ihaka with respectful curiosity, as if he'd declared that he was about to undertake some insanely risky activity, such as nude fencing.

The ambassador himself seemed unperturbed. He stroked his chin contemplatively and, when the man from Foreign Affairs had ceased gargling phlegm, said: 'If you're waiting for me to volunteer, Sergeant, you might want to make yourself real comfortable – maybe order in as well. Fact is, I wouldn't go up against a guy like this with anything less than an Abrams tank. I take it your attitude, in a nutshell, is that seeing as how he's our loose cannon, we ought to put him back in the rack?'

Ihaka raised his eyebrows in agreement: 'Well, put it this way, sir: I didn't join the police force to see if I could out-draw the Man from UNCLE.'

'No, I don't suppose you did,' said the ambassador with a slow smile. 'You just had a thing about handcuffs, right?' He put his elbows on the table, clasped his hands together, and looked around to take in everyone present. 'Contrary to the impression you might get from the movies, the vast majority of the men and women in the US security agencies are highly principled and dedicated servants of their country. But we have to face facts: there is the occasional rotten apple in the barrel; every now and again, one of these people goes rogue on us. Like a lot of things we could do without, it really started during the Vietnam war: what happened up there, particularly in Laos, has been well enough documented not to need my two cents' worth. There've also been some well-publicised instances of renegade officers running guns and other hardware to terrorist organisations and nations like Libya. Security considerations prevent me from telling you any more but the bottom line is this: we have a system for responding to these situations; we have people trained to deal with the likes of Mr Funke. One of them's heading this way as we speak.'

The minister stood up. 'Thank you, Mr Ambassador,' he said with a cheesy smile. 'On behalf of my government, let me reiterate how much we appreciate the speed and scale of the United States' assistance in this matter.' He rearranged his face and looked unaffectionately at Ihaka. 'Okay Sergeant, that's the assignment: you and your team find this character; the specialist sent by Washington will do the rest. If it should come to that, of course; hopefully, it can be resolved in a peaceful manner. Geoffrey here will fill you in on the rest of it. You're to act as the liaison officer. I trust I can count on you and your colleagues for the fullest co-operation.'

Ihaka's participation in the meeting was clearly finished. He stood up and nodded at the ambassador who nodded back.

Outside in the corridor the minister's offsider told Ihaka that the specialist was flying into Auckland from Los Angeles first thing the next morning; Ihaka was to meet the flight.

'Shit hot,' said Ihaka. 'Do I get to wear a shiny suit and hold up a sign? Tell me, has this new role of ours – sniffing out targets for visiting hitmen – been cleared with Mc-Grail?'

'Look Sergeant,' said the bureaucrat crossly, 'the Commissioner of Police was in the minister's office at midnight last night dealing with this matter. The decisions were made at that level and now you have a small role to play in carrying them out. If I was in your shoes, I'd focus on making it happen.' He walked a few paces down the corridor then stopped and looked back at Ihaka. 'Besides,' he said, a transparently malicious smirk spreading across his face, 'it's not a hitman, it's a hitwoman.'

Fifteen

Electra Crouch and her boyfriend Jake Latimer met for lunch at a new café in Kitchener Street, across the road from the art gallery. The café's decor was dominated by mirrored glass and stainless steel, giving it the clinical, high-tech sheen – and the atmosphere – of a state-of-the-art abattoir. Jake's gaze was drawn to the reflective surface like a rat to a rubbish dump and he was still shooting 'do you come here often?' looks at himself when the waitress arrived. It was only then, when he glanced across the table to check if Electra was ready to order, that he noticed she was sniffling tearfully into a handkerchief.

In the almost three months they'd been together, Jake had seen Electra cry twice. The first time was when an album deal fell through; the second was when she heard her father was dead. The album deal was a bummer but he'd been surprised at how hard she'd taken the news about her old man – going by her rare comments on the subject, she seemed to have as much filial affection as he did, and the way Jake felt towards his parents, if he won five million bucks in Lotto, he'd buy them a garden gnome. Second-hand.

Jake got rid of the waitress with a jerk of his head and asked Electra what was the matter. She stopped crying, mopped her eyes, blew her nose, drank most of a glass of mineral water and told him about her encounter that morning with Duane Ricketts. Jake blew his top, pounding the table so hard that the cutlery bounced and vowing to find that fucking Ricketts and kick his fucking head in. Despite her flushed cheeks and red-rimmed eyes, Electra was somehow able to look coolly unimpressed by this display of vicarious outrage.

'Quite finished?'

'Screw you,' he snapped. 'Why shouldn't I want to get the fucker back?'

'Get him back – what for? He didn't do anything to me.'

Jake, bemused, shook his head. 'What was all the blubbing in aid of then?'

Electra propped up her chin in the heel of her hand and looked away. 'Partly because I'm slutted that my father, on top of everything else, would try to get me involved with drugs. And partly, I don't know, the thought of him dying the way he did with nothing to show for it except a few bags of coke.' She stared at him defiantly. 'Pathetic I know but it just seemed to call for a few tears. Forget about Ricketts: I told him what I thought of him; that's all he's worth.'

Electra went to the toilet. When she got back to the table, she was still trying to marshall the welter of thoughts and memories and feelings that Ricketts had set loose, otherwise she might've picked up the overly casual note in Jake's voice.

'So, this special place of yours: where is it, just as a matter of interest?'

'Dale's dream home,' she said with a hollow laugh. 'The summer I turned six, Dad came over from Sydney and we went camping down at Coromandel – our last family holiday as it turned out. I guess it was make or break for him and Rayleen, and it broke. She was a beach babe in those days – just wanted to lie around in the sun and go for swims and that – but Dad had ants in his pants, you know, he couldn't hack doing nothing; plus, with his complexion, a day in the sun and he looked like a saveloy. Anyway, one afternoon he took me for a drive. We ended up in this place called Manacle, just north of Whangapoua. It's a neat little spot with a great beach and right there on the beach was this house you wouldn't believe, I mean a real mansion. It was weird in a way, seeing it there: you know how in the movies, some guy in the desert sees a mirage, a castle or something, out in the middle of nowhere? It was sort of like that.'

Electra's eyes took on a faraway look. 'So we're standing there doing the tourist thing, right? Gawking at it, when this old guy, like doddery old, came down the drive and said hi. He was wearing shorts and a daggy old towelling hat – Dad said afterwards he thought he was the gardener but the guy actually owned the place. Dad and him got talking about the house; it all went over my head but I read up about it later. It's famous: it was built, in the '30s I think, by this crazy English millionaire who just disappeared, never to be seen again; they used to call it Swarbrick's Folly after him.

'He asked us if we wanted a look around. Dad said sure, so we got the big guided tour. It was awesome, these amazing rugs and antiques everywhere, all done out in this dark wood: the sort of place you see in glossy magazines – lifestyles of the rich and famous sort of thing. Dad couldn't get over the master bedroom: it was as big as a tennis court with this humungous four-poster bed. The old guy even made Dad lie on the bed to try it out. As we were going, the owner bent down and looked at me and said "I think this little girl could do with a cold drink, let's see what we can find." We went into the kitchen and he got me a lemonade and a chocolate from a box of chocolates, Continental I think they were. It was almost full, the box, but he told me to take it; he said "Don't eat them all at once, darling, save some for a rainy day."

'On the way back to the camping ground, Dad said – I'll never forget this – "One of these days I'm going to buy that house and you know what, sweetheart? You'll spend your wedding night in that big bed." '

Electra looked at Jake. The faraway look was gone; the black eyes were as flat and hard as tarmac.

He said, 'So what's the moral of the story? Don't make promises you can't keep?'

She nodded. 'Especially to six-year-olds. They actually believe them.'

'Well maybe if his drug deal had worked out ... who knows? So according to Ricketts, what happened was, this guy Spurdle pulled a swifty but your old man got away with the coke? And then, it sounds like, went to this fucking mansion? Is the place still there?'

Electra shrugged. 'Far as I know. I read something about it being turned into a hotel.'

'So he must've broken in and hid the coke somewhere inside?'

Electra, who by now had lost interest in the subject, nodded. 'I guess – probably right in that big old bedroom he took such a fancy to.' She picked up the menu and began to study it. 'One thing's for sure, when it came to special places, I wasn't spoilt for choice: that was it – the one and only.'

*

The back porch of Duane Ricketts' Mt Roskill bungalow caught the afternoon sun, which made it a good spot to rest and regroup after a setback. For instance, if a scheme which he'd been counting on to deliver him once and for all from financial insecurity had just been blown away like dandelion seeds, he'd go and sit out there in an old armchair with a book and a beer and eventually doze off.

Ricketts had made an early start that day so he got only halfway through Jack Nicklaus' chapter on wedge shots and not much further through a Steinlager before he nodded off. He dreamt.

He was at a ball, a full black-tie affair. Across the dance floor Electra Crouch was talking to a man with his back turned so Ricketts couldn't see his face. Electra's hair was different, darker and more natural, framing her oval face, and she'd discarded the nosering and ear studs. She wore a low-cut, flared turquoise evening gown which reached to the floor. Her companion looked around to take in the scene; it was her father, Dale Varty. His hair was plastered down and parted in the centre and he wore a crimson cummerbund.

As if she felt Ricketts' eyes on her, Electra turned her head and looked at him. The look went on and on until its meaning became unmistakable. He walked across the room to ask her to dance. Before he could get the words out, she smiled enchantingly and glided into his arms. They danced without speaking, gazing into one another's eyes. Electra moved closer to him until they were joined from thigh to chest; her body was sinuous yet firm. She tilted her head back and slightly parted her lips and her eyes grew cloudy with desire. As he leaned down to kiss her, someone tapped him on the shoulder.

He glanced over his shoulder. Jumbo Adeyemi stood there, at once exotic and urbane in white top hat and tails, twirling the cane with which he'd administered the tap; in his other hand he had a small box which was gift-wrapped in gold foil.

'A little something to brighten up your dreary existence, man,' said Jumbo, handing him the box. Ricketts opened it. The box contained a curled and blackened slab of tongue which leaked blood from its serrated edge into the bed of cotton wool on which it rested. Jumbo winked at him, then bestowed a dazzling grin on Electra.

'Don't go wasting your time with this white boy, Miss Electra,' he told her. 'Why, his weeny little nudger would fit through that ring you've got on your pinkie finger with room to spare.'

Electra removed the ring and held it up in front of her face. 'Crikey,' she said. 'He must be hung like a hedgehog.'

'Indubitably,' said Jumbo. 'I, in sharp contradistinction, am blessed with a dangle like a bull elephant's trunk, which is why folks call me Jumbo.' He bent to kiss her hand. 'My vocabulary is even bigger; would you care for a game of Scrabble?'

Electra dimpled coquettishly and took his arm. 'That sounds too stimulating for words,' she giggled.

As Jumbo and Electra strolled off arm in arm, Ricketts became aware that silence had descended on the ballroom; the music had stopped in mid-waltz and the revellers had broken off their conversations to stare at him. Then, as if responding to the baton of an invisible choirmaster, they bellowed in unison and at mind-jarring volume, 'Ricketts, you cocksucker'.

Ricketts awoke with a whimper of relief which slid up the scale into an anxious bleat when he saw Tito Ihaka's contorted face hovering ten centimetres from the end of his nose; for a couple of unnerving seconds he thought the policeman was going to chew on his face, like a pit bull terrier. Instead Ihaka slowly straightened up, although he continued looking at Ricketts as if trying to decide where a bite would do the most damage.

'The neighbours are God-botherers,' said Ricketts, a little shakily. 'They're not too keen on that sort of talk.'

'Fuck the neighbours,' said Ihaka crisply.

Ricketts noticed that Ihaka was, by his normal standards, formally attired. 'Nice tie,' he said. 'Hundred per cent polyester?'

Although Ricketts wouldn't have thought it possible, Ihaka's expression became several degrees more malevolent; abruptly, he turned on his heel and stomped into the house. He came back with the neck of a beer bottle protruding from his meaty fist, leant against the side of the house and glared down at Ricketts who was still in the armchair.

'Where's the dope, Ricketts?'

Ricketts had gathered that this wasn't a social call but the question still took him by surprise. Even as he mouthed the automatic response 'What dope?', he could feel his face giving him away.

Ihaka poured beer down his throat for a while. 'The dope Varty told you about up in Bangkok. You got it here?'

Ricketts shook his head. 'Look, I don't know what you're talking about.'

Ihaka nodded as if the discussion was proceeding in line with his expectations. 'Tell you what: I'll get myself another beer and I'll take my time over it. While I'm doing that, you go and get the coke and put it in my car, out the front. Then I'll piss off and we'll forget the subject ever came up. Just bear in mind pal, this is it; this is the one and only favour you're ever getting from me. You pull another stunt like this, I'll put you away so fast, you won't even blink.'

Ihaka went inside. Ricketts stayed where he was. When Ihaka returned, so did his scowl.

'All right, cunty, you've had your chance ...'

'I haven't got it.'

Ihaka's eyes narrowed. 'Okay; where is it?'

'I don't know.'

When Ihaka started to call him filthy names, Ricketts interrupted again: 'Varty didn't tell me; he just said go and see Clegg.'

'Clegg? What the fuck was he meant to do?'

'Tell me where it was, I suppose.'

Ihaka studied Ricketts thoughtfully for a few seconds. 'This is going to put a rocket under the Clegg investigation – you realise that, don't you?' Ricketts shrugged. 'What I'm saying,' continued Ihaka, 'is if you're bullshitting, I'll come back and trample your balls into fishpaste.'

Ricketts shrugged again.

'I'll be on my way then.' Ihaka looked back from the foot of the porch steps. 'You've got nerve, Ricketts, I'll give you that. If I thought a trained fucking killer might turn up on my doorstep any moment, I wouldn't be sitting out on the porch having a wet dream.'

Ricketts yelled after him wanting to know what the hell he was talking about but Ihaka walked to his car without a backward glance and drove away.

*

Back at Auckland Central, Ihaka went straight in to see Detective Inspector Finbar McGrail.

'Ah, there you are, Sergeant,' said McGrail looking up from some papers. 'I hear you excelled yourself this morning.'

'Oh yeah?' said Ihaka guardedly, thinking, *here we go*.

'The minister's secretary said the American ambassador found you – and I quote – 'a breath of fresh air".'

Ihaka managed to look both surprised and slightly relieved. 'Yeah well, he seemed like a decent bloke – easy enough to do in that company, I suppose. You heard what's happening?'

'I did indeed. Extraordinary business but ours is not to reason why.'

'What's new, eh?' Ihaka's wary look faded. He tried, briefly and unsuccessfully, to squeeze self-satisfaction out of his expression. 'Still, the day hasn't been a complete dud – I reckon I know why Clegg was killed.'

McGrail's mouth quivered. 'Let me hazard a wild guess. Does it have anything to do with the shipment of cocaine Dale Varty brought across from Australia in 1983?'

Ihaka shoved his hands into his pockets. 'I thought you said the briefing would be a non-event?' he said resentfully.

'Oh it was, completely,' said McGrail blandly. 'Sergeant, why don't you close the door and take a seat?'

When Ihaka had sat down, McGrail opened a desk drawer and produced a cassette.

'This morning I had a ring from one of the partners at Trubshaw Trimble – Clegg's law firm. He asked if he could pop in for a chat – about this.' McGrail indicated the cassette; he put it in the tape machine on his desk and pressed a button.

A voice Ihaka didn't know said: 'Monday October 17th 1983, recording meeting with client Al Grills to discuss receiving stolen goods charge.'

McGrail stopped the tape.

'That's Clegg. The fellow who came to see me is the executor of his estate. In the course of going through Clegg's files – no doubt also with his Trubshaw Trimble hat on looking out for any nasties which might pop out of the woodwork – he found a key to a bank safety deposit box. That's where the cassette was.' Knowing instinctively what was running through Ihaka's mind, the inspector added: 'No Sergeant, he didn't tell me what else was in the safety deposit box and, under the circumstances, I thought it would be churlish to ask.'

Ihaka feigned a polite smile. 'Fair enough.'

McGrail fast-forwarded the cassette to the point he wanted. 'Now then,' he said. Intrigued despite himself, Ihaka sat up in his chair and craned forward.

A telephone rang. Clegg said, 'Clegg … yep … right now? I'm actually with a client … how long will it … a few minutes? … Okay, be with you in two ticks.' He hung up. 'Al, sorry about this, I've just got to duck upstairs and see the senior partner. Won't be long. Can I get Cath to bring you another coffee?'

Another voice, obviously Grills': 'No, she's right.'

'Okay, be back in a sec.'

A door opened and closed. A telephone receiver was picked up and a number dialled. Then Grills: 'Yeah, it's me ... You've heard from Varty? Shit hot, what's the story ... right ... right ... hang on, let me get a pen ... okay, what was it again? ... Otama beach, Thursday night? Okay ... you bet ... oh he'll be shitty all right ... yeah, what you said before, you don't do this sort of crap anymore ... yeah well let's face it, he's not going to turn round and fuck off back to Oz ... yeah ... yeah, picked it up this morning, a sawn off .22' – Grills laughed – 'he can't complain – hanging out with Terry Clark and co., he's fucking lucky he's lasted this long ... and I'll bring the stuff straight over to your place? ... Yep ... ten kilos, right? ... Sweet as ... okay, I better get off the phone, Clegg'll be back any mo ... yeah, see you.'

McGrail punched a button and the machine stopped. 'What do you make of that, Sergeant?'

'Varty set the deal up with whoever Grills is talking to but his partner decided to shaft him; the call was putting the finishing touches on the shaft. Except Grills fucked up big-time, right?'

McGrail opened the file on his desk. 'Grills' body was discovered by the side of the road that runs along Otama Beach on Friday, October the 21st. He died from massive head injuries as a result of a single blow with a shovel. The murder weapon belonged to the owner of one of the beach houses down there, near where they found the body. No-one was staying there at the time; the shovel had been left under the back steps where anyone could've picked it up.'

Ihaka snapped his fingers loudly lurching forward. 'Clegg must've warned Varty. When he heard the tape, he got in touch with Varty and told him what was going on.' He leaned back and closed his eyes. 'Grills is getting set to slot Varty; before he has a chance, Varty sneaks up on him and beats him like a drum; probably didn't mean to kill him. When he realised the guy was dead, he thought Christ, I've got to get out of here, dumped the dope somewhere, and buggered off.'

McGrail nodded. 'Makes sense.'

'You bet. I've just talked to that lying turd Ricketts. You know the real reason he was out at Clegg's place that day? Because Varty told him Clegg knew where the coke was. Varty must've cut him in on the deal as a pay back. Then when Varty shot through, they probably agreed to leave the stuff where it was till he got back. You could just about say this gives Leith Grills – Al's brother – a motive for killing Clegg. Speaking of Leith, you know he's working for Bryce Spurdle these days?'

'The drug dealer – supposedly retired?' McGrail shuffled through his papers. 'He's down here as a known associate of both Al Grills and Varty. Maybe it's Spurdle Grills is talking to on the tape.'

'Could be,' said Ihaka. 'Put it this way, it's a lot more likely that Spurdle's got Leith on the payroll to help him get his hands on that dope than to get rid of his missus.'

'Say again?'

'I told you about Spurdle's wife, didn't I, how she's got it into her head that he's hired Leith Grills to knock her off?'

McGrail, whose most fervent detractors acknowledged he had a mind like Colditz – once something had entered, it rarely escaped – shook his head very slowly from left to right and back again. 'Negative, Sergeant. Why should Spurdle do that?'

'Oh, she thinks he's found out she's been getting a knobbing from her gym instructor.'

'Well, if he has found out, she might have a point. Men have been known to kill their wives for less.'

'Men have been known to kill their wives for patting the family dog too often but we're talking about Spurdle here. Maybe if she was renting studs on his Amex card but that's about it. And let me tell you, there's no way this chick's paying for it; shit, she'd find herself a root in the Vatican.'

McGrail rubbed his chin reflectively. 'I see. Tell me, Sergeant, exactly what did you and the American ambassador talk about?'

Sixteen

It was a tense time in the Spurdle household. For reasons which escaped Bryce Spurdle, his wife Jody had been in a foul mood the previous few days. She'd bristled and snapped every time he opened his mouth, and when he'd asked her if it was that time of the month, a reasonable enough question under the circumstances, she'd thrown a wobbly and refused to make dinner. Discreet monitoring of the packet of tampons in her ensuite bathroom had ruled that out, so Christ knew what was eating her, the crabby little moll.

That was Monday night. Spurdle had dined on hamburger patties which, by the end of the meal, he'd come to suspect could have done with a little more defrosting in the microwave. Later, he lay in bed flinching at each gurgle from under the sheets in case it heralded the agonising abdominal ructions which often accompany food poisoning. Fortunately, it was nothing more than a particularly heavy build-up of the nocturnal wind which, in happier times, had provided him with much innocent amusement.

On Tuesday night, emboldened by an excellent bottle of Australian red wine and a large Cointreau and ice, he'd suggested that she might care to don a few choice items from her lingerie drawer and drape herself over the king-size bed to await his pulsating presence. Jody had been unimpressed by this love-talk: she'd called him 'a pisshead', threatened to throw up if he got within an arm's length of her, and implied that he'd pulsate about as much as the shrivelled-up parsnip which had been languishing at the back of the fridge since Waitangi Day. Then she'd plucked her dressing-gown from the wardrobe and flounced off to the spare room.

Wired on alcohol and unsated lust, Spurdle had, for the second night running, found sleep elusive. He'd flopped this way and that in the big bed, like a fish in the bottom of a boat, and tormented himself with bitter thoughts. Fuck, it wasn't as if his demands were excessive – he only put the hard word on her once every couple of weeks, if that. She'd been happy enough to lie back and think of her credit cards in the early days, when he'd spent more time in the saddle than Lester Piggott. That was then, before the deal was signed and sealed, he thought; now the bitch has got everything she wants, including a bloody long leash, one lousy squirt a fortnight's too much to ask.

Then on Wednesday night, the shit-train rolled through town again. He'd got himself fizzed up at the prospect of finally getting his hands on Varty's boatload of cocaine, but that'd turned out to be another pie in the sky. He'd sent Grills off to heavy Varty's ex-wife, a simple enough mission for someone as vicious and ugly as him, you'd think. Not on your fucking nelly: Grills had drifted back, red-faced and shaken, mumbling about how he'd been jumped by a short-arse Yank who'd stuck a pistol in his face. Then the deadshit dug his heels in and refused point-blank to have another go unless he got some firepower of his own. He was all set to head out to Pukekohe to collect a shotgun from a bloke he knew but Spurdle had given that the thumbs down, double quick: retrieving a swag of drugs which everyone had long since forgotten about was a very worthwhile exercise as long as it could be done nice and quietly, without attracting any attention, let alone that of the boys in blue. Leith Grills fired-up and brandishing a shotgun was not Spurdle's idea of stealth.

On Thursday morning Spurdle went into town and had breakfast at the Sierra café. He took his golf clubs and, on the way back, stopped in at the driving range in Northcote, where he flailed wildly at golf balls until his frustrations subsided.

He got home just before 1 o'clock and was pleasantly surprised to find there was a lull in the hostilities. Jody was in a civil mood and in the kitchen, preparing lunch. After grilled snapper, salad, a couple of glasses of chardonnay, and some bile-free conversation, Spurdle felt less at odds with the world. The phone call, which Spurdle answered, didn't hurt either.

'Is that Bryce Spurdle?'

The caller was male, the voice unfamiliar. He sounded young, whoever he was.

'Who's this?'

'You're the only B. Spurdle in the phone book but the question is, are you the B. Spurdle who went into a, let's say, business venture with Dale Varty a few years ago which didn't pan out?'

Who is this arsehole? thought Spurdle.

'Because if you are, I've got good news for you. I've located the product. The stuff that was brought in from overseas and went missing? I know where it is.'

Spurdle remained silent, wondering if it was some sort of set-up or perhaps someone pulling his tit.

'Are you out there?' asked the caller. 'Is there life on planet Spurdle?'

'I'm listening,' said Spurdle.

'Okay. I assume that means you're the guy. As I was saying, I know where the stuff is and I thought you'd be interested in that information.'

'Maybe.'

'Yeah, right … and maybe dogs like sniffing other dogs' backsides. How about we make a date to talk about it?'

Spurdle looked at his watch. 'You know the Sierra café on Ponsonby Road?'

'Sure do.'

'I'll see you there in an hour.'

'An hour's good. That'll give you plenty of time to top up the bank account.'

*

Spurdle took the Porsche this time but on the motorway he got stuck behind a cop cruising at right on the speed limit. He was almost ten minutes late when he pulled into a parking spot outside the Sierra. There was a long-haired guy, early to mid-20s, in dark glasses and black leather jacket sitting by himself at one of the outside tables. When Spurdle walked up to the entrance to the café, the guy took off his glasses and said, 'Yo, Bryce, you're late, dude.'

Spurdle stared down at him. 'Don't "yo" me, don't call me Bryce, and don't call me dude.' He sat down. 'Who are you, pal?'

Jake Latimer smiled confidently and shook his head. 'I think I'd prefer to remain anonymous ...'

'Is that a fact?' said Spurdle, raising his eyebrows. He leaned forward and lowered his voice. 'Let me explain how we're going to do this: first, you've got to convince me that I should take a blind bit of notice of you or anything you say. If you can do that, we'll go on to the next step. If we get to the stage of negotiating, then you're going to have to tell me who you are and where I can find you, otherwise forget it. See, the thing is, sonny, you're selling information and information's only worth anything if it's kosher. Now you, being so fucking sharp, are going to want money up front, right? Because otherwise you've got no leverage. You see the problem? I don't find out if what I've paid for is worth shit until after I've handed over the dough. So you're going to ID yourself: that way, if I pay for information which turns out to be bodgie, I can send someone round to your place to get my money back – and while they're at it, to stick a crowbar so far up your arse, you'll think you're getting dicked from both ends. Which probably wouldn't be a new experience for you.'

Latimer laughed, a little nervously. 'Hey, that's cool. I can dig it.'

'Well hoo-fucking-ray. Let's hear it, Flash.'

Latimer gave Spurdle a brief account of the events of October 1983 – managing to avoid any allocation of blame for the collapse of the enterprise – and of Varty's death in Bombat prison.

'So what?' demanded Spurdle. 'All that proves is you can read.'

'What else can I tell you, apart from where the stuff is?' asked Latimer plaintively.

'For a start, why don't you explain how you found out?'

Latimer took a deep breath: 'A guy I know was in prison with Varty, up in Thailand. Varty told him about, you know, the deal and how he hid the dope. He didn't tell him where but he dropped a few hints. I put that together with stuff I got from someone here, someone who was really close to Varty.'

'It sounds a bit fucking vague to me.'

'Shit, I can tell you which room in which building in which town. How much more do you want?'

'Have you actually seen the stuff?'

'Come on – would I be sitting here if I had? I only found out where it is myself a couple of hours ago.'

'Who else knows?'

'Only one other person; take it from me, they don't want anything to do with it.'

'How far out of Auckland?'

Latimer shrugged. 'Bit of a drive.'

'Coromandel?'

'Hey,' said Latimer holding up his hands. He smiled tentatively at Spurdle. 'Nice try.'

The older man didn't smile back. *Either this guy's not a bad actor,* thought Spurdle, *or he really believes he knows where the coke is.*

'Okay, let's say I believe you. How much?'

Latimer grinned twitchily and cleared his throat. 'Fifty grand.'

This time Spurdle did smile; it was an indulgent, almost fond, smile. 'You want to try again?'

'Jesus, there's a shitload of it …'

'Well, off you go and get it then. It's all yours. Of course, that means you have to take a few risks: you've got to find buyers, deal with all sorts of nasty bastards, shitting yourself the whole time they're going to stiff you or turn out to be undercover cops. And soon as word gets out that you're sitting on a big supply, there'll be a few hard shots around town making plans to take it off you.'

'Okay, okay. Tell you what, why don't you make me an offer?'

Spurdle stroked his nose and pretended to be doing some complicated mental arithmetic. 'Five grand.'

'Oh man, get real; that's a fucking insult.'

Seven minutes later they agreed on a price of $12,500 cash. Latimer waited at the Sierra while Spurdle went down to a bank in Ponsonby village and withdrew the money. On the way, Spurdle rang Leith Grills on his mobile phone and told him to put some gas in his car because he was going to be doing some distance.

*

Rayleen Crouch had her professional expression in place, nodded frequently and said 'Yes', 'Is that right?' and 'Uh-huh' at regular intervals. Despite the appearance of solicitous interest though, she was only half-listening. That was quite an achievement since most people would have been either fascinated or horrified – or perhaps even physically sick.

Crouch was in a counselling session with Jon, one of her clients. Jon was a 22-year-old heroin user with a fashionably wasted look and an Adam's apple which jutted as if he'd swallowed a large padlock; that was entirely possible since he made a habit of swallowing metal objects. It wasn't altogether clear to Crouch why Jon swallowed knives, forks, spoons and other even less digestible metallic items. A psychiatrist had told her that Jon had a death wish, which was possibly the least illuminating statement she'd ever heard. After she'd informed the psychiatrist that the same could be said about many, if not most, of the people one came across in welfare work, she pointed out it wasn't even all that logical an explanation seeing Jon had swallowed the contents of the average household's cutlery drawer several times over without managing to kill himself. Crouch tended to believe that, as was the case with most of the bizarre things her clients did, it was about half and half exhibitionism and a cry for help.

At this session, however, Jon was showing off by relating anecdotes about life on the street with a drug habit to support. The key to it appeared to be a willingness to engage in sado-masochistic homosexual acts for an appropriate fee; under normal circumstances, Crouch would've taken a professional interest since it was one of the few branches of deviant behaviour with which she was unfamiliar. On this particular afternoon though, not even Jon's lurid accounts of amyl nitrate, sodomy and the lash could hold her attention. She couldn't get her mind off what had happened at her house the night before: the intrusion of the very scary Leith Grills and his subsequent rout at the hands of the little American anti-drug policeman, who'd managed to be courtly and ever so slightly sinister all at the same time.

Like Grills, Funke had wanted to talk about her late ex-husband and his drugs but the combination of shock and Chivas Regal had left Crouch incapable of holding up her end of a chat about the weather. Fearing that Grills might return, she'd asked Funke to drive her to a friend's place in Epsom where she'd spent the night.

Jon eventually managed to gain Crouch's attention but by then it was too late. He'd just started telling her about well-known Aucklanders for whom the excretory functions formed an important part of sexual and para-sexual activity when she remembered she'd arranged to meet Funke at her place at 5 o'clock. She made her excuses and left.

Funke was already there, sitting behind the wheel of the dark-grey Fiat Tipo in which he'd ferried her to her friend's house the previous night. They went inside and she made coffee while he explained his assignment: the location and destruction of the shipment of cocaine which Dale Varty had talked about, in the process using up breath he could ill afford to waste.

'That's what that goon last night was after,' said Crouch. 'He's in it with Dale's partner back then.'

'Would you happen to know who that was?'

She shook her head. 'I'd only be guessing but Dale was thick as thieves with a shady character called Bryce Spurdle.'

Funke nodded. 'Well, ma'am, it doesn't surprise me one little bit that the underworld is showing an interest,' said Funke. 'There's a considerable quantity of cocaine involved here, so as you'll appreciate, it's real important that we get to it ahead of the likes of your gentleman caller.'

'I'm sorry, Mr Funke ...'

'Please, ma'am, call me Buddy.'

'Buddy, I'm sorry but I just don't have a clue where Dale would've hid it. You see, Dale and I had split for good by then. I wasn't in touch with him at all.'

Funke sighed. 'Ma'am, I'm sure sorry to bring this up. When Mr Varty was telling this Ricketts about the cocaine, he mentioned a daughter – she'd be your daughter too, I presume?'

'Electra?' she yelped. 'How the hell did she come into it?'

'According to the person who overheard the conversation, Mr Varty told Ricketts to go see her; our informant got the impression your daughter could point him in the direction of the drugs.'

Crouch waggled her head emphatically. 'That's ludicrous. I mean, for God's sake, Electra's only 18 now. She couldn't have been much more than six when she last set eyes on Dale.'

Funke shrugged. 'Well yeah, it does seems kind of strange but that's what our informant heard Mr Varty say. Now the thing that worries me is this Ricketts, who doesn't sound like a model citizen, is bound to try and get in touch with your little girl.'

Crouch considered this statement for a micro-second then bounded to the phone and rang her daughter.

'Electra? It's Rayleen.'

'Hi there.'

'Darling, are you all right?'

'Yeah, I'm okay. Why?'

'Have you seen or heard anything from a man called Ricketts?'

'Are you psychic or something? The guy bailed me up on my way to uni this morning ...'

'Honey, you stay exactly where you are; don't move, right? Promise me?'

'I'm not going anywhere but would you mind telling me what this is about ...'

'I'll be there in five minutes.'

Funke drove Crouch over to Datchet Terrace where Electra made them a pot of herbal tea and told them about Duane Ricketts, what he'd wanted, and how she'd sent him off with a flea in his ear. Then she told them all about the mansion in Manacle where the old man had given her an almost-full box of chocolates. All she left out was the promise her father had made on the way back to the camp-site.

When she'd finished, Funke looked from Electra to Rayleen and said, 'That's a fine young woman, right there. If more young people had her attitude to drugs, I'd be out of a job. Say, would you happen to know where can I pick me up a road map?'

Seventeen

Digby Purchase, the travel writer, had dined well: game soup to start, then seafood risotto and a half-bottle of Marlborough sauvignon blanc; that was followed by grilled tenderloin of beef, asparagus and gratin potatoes with a half-bottle of cabernet merlot from Martinborough. After a contemplative pause, he'd pressed on: a slice of orange syrup cake with mango sorbet and a glass of dessert wine, then cheese and port. And fingers crossed, the best was yet to come! As the grandfather clock in Manacle Grange's old billiards room chimed midnight, Purchase looked over the rim of his brandy balloon into Fleur Wolfgramm's tantalising green eyes and felt his thought processes disintegrate into a kaleidoscope of depraved images. In the course of his extensive travels and 20-year association with the tourism industry, Purchase had bedded a number of hotel managers – none of them, as it happened, of the female persuasion. It was an anomaly he fervently hoped to put right before taking his leave of Manacle Grange.

Digby Purchase was 46 years old, tall, pink, slender and bisexual. He had thick, very blond, almost flaxen hair which he wore longish, the Hitler-style fringe descending diagonally across his forehead to his left eyebrow. From time to time it would interfere with his vision, prompting an imperious toss of the head. With his expensive and somewhat fogeyish clothes, plummy drawl and air of languid boredom, Purchase did a passable imitation of a well-bred Englishman. The further afield he ventured, the more successful the impersonation tended to be; in London, where they occasionally come across the real thing, he was usually picked as an imposter in next to no time.

Over dinner Purchase reflected on the events which had brought him to Manacle Grange. There was no doubt about it, he decided; his guardian angel, who'd been conspicuous by his or her absence of late, was back in business. If that reception in Auckland hadn't been so naff, he wouldn't have drunk himself paralytic; if he hadn't done that, he wouldn't have slept through his alarm and missed the flight to Christchurch. And if he'd made it to Christchurch, he'd be facing the prospect, on the morrow, of a hike up a glacier or white-water rafting or whatever other hellish, not to mention life-endangering, activities the New Zealand tourism flacks could devise. Here, on the other hand, he faced the immediate prospect of a prolonged and sweaty grapple with the delicious Ms Wolfgramm. He made a mental note to ring and thank the public relations woman in the Tourism Board's Auckland office who'd suggested the alternative of a visit to Manacle Grange.

Indeed, Manacle Grange was most agreeable. And the wonderful thing about it was that, with an ounce of luck, he wouldn't have to write a single, sodding word about the place. The tiresome part of being a travel writer was that after the trip, when the fun and games were over, one had to write about it. But if the highlight of the trip was a stay in an exclusive hotel which had since gone out of business, you were off the hook. He'd lay odds the Grange would've closed its doors before his article was due – it was obviously a complete frost. When he'd arrived the day before, there were only two couples in residence: the Lees from Taiwan, who'd smiled a great deal, hadn't said a word, not even to each other, and, at breakfast, done stomach-turning things with their eggs; and the Australians, Barry and Marcie Pyves from the Gold Coast, who'd been rather more loquacious, cheerfully admitting to his bankruptcy and her plastic surgery within 15 minutes of being introduced. But the Lees and the Pyves had checked out that morning, leaving Purchase as the sole guest. And now the kitchen was closed, the staff had gone home, and Digby Purchase had Manacle Grange and its manager all to himself.

Purchase was the tourism writer for *Travel Weekly*, a London-based newspaper for the British travel industry. He'd been the editor for several years but had been demoted after spectacularly disgracing himself three times in quick succession. The first blot on his copybook came to light when he submitted an expenses claim relating to a trip to New York. Normally these were authorised without quibble, *Travel Weekly*'s publisher being too much of a gent to actually check how much of the company's money Purchase had spent, let alone assess the validity of the various items of expenditure. On this occasion however, the publisher's eye was caught by the column entry showing that during a three-day stay in the Big Apple, Purchase had run up a £365 laundry bill. Even allowing for the stratospheric charges of big-city five-star hotels, this seemed excessive.

Curious and uncomfortably aware that, as the authoriser, he was a major link in the chain of responsibility for fiddled expenses, the publisher called the accounts department and obtained Purchase's expense claims for his recent trips; all featured huge amounts for laundry. When an explanation was sought, Purchase confessed that, to avoid doing or paying for his laundry, he took a suitcase of accumulated dirty washing whenever he went on a trip and had it done in hotels at the paper's expense. While the publisher took a dim view of this, he would've been positively outraged if Purchase had told him the truth: that the clothes in the extra suitcase belonged to some of Purchase's bachelor acquaintances who paid him the going High Street rate to have their suits dry-cleaned and shirts laundered to five-star hotel standards.

Purchase was given a stiff warning. Nevertheless, two months later the publisher received an irate phone call from the marketing director of an upmarket holiday company who was aggressively insistent on knowing why the *Travel Weekly* representative on a just-concluded, no-expense-spared press trip to the Caribbean had been a semi-literate motor mechanic, when both the invitation and accepted practice specified a journalist. The mechanic concerned had posed as a freelancer commissioned by *Travel Weekly*, but his habit of throwing away press kits in the presence of the PR functionaries who'd prepared them, rather than in the privacy of his hotel room, aroused suspicion. The publisher's investigation established that Purchase had sent the mechanic on the junket as a contra payment for keeping his temperamental Triumph Stag roadworthy.

The incident in the sex club was the final straw. While attending a big annual travel exhibition in Berlin, Purchase had hosted the boss of one of Britain's largest tour operators, a major advertiser in *Travel Weekly*, to a night on the town. After dinner and visits to a few of the little bars along the Kurfurstendamm, Purchase took his guest to Mitzi's, a sex club in which he'd spent some horizon-expanding times during previous exhibitions. The tour operator had never seen a live sex show so they sat at the very front to enable him to savour the raw lubricity of the performances. Halfway through a protracted and disappointingly orthodox copulation routine, the late nights, long hours and booze caught up with the tour operator, who fell asleep in his chair. While his guest took time out, Purchase slipped away to a back room to renew acquaintance with a sparky little Uruguayan.

The humdrum fornicators were followed by the star of the show: Madame Herta, the Prussian Mistress of Pain. Herta wore stiletto heels and a skin-tight black leather bodysuit complete with zippered balaclava, and stalked onto the little stage cracking a whip and promising that all the naughty boys in the audience were about to get the spanking they so richly deserved. She was laying into her first victim in fine style when his ecstatic squeals were drowned out by an explosive series of snores from the tour operator, slumped in his seat at the foot of the stage.

Herta, who was actually Spanish rather than Prussian and possessed a haughty Castilian temperament, reacted angrily to what she interpreted as a provocative critique of her work. She strode to the front of the stage, wound up, and lashed the slumbering tour operator across the chest. The blow was sufficiently violent to do three things: it woke the tour operator up, it caused his left nipple to bleed profusely, and it shattered the expensive pair of designer spectacles in his shirt pocket. A scene ensued which ended with the tour operator being hustled out of the club by two bouncers, beefy neo-Nazis, who dragged him into an alley and gave him a methodical kicking as a small token of their admiration for Madame Herta and their resentment over Britain's role in the destruction of the Third Reich.

However, as the chimes of midnight died away, the humiliating demotion which followed the debacle at Mitzi's couldn't have been further from Purchase's mind. While, sexually speaking, a man of catholic tastes, Purchase did have a slight weakness for the youths of North Africa; at that moment however, the juiciest catamite in the casbah could have materialised in the old billiards room without attracting a second glance. There was something about Fleur Wolfgramm, about the faintly wicked gleam in her green eyes and the sensual mouth, which proclaimed that here was a woman who'd been around and enjoyed every stop on the circuit. If this one isn't a sack-artist extraordinaire, thought Purchase, I'm Yoko Ono.

Noticing she'd finished her Sambuca, Purchase threw back the rest of his cognac and reached for her glass.

'Allow me.'

She looked at her watch. 'Just a smidgin.'

Purchase hustled across to the small bar in the corner. The Sambuca bottle was empty.

'Out of this stuff, I'm afraid,' he said, holding up the bottle. 'What about a cognac?'

'Oh God, no thanks,' said Wolfgramm. 'It's far too late to be mixing drinks. I think I might call it a night.'

Purchase was seized with something close to panic. 'There must be more of it somewhere?' he gabbled.

'Probably in the library bar,' she said uninterestedly, 'but I can't be fagged getting it.'

'Don't worry, I'll get it,' said Purchase hastily. 'You stay right where you are. It's the second on the right down the corridor, yes?'

Wolfgramm shrugged. 'Yep, that's it.'

Galvanised by the twin imperatives of delaying Fleur Wolfgramm's retirement and getting more alcohol into her, Purchase broke into a run down the corridor. He yanked open the library door and was groping for the light switch when he heard a footfall in the corridor behind him. Thinking she'd come to cancel the Sambuca, he turned to plead. Largely because Purchase's mouth was open when the shotgun butt slammed into the side of his face, he sustained a multiple fracture of the jaw as well as being knocked senseless for several hours.

When Wolfgramm heard the bumps in the corridor, her first thought was that a guest had woken up with the dry horrors and gone on the prowl for a fizzy drink. Then she remembered that the only guest they had was the English ponce whom, if she wasn't very much mistaken, she'd shortly have to tell to fuck off, thereby blowing her strategy of getting the Grange some positive overseas press coverage. She went out into the corridor and found herself looking down the barrel of a pump-action shotgun and into Leith Grills' eyes. As scary sights went, there wasn't much to choose between them.

*

Grills waggled the shotgun which, in defiance of Spurdle's veto, he'd picked up from his mate in Pukekohe on the way down.

'Keep your trap shut,' he said in a low voice.

Wolfgramm opened her mouth but swiftly closed it again, deciding she didn't have anything to say which was important enough to justify ignoring a direct instruction from a shotgun-wielding throwback. With rising dread she saw the throwback's gaze was fixed on her bosom. For once though, Leith Grills had things other than breasts on his mind.

'You the manager of this joint?' he demanded.

Wolfgramm nodded, feeling a surge of relief as she realised that he'd been staring at her lapel badge.

'Show us the master bedroom.'

Without thinking, she stammered, 'I'm afraid it's occupied at the moment.'

'Too fucking bad for them,' growled Grills. 'Who's in there?'

She gestured hesitantly at the prostrate travel writer. 'Well, as a matter of fact, it's Mr Purchase's room.'

Grills glanced back at Purchase. 'Hoy blondie,' he said, 'I'm just going to have a geek in your room, all right?' Then to Wolfgramm: 'He says "Be my guest."'

Wolfgramm led Grills up the stairs to the master bedroom. He put down the sports bag which he'd had slung over his left shoulder and made a careful examination. It was a large, square, high-ceilinged room dominated by the massive four-poster bed. The head of the bed was against the left-hand wall, as you entered. On each side of the bed were small tables with lamps and beyond it, in the corner, was an old leather armchair. There were French doors in the wall opposite which opened out onto a balcony, and the bathroom was through a doorway in the far corner. A walk-in wardrobe faced the bed and alongside it was a chest of drawers with a mirror. Against the near wall were an antique writing desk with a high-backed chair and a wooden bench holding a battered leather suitcase.

Grills made Wolfgramm sit on the high-backed chair. He rummaged in the suitcase and pulled out three of Purchase's silk shirts which he tore apart, using the strips to tie her to the chair with her hands bound together behind the back of it. He balled up a shirt sleeve and shoved it in her mouth as a gag; she retched when the sour, mingled tang of deodorant and body odour hit the back of her throat. Then he searched the bedroom. It took him 15 minutes to find what he was looking for.

About the time that Grills, on his hands and knees in the walk-in wardrobe, spotted the scratches on the skirting board and the indentations around the carpet tacks indicating that the carpet had been lifted and replaced, Buddy Funke gently pushed open the front door of Manacle Grange and slipped into the impressive entrance hall. He cocked his head and listened for half a minute. The ground-floor lights were on but the great house was quiet. Moving soundlessly in his rubber-soled walking shoes, Funke went through the hall towards the stairs with the gleaming dark-wood banisters and ornate fretwork. As he reached the stairs, he glanced down the corridor running through to the rear of the house and saw splayed feet protruding from a doorway. He investigated. The feet were attached to an unconscious man who'd either wandered into the path of a longhorn stampede or been taken out by someone who employed direct and brutal methods. Believing the latter scenario to be the more likely, Funke drew the .38 revolver from his belt.

Halfway up the stairs Funke heard the murmur of a male voice. On the landing he looked left and right; the first door on the right was open and the lights in the room were on. An exclamation of triumph – 'you fucking beauty' – floated through the doorway. Funke flattened himself against the wall and inched down the corridor.

Holding the revolver out in front of him in both hands, Funke slid round the doorway moving fast and low. His eyes and the .38 moved as one, sweeping the room in an arc from left to right. A large backside poked rudely out of the wardrobe at the far end of the room; its owner, presumably the speaker, remained absorbed in whatever he was doing in there. A woman was tied to a chair and gagged. Funke held a finger to his lips as she rolled her eyes and jerked her head towards the bottom.

Funke glided across the room. The wardrobe was big enough to stable a giraffe but all it contained was a blue blazer on a hanger, a spare pillow and blanket on a shelf above the rail, and the man he'd tangled with at Mrs Crouch's place the night before.

Grills had pulled up the carpet in the corner, peeled it back and lifted a few short lengths of floorboard. There were some tools and half a dozen plastic bags of white powder on the floor beside him. In front of him, propped up in the corner, was a shotgun. As Grills lifted out two more bags, Funke placed the revolver's muzzle against the nape of the kneeling man's neck. Grills froze.

'Make a move for that shotgun hoss, you're gone,' said Funke. He stepped back two paces. 'Now you just back on out of there on your hands and knees.'

Grills did as he was told. When he was all the way out of the wardrobe, Funke told him to get up and put his hands behind his head.

'We can't go on meeting like this,' said Funke smiling pleasantly; Grills sent back a murderous glare. 'What was that you were rooting around after in the closet there, boy? Found yourself a big mess of nose candy?'

'Go fuck yourself,' said Grills through clenched teeth.

'Later maybe,' said Funke affably. 'If I don't get a better offer. Going by the shape of that pilgrim downstairs and the way you've trussed up the little lady, you're some piece of work. Seems to me I better get the cuffs on you, pronto. We're going down the stairs and out to my car, okay? Keep in mind, you as much as shuffle and I'll give you the gun.'

Grills led the way down the stairs. In the hall, Funke plucked a plump cushion off an armchair and held it behind his back.

Funke's Fiat was parked a little way down the drive behind a white Holden Berlina.

As they passed the Holden, Funke asked, 'Say, this your heap?'

Grills said it was.

'I got a better idea. Open the trunk.'

Grills gawked at him, nonplussed. 'What?'

'Open the goddam trunk,' snapped Funke, pointing the pistol at the rear of the car.

Grills fished in his pocket for the car keys and opened the boot.

'Get in,' ordered Funke.

Grills hesitated. Funke extended his right arm and pointed the .38 at Grills' head. 'Oh, I get it – you'd prefer to die. Well, that's okay.'

Grills clambered awkwardly into the boot and stretched out on his side. Funke looked down at him, smiling thinly.

'Ain't you a good boy? Now get on your back and put your hands behind you, underneath your body.'

When Grills had got himself into a satisfactorily defenceless position, Funke planted the cushion on his chest, rammed the gun barrel into it and shot him twice through the heart. The manoeuvre was executed with the deft economy of a poultry farmer wringing a chicken's neck. Funke closed the boot, stuck the pistol in his belt, slipped the car keys into his pocket and walked back up the drive, softly whistling 'Rose of Alabama'. He stopped whistling when a tall figure in a long raincoat and with a stocking mask over his face stepped out of the shadow of the house and pointed a sawn-off rifle at him.

'Very neat,' said the masked man. 'I take it you've done this sort of thing before?'

*

Funke adopted a quizzical expression. 'If it's a room you'd be wanting,' he said earnestly, 'I don't think you'll need the rifle. Near as I can tell, the place is about empty.'

'Thanks all the same but I'd say I'm here for the same reason as you.'

'Who're you?'

'As they say in the movies, I'll ask the questions,' said the newcomer who sounded as if he was enjoying himself. 'Now slowly take out the gun, drop it on the ground and get your hands up. Otherwise, as you were just saying to the poor bastard in the boot, a bullet between the eyes can be easily arranged.'

Funke discarded the revolver. The man in the stocking mask motioned him back and without taking his eyes or the rifle off Funke, stooped and picked up the .38, which he slipped into his coat pocket.

'Okay, pardner,' he said. 'I presume you've found the crank; let's go and get it.'

Hands in the air, Funke led the way into the Grange and up to the master bedroom. Fleur Wolfgramm stopped struggling to get free and looked in bewilderment at the man in the stocking mask, wondering why Manacle Grange had all of a sudden become a mecca for men with guns.

The new arrival looked at her. 'Well now, I was expecting to interrupt something but this is downright kinky.'

'It's over there,' said Funke. 'In the closet.'

The other man seemed to smile under his stocking mask. 'Then why don't you hop in there and get it?'

Funke went into the wardrobe and collected the bags of cocaine which Grills had extracted from their hiding-place. He brought them out and dumped them on the foot of the bed.

'There's more,' he said.

'I should hope so,' said the tall man. As Funke went back to the wardrobe, the newcomer strolled over to Wolfgramm. Holding the sawn-off rifle in his right hand braced against his hip, he used his left hand to remove the gag then perched on the end of the bed.

'I can see you're tied up right now,' he said, 'but when do you …'

Funke backed out of the wardrobe and spun around, bringing up Grills' shotgun. The man in the stocking mask's buttocks were scarcely off the bed when Funke fired from the hip. The blast took the masked man in the chest and flung him back onto the big bed where he sprawled. With his lacerated torso and outspread arms and legs, he looked like a dissected frog.

Funke walked over to the bed and retrieved his revolver from the pocket of the raincoat. He looked down at the dead man and said, 'Sleep tight, little buddy.'

He went out into the corridor and listened for a minute then opened the French doors and did the same on the balcony. During the 20 minutes or so she'd been tied to the high-backed chair, Wolfgramm had formed the view that firstly, she was in pretty dodgy company and secondly, her chances of getting through the night in one piece were somewhere between poor and ratshit. After witnessing the man in the stocking mask go out backwards, she decided that she'd over-estimated both the company and her chances.

Funke came back into the bedroom closing the French doors behind him. 'You the manager, right?' he asked.

She nodded.

'Tell me sugar, how many more folks am I going to have to shoot?'

She shook her head. 'None.'

'Well that's a relief.'

Funke pulled up the dead man's mask. He was about 40 with a long nose and good teeth. Although the face was screwed up in a death snarl, Funke was sure he hadn't seen him before. He wiped off the shotgun and placed it and the sawn-off .22 beside the dead man then pulled the bedspread over the body from both sides of the bed, wrapping it.

He got the rest of the cocaine out of the wardrobe, replaced the floorboards and rolled the carpet back. He put the 20 packets of cocaine into Grills' sports bag and slung it over his shoulder. Then he untied Wolfgramm.

She stood up rubbing her wrists. 'This is a drugs thing, right?' she said.

Funke looked amused. 'Yeah, kind of. In case you're wondering, I'm the good guy.'

She said, 'Oh?'

Funke chuckled. 'More to the point, I'm the one still standing. Now help me tote this boy downstairs.'

With Funke at one end and Wolfgramm at the other, they carried the dead man outside and deposited him in the boot of the Berlina. Leith Grills had often dreamed of coming face-to-face with the man who'd killed his brother but the fact that they were both dead rather robbed the encounter of drama.

Funke forced the boot shut on the two corpses and flipped out his ID.

'I'm a sort of cop working for the US Government. I realise this-all ain't exactly by the textbook but shit, you know, that's the way things work out sometimes; nothing for it but to go with the flow. Right now I need you to help me out.'

'How?'

'Drive this car back to Auckland – can you do that?'

'With those guys in the boot?'

'Honey, those guys are deader than Davy Crockett. They ain't going to give you any problems.'

She shrugged. 'Okay.'

'All right. You get yourself in the car.'

Wolfgramm got into the driver's seat. Funke went over to his car then came back to the Berlina.

'Here's the keys. Give me your hand.'

She offered her right hand. Funke produced a pair of handcuffs; he snapped one bracelet over her wrist and attached the other to the steering wheel.

'Go nice and steady now. I'll be right on your ass. If you do anything fancy, make a run for it, step on the gas or take a wrong turn, I'm going to start shooting. You understand me? We'll drive to Auckland and head to the airport, to the car park at the international terminal.'

At 4.05 a.m. Fleur Wolfgramm steered Grills' Holden Berlina into the car park at the international terminal at Auckland airport. She drove to the middle of the near-empty parking area and stopped. Funke pulled up beside her and got out of his car. He took the keys out of the ignition, uncuffed her, used a handkerchief to wipe the steering wheel, the driver's doorhandle and around the boot lever and then locked the car. He told her to get into the Fiat and got in on the driver's side.

'You're going to have to stick with me for a day or two, sugar.'

'Do I have a choice?'

'Sure you do. You can stick with me or join those fellas in the boot. Be a squeeze but I reckon there's room for one more.'

'You talked me into it.'

Funke started the car. As they drove away from the airport towards Mangere, he asked, 'You ever hear mention of a party called Bryce Spurdle?'

'I have as a matter of fact. He's rich.'

'I'm mighty pleased to hear that. You wouldn't happen to have any idea where he hangs his hat?'

'You want to get in touch with Spurdle?'

Funke nodded.

'That shouldn't be too hard. He's married to a girl I used to work with.'

Funke twisted around and grinned at her. 'There you go. I'm already glad I didn't pop you.'

Eighteen

Whenever anyone asked her where she was from, C.C. Hellicar's eyes would light up and she'd reply, 'As a matter of fact, I was born in Between.'

It was quite true: C.C. – the initials stood for Candice Clara but she'd been C.C. as long as she could remember – was born in the one-store town of Between in Walton County, Georgia. She was a home birth, arriving two weeks early and at such short notice that her mother had no chance of getting to the hospital; she'd just leaned out the window and hollered for her neighbour. When C.C. was seven, her mother died and she and her father moved a few miles up the interstate to the county seat of Monroe, an hour's drive north-east of Atlanta, where her aunts lived.

Being born in Between was the first of several unusual things about C.C. Hellicar. Another was that she'd lost her virginity and killed someone on the very same night. One assumes that doesn't happen very often; just how rarely is a matter for speculation, given the lack of statistical data; C.C. herself, for instance, had never revealed just how much she'd managed to pack into that eventful night. The fact that she shot a man dead at approximately midnight on a sultry August night in 1983 was a matter of public record but being a well-brought-up young lady of good Southern stock, she was extremely discreet about such matters as ceasing to be a virgin. The only other person who knew the full story was her third cousin Wesley Teuton, her partner in the necessarily brisk and furtive act of intercourse which took place in the back seat of his father's Thunderbird in the parking lot of the Dairy Queen hamburger joint and ice-cream parlour. Earlier that evening they'd been to the movie *Alien* and thinking about it later, C.C. wondered if it was the sight of Sigourney Weaver in her panties which had inspired Wesley to do what she'd been waiting for him to do for the several weeks since her sixteenth birthday.

When Wesley heard next morning what his date had done for an encore, it merely served to reinforce his conviction that he'd be the worst sort of fool to flaunt his carnal knowledge of C.C. Hellicar. He'd initially come to this conclusion as he was driving C.C. home, although, at that stage, his concern was focused more on her father. Willard Hellicar was celebrated throughout Walton County as a hard-ass, a dead shot with anything from a sleeve piece to a semi-automatic carbine, and a fiercely proud and protective parent to his only child. The closer he got to the Hellicar place, the more nervous Wesley became at the thought of having to look his date's father in the eye. Willard Hellicar had icy blue eyes – which, disconcertingly, his daughter had inherited – and Wesley feared that when those cold orbs began boring into him, he'd go to jelly and let on what had transpired in the car park.

So when C.C. asked him did he want to come in for a cold drink and a piece of pie, Wesley declined saying he'd be in big trouble if he didn't get his daddy's car back by midnight. In fact, time was slipping away so if it was okay with her, rather than walk her to the door, he'd get right on his way. C.C., who'd baked the pie that afternoon especially, shrugged, gave him a chilly look, got out of the car and walked up the path towards the house.

The Hellicar place was set back from the road behind a couple of old willows. When C.C. was about ten metres from the front porch, the door opened and a man came out. When he stepped into the pool of light from the lamp above the front door, C.C. observed that he was large and black. While her father was not particularly racially prejudiced – at least not by the standards of many Georgians of his generation – neither did he make a habit of inviting blacks into his home to sip his Wild Turkey. The fact that the black man had a tyre iron in one hand and a canvas sack in the other added to her suspicion that it hadn't been a social call.

C.C. and the robber, as she'd characterised him, looked at one another for a few seconds without speaking. Then she yelled 'Daddy' at the top of her lungs.

'Your Daddy ain't going to help you,' said the robber, grinning broadly.

He started down the porch steps, lazily swinging the tyre iron. C.C. opened her purse and took out the nickel-plated .22 automatic her father had given her on her thirteenth birthday and which she practised with once a fortnight at the firing range.

The robber's grin got even wider 'Well lookee here,' he said. 'Missy's got herself a popgun. You ever used …'

C.C. aimed at his gleaming white teeth and, as she did 19 times out of 20 at the firing range, hit the target. The bullet took a deviation off the intruder's upper jaw and proceeded upwards to the brain. He was dead before he hit the ground. C.C. averted her eyes as she ran past him. She raced up the steps and into the house where she found her father lying face down at the foot of the stairs. He was in his dressing-gown; his hair was matted with blood which leaked from a weal on the back of his head but he was still breathing. She was about to call for an ambulance when he groaned and rolled over onto his back.

Willard Hellicar sat at the kitchen table holding a tea towel full of ice-cubes to his wound and taking hefty gulps from a tall glass containing four fingers of bourbon and the left-over ice. He was telling his daughter how he'd been upstairs waiting for her to get home and how he'd come over a little peckish and remembered the blueberry pie she'd made, when she interrupted to say there was a man in the front yard with a hole in his head.

Willard put down his glass. 'Darling, did I hear you right?'

'I shot him, Daddy – the robber. He came out the front door just as I was walking up the path. He was coming at me with the tyre iron so I shot him.'

'Jesus Christ almighty. Is the son of a bitch dead?'

'I didn't look real close but I'd say so.'

They went outside. C.C. stayed on the porch while Willard went over to where the man lay. He put his hands on his knees and peered at him. 'That's a dead nigger,' he said finally. 'No two ways about it.'

'Please Daddy,' said C.C. reproachfully, 'don't call him that.'

Willard Hellicar studied his daughter with frank amazement. 'C.C., you just blew this no-good's head off and now you're chastising me for calling him a nigger?'

'There's no call to use that word,' she said stubbornly. 'Besides, race didn't enter into it – I would've shot him whatever colour he was.'

Willard smiled wryly. 'That's my girl. Now tell me, where were you at when you pulled down on him?'

C.C. came down from the porch and showed him. 'I was right here. I called out for you and he said you weren't going to help me. Then he started down the steps sort of swinging the tyre iron. He was in the course of asking me if I'd ever used the gun. I guess he found out, huh?'

'You're damn right he did. You hit him dead centre from seven paces away in the dark.' Willard shook his head. 'Honey, I knew you was good with a gun but that's something else.'

C.C. frowned. 'Well, I just didn't see any way round it, Daddy. He indicated that he'd done you harm so I figured he wasn't going to want a witness.'

Willard started shaking his head again. 'Damned if you ain't got ice-water in your veins, C.C. Maybe you should forget about going to college; go off to Africa, be a big-game hunter instead. Now how about you run inside and fetch an old towel or something to put over this boy's face because we're going have to drag him into the house. I remember the sheriff telling me one time, anyone comes into your home without an invite, you can shoot the son of a bitch and no jury in Walton County's going to worry about the details – it's just straight ahead self-defence, no matter what. Course, the fact that he's an Afro-American and we ain't won't hurt none neither.'

There were other unusual things about C.C. Hellicar: for instance, that she'd spent 18 months at the US Army Special Forces training camp at Fort Bragg in North Carolina; that she worked for a company based in Scottsdale, Arizona, which provided security advice, training and protection to government agencies, corporations and private citizens in many parts of the world; that the company she worked for was secretly owned and funded by the CIA – a 'proprietary' in CIA jargon; and that she was what Everton Sloan III had referred to as a 'cleaner'.

*

Just before 7.15 a.m. the small crowd pressed forward as the first passengers came out through the Arrivals gate, pushing their trolleys and looking around expectantly for familiar faces. Tito Ihaka made his way to the front of the crowd and checked a luggage tag to make sure they were off the United flight from Los Angeles. He heaved a sigh of resignation and held up the sign which had been behind his back saying MS HELLICAR in block letters.

A few minutes later the crowd had thinned out and Ihaka was leaning against a wall holding the sign to his chest, staring at the ceiling and whistling tunelessly to himself when a female voice said: 'Maybe you should go easy on the steroids, Ms Hellicar.'

The speaker had short, dark-blonde hair, high cheekbones and the palest blue eyes Ihaka had ever seen. She was standing a few metres away in a pose of studied nonchalance, one long leg crossed in front of the other and hands thrust into the pockets of her loose-fitting pleated trousers. The trousers were the lower half of a light-grey Donegal tweed suit under which she wore an embroidered waistcoat and a white shirt. With her cool gaze, athletic, square-shouldered build and lean, sculpted face, she looked conditioned and purposeful. The accent though was pure Southern belle.

She extended a hand. 'I'm C.C. Hellicar.'

They shook hands. She had a firmer grip than plenty of men Ihaka had shaken hands with, the Minister of Police for one.

'Detective Sergeant Tito Ihaka.'

She raised an eyebrow. 'Tito? As in the late, great Communist?'

'That's the one. My old man was a bit of a red.'

'You say "was" – did he lose the faith?'

'No, "was" as in he's not around anymore. He was a believer till his dying day.'

'I'm sorry. My momma was a McGovern Democrat; in Walton County, that's just one step up from being a Communist. She passed away too.'

Ihaka nodded. 'Yeah, well that's where worrying about the future of mankind gets you.' He pointed at the metal suitcase on the floor beside her. 'Is that the lot?'

'Uh-huh but you don't have to carry it for me.'

He shrugged. 'We're old-fashioned down here.' He picked it up; it weighed a ton but she hadn't bothered with a trolley. *What the hell am I doing*, he wondered, *volunteering to carry Wonder Woman's bag?*

'You got a matching pair of elephant guns in here?'

She smiled. 'I overpacked. I wasn't sure what to expect in the way of weather. Actually, I do have some equipment in the diplomatic bag.'

'Right, that's being taken care of. It'll be delivered to the police station in town.'

Ihaka led her out to the unmarked car which was parked in front of the terminal's main entrance, in a restricted zone. He put the suitcase in the boot and they got into the car. As they drove away from the airport down George Bolt Drive she asked, 'Are you a Maori?'

'Sure am.'

'I'm afraid all I know about Maoris is what was in the *Welcome to New Zealand* movie they showed on the airplane.'

'I bet it was full of women swinging little balls and blokes in grass skirts poking their tongues out?'

'There was some of that.'

'We're reasonably civilised. Personally, I haven't eaten anyone since my twenty-first birthday party.'

Feeling that the conversation had taken an unpredictable and possibly difficult turn, Hellicar smiled politely and looked out the window.

'Sorry, it's not the scenic route,' said Ihaka.

She shrugged. 'It never is. They don't put airports in the nice part of town.'

'I guess you see a few airports in your line of work?'

'A slew of them.'

'You're from the South, right?'

'Yes sir. As a matter of fact, I was born in Between.'

Ihaka glanced at her, puzzled.

'The town of Between. It's in Walton County in the state of Georgia.'

'A place called Between? You're kidding?'

'Absolutely not. We got another town's called Social Circle.'

'No shit? Georgia – that's redneck country, isn't it?'

She looked amused. 'The South's come a ways since the Civil War, Sergeant. You gave up eating folks when you turned 21; me, I freed my last slave.'

Ihaka chuckled. 'Those were the days, eh? So this is how you spend your life – flying round the world weeding out the bad apples, as the ambassador called them?'

Ihaka had his eyes on the road so he missed Hellicar's thoughtful glance.

'What I do is classified information – I'm not at liberty to discuss my work and all that jazz. Besides, we should be talking about Harold Funke. You got a fix on him?'

'Not yet but we've got some leads,' he said with more confidence than he felt. 'He sounds like a dangerous bastard.'

She went back to looking out the window. 'That he is. You wondering if I'm up to it, huh?'

'No, just curious – we don't get much of this James Bond stuff. I mean, we've got a unit called the Armed Offenders Squad – a bit like your SWAT teams, cops who get special weapons training and dress up in black uniforms and all that shit; makes them think they're fucking Rambo. No offence but on the face of it, you sort of wonder what you can do that a bunch of them couldn't.'

'No offence taken,' she said mildly. 'There's guys in SWAT teams can put a round up a bug's ass halfway across town as long they've got all day to get themselves set; the same guys couldn't hit the Dixie Flyer from five yards away if they have to do it bang' – she snapped her fingers – 'like that.

Especially not when they know that if they don't hit the target first time, they're going to die. How many of these guys who think they're Rambo would you say have been in that situation?'

'Bugger all. But you have?'

'Uh-huh,' she said. 'And as you can see, I'm still here.'

Neither of them spoke for a few minutes. When they stopped at the lights at Hillsborough, Ihaka turned to her and said, 'So what does the C.C. stand for?'

'Candice Clara.'

'Anyone ever call you Candy?'

'Not at home. Maybe every once in a while at school – some of the boys.'

'Let me guess: they used to say, "Hey Candy, you look good enough to eat", right?'

Hellicar batted her eyelids at him. 'That's truly amazing,' she said in an awe-struck tone. 'How in the world did you know that?'

Ihaka pretended he hadn't picked up the sarcasm. 'It's a gift. My grandmother was a full-blooded Maori; she could tell things about people just by looking at them. I sort of inherited it.'

'That's fascinating.' She looked away. 'What else can you tell about me?'

He studied her profile for a few seconds then nodded sagely. 'The boys who said you looked good enough to eat? I bet none of them ever did.'

Hellicar turned her head slowly and fixed her wintry blue eyes on Ihaka. The effect was slightly unnerving and left him with the strong feeling that, despite his determination not to, he'd seriously underestimated her.

'I hate to be the one to tell you this, Sergeant,' she said in her honeyed drawl, 'but you ain't in your grandmama's league.'

*

By 11 a.m. that Friday the temperature in Wellington had crawled up to eight degrees Celsius where it rested on its laurels. Depending on whether you were a local or a visitor, there was a stiff breeze or a gale whipping off Cook Strait. Lumps of black cloud bumped along the ridges above the city and drenching rain slanted in on the wind. In the office buildings and in the toytown houses clinging to the hillsides and dotted though the gorges, people shivered and moved their chairs closer to the nearest source of heat.

Perhaps the only person in the capital who wasn't complaining about the weather was the diplomat Jason Maltby. Oblivious to the elements, he plodded up the 112 steps from the street to his brother's Kelburn house, reflecting that if he had to suffer stress, far better to do so in Wellington than Bangkok; if he'd had a morning like this in Bangkok, he'd need to be wrung out like a sodden sponge. Inside, Maltby changed his shirt then sat at the kitchen table with a cup of instant coffee and considered his next move. Eventually he reached a decision. He rang directory service and obtained the phone number for D. Ricketts of Mt Roskill, Auckland.

It was a blustery, overcast day in Auckland with a good drying wind blowing from the west. Duane Ricketts was hanging out his washing when he heard the phone. He went inside and answered it.

'It's Jason Maltby here, from the embassy in Bangkok. Remember me?'

'Jason, I hope you're not ringing to tell me they've set a date for my trial? That'd be a waste of taxpayers' money.'

'No, nothing to do with that. I'm in Wellington actually, back on a couple of weeks' leave. The reason I'm ringing is that I was called into a meeting at the department this morning, about this DEA man from Bangkok, Harold Funke. Does the name mean anything to you?'

'Not a thing. What's the DEA?'

'The American Drug Enforcement Administration. It's a gigantic anti-drug police stroke intelligence organisation; they've got offices all round the world.'

'You don't mean to tell me they haven't got more to worry about than me and my two lousy heroin cigarettes?'

Despite his anxiety, Maltby couldn't help smiling: the same old Ricketts. 'I think it'd be safe to say that the DEA has got one or two more pressing matters on its books. No, it appears this Funke character's swapped sides and come to New Zealand chasing after a consignment of cocaine that was once the property of our late mutual acquaintance, Dale Varty.'

Eh?

'Hello, Duane? Are you still there?'

'Yeah, I'm still here. I'm just having a bit of trouble working out what it's got to do with me.'

'Not a lot really. The truth is, I'm ringing to ask a favour ...'

Maltby paused to give Ricketts an opportunity to make encouraging noises. No noises, encouraging or otherwise, were forthcoming.

Eventually Maltby ended the silence. 'Yes, well, I suppose you've got no particular reason to do me a favour,' he said awkwardly

'Rule number one, Jason – don't promise to do someone a favour until you know what it is.'

'That's sensible, I suppose. Well, during your police force days or since, have you come across a detective sergeant called Ihaka?'

What the fuck is this? wondered Ricketts. '*This is Your Life*'? 'Yeah, I know the fat prick. What about him?'

'Ihaka's in charge of finding Funke, who by all accounts is a nasty piece of work. Up in Bangkok, they think he murdered the ladyboy, Brandi – the one Varty … got involved with.'

Yesterday Ihaka was crapping on about a trained killer, thought Ricketts; *this must be the guy. But what's the connection to me?*

'Funke rang me in Bangkok, just after you'd left,' continued Maltby. 'He fed me a cock-and bull-story which, I'm afraid to say, I swallowed. He claimed he had to do a report on Varty and needed various details including next-of-kin; I gave him the name and address of Varty's ex-wife. The favour is this: could you alert Ihaka that Funke's got this woman's name and address? I wouldn't want to have it on my conscience if anything happened to her. If you're wondering why I don't do it myself, the truth is I'm in a certain amount of hot water as it is; if word got around that I'd dished out this information over the phone to the representative of a foreign agency, and a corrupt one at that … well, put it this way, I'd be for the high jump.'

'Shit, that's no big deal,' said Ricketts, thinking, *Christ, old Maltby's sounding as flat as I feel.* 'What's her name?'

'Rayleen Crouch. She lives in Grey Lynn.'

'No sweat. I'll pass it on.'

'Thank you, Duane, I appreciate it. It's quite embarrassing really. I should've smelt a rat: I mean, Funke even wanted to know about Varty's daughter, God only knows why. Luckily I had enough sense not to …'

'Jason, hang on a moment, would you? Just let me think.' *The ladyboy? Is that it? He was on the stairs; maybe he overheard what Varty told me.* 'You said they think this guy Funke killed the ladyboy?'

'That's right. And it's not the Thai police saying it either; that came from the US embassy.'

Ricketts thought, *Holy shit*, said goodbye and hung up.

Nineteen

The telephone conversation went pretty much as Duane Ricketts had anticipated.

'Ricketts,' hissed Tito Ihaka, as if administering a terrible curse. 'What the fuck do you want?'

'It wasn't very nice of you not to tell me about Funke.'

'What's your problem, Ricketts?' demanded Ihaka caustically. 'Have you lost it completely or what? I thought I made myself clear: I wouldn't piss on your face if your eyebrows were on fire.'

'You're taking this rather personally, aren't you?'

'This is different: when you decided to go after the dope, you crossed the line. You're one of them now.'

'Who's them?'

'Them's everyone who's not us.'

'You're full of shit, Ihaka. Since when haven't I been on the outer?'

'Some people thought you were hard done by; some people still had a bit of time for you. Not any more they don't.'

'Some people being you?'

'Especially me.'

Pompous turd, thought Ricketts. 'In that case you obviously won't be interested in any assistance from me?'

'Hang on,' said Ihaka. 'Who told you about Funke?'

'That's the pleasantries over with, is it? Tell me something first: have you got a handle on this prick yet?'

'Funke? We're following some leads.'

'In other words, you haven't got a fucking clue.'

Ihaka grunted affirmatively. 'Let me put it this way: Mr Funke's movements since Tuesday night – when he purchased a .38 Smith & Wesson revolver and enough ammo to wipe out the Eden Park cheerleaders – and his current whereabouts remain shrouded in mystery. As of now, our strategy is to hope that he walks into Auckland Central and gives himself up.'

'Well, they say the simple plans are often the best. To answer your question, the person who told me about Funke was the same person who told me he's got hold of the name and address of Varty's ex-wife.'

'How?'

'Pass.'

'What does she know?'

'Nothing, according to Varty. Funke mightn't believe that of course; he might cut chunks out of her until he's convinced otherwise. Just a thought. Her name's Rayleen Crouch, she lives in Grey Lynn. To save you looking in the phone book, there's an R. Crouch at 108 Crimea Avenue.'

'Okay, we'll drop in on her. You still haven't said who told you – and don't fuck around, eh? This is serious shit and we need all the help we can get.'

'Ihaka?'

'Yeah?'

'Are you familiar with the saying "Get a big dog up you"?'

*

That Friday afternoon some light was shed on Harold 'Buddy' Funke's mysterious comings and goings.

Ihaka and Detective Constable Johan Van Roon went to 108 Crimea Avenue where the doorbell wasn't answered. The next-door neighbours supplied the information that Rayleen Crouch was some kind of social worker; with assistance from the Social Welfare Department, they tracked her down to a youth hostel in Mt Albert. Crouch filled them in on how Funke had popped up out of the blue with his badge and gun, shooed Leith Grills off the premises and discovered, courtesy of their daughter, where her ex-husband had hidden his cocaine.

When Van Roon went off to ask the Whitianga police to send a reconnaissance team to Manacle Grange, Ihaka commented to Crouch that the news of Funke's villainy didn't seem to surprise her a great deal.

Ihaka's exploratory prod likewise failed to draw much of a reaction. 'Sergeant, I've been a social worker for 15 years,' she said in a somewhat world-weary tone. 'Very little surprises me any more. Besides, it's every man for himself these days, isn't it?'

At 3.40 p.m. the Whitianga police unit reported from Manacle Grange that they'd discovered direct physical evidence of one crime and prima facie evidence of several others: the previous evening, the hotel's sole guest, an English journalist, had suffered a broken jaw when ambushed by an unknown party; there were pellets in the bedposts and wall and traces of blood on the sheets in the master bedroom, indicating that someone had been in the line of fire when a shotgun was discharged; the hotel's manager had disappeared without taking her clothes, toiletries or car with her; and three of the journalist's silk shirts had been torn to shreds. While the shirt-ripping didn't have quite the sinister implications of the other discoveries, the journalist was making as much fuss about it as a man whose jaw was broken in three places could possibly make.

Ihaka estimated that, left to themselves, the boys from Whitianga would be pushed to make sense of it all before the turn of the century so he sent Van Roon down to give them a hand. In just over two hours' time C.C. Hellicar, who'd planned to spend the morning catching up on her sleep and the afternoon working out, was coming in for a full briefing. For various reasons, some of them personal, Ihaka was very keen to have something of substance to report. The way things were going, though, it looked like he'd once again be subjected to unsettling scrutiny from those frosty, eerily pale blue eyes.

*

When he'd finished exchanging endearments with Ihaka, Ricketts drove over to Westmere to see Electra Crouch. She wasn't home. He moved his car a bit further down Datchet Terrace and parked on the other side of the road, facing back up the street. From there, he had a good view of the building and would see her and anyone else coming whereas they weren't likely to notice him. Then he settled down to wait.

Datchet Terrace wasn't a hive of activity that afternoon. In two hours, Ricketts observed 22 cars, 13 pedestrians and 4 children on bicycles. None of them warranted close attention except perhaps for the boy who spat copiously on his rear window and scuttled away cackling gleefully. At 2.15 p.m. a black Porsche cruised down the street, coming to a halt outside Electra's apartment building. A stocky man, well into middleage, got out. He wore a striped, long-sleeved body shirt, jeans with a big-buckled belt, desert boots and aviator sun-glasses. His hair was thick, bushy and unnaturally black: it covered his ears like eaves, curled onto his collar and smothered his forehead. The overall effect was of a man who, for some reason, had been pleased with his appearance 20 years ago and had retained the look ever since. He went into Electra's apartment building only to emerge a couple of minutes later. He got back into his car and just sat there. Ricketts found this behaviour both interesting and slightly worrying.

For the first time, Ricketts felt he could've done with a mobile phone. While it seemed unlikely that Funke would

choose something as ostentatious as a Porsche for trans-
portation, it would've been comforting to have had the op-
tion of calling in the seventh cavalry. As things stood, if he
went to find a phone box, Electra might come home and
Funke, if it was him, would have a free hand to do whatever he had in mind. At 2.47 p.m. Electra Crouch resolved
the dilemma by walking down Datchet Terrace and entering number 13A. The man in the Porsche had a good, long
look at her as she walked past, then put his head back on
the headrest. Ricketts didn't read too much into the look, figuring Electra probably attracted plenty like it.

Ricketts wrote the Porsche's registration number on the
back of a credit card docket. He got out of his car, crossed
the road, went into number 13A, climbed the stairs to the
second floor and knocked on the door to flat 3.

'Who is it?' called Electra.

'Duane Ricketts. I need to talk to you – it's important.'

'No way is it important enough. Piss off.'

'Electra, listen, there's an American called Harold Funke
who might try to contact you …'

'First with the news again, Ricketts.'

'Eh?'

'You're only a day late, that's all. Funke was here yesterday.'

'Jesus, what did he want?'

'The same as you. One slight difference though – he's a
cop. Go away Ricketts and this time, stay gone.'

'Just a sec. Did he get in touch with you through your
mother?'

'What difference does it make?'

'Electra, Funke's a bad guy. He's a killer.'

'Oh fuck off Ricketts, you wanker. I saw his badge.'

'Yeah, I know what he is but he's bent – he's after that
cocaine. Don't take my word for it: ring Detective Sergeant

Ihaka at Auckland Central. Better still, ring your mother; the cops would've talked to her by now.'

There was a long silence before she said, 'Well, whatever he is, he got what he wanted.'

'You told him where it is?' When she didn't reply, Ricketts continued: 'Well shit, how were you meant to know? There's something else: a bloke's been sitting outside in a Porsche for half an hour, waiting for someone. Do you want to have a look, see if you know him? It might be Funke.'

A minute later the door opened. Her outfit – blue jeans, a man-sized white shirt worn outside the jeans, boots with high heels – was less of a uniform than what she'd had on the day before. The expression had softened a little too but was still a long way from tender.

'How's business, Ricketts?' she said with heavy irony. 'Got a few kids hooked today, did we?'

Ricketts let it go. 'Is that Funke out there?'

She motioned Ricketts inside with a jerk of her head and shut the door. 'Can't tell from up here. He wasn't in a Porsche yesterday though.'

'Maybe he's sold the dope and traded up.'

Electra wasn't sure if the remark was offensive or merely inane. Before she could make up her mind, there was a thunderous knocking at the door.

*

Electra jumped. Ricketts motioned her away from the door. A short, narrow hallway ran from the flat's entrance through to the living room; the kitchen was off the hallway on the left. He stepped into the kitchen and grabbed a chopping knife off the bench.

The knocking started again. When Ricketts nodded, Electra asked, 'Who's that?'

'Is Jake Latimer in there?' The man didn't sound young but he was definitely angry.

'Jake's not home.'

'When the hell will he be?'

'I don't know.'

'Give him a message – he'll know who it's from. It's real simple: tell the little fucker he's in deep shit. Tell him I didn't get what I paid for and I want my money back. If I don't get it, he'll be in a wheelchair before the weekend's out.'

'I don't know what you're taking about. Jake didn't say anything about this …'

'No kidding? Well let me fill you in. I paid the cunt for information – where I could find something that belongs to me. The bloke I sent to pick it up hasn't come back so either Latimer dudded me or he doubled up – got greedy and did the same deal with someone else. If he did that, he'll end up in a fucking coffin, never mind a wheelchair. Tell him he's got 24 hours.'

Message delivered, he stomped off. Ricketts put down the knife; from the kitchen window he watched the middle-aged man come out of the building, get into the Porsche and drive off. He went through to the living room where Electra was sitting at a small table with her head in her hands, staring at the tabletop. He perched on the end of a sofa, feeling the sensible course of action was to keep quiet until invited to say something. Electra sat motionless for a couple of minutes then suddenly sprang to her feet and stormed out. Ricketts heard her going from room to room. After a minute or two, she reappeared and sat down at the table, pale and stiff with tension. In a voice creaking with rage, she said: 'Fucking lowlife fucking pimp.'

It didn't necessarily call for a response but Ricketts decided to chance it. 'He's done a runner,' he said, not bothering to make it sound like a question.

Without looking up, she bobbed her head in a short, angry nod.

'You told him where the dope was; he sold the information to the loudmouth in the Porsche who would've made it part of the deal that no-one else knew. When Jake found out Funke was in on the secret, he realised he was in big trouble so he took the money and ran.'

Another abrupt nod.

'Well, you've got to ask yourself one question.'

She turned her head slowly.

'Do I let him get away with it?'

The fury in her eyes dimmed to resignation. Her shoulders drooped and she resumed staring at the tabletop. Eventually she said in a brittle voice: 'Looks to me like he already has.'

'Only if you let him,' said Ricketts.

'There's stuff-all I can do it about it now,' she said sulkily.

'You could tell the cops: whatever's going on, it's got to be illegal and Latimer's dealt himself in. Or you could sick his Porsche-driving mate onto him – that's what I'd do.'

Electra switched on the scorn. 'A, I don't know who the guy in the Porsche is, B, I don't know where Jake is. Apart from that, it's a really great idea.'

Ricketts produced the credit card docket. 'A's not a problem. I got the number of the Porsche – I can find out who owns it in five minutes. And I bet you could work out where Jake's gone if you put your mind to it.'

Electra's eyes narrowed and she sat up straight.

'Put yourself in his shoes: he's hit the jackpot but now he needs a place to hide. Where would he go? What would he do with the dough? I mean, you lived with the guy; you must have some idea?'

Electra thought about it, nibbling her bottom lip as she did so. It seemed to work: 'He bought a Lotto ticket every single week; man, it was like a ritual. I must've heard him say a hundred times that if he hit, you know, if he won big, he'd buy a Harley-Davidson. And if he got a Harley, he couldn't help himself, he'd have to show it off to his best friend, Lenny. He lives up near Whangarei.'

Ricketts asked to use the phone. He rang a guy he knew at Telecom and asked him to check if there'd been any STD calls made on Electra's phone in the previous couple of days. There'd been one – at 8.55 that morning, to Whangarei.

Ricketts passed the number to Electra. 'Recognise it?'

She got a Filofax out of her backpack and checked it. It was Lenny's number. Warily, almost formally, they exchanged nods of acknowledgement.

He said: 'Okay, now let's find out who he's got on his tail.'

Ricketts rang another contact, this time in the Ministry of Transport. It was obvious from his reaction that the answer struck a chord.

'Well?' she said when he put the phone down.

Ricketts gave her a careful look. 'The Porsche belongs to Bryce Spurdle.'

Electra, expressionless, kept her black eyes on Ricketts for half a minute then asked if he wanted a cup of tea. On her way through to the kitchen, she said over her shoulder: 'They're not meant to do that, are they? You know, just hand out information to anyone who rings up?'

'I'm not just anyone – they know me.'

'How come?'

'Remember I said yesterday that I find people for a living? It's a hell of a lot easier if you can access that sort of information. That's a matter of getting to know the right people – and maybe making it worth their while.'

Electra brought two mugs of tea into the living room and handed one to him. 'Is that how the cops do it?'

Ricketts smiled. 'The cops do all sorts of things; anyway, they've got most of that stuff at their fingertips.'

'Do you reckon they'd know the number of Funke's car?'

Ricketts sipped his tea and remembered what Ihaka had said. 'I doubt it. Why?'

'I wrote it down.' She half-smiled self-consciously. 'Electra Crouch, girl detective.'

'Why'd you do that?'

'When I was living at home, every time a guy came round to pick me up, when he wasn't looking, Rayleen – that's my mother – would take down the number of his car in case, I don't know, we ran away together or something – you know, the boy turns out to be Jack the Ripper Junior. Yesterday I was at the kitchen window when she got into his car and I thought, hey, look at her, getting into a strange man's car, blah blah.' She shrugged. 'And I wrote it down.'

The first thing the cops would've done, thought Ricketts, *was check the car rental companies. If Funke had hired a car, he would've used false ID but they would've been looking out for that.* He asked her for the number and rang his man at the Ministry of Transport again; the car was a Fiat Tipo registered to a Mrs Ada Merchant of Crescent Lodge in Eden Crescent. *That's weird*, he thought, *surely to Christ Funke wouldn't be tooling around in a stolen car, running the risk of being spotted by every cop on the road? Unless he just used it once and dumped it.*

'So?' said Electra.

He told her. 'It's a bit strange. I might just check this Crescent Lodge place out.'

'You find people, right? How'd you get into that?'

'I used to be a cop. When they kicked me out, it seemed about the only thing I was qualified for.'

She looked at him disbelievingly. 'You got kicked out of the cops?'

Ricketts nodded.

'What for?'

'How do you feel about horses?'

She frowned. 'Horses? What about them? They don't do much for me.'

Ricketts smiled a little grimly. 'If everyone had that attitude, I'd probably still be a cop.'

Twenty

Jody Spurdle, wearing skin-tight, calf-length leggings and a barely adequate halter-top, was doing stretches on an exercise mat in the TV room to a Cindy Crawford work-out video when her husband got home. She heard him coming from the letterbox 400 metres away because he gunned the Porsche up the drive at the sort of speed white people in expensive cars pass through parts of South Auckland where that particular combination is as unfamiliar as it is provocative. *Oh gross,* thought Jody, as the Porsche slid to a halt in a spray of gravel outside the front door; *he's got the runs again.*

About once a fortnight Bryce Spurdle got together with a few cronies for a long lunch. More often than not, these bouts of gluttony and heavy drinking played havoc with his digestion; if he didn't keep his eye on the clock – for instance, if he dallied over a final cleansing ale – he ran the risk of experiencing, at some point during the drive home, a swift and terrible build-up of what he called 'nozzle pressure'. Faced with the messy, ignominious and downright dangerous prospect of soiling himself at the wheel of a vehicle doing 100-plus kph along the motorway, he'd put in a supreme physical and mental effort involving clenched buttocks and what sports psychologists call 'visualisation' – overcoming the pain and stress of competition by imagining the moment of eventual triumph; in Spurdle's case, that was the blissful relief he'd obtain a millisecond after his bottom made a hard landing on a lavatory seat.

Jody had become well acquainted with the syndrome: he'd roar up the drive, pull up out the front with a squeal of rubber, and hit the ground running. So when, that afternoon, he slammed the front door behind him with an impact which rattled every window in the house, it occurred to her that perhaps he wasn't answering a bellow of nature after all; usually, he didn't waste time slamming doors or saying hello or doing anything at all which might slow his progress to the toilet reserved for his exclusive use which adjoined his den-cum-snooker room.

She stopped the video and went to investigate. She found her husband in the den. He was behind the bar sloshing dark rum into a glass and scowling like a spoilt brat on Christmas morning. He dumped some ice and a dollop of Coke into the glass and gulped massively.

'Something wrong?' she asked.

Spurdle wrenched off his sunglasses, dropped them on the bar and glared at her. 'Yes, as a matter of fact there is,' he said in a clipped, snide way. 'But what the fuck would you care?'

'What's that meant to mean?'

He responded with a surly shake of his head and came round to the other side of the bar where he sat on a high stool with his back to her. 'Forget it,' he grumbled. 'You better get back to your work-out before your arse goes soft.'

She walked over to him. 'For crying out loud, Bryce ...'

'Look, it's business, all right? You wouldn't want to know. You never have before so why change the habits of a lifetime?' He looked away and swallowed more rum and Coke.

'Well, I'm interested now – better late than never, isn't it?'

'What's the matter, sweetie?' he sneered. 'You worried the money tree's got dry rot?'

Jody drew in her breath angrily. 'Jesus, Bryce, you can be such an arsehole when you put your mind to it.'

Spurdle tossed back the rest of his drink and got up to make another one. He glanced across the bar at Jody. She was doing the petulant act: lips pursed, head on one side and hand on her hip. *Look at her*, he thought bitterly, *standing there like a gym slut. "Hey guys, check this out – flat stomach, tits like lawn bowls and a bum like a boy scout." Which reminds me; last time – when was it, Tuesday night? – I had the gall to suggest a root, I got dumped on from a great height, yeah, including that fucking crap about having as much jab as a shrivelled-up parsnip.*

Throughout their brief courtship and seven-and-a-half-year marriage, Spurdle had fretted at the thought of Jody learning of his murky past and had gone to some lengths to conceal it from her. But the recollection of her calculated slur on his virility, on top of the succession of maddening frustrations, caused something to snap. He was seized by an overpowering urge to jolt his glamorous young wife from the polka-dot bandana restraining her dyed-blonde hair all the way down to her pink toenails.

He put down the rum bottle, placed his palms flat on the bar, hunched his shoulders and, adopting what he imagined was a silky and slightly menacing tone, asked: 'You really want to know what I'm pissed off about, do you?'

'I asked, didn't I?'

He hoisted his eyebrows another centimetre. 'Are you quite sure about that?'

'What's all the drama in aid of, Bryce?' she said, starting to feel faintly uneasy. 'If you're going to tell me, tell me; if you're not …'

'Okay,' he said, in an 'I'm a reasonable man' voice. 'I'll tell you.'

And he did.

· · Despite Spurdle's sudden, reckless desire to lob a dirty great rock into the calm pond of his wife's pampered and complacent existence, there were, inevitably, limits to his candour. He told her that he'd funded Varty into the drug deal when in fact he hadn't put up a cent: the ten kilos of cocaine were technically the property of the moribund Mr Asia syndicate; Varty simply commandeered it and also paid for the charter of the yacht. Spurdle claimed Varty had double-crossed him – when it had been the other way around – and that Varty had murdered Al Grills, a misrepresentation which owed as much to ignorance as invention. The narrative concluded with Jake Latimer pocketing the $12,500 and Leith Grills' as yet unexplained failure to return from his mission.

Jody listened to her husband with mixed feelings which, contrary to his expectations, did not include shocked disapproval of his would-be drug trafficking, past and present. Her chief reaction was mortification: not only had she been hideously wrong to believe that Bryce wanted her out of the way, she'd also brought in the police. And now of all times, with this stuff going on! The minute she got the chance, she'd ring Sergeant Ihaka and tell him it was all a dreadful mistake.

Having dropped his bombshell, Spurdle awaited the fallout. He'd anticipated confusion, tears, anxiety rising to panic and other manifestations of scandalised dismay. What actually happened was that Jody leaned down and kissed him softly on the cheek.

'Poor thing, no wonder you're upset,' she said tenderly. 'God, I don't blame you one little bit. I'm just going to jump in the shower; why don't you relax, put your feet up, have another drink, and think about what you'd like for dinner.'

Spurdle was deflated. He was still puzzling over it 20 minutes later when something happened to temporarily deprive him of the capacity for rational thought. Cooing noises floated down the stairs from the bedroom. Jody was calling him in a teasing and suggestive little girl voice; it was a voice he hadn't heard for several years – indeed, a voice he'd given up hope of ever hearing again – and to which he responded as instantly, eagerly and pathetically as a goofy dog to its master's summons. His heart thumped wildly; his hands shook; blood surged to his groin emphasising that his jeans were a shade too tight for comfort. He put down his drink and half-fell, half-dismounted from the bar stool.

'Yes, dear,' he croaked tentatively, praying that his ears hadn't deceived him or worse, that the minx hadn't decided that mere denial was no longer sufficient and the time had come for a more exquisite form of torment.

'Come and have a look at this,' she said playfully. 'I need a second opinion.'

Spurdle shambled up the stairs. Jody sat on the end of the bed; she was wearing a diaphonous black teddy which reached to the top of her thighs, a garter belt with sheer black seamed stockings, and bright red, spike-heeled shoes which matched her lipstick. She leaned back, shoulders squared and legs slightly parted and extended, as if offering every silk-wrapped, semi-visible square inch of herself for his drooling inspection. Spurdle goggled; he felt weak at the knees and was vaguely aware that, below his belt, something was twitching and leaking like a beheaded snake.

'Well?' she said huskily. 'What do you think?'

*

Half an hour later Bryce Spurdle lay on his back in the king-sized bed. His eyes were closed, his mouth was open and he was making little snuffling sounds punctuated, every now and again, by a barnyard grunt. Next to him, Jody sat up in the bed with her back against the headboard, one hand behind her head, one slim, brown arm draped over her now uncovered breasts. *Good thinking, kiddo*, she told herself: whisking Bryce off to bed had killed two birds with one stone – got him out of that filthy mood and taken the edge off her guilty conscience. A few more of those performances – she'd been a raunchy little trollop if she did say so herself – and they'd be square …

Jody swore under her breath as she remembered that she'd volunteered to cook Bryce the dinner of his choice. The state he was in, he'd agree to anything so she could suggest going out instead; on the other hand, maybe she should rack up the brownie points while the going was good. She was weighing it up when the bedside phone rang. She answered it as Bryce snorted and rolled onto his side.

'Jody?'

'That's me.'

'Long time, no yakety-yak, chickie – it's Fleur, Fleur Wolfgramm.'

'Fleur! Where are you?'

'I'm in town for a couple of days. Any chance of catching up?'

'You bet. When do you want to do it?'

'How would tonight suit?'

'Tonight?' Jody glanced down at her husband who'd pulled a blanket over his head. 'Tonight could be difficult. Bryce and I had something planned, sort of.'

'Actually I'm meeting someone tonight …'

'You old tart,' said Jody with a giggle. 'Tell me more.'

Wolfgramm coughed. 'No, it's not like that. He's a client; but I was telling him a bit about Bryce and he's really keen to meet him – he thinks they've got lots in common and could do some business together. Trouble is, he's American and he's about to head off overseas.'

'Hey, well why don't you and your friend come out to our place for dinner tonight? We were tossing up on eating out or staying at home; if I'm going to cook, it makes no odds if it's two or four.'

'That'd be great. Are you sure it's okay though? We won't be interrupting anything, will we?'

Jody said no, but if she'd rung a few minutes earlier ...
Fleur said she hadn't realised the late afternoon bounce was
back in fashion and they both sniggered. Then Jody gave
directions and said to come any time from 7.30 on and Fleur
said the Spurdles obviously couldn't wait that long and they
sniggered some more and exchanged 'see you soons' and
hung up. It wasn't until Jody was under the shower that it
struck her that the last she'd heard of Fleur, she'd been running an upmarket boutique hotel somewhere on the Coromandel. Surely it couldn't be the same place that Bryce was
talking about ...

*

Duane Ricketts left Electra Crouch's flat in Westmere at 4
o'clock that Friday afternoon. He drove along Jervois Road,
down College Hill and past Victoria Park into the city. He
parked in the Shortland Street car park, walked up the hill
and turned left into Eden Crescent. Crescent Lodge was a
boarding house, all right. Out of curiosity he went back
down the street checking cars and numberplates and soon
came across the Fiat Tipo that Electra Crouch had seen
Funke in. Ricketts was considering the implications of it all
when he felt a seismic tremor at the very back of his mind.
He walked up past the Hyatt Kingsgate hotel and sat on a
bench in Albert Park; after 20 minutes' concentrated
thought, he had a plan.

He retrieved his car from the car park and drove back to
13A Datchet Terrace where he outlined the plan to Electra.
She listened impassively and, when he'd finished, asked a
couple of reassuringly intelligent questions.

'It's a punt,' he said, 'pure and simple. It might be a complete waste of time but I reckon it's worth a try. What do
you reckon?'

She nodded. 'Definitely.'

'What about your bit?'

'Yeah, I'm in.'

'You realise you'll have to lose the nosering and look ... normal?'

She smiled lopsidedly. 'The nosering's no big deal; it can always go back. Looking normal's a lot to ask of a girl though: the clothes are the worry – I mean, what do women detectives wear?'

*

At precisely 6 o'clock that evening a meeting commenced in a small conference room on the eighth floor of the Auckland Central police station. The participants were Detective Sergeant Tito Ihaka and Detective Inspector Finbar McGrail of the Auckland district police and C.C. Hellicar, whose title, affiliation and, reflected Ihaka, no doubt shoe size and favourite flavour of ice-cream were classified information. She was all in black: black Levis, a loose black zip-up jacket over a black skivvy, and black, ankle-high gym shoes. Ihaka wondered if they were her work clothes.

Ihaka was reviewing the events at Manacle Grange when there was a knock at the door. A constable entered with a metal briefcase for Ms Hellicar which he placed on the table.

'As I was saying,' continued Ihaka, 'the coke must've been stashed under the floorboards in the wardrobe. It's gone and so's the manager; the obvious conclusion is that Funke took them both.'

'Why take the manager?' asked McGrail.

'We think she might've gone feet first. At this stage, we're working on the theory that he used the shotgun on her but didn't want to leave the body. The pommie journo was lucky; he didn't get a look at Funke.'

'I'm a little confused, Sergeant,' said Hellicar. 'I understood Funke had a Smith & Wesson .38?'

'He did but that doesn't mean to say he couldn't have got himself a shotgun as well; they're not that hard to get hold of.'

'Why would he want one?' she asked mildly. 'It's unwieldy, difficult to conceal, and he's got himself a perfectly good pistol; beats me why he'd bother with a shotgun. Besides, if it was just a matter of getting shed of her, Funke wouldn't use a shotgun, especially at that time of night; he'd know that many ways of doing her with his two hands, he'd be plum spoilt for choice.'

One of Ihaka's attributes, which certainly wasn't shared by all ranking officers at Auckland Central, was that he recognised good sense when he heard it, even when it was being employed to undermine his position; allied to that, he never wasted time or breath defending a position he knew to be indefensible. Even so, he felt a rush of irrational but intense irritation when he saw, out of the corner of his eye, McGrail nodding agreement.

'I must say, that seems like sound thinking to me,' said McGrail, bestowing a warm smile on Hellicar. *Hello,* thought Ihaka. *McGrail's got a stiffy.*

Ihaka nodded at Hellicar. 'Yeah, you're probably right; Funke wouldn't use a gun unless he had to. Maybe someone else brought the shotgun to the party.'

'My word,' said McGrail turning to Hellicar again. 'The sergeant's a moving target tonight.'

Hellicar grinned as if she was enjoying the by-play. Ihaka maintained a polite smile which didn't entirely disguise a desire to rip out McGrail's tongue and strangle him with it.

'Such as who?' asked Hellicar.

Ihaka told her about Leith Grills' barging in on Rayleen Crouch, his association with Bryce Spurdle and Spurdle's suspected involvement in the drug shipment. He added: 'We tried to bring Grills in this afternoon but couldn't get our hands on the bugger; his wife said he's out of town and she doesn't know when he gets back.'

'How would Spurdle and Grills have found out about Manacle Grange?' asked McGrail.

'I guess the same way as Funke,' said Ihaka. 'Through the daughter. Seems like she's the only one who knew the dope was down there. We'd better talk to her.'

'What about your sparring partner, Ricketts?' said McGrail. 'What's he up to? He's known about the drugs all along and I can't see him standing on the sidelines.'

'Who is he?' asked Hellicar.

Ihaka gave her a brief and unflattering summary of Ricketts and where he fitted in. 'I wouldn't bet on it,' he said, 'but I think I might've warned him off. Ricketts came back from Thailand looking to make a score, no two ways about that, but only if he could've breezed it: walked in, got the stuff, walked out and off-loaded it – no law, no complications, no heavy stuff. My gut feeling is that Ricketts would play the odds. Once it got too high risk, he'd flag it away.'

Ihaka ran them through what was being done: a nationwide alert for Funke; a watch on all ports; another, more painstaking, check of hotels, motels, and boarding houses; a blitz on informants; and surveillance of known and suspected major drug dealers, including Spurdle, whom Funke might contact.

'It's a waiting game now,' he concluded. 'Funke won't want to take the stuff out of the country and in through Customs somewhere. He'll try to sell it here and that means putting the word out, moving around, seeing people. We'll get a tip-off or a sighting – just a matter of time.'

'What about this guy Ricketts?' asked Hellicar. 'You got someone on him?'

Ihaka shook his head. 'Waste of manpower. If we put him under surveillance, Ricketts would spot it; if we put a tail on him, he'd lose it. He's good at that shit – better than most of our guys anyway.'

McGrail gave Hellicar another winning smile. 'On that score at least, the sergeant and I are as one.'

The meeting wound up shortly afterwards. McGrail lavished some more of his limited supply of charm on Hellicar, then left the room.

'He surely is a nice guy,' she said.

Ihaka lurched over to the large plastic rubbish bin in the corner, bent over so his head was almost in it, and did a disconcertingly convincing imitation of someone being violently and noisily ill.

He turned around wiping his mouth with the back of his hand. 'They don't come any nicer than McGrail,' he agreed. He nodded at the briefcase. 'Is that your gear?'

Hellicar stopped staring at Ihaka and shook herself to make sure she hadn't imagined the vomiting routine. *It's not me*, she told herself. *I didn't take a sleeping pill on the plane; I'm not hallucinating; he really did do that.*

'Yes, that's it,' she said distractedly.

'Can I've a geek?'

'A what?'

'A look. Can I've a look at your equipment.'

'I'll show you, Sergeant, if that's what you really want,' she said watching him suspiciously. 'Just don't offer to show me your nightstick.'

Ihaka looked affronted. 'The thought never entered my head.'

'I dare say there isn't room – not with the other stuff you've got in there.'

While Ihaka pondered that remark, she spun the combination locks and snapped the briefcase open. It contained a sleek, compact black automatic pistol with a moulded finger-grip butt, a spare magazine, a box of ammunition and a plastic stock.

Ihaka wolf-whistled. 'That's a mean-looking unit. What is it?'

She picked up the pistol and ejected the empty magazine from the butt. 'A Heckler and Koch VP 70; nine millimetre, takes an 18-round load.'

She opened the box of ammunition and began feeding bullets into the magazine.

'What's this?' asked Ihaka, tapping the stock.

'A stock; you can fix it to the pistol and brace it against your shoulder – like a rifle butt – and set it to fire in three-shot bursts. For those times when you just can't afford to miss.'

'I thought they were all like that?'

She nodded. 'To tell the truth, I've only ever used the stock at the firing range.'

'State of the art bang-bang,' he said in a hucksterish American accent.

She shrugged. 'It's a good weapon for sure but it just suits me – nice weight, good feel. I got the grip – see how it's moulded? – custom-made to fit my hand.' She slipped the last bullet into the magazine, slid the magazine into the butt and aimed across the room. 'It gets the job done.'

Twenty-One

At 7.05 that Friday evening Duane Ricketts drove his baked-bean-orange Toyota Corolla down Eden Crescent. He was dressed in a blue shirt with a button-down collar, a cheerfully patterned tie, a dark-green check woollen jacket and off-white chino pants. They were his good-news clothes; he wore them when he took a runaway back to Mum and Dad or, failing that, gave them a phone number and a polaroid of the stray displaying clear eyes, clean fingernails and a haircut that wouldn't frighten the neighbours. His bad-news outfit was white shirt, plain tie and dark suit. He wore it when he had to explain to parents that they still had a child but he or she bore no resemblance to the one they missed; or to break the news that a long-lost brother, the clever one everybody said was going to be famous some day, spent most of his life on a bench in Myers Park with a cask of Lincoln Road muller-thurgau and hadn't changed his underpants since the fall of the Berlin Wall.

A transformed Electra Crouch was in the passenger seat. She'd borrowed a thigh-length tweed herringbone coat, belted at the waist, from the woman in the ground-floor apartment and wore it over black leather trousers and a black turtleneck sweater. The nosering, the earstuds, the chestnut tint and the gel had all been discarded; the hair – now glossy-black – fell naturally, curling onto her forehead and below her ears. Electra looked older than 18 anyway but Ricketts had suggested that a bit of make-up might add a useful year or two. Not one for half-measures, she'd put on lipstick, eye shadow, face make-up and, judging by the alluring scent, some rather expensive perfume.

Ricketts had déjà vu when the new-look Electra Crouch came out of her bedroom and struck a catwalk pose: the clothes were different but otherwise she looked uncannily like she'd done in his dream. He had mixed feelings on the more pertinent issue of whether it amounted to a convincing impersonation. *She'll pass for early 20s all right, he thought, but apart from that she looks about as much like a working policewoman as Madonna does.* He hoped that whoever ran Crescent Lodge based their expectations of policewomen on American TV shows.

The Fiat Tipo was still there. Ricketts drove past the boarding house, U-turned and double-parked facing back down the street. After a few minutes' wait, he got a parking spot where he wanted: across the road from Crescent Lodge and a little way up the street so anyone going from the boarding house to the Fiat would walk away from them, not towards them. It was almost dark but there was a street light right outside Cresent Lodge, illuminating the entrance.

'Okay,' said Ricketts. 'Let's run through it again.'

'What for?' she said. 'We've done it to death.'

'Humour me.'

Electra put her chin on her chest. 'Okay,' she sighed. 'I don't touch anything; I don't use names; I leave the talking to you; I look reassuring and professional; I refrain from smoking. As soon as we get into the room, I ask to use a phone; I ring the flat and pretend to have a conversation with Ihaka then I keep them occupied till you're finished. If I see Funke coming, I take off.'

'And if they ask you what's going on?'

'I tell them to mind their own fucking beeswax.' She glanced sidelong at Ricketts who seemed to have left his sense of humour back at the flat with the nosering. 'Sorry, got that wrong. I say I've been assigned to tag along with you but don't really know what it's all about. If they don't get the message, then I tell them to mind their own fucking beeswax.'

It was Ricketts' turn to sigh. 'This is not a game.'

'I know, I know, I know. Don't worry about it, I'll be fine. I do this before a concert – kid around, get loose. You should try it. Speaking of music, you got any?'

'There's a few tapes in the glovebox.'

She opened the glovebox, brought out half a dozen tapes and shuffled through them. 'Oh, I get it,' she said. 'You can have whatever you want as long as it's Van Morrison?'

'What's wrong with Van Morrison?' said Ricketts testily.

'To me he's like, you know, Mozart, Beethoven – guys like that.'

'In other words, he's a kraut who's been dead for a couple of hundred years?'

'I didn't mean …'

'What you're trying to say is boring old farts listen to Van Morrison – correct?'

She said, 'If the hairpiece fits,' and started laughing. 'What I was actually trying to say is people who listen to him obviously aren't into what's happening right now.'

'Like The Homo Dwarves? Choice name – where'd you get it from?'

She shrugged. 'Just made it up. We wanted a name that'd get up people's noses.'

'I hate to disappoint you but it doesn't get up mine – then again, I'm not a homo or a dwarf.'

'Nor's my mother; nor are most of the people who've whinged about it.'

At that moment a couple came out of Crescent Lodge. The man was middle-aged and short with a broad, tanned face and not much hair. He was wearing a dark reefer jacket and light trousers and carried a shopping bag. The woman was younger, stylishly dressed and quite striking, with a mane of dark hair. They walked across the road towards the Fiat.

'That's him,' said Electra quietly.

'What about the woman – you know her?'

She shook her head. 'No. She looks a bit glam for him though.'

'Yeah, doesn't she?'

The couple got into the Fiat. The woman was a new factor but Ricketts couldn't see that it changed anything. As soon as the Fiat turned out of Eden Crescent, he got out of the car and got a boxy black plastic briefcase out of the boot.

'Let's go,' he said.

*

They crossed the road and went into Crescent Lodge. It was a narrow, three-storey wooden building which had seen better days; even in its prime, Sunday drivers wouldn't have made detours to admire it. The foyer was deserted except for three china ducks flying in close formation across chintzy blue floral wallpaper. Below the ducks was a sofa which looked old enough to have farthings in its crevices.

The little office beyond the reception counter was unoccupied so Ricketts halloed loudly. A door opened down the corridor which ran off the foyer. A woman poked her head out, saw them and bustled down the corridor. She looked in her 60s: well-lined, iron-grey hair, and eyes which twinkled behind the reading glasses.

She beamed at Electra. 'Well, look at you,' she said. 'Aren't you the pretty one?' She glanced uncertainly at Ricketts who realised that she was having the same thoughts about the two of them as they'd had about Funke and his female companion a few minutes earlier. 'Now then, would you be wanting a room? We do have a vacancy.'

'Actually, madam, we're from the police,' said Ricketts flashing his fake identification. It was an extremely convincing forgery, as were the documents in his wallet identifying him as a health inspector, a Telecom engineer and an officer of the Social Welfare Department. The forgeries had been done for him by a Dutch screen-printer who lived in Huapai and who'd been the first person Ricketts rang after he was kicked out of the police force. The purpose of the call was to warn the Dutchman that the police knew about the 20 or 30 marijuana plants he had in his garden and would be coming round to arrest him shortly.

'I'm Detective Sergeant Wright,' he said, 'and this is Detective Constable Edgar. Are you Mrs Ada Merchant?'

Her eyes grew big. 'Goodness me. Yes I am, but what ...'

He produced a small notepad from his jacket pocket. 'Mrs Merchant, are you the owner of a Fiat Tipo?' – he flipped the notepad open and read the car registration number.

'Yes,' she nodded vigorously. 'Yes, that's my car. I've had it for three years now. Everyone told me to get a Japanese car. Don't get a Fiat, they said; they're unreliable and they rust. But do you know, I've never had a problem with it – not even the slightest speck of rust. You didn't catch me on one of those hidden cameras, did you, going through a red light? I'd be surprised if that's the case, Sergeant; I'm normally very careful ...'

'Mrs Merchant, have you lent your car to anyone recently?'

Comprehension eventually arrived on Mrs Merchant's face, bringing up the rear in an almost comically predictable procession of expressions. 'Yes, yes, of course I have. I lent it to Hank – that's Mr Williams, my American guest. Did he go through a red light? I'd be a little cross if he did because he promised ...'

'Mr Williams is a guest here?'

'That's right. You see, he was involved in some sort of dreadful traffic accident back home – Oklahoma, I think he said he's from. Not his fault, he assures me, but there's going to be a court case and in the meantime, his licence has been suspended which means the poor man couldn't hire a car; that would've completely mucked up his holiday so he suggested that I hire one – whatever sort I wanted, he'd pay for it – and he'd use my Fiat.' She lowered her voice. 'Guess what I did? I hired a BMW.' She emitted a little squeak of delight. 'You should see people's faces when they see me in it.' Her face dropped. 'Golly, I didn't break the law, did I?'

'Don't worry Mrs Merchant, this has got nothing to do with you and not much to do with your car. We're only interested in it because that's how we traced your guest, Mr Williams. To cut a long story short, we don't think he's who he says he is. We believe his real name is Funke and that he's wanted by the authorities in Thailand. Is he here now?'

'No, you've just missed him – he's gone out for dinner with his lady friend.'

'Mrs Merchant, we need to establish as quickly as possible whether this is the man we're looking for; for that reason, I'd like to have a look in his room. You've obviously got a spare key?'

She looked dubious. 'Well, yes, but don't you need a search warrant for that sort of thing?'

'Not if you let us in,' he said. 'After all, it's your room; you can go in there whenever you like.' Ricketts lowered his voice confidentially. 'Between you and me, Mrs Merchant, this is a pretty serious matter with all sorts of international ramifications. All we're after is confirmation of identity; I'll be in and out in two ticks.'

She nodded agreement, fetched the key from the office, led them upstairs and let them into Room 7. It contained a neatly-made three-quarter-sized bed, a hand-basin, a small writing desk, a bedside table with a reading light, a chest of drawers and a wardrobe. Perfume hung in the air.

Mrs Merchant wrinkled her nose like a guinea pig. 'Mr Williams' friend certainly splashes on the perfume.' She looked at Electra. 'Yours is much nicer, my dear, much more subtle.'

Electra rewarded her with a gorgeous smile. 'Why, thank you, Mrs Merchant. To tell the truth, I'm a bit of a beginner when it comes to the smellies. Look, is there a phone I could possibly use? I should check in with headquarters.'

Mrs Merchant, who appeared to entertain fewer reservations about Electra than about Ricketts, said of course there was. As soon as they'd gone downstairs, Ricketts closed the door and took a pair of skin-tight plastic gloves from his briefcase. He put them on and tried the wardrobe; it was locked. He took a small jemmy from his briefcase and forced the wardrobe door. Inside were a couple of shirts on hangers, a shopping bag containing a blouse, brassiere and briefs, and a large Samsonite suitcase with a combination lock. He pulled the suitcase out of the wardrobe and checked it was locked, then used the jemmy to lever it open. It contained some carefully folded clothes, US passports in the names of Harold Funke, Donald Surface and Lyle Gorse, an airline ticket with an open return to Los Angeles, and 19 plastic bags of white powder, which was one less than Dale Varty had said there'd be. Ricketts removed the bags and replaced them with 19 of the 20 bags of icing sugar he'd brought with him in the briefcase. He'd picked up the icing sugar at a supermarket earlier that evening and repackaged it in self-sealing clear plastic bags.

Ricketts closed the suitcase, returned it to the wardrobe and put the 19 bags of what he was reasonably confident was cocaine into his briefcase. He left the room locking the door behind him, took off the gloves and put them in his jacket pocket and went down to the foyer where Electra and Mrs Merchant were agreeing to disagree about Mr and Mrs Rachel Hunter: Electra didn't have a lot of time for either of them while Mrs Merchant seemed to think that Rod Stewart was a bit of a lad and that there were worse things in life than being rich, famous and regarded as a bimbo – running a slightly down-at-heel boarding house, for instance.

'What do you think, Sergeant?' asked Electra with a malicious glint in her eye. 'I bet you're a big Rach fan?'

Ricketts gave her a prim little smile and said, 'I think she's a wonderful ambassador for New Zealand.' He turned to Mrs Merchant. 'Your guest's definitely the man we're looking for. You were saying he's got someone with him?'

'Yes, a friend of his; they met overseas apparently. She's from out of town – that's why she used his room to get changed.'

That's one theory, thought Ricketts.

Ten minutes later he rang Auckland Central police station from a phone box on Dominion Road. Without identifying himself, he informed the constable to whom he was put through that Harold Funke was staying in Room 7 of the Crescent Lodge boarding house, driving a Fiat Tipo the registration number of which he provided, and in the company of a rather attractive brunette. He thought about adding that the brunette could be an accomplice or a girlfriend or both, or possibly even some sort of hostage, but decided against. It was complicated enough already.

*

At 7.45 p.m. the two-person police surveillance team stationed in a small stand of pine trees in the paddock across the road from the entrance to the Spurdle property reported in to operation control at Auckland Central. They'd got the registration number of a car which had just gone up the Spurdle's drive but weren't entirely in agreement over the make and model: Constable Beth Greendale, whose brother was a mechanic and who knew a bit about cars, had seen enough through her night-sight binoculars to be reasonably confident it was a Fiat Tipo; Constable Jarrad Renshaw, who didn't have a brother, didn't know much about cars, and whose idea of a good time wasn't blundering around in the dark putting his foot in cowpats, described it as 'just another fucking Japanese hatchback'. They also reported that there were two passengers, a male and a female; beyond that, their descriptions fitted every pale-skinned man and woman on the planet who didn't have two heads.

Five minutes after Ihaka received that information, along with details of the car's registered owner, he was handed a note of the anonymous tip-off about Funke. After a brief discussion with McGrail, Ihaka dispatched a police team, including several members of the Armed Offenders Squad, to Crescent Lodge. Then he walked along to the conference room where C.C. Hellicar was writing postcards and listening to John Hiatt singing about lipstick sunsets on her Walkman.

Ihaka stood in the doorway looking unusually serious. Hellicar put down the ballpoint and took off her earphones.

'Feel like going for a drive?' he asked.

'Anywhere in particular?'

Ihaka nodded. 'Spurdle's place. He's got company.'

Hellicar's eyes narrowed and she reached for the metal briefcase. 'Is it him?'

'Could be.' He paused. 'I've got a feeling it will be.'

She stood up with a faint smile. 'Oh right, your gift. So I guess you already know how all this is going to work out?'

'Yeah – Funke's about to become defunct.' He stood aside to let her through the door then caught up with her. 'Listen, will you be heading off straightaway or can you stick around for the weekend? Reason I ask is my family's got a beach house up north. I could take you up there, show you a bit of the country.'

Hellicar's cool look wasn't entirely devoid of either amusement or curiosity. 'You mean just you and me?'

Ihaka shrugged. 'Up to you. If it'd make you feel more comfortable, bring your two mates – Heckler and Koch.'

Twenty-Two

Buddy Funke halted the Fiat Tipo outside the Spurdle mansion and switched off the motor. He gave Fleur Wolfgramm a long, calculating look and said, 'You've played it real smart so far, sugar; don't go blowing it now.'

Part of Fleur Wolfgramm – the logical, cynical and therefore pessimistic part – was faintly surprised to be still alive. The other part – the upbeat, extrovert, slightly New Age part which was responsible for most of the really stupid things she'd done in her life – had drawn comfort from the fact that Funke had been a gentleman when he'd had ample opportunity to be a beast. From the outset, her strategy had been to do whatever it took to stay alive till they got to the Spurdles and then hope that something turned up. The first bit had been a piece of cake – whatever it took had proved to be very little – but the menace now unmistakable behind Funke's amiable demeanour suggested that the next bit might be a lot trickier.

'What do you mean?' she said anxiously. 'Why should I do that?'

'No reason that occurs to me,' he said with the wry delivery of a cracker-barrel philosopher, 'but folks have a habit of giving in to temptation just because it's there; sometimes they ain't even that shook on what it is they're giving in to. Me and Mr Bryce Spurdle are going to talk business tonight and I don't expect he'll want to do that in front of the women-folk. Remember now, just because I'm not there keeping an eye on you is no reason to cut the fool. We've got along just fine, you and me, but if anything untoward happens, you'll answer for it.'

Wolfgramm nodded. 'Message received,' she muttered. 'I'll say this for you, you know how to put a girl in a party mood.'

Bryce Spurdle had been stunned and immensely gratified by his wife's second coming as Susie Homemaker in crotchless panties. As the afterglow faded, however, gratitude inevitably gave way to suspicion. Whatever else he was, Spurdle was a realist and, after a few seconds' wishful thinking, he dismissed the possibility that it'd been a genuine and spontaneous expression of her true feelings. Before it began to gnaw at him, he had one of those rare moments of clarity when one grasps that the easy and obvious course of action is also the most sensible. *What the fuck am I worrying about?* he asked himself. *Who gives a fat rat's arse what she's up to? Get your snout in the trough, mate; make the most of it while it lasts.*

Bucked both by his rigorous reasoning and the conclusion to which it led, Spurdle refrained from throwing a tantrum upon being informed that a pair of strangers was coming to dinner. While Jody prepared his favourite meal – Mediterranean roast lamb and sticky toffee pudding – he browsed contentedly in the mini-wine cellar beneath the stairs, savouring the aroma of roasting garlic and balsamic vinegar which wafted down the hall from the kitchen. He liked to take his time choosing wine, especially on an occasion like this when he had to balance his ebullient mood and desire to do justice to Jody's culinary exertions against his profound aversion to wasting expensive wine on other people.

The Spurdles and their guests were having pre-dinner drinks in the lounge. Bryce was doing the honours: champagne for the ladies, Scotch for Funke, more dark rum for himself. Jody and Fleur were already gabbling like auctioneers while Funke stood on his own, quite relaxed, with one hand in his pocket and the other holding a shopping bag.

Spurdle eyed him surreptitiously as he poured the champagne; he wondered briefly what was in the bag before turning his mind to the much more interesting question of whether their guests were sleeping together. Not surprisingly, given that his assumptions about other people's sex lives owed far more to his dirty mind than to empirical evidence or even probability, he concluded that they were.

The drinks were distributed and toasts exchanged. The women took perfunctory sips and carried on with their exclusive conversation. Spurdle was swirling his drink around trying to think of something to say when Funke saved him the trouble.

'You got the message that I have a business proposition for you?' he murmured.

Spurdle, who associated that approach with losers, conmen and white-collar thieves, looked as unenthusiastic as the circumstances permitted and said, 'Yeah, Jody mentioned it.'

'How about we get to it right away?' said Funke. 'Would there happen to be a little corner we can go so's we don't bore the ladies?'

Spurdle glanced at Fleur and Jody, thinking that for all the ladies cared, he and the Yank could get naked and shave each other's body hair. 'Okay,' he said. 'Let's do that. Girls, we're just slipping down to the den. The champagne's in the ice-bucket – help yourselves.'

They went into the den. Spurdle was hitching himself up onto a stool when Funke plonked the shopping bag down on the bar in front of him.

'A little something from me to you.'

Spurdle looked bemused and slightly apprehensive. Funke grinned and pointed at the bag. 'Well?' he asked. 'You going to have a look?'

Spurdle pulled the bag towards him. He peered into it suspiciously then glanced sharply up at Funke who winked back. Spurdle reached into the shopping bag and brought out a plastic bag of white powder. He looked at it for a few seconds then placed it on the bar and pushed it away.

'What's that then?' he said with a jerk of his chin.

Funke turned the bag over to show that it had been opened and then patched with sticking plaster. 'That, my friend, is cocaine de luxe and I ought to know – I'm a goddam expert.'

'Just what the hell makes you think I'd want it?' asked Spurdle, working up a little truculence.

'Well now,' said Funke with a thin smile, 'I hear tell you're a man who'd know what to do with it; a man who understands that this stuff's just about the most efficient way of generating cash money ever invented.' He pushed the bag back towards Spurdle. 'That's a present; call it an expression of goodwill. There's 19 more where that came from: all up, ten kilos of top of the range nose candy.'

Spurdle stared at him. 'Who are you, pal?'

'Don't take this the wrong way but I work for the DEA. You know what that is?' Spurdle, eyes wide, nodded. 'The Brits have got a saying about someone being a poacher turned gamekeeper. That's sort of what I am, except contrariwise.'

Spurdle's eyes narrowed. 'This could be a set-up.'

Funke shrugged. 'That goes both ways,' he said mildly. 'For all I know about you, you could be taking it in the tail from the chief of police. Let me tell you how it came my way; that might explain a few things. I found it in a little place called Manacle ...'

Spurdle flushed a dark, angry red and wriggled off the bar stool. 'You got it from Manacle Grange?' he demanded, his voice rising. 'That makes it my fucking cocaine. I paid for it twice over and got ripped off both times. How the fuck did you get hold of it?'

'Well, let me tell you, it wasn't easy,' said Funke who seemed to be finding the conversation increasingly enjoyable. 'But what counts is, I've got it, and as we both know, in this business possession is ten-tenths of the law – everything else is for shit.'

'Wait a fucking minute,' said Spurdle. 'Now I've got you taped; you're the one who pulled a gun on Leith Grills the other night, over at Rayleen Varty's place.'

'Yup, that was me all right,' agreed Funke. 'That old boy work for you, did he?'

Spurdle caught something in Funke's tone. 'Yeah, now and again. In fact I've been expecting to hear from him all day. I don't suppose you came across him down at Manacle Grange?'

'I did as a matter of fact,' said Funke. 'The way he was waving that shotgun, it would've been hard to miss him.'

Spurdle did a double-take. 'A shotgun? Jesus Christ, what happened?'

'It's a sad story; suffice to say, I'm here and he ain't; I got the cocaine and all your Mr Grills has got is a couple of holes that the Lord didn't give him.'

Spurdle gawked at Funke, transfixed. 'You shot him?' he asked hoarsely.

'Yes sir, I did,' said Funke briskly. 'The boy left me no choice. Like I say, he was waving that shotgun like he was John Dillinger himself. That's by the bye, time's a-wasting. Are you and me going to do some business, or should I take my custom elsewhere?'

Spurdle shook his head in bewilderment and went behind the bar to make fresh drinks. He pushed Funke's Scotch across the bar to him, took a distracted swig of his rum and Coke, then stood with his hands flat on the bar and head bowed. Two minutes passed. Then he looked up at Funke, heaved a sigh of resignation, and said, 'How much?'

'All right,' said Funke. 'In my experience, which as I say is considerable, merchandise of this quality wholesales at around 200 grand a kilo and retails at about 500 grand. I'm talking American; in your money, that's around 320 whole-sale, 800 on the street. Working off those numbers, you – being the wholesaler – would aim to make around three million of your dollars on ten kilos. That sound about right to you?'

'It sounds fucking high to me.'

'Sure it does, because right now you're a buyer. I'm about to make you the offer of a lifetime, amigo: the stuff's yours for 750 grand.'

'NZ or US?' asked Spurdle quickly.

'NZ. That means if you're even semi-reasonable, you'll make at least three times your money. If you're good, you'll quadruple it without working up a sweat.'

Spurdle knew he was being offered a good deal and forced himself to keep a poker face. 'Even if it's as good as you say, that's still pretty steep ...'

'Uh-uh,' said Funke waving his index finger. 'That ain't a negotiating position, that's the price. It's cheap and you know it.'

'Well, maybe ...'

'No goddam maybe about it,' said Funke emphatically. 'Christ almighty, when I think of the shit I had to go through to get it ... by the way, there is one condition.'

'Oh? What's that?'

'We do the deal tomorrow morning at sun up.'

'The fuck we will,' yelped Spurdle. 'Where the hell am I going to get the money? It's Friday night in case you hadn't noticed ...'

Funke's eyes went dull and his mouth set like a closed vice. 'How about you quit flapping that tongue, brother?' he said softly, hunching across the bar. 'I'm not offering you the best deal you ever had on account of I particularly like you – because I'm bound to say, I've known you for half an hour and you ain't grown on me even a little bit. The fact is, I figure I've pushed my luck about as far as it's going to go; I want to be on the first plane out of here tomorrow morning so I'm giving you a discount for short notice. Now you're asking me where you're going to get the money from on a Friday night, like I'm some kind of jerk who couldn't find his dick in a double bed. If I seriously thought you had to get the money from a bank, I wouldn't be here because that would give me two good reasons not to deal with you: in the first place, it would mean you're dumb because the bank's going to report a withdrawal that size; second, it would mean you ain't a player. Anyone who buys and sells dope has access to a mess of cash whenever: either he's got a stash or he knows people whose business is selling money. Now make up your goddamn mind – are you in or out?'

Spurdle didn't reply right away but that didn't worry Funke because he knew from the look in his eyes what the answer would be. While he waited for Spurdle to get around to it, Funke sipped his Scotch and idly wondered how much the son of a bitch had in his secret safe.

*

Tito Ihaka pulled over to the side of the road about half a kilometre from the entrance to Spurdle's drive, flicked off the headlights and turned to C.C. Hellicar.

'I've got an idea,' he said.

She kept looking straight ahead. 'Sergeant, this is not a good time to be having ideas,' she said. 'Let's not complicate things. Why don't you just get me thereabouts and then stay out of the way?'

'No, this is a shit-hot idea. See, I've got a valid police reason for dropping in on the Spurdles. When I show up, Funke'll be so busy worrying about me, you can sneak in and zap the bugger.'

Hellicar appeared to be considering it. 'It makes sense I guess; there's just one slight flaw.'

'What's that?'

Hellicar twisted around in her seat and gave him a very direct look. 'Funke might just shoot you on sight.'

Ihaka's forehead furrowed. 'Thank Christ there's not a major flaw.' He shook his head. 'I doubt it; he's got no reason to think we're onto him and I've got a reason for being there. Sure, he's going to watch me like a hawk but that's what we want him to do.'

'Tito,' said Hellicar gently. 'I appreciate it and all but I really don't think this is a good move. You being a cop isn't worth a Yankee dime to Funke. He's going to be eat up with suspicion the moment you set foot there; half a second after he decides something's going down, you'll have a .38 in your face.'

'It's just a matter of timing,' said Ihaka blithely. 'Shit, I'm not planning to spend the night with the prick; I'll wait till you're up there before I go. So we're talking what? A couple of minutes. It's a tried and true tactic – create a diversion and whack the fuckers when they're looking the other way.'

Hellicar sighed and looked up at the car roof. 'I don't understand; you're not a macho dimwit or some idiotic kid who thinks it's like the movies and the good guys always walk away. It's not even your responsibility.'

In a whiny country and western voice Ihaka sang 'Tito, don't be a hero.' Hellicar threw up her hands and said 'Goddammit.'

'You're dead right about me not being macho or naïve,' he said, 'but you've got the other bit wrong. Okay, Funke's one of yours but this here's' – he gestured at the surrounding darkness – 'my neck of the woods. More to the point, if Funke gets past you, then me and the other blokes will have to have a go and that could get ugly – don't forget there are three other people in the house. In my professional opinion, it's the best chance of getting the job done without things getting out of hand.' He paused and leant back in his seat. 'Besides, I hate having nowhere to go on a Friday night.'

Hellicar nodded solemnly. 'Well shit,' she said, 'why didn't you just say so in the first place.'

Ihaka started the car. 'The surveillance guys say it's about 400 metres from the road up to the house. I'll drop you just before the gate and give you quarter of an hour or so to get up there. What time do you make it?'

'Twenty-five after nine.'

'Okay. I'll knock on the door at a quarter to ten. The back-up's in the paddock across the road; they'll block off the entrance. How long should they wait?'

'Me and Funke haven't got a whole heap to talk about; whichever way it goes, it'll be over and done with pretty damn quick.'

*

At 9.44 p.m. Ihaka drove up to the Spurdle residence, parked behind the Fiat Tipo and rang the doorbell. A minute later, a flushed Bryce Spurdle opened the door. Ihaka introduced himself and asked to speak to Mrs Spurdle.

Spurdle liked to see himself as a man in control of his destiny but recent events had left him feeling like a body surfer caught by one of those sudden monster waves which dribble in innocuously, pause about 20 or 30 metres out from the shore, rear up and then hurl themselves at the beach like dam-bursts. He felt like he'd been picked up and catapulted by an irresistible force – churned, flipped, dragged, bounced and finally dumped on the beach, breathless, disoriented and tingling with exhilaration. The only thing missing was sand in his crack. On top of all that, he'd drunk six double rum and Cokes, a couple of beers and two-thirds of a bottle of wine in the space of a few hours. The net result was that he'd achieved a state of fuzzy detachment and while it seemed strange that a cop should turn up out of the blue wanting to talk to his wife, he couldn't actually find it within himself to give a flying fuck.

So he shrugged and said, 'You better come in then. Bit bloody inconvenient though; we've got people for dinner.'

'It won't take a moment.'

Spurdle led Ihaka down to the dining room where the others were sitting at the long, polished wood table politely waiting for him to come back before they started their desserts. Spurdle paused in the doorway, waited till he had everyone's attention, then said loudly, 'Babe, there's a cop to see you,' adding, as if oblivious that Ihaka was right behind him: 'big bastard he is too.'

Having made his dramatic announcement, Spurdle sat down at the head of the table with his back to Ihaka and began a minute inspection of his dessert. Ihaka came into the dining room which was between the lounge and the kitchen; the lounge was on his right through open double doors and the doorway to the kitchen was on his left. An anguished Jody Spurdle sat bolt upright gaping at him from the far end of the table; a woman he didn't know was on the lounge side of the table looking queasy and shaking her head at the middle-aged man opposite her. He was clearly unhappy but there was something not quite right with his eyes so it was difficult to tell whether the focus of his displeasure was the woman, Ihaka or Spurdle, who was attempting to completely submerge his sticky toffee pudding in whipped cream.

'Evening,' said Ihaka ducking his head. 'Sorry to barge in but I wondered if I could have a quick word with you, Mrs Spurdle.'

'What about?' she stammered

'Well ...' said Ihaka, hesitating. 'It's to do with what we discussed the other day.'

Jody had gone quite pale. 'I don't know what you're talking about,' she said shakily. 'Please go away.'

Funke got up from his chair, walked around the table to stand in front of Ihaka, and drawled: 'Just what in the hell is going on here?'

Ihaka studied him with that look of barely concealed contempt which police officers automatically bestow on uppity members of the public. 'I was talking to Mrs Spurdle. I'm following up a matter she brought to our attention ...'

'She says that ain't so.'

Ihaka shrugged indifferently. 'That's understandable. It's a little embarrassing.'

Funke persisted. 'It must be pretty damn serious for you to come all the way out here at this hour.'

Ihaka ignored him. 'Mrs Spurdle, we talked to Leith Grills tonight ...'

'You use a fucking ouija board?' snapped Funke. He reached under his reefer jacket for the revolver which he had stuck in his belt at the small of his back, pulled it out and held it under Ihaka's chin.

'Do you know who I am, boy?' he said.

'Clint Eastwood's midget brother?'

Something's all-to-hell wrong here, thought Funke. *This asshole should be filling his pants instead of standing there cool as you please, giving me a fuck-you look.*

Out of the corner of his eye, Funke saw a black shape in the kitchen doorway a few metres to his right.

'Put the gun down,' said C.C. Hellicar firmly.

Funke kept the .38 a few centimetres from Ihaka's chin and turned his head slightly. A young woman was wrapped around the jamb of the door showing as little of herself as possible. She had an automatic on him, holding it very steady in both hands. Funke remembered that hot afternoon in 1962, the store on the back road down around Sierra Blanca and the white trash storekeeper who'd blown away Lyle Gorse. *She's pointing her piece just like that storekeeper,* he thought – *still as death itself. Something tells me this little gal ain't going to chew on it.*

'Where'd you spring from, honey?' asked Funke in his most laconic tone.

'Langley sent me.'

'Langley huh? Well I guess they didn't send you all the way down here to give me counselling.' Funke's eyes swung back to Ihaka. 'Looks like we got ourselves a Mexican stand ...'

Hellicar shot Funke in the exact centre of his right cheek. The bullet exited through his left cheek along with a fine hail of splintered teeth and gum, went through the open double doors and shattered the most valuable piece in Spurdle's Toby Jug collection before burying itself in the antique sideboard at the far end of the lounge. Funke spun around and fell face-first, losing hold of the .38. He lay on his front, groping blindly and feebly for the pistol. Holding the automatic pointed to the ceiling, Hellicar walked purposefully across to Funke and stood astride him. She extended her arms, took careful aim, and shot him twice in the back of the head.

In the echoing silence, Jody began to cry hysterically; Fleur Wolfgramm gripped the table with both hands and stared sightlessly at her untouched sticky toffee pudding while Bryce Spurdle goggled at Funke's body in drunken disbelief and reached for his wineglass with a trembling hand.

Satisfied that none of them posed a threat, Hellicar turned to Ihaka who hadn't moved anything except his eyeballs since Funke had pulled the gun.

'You okay?'

Ihaka nodded and took a very deep breath.

'You know, he hadn't cocked the .38; that made the shot a little safer.'

Ihaka forced a smile. 'I feel a lot better for knowing that.'

After 30 or so seconds, the frozen concentration began to recede from Hellicar's pale blue eyes and her mouth formed a lopsided, mirthless smile.

She hefted the automatic: 'You still want to take us to your beach house?'

Twenty-Three

The United States Government terminated its occasionally awkward 27-year association with Harold 'Buddy' Funke at precisely 9.53 p.m.

By 10 p.m. the back-up team had completely secured and sealed off the Spurdle property. At 10.17 p.m. four unmarked vehicles passed through the police roadblock and swept up the drive; a few minutes later, two of them swept back down the drive and headed into town. The first, a black Toyota Landcruiser four-wheel-drive fitted out as an ambulance, was driven by an armed constable; his passenger was a police pathologist and his cargo was a body bag containing former special agent Funke. While to the untrained eye the second car looked like an ordinary old Commodore, it was in fact a modified version from the Holden Special Vehicle facility in Notting Hill, Victoria: it had a 5.7-litre V8 engine, a top speed of 243 kph, could reach 100 kph from a standing start in 6.6 seconds and was by some distance the most sought-after car in the Auckland Central fleet. On this occasion it was being used to ferry an uncharacteristically subdued Detective Sergeant Tito Ihaka to his home in Sandringham and a characteristically enigmatic C.C. Hellicar to her city hotel.

The police contingent which remained was led by Detective Inspector Finbar McGrail whose first priority was to convince the Spurdles and Fleur Wolfgramm that it was really none of their business if Americans wanted to shoot one another in their dining room. It was a slow process: the trio were suffering varying degrees of shock and needed medical treatment and gentle handling. What with one thing and another, it wasn't until close to midnight that Wolfgramm mentioned the car out at the airport with two dead men in the boot. By the time the squad car from the Otahuhu police station got there, it was too late.

At five minutes to midnight, Derril Shine, 23, had driven his lime-green Toyota Starlet very slowly and with the head-lights switched off into the international terminal carpark. In the passenger seat was Apollo Laulau, a 21-year-old Fijian-Samoan whose main interest in life was collecting baseball caps. Both men were unemployed; while they were vaguely familiar with the concept of earning an honest liv-ing, neither of them had ever actually given it a try.

The pair had been drinking in the public bar of a Man-gere Bridge tavern. During a game of pool, an acquaintance had told Shine, who constantly advertised his availability for any criminal enterprise which didn't require seed money and didn't involve heavy-duty violence, that there was good money to be made supplying stolen cars to a second-hand car yard-cum-chop shop in Te Atatu. Shine had thought about this for a minute or two then left the bar and driven his Starlet to the airport. After checking the Arrivals board to see when the last flight of the night got in, he'd gone back to the tavern to discuss commission, preferred models and delivery procedure with his acquaintance and to enlist Laulau as his driver.

There were fewer than three dozen cars in the car park. After eliminating those with alarms or steering-wheel locks and models which weren't in demand, Shine chose the Holden Berlina parked on its own in the centre of the car park. He got a jack out of his boot, smashed the Berlina's passenger-door window, raised the bonnet and hot wired the engine. With Laulau following in the Starlet, Shine drove the Berlina to the house in Glen Innes where he'd lived by himself since his co-tenants had taken up residence in Mt Eden prison. Shine wasn't sure how long he'd be able to stay in the $200-a-week accommodation; it was really a question of when the penny dropped and the landlord realised he had neither the inclination nor the means to pay the rent.

Shine parked the Berlina out the back of the house and he and Laulau went inside for one last drink. What started as a celebratory Drambuie and beer chaser soon developed into a drinking race, the outcome of which was settled by Laulau's abrupt loss of consciousness. Shine went into the bathroom, induced a prodigious vomit by putting two heavily-nicotined fingers down his throat, and then collapsed on his bed.

He woke up at 10.25 the next morning. He didn't feel refreshed or alert or particularly well, so apart from the vile taste in his mouth, it was much like any other morning. It had been a good idea to make himself sick; next time he'd have to remember to clean his teeth afterwards. Laulau was still slumped on the couch, so Shine made himself a cup of tea and went outside to inspect his new car.

As he sat behind the steering wheel sipping his tea, it occured to him that there might be something in the boot worth stealing; he pulled the boot release lever and got out of the car. That was when he noticed the smell. *Fuck me, that's off*, he said to himself. *The coconut's probably shat himself.* When Shine lifted the boot lid, the smell, a greasy, noxious, choking blend of rotten fat and open drains, intensified dramatically. The stench and even more shocking sight caused him to gag shudderingly before he could slam the boot shut and reel away.

Trembling with nausea and anxiety, Shine sat on the back steps and reviewed his options. He could simply deliver the car and its contents as arranged, thus shifting the problem of the bodies in the boot onto someone else's plate; if he did that, the someone else would probably hunt him down and beat him paraplegic with a baseball bat. Or he could transfer the bodies from the boot to another location, then deliver the car; it took him less than five seconds to decide that, on the whole, he'd rather be beaten with a baseball bat. Or he could just pull the pin and dump the frigging thing.

It wasn't a difficult decision. When he'd reached it, Shine went inside and shook Laulau awake. The Fijian–Samoan, whose complexion had taken on an unhealthy and rather un-Polynesian grey sheen, groaned and sat up, rubbing his bleary eyes.

'Let's go, bro,' yelled Shine. 'Arse into gear time. I'm going to have a quick shower. Do something useful for once in your life and check out the boot on those wheels.'

Shine waited till his accomplice had shuffled outside before taking up a position at the kitchen window. It wasn't so much the amount Laulau threw up or the distance it travelled which impressed Shine; it was the fact that the yellow-green gushes continued even after he'd fallen into a dead faint.

They abandoned the Berlina an hour later behind the Remuera golf course in Abbott's Way, then Shine dropped Laulau off at his aunt's house in Mt Wellington. Laulau told his aunt he had food poisoning and went straight to bed.

*

The Ihaka family retreat was a rough-and-ready weatherboard pole-house at Tauranga Bay, on the south head of Whangaroa Harbour, about two hours' drive from Cape Reinga. It had three bedrooms and a small kitchen with a worn formica bench and a museum-piece fridge which heaved and rattled like a Sopwith Camel when Ihaka switched on the power. There was a large all-purpose room with a bare wooden floor and an assortment of battered and ill-matched furniture, cast-offs from several clan members' homes; sliding glass doors opened onto an enormous deck which extended to within a girlish stone's throw of high water mark.

It was a fine, warm, still day. Hellicar stood on the deck and surveyed the half-mile or so of empty yellow beach. The curtains were drawn in the other beach houses and the only sound was the soothing rinse of the incoming tide.

'Is it always like this?' she called to Ihaka who was putting food into the fridge. 'Not another soul in sight?'

He came out onto the deck and sucked down a lungful of sea air. 'Yeah pretty much, except for a couple of weeks at Christmas. Put it this way, I've never seen a Jap with a camera here.'

'You have a problem with the Japanese?'

Ihaka shook his head. 'I just don't want busloads of the little buggers clogging up my beach. Same goes for German backpackers, Aussies in campervans or, for that matter, dickheads from Auckland with their caravans and spastic kids.'

'Isn't that a tad selfish?' She waved an arm. 'I mean, there's not exactly a shortage of space.'

He squinted into the sun. 'Depends on your point of view,' he said. 'Some of us need more than others.'

Ihaka manhandled a 12-foot aluminium runabout with a 2-stroke seagull engine out of the kitset lock-up shed behind the beach house and they carried it down to the sea. They spent the afternoon puttering along the coast and in and out of little bays where Ihaka dived and foraged for shellfish. Hellicar sat in the bow sunning her long legs and wondering how much of Ihaka's catch was edible by normal people's standards.

The sun was losing its warmth and Ihaka was thinking of calling it a day when Hellicar suddenly took off her shorts and T-shirt and slipped over the side in her bra and underpants. She swam back and forth parallel to the shore, 100 metres at a time, for 20 minutes, and then effortlessly hauled herself back into the boat.

She had a body off a billboard and Ihaka took his time over passing her a towel. She snatched it from him, mimicking his bug-eyed stare.

'You look pretty fit,' he said hurriedly. 'I suppose you have to be?'

She smiled briefly and sardonically and wrapped the towel around herself. Then she leaned back and studied Ihaka who was sprawled in the stern, fishing rod in one hand and a can of beer in the other, wearing only football shorts.

She said: 'What about you – do you work out?'

Ihaka drained the can, crumpled it, resisted – only just – the urge to belch and said, 'Shit no.'

'You should.'

Ihaka got two cans out of the Esky and tossed one to her. 'What for? I was born fat; my father was fat; my uncles are fat; my grandfather was fat. It's a tribal tradition. You honkies don't understand such things.'

Hellicar nodded solemnly, as if acknowledging a wisdom deeper than hers. 'I didn't say you were fat. Right now you're just a big guy but if you're not careful, it'll sort of creep up on you. If that chest ever slips,' – she clicked her tongue – 'you'll be bumping into folks before you're close enough to recognise them. What'd your daddy die of?'

'Heart attack.'

'How old was he?'

'Fifty-one.'

'Doesn't that tell you something?'

'Yeah, it tells me that only fuckwits believe hard work never killed anyone. You want my opinion, a gym is a place where you pay for the privilege of breathing other people's body odour.'

Hellicar raised her eyebrows. 'How about jogging?'

'Last time I went for a run, a dog bit me.'

She blinked and fought back a giggle. 'Really? Where?'

'I was coming down Sandringham Road ...'

'I meant what part of your anatomy?'

'The backside, if you must know.' Unconvinced by her straight face, he added: 'It wasn't funny – it hurt like buggery. Plus, I couldn't crap normally for about three weeks.'

Hellicar's better judgement told her to change the subject but she couldn't help herself. 'Why was that?'

'The fucking mongrel took a dirty big piece out of my right cheek; I couldn't sit down so I had to get up on the dunny seat and perch there.'

In her mind's eye, Hellicar saw Ihaka squatting on a toilet seat like a sumo wrestler. She bit her lower lip quite hard and said, 'Forget I ever raised the subject. You're happy with the way you look, that's fine. What the hell's it got to do with me, right?'

Ihaka waited a minute then said, 'I don't suppose the sort of blokes you go for belong to Weight Watchers?'

She frowned. 'We seem to be at cross-purposes: I was talking about looking after your health.'

He nodded. 'The conversation's moved on; I'm just asking: what's your type?'

'I don't have a particular type,' she said firmly. 'You know, it's not like having a preference for a certain brand of toothpaste.'

Ihaka was expressionless but his brown eyes gleamed. 'Okay, well put it this way: what does the man in your life right now look like?'

'The invisible man,' she said with a finality which indicated the subject was closed. 'Now turn around.'

'Why?'

'Because I'm about to take off my wet things and put on my dry things.'

'We're a bit tight on room down this end. How about if I just close my eyes?'

'How about I put this bucket over your head?'

*

They went in, showered and changed. Ihaka prepared the shellfish, steaming the mussels and pounding the black, rubbery pawa tender before frying it with bacon. To Hellicar's surprise, she almost enjoyed it. He barbecued a couple of steaks which they ate out on the deck with a salad and a bottle of red wine.

A little later Hellicar brought out the ghetto-blaster she'd found in one of the bedrooms and put on a tape.

She stood with her hands on her hips. 'You want to dance?'

Ihaka stood up. 'I'm not exactly poetry in motion.'

Hellicar shrugged. 'So we won't win the steak knives.'

The song was a slow country lament. At first Ihaka kept a respectful distance but little by little the gap closed till they were close enough for him to feel her breath warm and ticklish on his neck. She put her head on his chest and began, very softly, to hum the song. At the exact moment that Ihaka realised he'd been unconsciously holding in his stomach, his mobile phone rang.

They stopped dancing and looked at one another.

She said, 'Wrong number, maybe?'

Ihaka tried to smile but didn't even get close. He went inside, snatched up the phone and snarled incoherently. Almost curtly and certainly without a hint of apology in his Ulster brogue, Finbar McGrail said: 'Whatever you're doing, Sergeant, stop doing it and get in here.'

Ihaka held the phone away from his ear and looked out to the deck where Hellicar stood with her arms folded and head slightly cocked, watching him. He drew a finger across his throat, then said to McGrail: 'What's happened?'

'We've just found Leith Grills in the boot of his car, shot twice in the chest at point-blank range. There was another body with him – European male as yet unidentified: about six foot two, 40-odd, a shotgun job; Funke's work, both of them. That's the first thing. The second thing is the cocaine we recovered from that boarding house turned out to be icing sugar. Just before we got there, a man and a woman posing as detectives showed up looking for Funke and talked their way into his room.'

Ihaka said flatly: 'Ricketts.'

'It looks like him from the description; it definitely feels like him.'

Ihaka chuckled bitterly. 'You've got to give the bastard marks for persistence. You hit his place yet?'

'We're just about to.'

'You won't find an aspirin. You won't find him either.'

'I share your conviction, Sergeant; that's why you're needed.'

'Okay. I'll be a few hours though – I'm up north.'

Ihaka ended the call and said quietly, 'Cunthooks.' He walked out on to the deck and said to Hellicar: 'We'll have to finish the dance some other time.'

She turned away to look out to sea and murmured, 'No time like the future.'

*

Ihaka was right in thinking that Duane Ricketts would have more sense than to hang around at home waiting for the police to show up. What Ricketts did do, just to keep abreast of developments, was ring his next-door neighbour, the 69-year-old pensioner, Clarrie Scudamore.

It was the first time they'd spoken for almost a year, since the night Ricketts had knocked on his neighbour's front door and asked if he could have a lemon from the abundant crop on the tree in Scudamore's back yard.

Scudamore had eyed him suspiciously: 'What for?'

'I'm making someone a gin and tonic and I'm clean out of them.'

If Ricketts had been aware that Scudamore, a Seventh Day Adventist, was almost fanatically anti-drink, he would've said something else. Then again, if he'd known that Scudamore was almost certainly the meanest person in Mt Roskill, a suburb where charity begins and ends at home, he wouldn't have bothered to ask; he would've simply vaulted the fence and taken a lemon off the tree.

Without really bothering to conceal the satisfaction it gave him, Scudamore had said 'Grow your own,' and shut the door.

When Ricketts rang at about 10 o'clock that Saturday night, Scudamore, his voice hovering uncertainly between curiosity and indignation, demanded to know what on earth was going on over there. At the other end of the line, Ricketts smiled to himself.

'What do you mean?'

'You know perfectly well what I mean; there are police everywhere – they've even got dogs. I think you owe me the courtesy of an explanation.'

Ricketts didn't feel he owed Scudamore the courtesy of an explanation or even courtesy for that matter, so he hung up in his ear and dialled Bryce Spurdle's number.

Spurdle had his feet up watching television. He stared balefully at the phone on the coffee table when it began to ring; eventually he decided that seeing everything that could go wrong had already done so, there was no reason not to answer it. He picked it up and said a guarded hello.

'Is that Bryce Spurdle?'

'Yeah.'

'This is Duane Ricketts. The name mean anything?'

'Nup.'

'I was the last person Dale Varty spoke to.'

'I'm happy for you.'

'That makes two of us: he told me where he hid that cocaine. I made the mistake of telling Jake Latimer. Does that name ring a bell?'

Spurdle sat up straight. 'Loud and fucking clear. That shitbag ...'

'Yeah, we'll get to him in a minute. The reason for the call is I was wondering if you're still interested in the dope? Because if you are, I can deliver.'

'You're full of shit, pal,' said Spurdle crisply.

'How's that?'

'You haven't bloody got it; the cops have.'

'All the cops've got is a lifetime's supply of icing sugar. You know where the coke was, right? An American guy called Funke got hold of it and brought it back here. He was staying at a boarding house in town; when he went out, I got into his room and did a swap.'

'When was this?' asked Spurdle, a note of cautious interest entering his voice.

'Last night.'

'What time last night?'

'Early on; about eight.'

'How much coke was there?'

'Nine and a half kilos in 19 bags. Funke must've had one with him.'

There was a long silence.

'Well?' said Ricketts eventually.

Spurdle grunted non-committally.

'As a matter of interest, why'd you think the cops had it?' asked Ricketts.

'Because Funke was round here last night giving me the same sales pitch. The cops showed up and blew him away, right in front of us. Fucking choice, eh? My wife's a nervous wreck.'

It was all the same to Ricketts whether Funke was in a hole or behind bars as long as he was out of circulation. 'So what about it – are you interested?'

'Depends on the price, doesn't it?' said Spurdle. 'It's going down by the hour; the heat's on big-time.'

Ricketts suggested a round million; Spurdle said piss off, there was no way in the fucking world he'd go over a hundred grand. Ricketts said okay, see you later and Spurdle back-tracked, saying hang on a minute, have you got a fucking plane to catch too? Eventually they reached agreement in principle on $450,000, Spurdle saying he wanted to sleep on it, think about whether he really wanted to go through with the deal.

You mean to check me out, thought Ricketts. After they'd arranged to talk again in the morning, Ricketts tossed in the sweetener: he told Spurdle where he could find Latimer.

Ricketts hung up and walked through to the living room of the house in Huapai owned by the Dutch screen-printer who was sitting cross-legged on the floor rolling a joint.

Ricketts watched him for a few seconds. 'Do you ever worry about what that stuff's doing to you?' he asked.

The Dutchman stroked his long beard and thought about it. 'Not for long,' he said eventually. 'I can never remember what I'm meant to be worrying about.'

Twenty-Four

Jake Latimer's friend Lenny had led a fairly pointless existence at the taxpayer's expense on two hectares just outside Whangarei since the day he'd stooped to pick up a ballpoint pen, with which he'd been making inane, semi-literate additions to a management memo on the staff noticeboard, and put his back out. The resultant discomfort – a conveniently imprecise measure of suffering – was his entry visa to the never-never land of accident compensation where time crawled by like a Moscow bread queue and with each month that passed, it got harder to find reasons for getting out of bed in the morning.

Not long after 9 o'clock on Sunday morning, Latimer rode his second-hand Harley Davidson 1200 Sportster down the drive from Lenny's weatherboard bungalow to the main road. He paused when he reached the road, put on his helmet, gave the machine a couple of wasteful but mildly arousing revs, then swung it to the left and roared off down Highway 14 towards Maungatapere. He didn't notice the white Toyota van parked on the verge a little way back up the road. Even if Latimer had noticed the van, he wouldn't have given it a second glance; as far as he was concerned, the whole point of having a Harley was that people – especially the sort of dildos who drove Toyota vans – looked at you, not the other way round.

The man sitting behind the wheel of the Toyota van was called Rowan Mayweed and no-one had ever accused him of being a dildo, at least not to his face, which was red and lumpy with mean eyes and a nose you could clear scrub with. For a second or two he thought about going after Latimer before deciding that by the time he got rolling, the prick would be halfway to Dargaville. He'll be back, Mayweed told himself; he lit his tenth cigarette of the morning and settled down to wait.

Mayweed was 47 years old and weighed 125 kilograms. He owned a takeaway in Whangarei which did a reasonable burger and excellent fish and chips. The fish was always snapper or terakihi and the chips were made on the premises from garden-fresh potatoes by a refugee from East Timor who found that peeling potatoes and cutting them into chips took just enough concentration to keep her mind off things she preferred not to think about. For all Mayweed cared, the takeaway could've served deep-fried penguin. He left his staff to run it as they saw fit; the only reason he'd bought the business in the first place was to enable him to launder money generated by his marijuana plantation in the Tangihua forest.

Mayweed was spending Sunday morning sitting in his van on the side of the Dargaville road because his old acquaintance Bryce Spurdle was paying him to. They went back to the early '70s when Mayweed had been a bouncer at an Auckland night spot where Spurdle staged rock concerts. The law of supply and demand had brought them together: whenever possible, Spurdle avoided doing his own dirty work; Mayweed, on the other hand, was only too happy to do his own and, for the right price, anyone else's.

Mayweed heard Latimer returning from his 50-minute spin before he saw him. He started the van and drove off the verge onto the road as the Harley Davidson zoomed over the hump 100 metres away and decelerated for the turn into Lenny's drive. Mayweed indicated that he was turning into the driveway as well; observing New Zealand's quirky rule of the road which gives right of way to the person making a right turn, he slowed to a halt to let Latimer go first.

As Latimer turned into the drive, Mayweed mashed his foot down on the accelerator. The van catapulted forward and rammed into the back of the motorbike. Latimer went over the handlebars like a human cannonball, did a ragged somersault, landed on the point of his right shoulder and slid up the gravel drive on his front. The Harley skidded away on its side in a shower of sparks, flipped and slammed into a tree, rupturing the fuel tank. There was a dull, thumping explosion and a column of bright orange flame leapt several metres into the air before dying down to little pockets of fire which licked at the charred and twisted metal.

Mayweed got out of the van and strolled up the drive towards Latimer who was staggering to his feet. His right arm hung uselessly and crimson grazes glistened through his torn leathers. Mayweed waited till Latimer had removed his helmet then said, 'Bryce Spurdle says g'day,' and punched him very hard in the mouth. Latimer fell over and Mayweed, who'd come prepared in heavy work boots, kicked whichever part of his anatomy Latimer was unable to shield with his functioning arm. After a dozen or so deliberate and percussive boots, Mayweed decided that if he kept it up for much longer, he'd either kill Latimer – and he certainly wasn't being paid enough to do that – or have a heart attack. He stopped kicking and bent over with his hands on his knees, gulping in air.

When Mayweed had got his breath back, he squatted on his haunches and said, 'All right twat-features, where's the money?'

Latimer's lips fluttered but all that emerged were a few little blood bubbles.

'The money you rooked Spurdle out of,' prompted Mayweed. 'Have you got it on you or is it up there in the house?'

Latimer groaned pitiably; unfortunately the only person who could hear him was Mayweed and he hadn't felt a flicker of pity towards anyone but himself since his voice broke.

Latimer's groans became an inaudible whisper. Mayweed hunched down and cocked an ear. 'Say again?'

'I spent it,' croaked Latimer. 'On the bike.'

Mayweed looked over his shoulder at the smouldering wreck and said, 'Oh fuck.'

*

Duane Ricketts got up late and went for a run. As often happens, the combination of fresh air and exercise cleared the head and sharpened the thought processes; by the time he got back to the Dutch screen-printer's house, having covered seven mostly flat kilometres in 37 minutes, he'd worked out what he had to do.

He showered, dressed and poached some eggs for himself and his host. At midday, as arranged, he rang a service station in Albany. Spurdle answered the phone.

'So, how'd I scrub up?' asked Ricketts.

'Eh?'

'That's what you've been doing, isn't it – checking up on me?'

'I made a couple of calls,' admitted Spurdle. 'I hear your name's getting some airplay down at Central; sounds like you're pulling a bit of heat.'

'Yeah, I heard the same thing,' said Ricketts nonchalantly. 'All the more reason to move quick. I take it we have a deal?'

'Looks like it. What've you got in mind?'

'The sooner the better as far as I'm concerned – like tonight.'

'That's as good a time as any, I suppose. Where?'

Here we go, thought Ricketts. 'What about Cornwall Park?'

'No way,' said Spurdle. 'It's too big and too dark – a recipe for a fuck-up. Besides, you wouldn't want to be wandering around in there in the middle of the night, would you? It'd be wall-to-wall perverts – sheep-shaggers, you name it; the place'd be crawling with them.'

'You got a better idea?'

'What about a movie theatre?'

'Oh, you want an audience, do you?' said Ricketts sarcastically. 'I thought the idea with drug deals was to keep them private. Shit, if you do it at the movies, someone gets a look at you when you buy your ticket, people notice you when you get up and walk out in the middle of the film. It's asking for trouble.'

They traded ideas for a few minutes; Spurdle's didn't get any better and Ricketts' were designed to be rejected. When he sensed that Spurdle had run out of suggestions and patience, he said: 'Well, what about Westhaven Marina? Sunday night: if we leave it late enough, the place'll be deserted but it's not like you're in the middle of nowhere. You got easy access, we can be in and out in a couple of minutes.'

Spurdle went for it.

'What time do you want to do it?' asked Ricketts. 'Midnight, one o'clock, later than that?'

'One o'clock'll do. How will I know you?'

'If the theory's right, we'll be the only people there, won't we? On that subject, let's be sure we understand each other: this do is by invitation only and the only people with invites are you and me, right?'

'Suits me.'

'I'll be driving an orange Toyota Corolla.'

'I'll bring the Merc – it's a 360, dark-green.'

'Yeah, why not? Tell the world crime does pay.'

Next Ricketts rang an old friend from his cricketing days who'd since made himself rich by writing stunningly simple-minded advertising jingles which burrowed into the subconscious like borer. Among the rewards he had to show for this curious knack was a two-million-dollar, three-storey apartment in Shelley Beach Road, Herne Bay, overlooking Westhaven Marina.

When the jingle wizard answered the phone, Ricketts offered him and his wife an all-expenses paid night at the Hotel du Vin.

'I don't think so, Ricketts. You wouldn't make an offer like that unless there was a truly evil catch.'

'There's no catch,' said Ricketts earnestly. 'Only thing is, it's got to be tonight.'

'That's it? Somehow I don't believe you, Ricketts; I can recognise a bribe when it's dangled in front of me. Just tell me what it is you're up to so I can marvel at your bare-faced cheek for a moment or two before I tell you to stick the Hotel du Vin up your pipe.'

'Trust me, I used to be a policeman. You might as well leave us a key though, just in case.'

In the following ten minutes Ricketts used every trick in the book, except telling the truth, to talk the advertising man round. In the end and despite his misgivings, the advertising man gave in, deciding – without being entirely sure why – that he wanted to stay on side with Ricketts.

When he got off the phone, Ricketts went through to the kitchen where the Dutch screen-printer was washing the breakfast dishes.

'Go easy on the weed today, eh?'

The screen-printer looked blankly at Ricketts through his granny glasses and waited for an explanation.

'I might get you to give me a hand tonight – nothing too demanding but I wouldn't want you to fall asleep on me.'

The Dutchman shrugged and looked at his watch. 'Sure. But that still leaves the afternoon.'

Ricketts showed his teeth in a grin which the screen-printer knew from experience and distrusted deeply: 'Did I forget to mention that we're having a visitor? There's a policeman I want you to invite out here for afternoon tea.'

*

At that moment the policeman in question, Detective Sergeant Tito Ihaka, was, for the second time in three days, hanging around in the international terminal at Auckland Airport waiting for C.C. Hellicar.

When she'd completed check-in for her flight to Los Angeles, Hellicar walked over to him. She produced a sheet of notepaper from her handbag and gave it to him.

'That's my daddy's address and phone number in Monroe, Georgia,' she said. 'You ever fixing to come to the States, doesn't matter what part, you get in touch with him, okay? He'll pass the message on. I figure the likelihood of me being sent down here again is next to zero but' – she hunched her shoulders – 'I'm due a right smart amount of vacation and they've got to let me take some sooner or later.' She tilted her head and looked at him, her pale blue eyes shining. 'How about it, Tito – you being able to see the future and all: do we ever get to finish that dance?'

Ihaka closed his eyes trance-like for a few seconds then nodded: 'Yep – what's more, we walk away with the steak knives.'

The smiles they exchanged were affectionate, knowing, wistful and perhaps also a little relieved.

'Okay,' she said briskly. 'We've both got to go. Give me some Southern sugar and be on your way.'

They kissed, an awkward, in between sort of kiss, half on the cheek, half on the lips. It was the kiss of a man and a woman who'd felt something happen between them, a moment electric with possibilities, but who recognised that the moment had passed and it was pointless to pretend otherwise.

She squeezed his hand. 'Go carefully now, you hear?'

'You too, Candice Clara.'

Ihaka turned and walked out of the terminal, as certain as he was of anything that he'd never set eyes on C.C. Hellicar again.

Twenty-Five

$\mathcal{B}$earing bad tidings is a thankless task, no matter how you go about it.

Members of the 'cruel to be kind' brigade believe in getting straight to the point and can be recommending a crematorium before the next of kin is sitting comfortably. Others prefer to break it gently and sidle up to the unwelcome news via the weather, the soaps and Andre Agassi's new haircut.

Rowan Mayweed tried a middle way when he rang Bryce Spurdle on Sunday afternoon – the old 'I've got good news and I've got bad news' approach. It didn't get him very far.

'Fucking what?' barked Spurdle. 'Rowan, I don't want to hear this shit. I feel like Rose Kennedy I've had that much fucking bad news lately; I'm up to here with it. All I wanted to hear from you is that you've done the business. Instead, I get this fuckhead good news, bad news routine.' He paused and released a deep, angry sigh. 'All right, let's have it,' he continued in a long-suffering voice, dragging out the words. 'Give us the bad news first.'

Mayweed, who was calling from his split-level brick house at Whangarei Heads, squirmed in his easy-chair thinking, *Fucking Bryce, he's going to make a meal of this.*

'I'll tell it to you as it happened,' said Mayweed, calculating that if he arranged the facts in chronological order, there was a slim chance that Spurdle would understand and be appeased. 'Latimer went out for a burn on his motorbike this morning. When he got back, I followed him into the driveway and shunted him right up the arse. He went for a row of shitcans; the bike hit a tree and boom, up in flames.'

Spurdle chuckled, a low, grimly satisfied noise from deep in his throat. Mayweed was encouraged.

'He wasn't looking too flash by this stage, your little mate; he's got a busted arm for sure and I reckon they'll be digging gravel out of him for a week. Before he'd worked out which way was up, I decked him, then slippered the crap out of him. Tell you what mate, you got your money's worth; I'd lay odds the bastard's in plaster from his gob to his knob.'

'Well Rowan, that all sounds tickety-boo,' said Spurdle with transparently false good humour. 'Pity you have to spoil it. So what's the bad news?'

'The bad news is he's already spent your money.'

'Spent it?' screeched Spurdle. 'How the cunting hell does a turd like that blow twelve and a half grand in a couple of days?'

'He bought the bike,' said Mayweed wearily.

'He bought the bike,' repeated Spurdle in a voice filled with wonder. 'Would that happen to be the same bike you shunted into a tree and blew to shit?'

'Yeah, the same fucking bike. I dragged the prick up to the house and made him show me the paperwork. He got it last Friday from a place in New North Road, specialises in second-hand Harleys. Cost him thirteen grand.'

After that, things went rapidly downhill. Spurdle said you'd have to be thick as pigshit, Christ, a little arsewipe like Latimer with a Harley-Davidson, it was fucking obvious what he'd done with the money. Mayweed retorted that it was bloody easy to be wise after the event and if that was the thanks he got for putting himself out to do a bloke a favour, next time he wouldn't bother. Spurdle came back with favour my fuzzy arse, it was business and Mayweed hadn't kept his side of the bargain so if he thought he was going to get paid, he better think again and what's more … it was around about there that Mayweed told him to go fuck himself and hung up.

*

After he'd put down the receiver, Spurdle looked at himself in the mirror behind the bar and said, 'Tithead.'

The bike going up in smoke wasn't such a big deal. He knew a guy in the insurance game who'd dummy up a false claim for a few hundred bucks; all he needed to do was get a tow-truck operator from Whangarei to pick up what was left of the bloody thing and talk the bloke in the bike shop into giving him a copy of the receipt. There wasn't any point in getting shitty with Mayweed but you just can't help yourself sometimes, can you? No point in ringing him back either: when Rowan gets that beak of his out of joint, it stays that way for a fortnight.

And a fortnight was no good to Spurdle; he needed Mayweed that night.

Half an hour later Spurdle was still sitting at the bar in his den cursing his quick temper and racking his brains trying to think of someone who could step into Mayweed's shoes when his wife walked into the room.

It wasn't the first time Spurdle had seen Jody looking ropey – exhausted or ill or hungover, or even, on a couple of memorable occasions, all three – but he'd never seen her in this state. Her face was drawn and blotchy and her unwashed hair hung in oily tangles; her shoulders sagged, her hands plucked at the belt of her white towelling robe and her red-rimmed eyes were darting around like a frightened bird's.

'Hi,' she said in a dull voice. 'I heard you on the phone a while ago, shouting. Anything wrong?'

'Shit, I didn't wake you up, did I?'

She shook her head and flopped down on a sofa. 'I've been awake for ages.' She yawned nervously and took a deep breath, steeling herself: 'I owe you an explanation. You must be wondering what the hell that was all about the other night with the cop.'

Spurdle shrugged. 'Oh well …'

'I made a really, really terrible mistake,' said Jody, her voice quavering on the edge of tears.

He joined her on the sofa. 'Hon, this'll keep. Why not leave it till you're feeling better, eh?'

Her lower lip wobbled and her breathing became jerky. 'I want to get it off my chest.' She looked away, sniffing. 'What he was talking about, Ihaka, was me going to the police because I thought you'd hired Leith Grills to kill me.'

Jesus, thought Spurdle, *it's all got too much for the poor little bitch. The men in white coats will be here any minute; I mean, look at her, opening and closing her trap like a goldfish and eyeballing me as if I've sprouted tusks.*

'Did you hear what I said, Bryce?'

He patted her hand. 'Well, I heard you say something, sweetie …'

'I picked up the phone one day when you were talking to Grills. The guy totally freaked me out anyway and when you said you'd changed your mind and wanted him to get onto the wife … I just got it into my head that's what you meant.'

'I'm missing something here,' he said warily. 'No matter how much Grills gave you the creeps or what you heard me say to him, I don't see how you got from there to the idea I was … up to something like that. Didn't you ever just sit down and ask yourself why? Why would I want to do it?'

She sobbed and buried her face in her hands. 'I thought you must've found out I was having an affair.'

He frowned at his wife's bobbing head. 'An affair? Who with?'

'A guy called Troy Goatley,' she said in a strangled voice.

Spurdle went over to the bar, opened a beer and poured a little cognac into a liqueur glass. 'Who's he?'

'I met him at the gym in Takapuna – he runs the weights room.'

'How long have you and him been …'

'Since late last year. It's finished, I broke it off.'

Spurdle drank his beer and idly wondered how Jody would react if he told her that the private detective who'd been keeping an eye on her on and off since before they were even married had reported the affair several months ago; or that in the safe under the floorboards in the wine cellar there was a large manila envelope containing audiotaped and photographic evidence of her infidelity; or that some nights when she went to bed early, he'd get the envelope out and … Yes well, he said to himself, I think it's safe to assume she'd react negatively; extremely fucking negatively; so fucking negatively that he might go into the kitchen tomorrow morning and find the cat having his dick for breakfast.

He went back to the sofa, gave her the drink, and draped a protective arm around her shoulders. 'Look, baby, we've been through a fair bit in the last few days. As far as I'm concerned, whatever's happened has happened – it's over and done with. I think we ought to just get on with life, you know, start again with a clean slate. What do you say?'

She put her face against his chest and snuffled wetly on his shirt; he rested his chin on the top of her head and patted her back, making soothing noises. They stayed like that until Jody had cried herself out, which took a few minutes. Well before the tears dried up, her husband's eyes opened wide and then narrowed to a thoughtful squint. He was having an idea.

At 9 o'clock that night Jody, more like her old self, and Bryce were curled up on the sofa in the TV room watching a movie; on the low table in front of them were the remnants of a home-delivered pizza and an almost empty bottle of wine. When the ads came on, Spurdle disengaged his arm, looked at his watch and said by the way, he had to pop out for a while later on.

Jody's head swivelled. 'What for?'

He winked at her. 'To see a man about a dog.'

'No, come on Bryce,' she began before noticing his foxy, guarded expression. 'It's those drugs again, right?'

He nodded.

'Why don't you just give it away, babe? I mean, God, are they really worth all the aggro?'

Spurdle leaned towards her, his face set and serious. 'I've been waiting more than ten years to get my hands on this stuff. Remember I told you how Varty brought it over from Australia then did the dirty on me? Ever since then, it's been there at the back of my mind, nagging away at me, but there wasn't a bloody thing I could do about it; only Varty knew where it was and he was in the clink in Thailand.' His voice got harsh. 'Well now it's out there, up for grabs. Each time I get close, there's some sort of last minute fuck-up; each time that happens, it makes me more determined that if any bastard's going to end up with it, it's going to be me.'

'Okay, okay,' she said, taken aback by his intensity. 'I didn't realise it meant that much to you. Who's this guy you're meeting?'

'Ricketts his name is; he was in that Thai jail with Varty.'

'Can you trust him?'

He sniggered. 'Babe, this is dope – you can't trust anyone.'

'Will it be dangerous?'

Spurdle shrugged. 'No reason it should be. I ran a check on this guy and he doesn't sound like he's a hard man – he's small time, a bit of an amateur. But you never know:

as I said, it's the dope business … and yeah, I would feel better if I had someone with me, preferably someone built like a brick shithouse. Unfortunately poor old Leith can't make it.'

Jody swallowed hard. 'There must be someone else.'

'I had a guy in Whangarei in mind – that's who I was talking to this afternoon.' He smiled wanly. 'The negotiations broke down.'

'Bryce, I'm sorry but I've got to say, I think it's just crazy for you to go by yourself …'

'Well that's fine honey, but this isn't a lot of people's idea of fun. Besides, you're talking about a guy who looks the part and can handle himself.' Then, tentatively. 'I can only think of one possibility and that's pretty bloody remote.'

'Who's that?'

'Goatley.'

Jody stared at him, open-mouthed.

'You were saying he runs the weights room. I imagine he'd be a pretty well-built sort of a bloke?'

She nodded slowly. 'He's big all right and, you know, seriously into that scene.'

'What do you reckon – think you could talk him into it?'

Jody Spurdle held her husband's gaze for the first time that day. 'I think so.'

*

At 12.50 a.m., Monday, Spurdle drove his dark-green Mercedes 360 down Curran Street, under the harbour bridge and into the Westhaven Marina. He cruised very slowly past the yacht club buildings down to the parking area on the end of the seawall. To his left, Waitemata Harbour shifted and rustled like a great, dark duvet over a restless sleeper; to his right, row upon row of yachts and launches sat in their moorings like ducks, their lines clinking and creaking in the breeze. There were no cars and no lights showing in any of the buildings. The car park was slick from recent rain and the low, starless sky threatened more before the night was much older. Spurdle turned and circled back to the foot of the harbour bridge. Satisfied by what he'd seen and hadn't seen on the slow tour, he drove back to the far end of the seawall and turned off the engine.

A couple of minutes passed. Troy Goatley, who lay cramped and foetal on the back seat, deferentially broke the silence. 'Jody – Mrs Spurdle – wasn't too specific about exactly what it is you want me to do.'

'Just look mean,' said Spurdle staring straight ahead. 'And if I tell you to do something, don't ask questions, just do it, all right?' Headlights came around the harbour's edge and up past the yacht clubs. 'Here he is. Stay put until I give you the word.'

Spurdle got out of the car leaving the door open. He zipped his brown leather jacket up to the throat and hunched his shoulders against the chill. The Toyota stopped a few metres away; the lights and engine were switched off. Ricketts, wearing a windcheater and jeans, got out of the car.

He said, 'Yo ho ho and a bag of cocaine.'

Spurdle, who didn't seem to think it was the time or place for levity, was curt. 'Let's see it.'

Ricketts reached into his car and brought out a sports bag. He put it on the ground, unzipped it, and held up a plastic bag of white powder for Spurdle's inspection.

'Show me yours,' said Ricketts.

Spurdle smiled unpleasantly and called over his shoulder: 'Troy, bring out that suitcase, would you?'

The back door of the Mercedes opened and Goatley extricated himself. He was a head taller than Ricketts; pectorals

like hubcaps swelled out of the low-cut singlet he wore under an unbuttoned denim jacket and his jeans were stretched
taut over slab-like thighs. Moving with a tight-buttocked
body-builder's strut, he went and stood, glowering, beside
Spurdle.

'This is Troy,' said Spurdle. 'He can benchpress 170 kilos.'

Ricketts raised his eyebrows. 'Who counts for him? This
is out of order, Spurdle. It was meant to be just you and me,
remember?'

Spurdle's unpleasant smile grew wider. 'I'm scared of the
dark. Troy, search him and the car.'

Goatley walked across and glared down at Ricketts who
shrugged and held out his arms. Goatley patted him down
and then searched the car, boot and interior. He backed out
of the car dangling a pair of binoculars.

'Nothing much in here except these, Mr Spurdle.'

'Okay. Bring me the bag.'

Goatley dumped the binoculars on the driver's seat and
took the sports bag to Spurdle. He produced a Swiss army
knife from the pocket of his leather jacket, slit open one of
the plastic bags and dabbed some white powder on his
tongue.

He winked at Goatley. 'The real thing, as they say.'

He zipped up the bag and put it in his car. 'You know,
Ricketts,' he said putting on a reflective air, 'it seems to me
there's something not quite right about all this. I mean, a man
would have to be a major dipstick to pay 450 grand for something that belongs to him, don't you reckon?'

Ricketts shook his head. 'Forget it, Spurdle. I don't give
a shit about the history of it. I'm selling, you're buying, we
agreed a price. End of story.'

Spurdle's smirk faded. 'Yeah, end of story's right.' He
knelt, flipped open the suitcase and began taking out brick-
sized wads of bank notes which he tossed one by one

to Ricketts. 'How many's that – six? That's over 20 grand; take it and be fucking grateful. Now piss off before I change my mind and get Troy to chuck you in the tide without a cent.'

Ricketts dropped the money on the driver's seat of his car and picked up the binoculars. He said 'catch' and lobbed them to Spurdle.

'See that place up there with all its lights on?' He pointed across the rows of boats to the cliff overlooking the approach to the harbour bridge and the marina. 'Take a close look.'

Instantly suspicious, Spurdle's eyes flicked from Ricketts to the lit-up building and back to Ricketts. Then he used the binoculars. The building was a three-storey apartment which blazed with light against the dark background. A wild, piratical figure stood on the balcony in front of the huge top-floor window. He had a bushy, nipple-length beard and wore John Lennon spectacles, a camouflage jacket and a red bandana on his head. He looked to Spurdle like one of those psycho gun-nuts, the sort who subscribe to *Soldier of Fortune* magazine and either join the French Foreign Legion or go down to the local shopping centre and shoot anyone with ginger hair and freckles. The fact that he was examining Spurdle through telescopic sights attached to a rifle contributed powerfully to this impression.

Spurdle lowered the binoculars, noticing that Ricketts had switched on his headlights, illuminating him and Goatley in the beam.

'There's a guy up there with a gun,' he said as if uncertain whether to believe the evidence of his own eyes.

Ricketts nodded. 'Yep, a friend of mine. He's a professional hunter,' he added helpfully. 'He's got a night-vision scope and in case you're wondering about the range of that rifle, he was telling me before he could pick off a windsurfer coming round North Head from up there. He could drop you and that overgrown mongol like sacks of shit.' He paused to let the threat sink in. 'You're going to cough up, Spurdle, to the dollar. You can hand it over, or I guess I'll just have to step over your corpse and help myself. Up to you.'

Goatley took the binoculars from Spurdle and had a look for himself. He said, 'Mr Spurdle, maybe you should ...'

'Shut up and get in the car,' snapped Spurdle.

Goatley put the binoculars on the ground and got into the car. Ricketts told Spurdle to slide the suitcase over to him. He quickly checked the contents then gave Spurdle a pleasant nod. 'Let's do this again some time.'

Spurdle got into the Mercedes and started the engine. As he pulled away, he lowered the window. 'You think you're fucking smart, don't you?' he said, his mouth twisting with pique. 'Just remember this, little man – it's not over till I say so.'

He nudged the accelerator and the Mercedes surged forward, hissing across the wet tarmac. Ricketts watched him go and said softly, 'Dale Varty sends his best.'

Coming out of Westhaven up the hill into Shelley Beach Road, Spurdle found his way blocked by three police cars parked across the road in a U formation. Before he could reverse, a fourth unmarked car pulled away from the kerb and stopped right behind him. Detective Sergeant Tito Ihaka got out of it as policemen converged on the Mercedes from both sides of the road.

Ihaka looked in the driver's window and said cheerfully, 'What are you doing out and about at this time of night, Mr Spurdle? You should be home, tucked up in bed with that spunky little wife of yours.'

When the police found the cocaine and Ihaka told Spurdle and Goatley they'd have to come down to Central and play 20 questions, Spurdle exploded saying it was a set-up, the dope wasn't his, it belonged to this cunt Ricketts who'd still be down in the marina, he was the one they wanted. Ihaka smiled enigmatically, shepherded him into the back seat of a police car, and climbed in beside him.

As the car moved away, Ihaka turned to Spurdle and flashed a grin of pure, cold malice. 'I'll let you into a little secret, snotball,' he said. 'Ricketts is one of us.'

Twenty-Six

Fingerprints taken from the unknown dead man, shoe-horned along with the also-dead Leith Grills into the boot of the latter's car, matched those of Clive Anthony Nigel Balfour, who in August 1976 had been convicted of robbery with violence. The then-22-year-old's crime spree had begun on a Sunday evening at the White Lady pie cart in Newmarket, taken in a couple of service stations, a take-away and a dairy, and culminated the following Thursday afternoon in the Royal Oak branch of the Auckland Savings Bank.

Balfour's *modus operandi* involved a stocking mask, a line of banter which, while glib, was nonetheless appreciated by his victims, who took it as a sign that he didn't really want to shoot them and wouldn't do so unless he absolutely had to, and an imitation Colt .45 Peacemaker which his grandfather had given him for his eleventh birthday. Clive Balfour senior, a prosperous car dealer, had bought it at the Neiman-Marcus department store in Dallas and it was about as realistic as toy guns get, 700 grams of die-cast, steel-zinc alloy. However, it wasn't realistic enough to fool a firearms buff like Roy Codd, who happened to be in the bank when Balfour entered wearing his stocking mask, brandishing his toy gun and telling the bank staff that if they didn't hand over a great deal of money, he'd have to come back next week.

Codd detached himself from the queue and confronted Balfour. 'That's not a real gun,' he said in a very loud voice.

Balfour looked puzzled and twisted the toy gun in his hand, examining it from several angles. 'Are you sure?' he said dubiously.

'I've been a gun collector for 20 years,' sneered Codd. 'I know a fake when I see it.'

Balfour shrugged. 'Okay, let's see.'

He placed the muzzle against the prominent cleft in Codd's chin and thumbed back the hammer. As sure of himself as he was, Codd couldn't help flinching and clamping his eyes shut. Balfour flipped the gun in the air, caught it by the barrel and chopped the butt down on Codd's receding hairline. The firearms buff folded up like a deckchair, rivulets of blood streaming from his split scalp to form intricate patterns on his face. Balfour looked around and tersely enquired if anyone else wanted to make fun of his gun.

That morning Balfour had held up a dairy in Remuera. Although he'd worn the stocking mask, the owner of the dairy had recognised him, which wasn't really surprising seeing the Balfour family home was just around the corner and young Clive had been coming into the shop at least once a week for a decade, buying soft drinks and frozen buzz bars in summer and hot pies in winter, and shoplifting girlie magazines all year round. The dairy owner had long since tumbled to the shoplifting but turned a blind eye. He did so partly because the Balfours were rich, important and good customers and partly because the Balfour kid was different: weird, disturbed, call it what you like, the guy was a loose unit. In fact, if the stories were anything to go by, the wrong side of Clive Balfour was one of the more dangerous parts of town. Better a few copies of *Men Only* and *Playboy* taking a walk, felt the dairy owner, than a Molotov cocktail through the shop window or getting home to find Maxie the Scotch terrier nailed to the front door.

The disturbing stories which circulated about Clive Balfour dated back to his expulsion a few years earlier from Prince Albert College, the posh private school for boys in Meadowbank. He'd set fire to a prefabricated office used by a biology teacher with a reputation for being swift to send for the cane and extremely methodical when it arrived. The teacher wasn't in his office at the time but a dozen or so cartons containing the fruits of two years' research towards a doctorate were. Balfour's arson earned him a suspension, the headmaster choosing to believe his excuse that it was a practical joke which had got out of hand even though the facts cried out for a less charitable interpretation. Cynics suggested that Grandfather Balfour's generous donation to the college building fund was coincidental only in the sense of timing.

The incident which caused his expulsion took place a few months later during the college's annual cadet training week when the boys dressed up in heavy black boots and khaki serge uniforms which chafed like sandpaper and spent the hottest three or four hours of the day drilling on the parade ground. During a lull in the square-bashing, Corporal Balfour and his platoon were sent to the firing range to waste ammunition and be bawled at by a firearms instructor from the Papakura Military Camp.

Eventually Balfour grew tired of the abuse. He pointed his loaded .22 rifle at the instructor and told him that if he didn't shut up, he'd shoot him; when the instructor shut up, Balfour told him that if he didn't apologise to the whole platoon, he'd shoot him; when the instructor apologised, Balfour told him that if he didn't strip naked and crawl up the drive, through the school gates and all the way back to Papakura, he'd shoot him. The instructor stripped off and started crawling. It was never fully established whether Balfour had taken into account the fact that, en route to the school gates, the instructor would crawl past two matrons' flats, the chapel, the staff common room and the playing fields where 600 boys were being trained for the last war.

Armed robbery was rather more serious than shoplifting so the dairy owner rang the police, who were waiting for

Balfour when he returned to his parents' house after the bank job. He was tried and convicted; before sentencing, the magistrate called for a psychiatric evaluation which duly pronounced Clive Balfour schizophrenic. He was thereupon bunged into Kingseat Hospital and largely forgotten about.

*

On Sunday afternoon Balfour's parents were tracked down to their retirement home at Algies Bay; that evening they drove to Auckland to identify the corpse. Not that there was much doubt about it, especially after Balfour's Honda Civic had been found parked behind the church hall, two blocks from Manacle Grange.

Detective Inspector Finbar McGrail was keen to trace Balfour's route from Kingseat Hospital to the boot of Grills' Holden Berlina. Balfour's parents told him that Clive had responded to treatment and, after leaving hospital in mid-1979, had worked for a couple of years on a South Island high-country farm. He'd suffered some sort of relapse and had to come back to Auckland; at the end of 1983 he'd gone overseas, working firstly on a cattle station in Australia's Northern Territory and then on ranches in Zimbabwe and Kenya. He'd returned to Auckland in 1992 and bought a cottage in Parnell and a farmlet at Clevedon with money left to him by his grandfather; since then he'd divided his time, as the glossy magazines say, between the two properties.

His parents admitted that, living up at Algies Bay as they did, they hadn't seen a lot of him and knew next to nothing about the company he kept, not that he'd ever kept much. Balfour, it seemed, had always been a loner and living on large, isolated farming properties had made him even more solitary. As far as they were aware, he hadn't been in trouble with the law since 1976, he wasn't a drug user, and had no connection with Manacle Grange.

McGrail didn't for a moment doubt that, by their lights, Mr and Mrs Balfour had been caring parents to their only child; he also suspected that, deep down, they'd always feared he'd come to a sad or bad end. If that was so, he reflected lugubriously, Clive Balfour had died up to his parents' expectations.

Fleur Wolfgramm had testified that Balfour had been after Varty's cocaine. The question was how had he known where to look? McGrail hoped to find the answer in Balfour's Parnell cottage.

*

The police search team arrived at the two-bedroom cottage in Bath Street at 2.15 on Monday afternoon. It was sparsely furnished, almost monkish, and spotlessly clean.

'It's odd, this,' mused McGrail to Senior Sergeant Ted Worsp, a veteran cop who'd been added to the investigation because he'd arrested Balfour in 1976 and was therefore assumed to possess some insight into the dead man; thus far he'd kept it to himself. 'This could be a motel; it doesn't tell you a thing about the man. People who live on their own usually go the other way – they go overboard putting their personal stamp on the place.'

A few minutes later Worsp was in the guest bedroom, which contained a bed and a mattress, an empty wardrobe, an empty chest of drawers and the cheap rug on which he was standing.

'Fucking waste of time, this,' he grumbled to Constable Johan Van Roon. 'Doesn't look like he even lived here. What about the place out at Clevedon?'

Van Roon shook his head. 'It's just a hut apparently. They found sweet FA there.'

The floorboards creaked beneath Worsp as he turned to leave the room. Given his considerable weight, this in itself wasn't unusual but the creak was loud enough to make him lurch backwards. As he did so, he felt the floor sag alarmingly.

'Bloody hell, this floor's a bit dodgy,' said Worsp. 'Watch this.'

Worsp bent at the knees and heaved his bulk a couple of centimetres off the ground. When he came down, there was a sharp, splintering crack and the floor gave way. Worsp continued to travel south, plunging straight through the floorboards and disappearing from view. It transpired that he'd conducted his little demonstration on the trapdoor to a cellar which Balfour obviously found more congenial for everyday living than the cottage's above-ground rooms. The cellar had a metal-framed camp-bed and a sleeping bag, an old armchair, a small table and a chair, a mini-fridge filled with bottles of Fanta and tubes of luncheon sausage, piles of newspapers and periodicals ranging from the learned to the juvenile, and a bookcase. Among the authors represented on its shelves were L. Ron Hubbard, Erik Von Daniken, Janet Frame, William Burroughs, James Ellroy, Roald Dahl, Aleister Crowley, Laurens van der Post and Barry Crump.

On the table was a scrapbook containing newspaper articles about the deaths of Al Grills and Bart Clegg and twelve 94-leaf hardback A4 notebooks filled with spidery, illegible scrawl. Sitting on top of the bookcase was a champagne flute which, to the teetotal McGrail's inexpert eye, looked very much like the one Clegg had been drinking from just before someone jammed him under the seat in his spa pool and left him to simmer.

*

Two days later, on Wednesday, 27 April, Rayleen Crouch returned to her Grey Lynn villa after a hard day's social work to find McGrail and Detective Sergeant Tito Ihaka waiting for her. McGrail introduced himself and said that if she had a few minutes, there were a couple of loose ends he'd like to tie up; she said that was the best thing to do with loose ends and invited them in for a cup of tea.

While she made the tea, Ihaka leaned against the wall looking mildly curious. McGrail sat at the table in the kitchen-cum-dining room and did the talking.

'Ms Crouch, do you know a man named Clive Balfour?'

She screwed up her face. 'Rings a bell ...'

'Balfour suffered from a psychiatric disorder; he was in Kingseat during the late '70s and had ongoing counselling after his release. I saw your name on a document and got the impression that he'd been – I'm not sure what the term is in your field – a patient? of yours.'

'A client – we call them clients. Yes, I remember him now. God, it seems like a lifetime ago; that's social work for you – time flies when you're having fun. He was diagnosed schizophrenic, wasn't he? I seem to recall he wasn't too bad as those cases go. I mean, he had his moments, sure, but he was quite rational and socially capable most of the time. What about him?'

'He's dead, I'm afraid. The American, Funke, shot him.'

'What?' gasped Crouch. 'What's going on? Last I heard, someone had shot Funke.'

McGrail's brows beetled. 'Heard from whom, as a matter of interest?'

'My daughter,' she said defensively.

'Of course – and she would've heard it from Ricketts; their alliance had slipped my mind.'

'Where on earth did Balfour run into Funke?' asked Crouch.

'Their paths crossed last Thursday night at Manacle Grange, which is really why we're here. You see, Ms Crouch, so far we've found just the one link connecting Balfour to your ex-husband's treasure trove, which of course was the reason for him being at Manacle.' McGrail's lips formed a tentative, slightly apologetic smile. 'That connection is your good self.'

'I'm sorry,' she said with a frown. 'I'm not sure what you're getting at.'

'Well it's quite simple: only a handful of people, of whom you were one, knew prior to last Thursday night where the cocaine was. As far as we know, you're the only member of that select group, if not the only person involved in this whole business, who knew Balfour.' McGrail smiled thinly again but this time without a hint of an apology. 'So we were wondering if you sent him to Manacle Grange.'

She paused in the act of pouring boiling water into a teapot, glanced at McGrail, and then re-focused on pouring. 'That's pretty off-the-wall, Inspector,' she said casually. 'I've had nothing to do with Balfour for at least ten years. More to the point, why would I do that? How do you have your tea by the way?'

'Black for me, thank you; milk and one sugar for the sergeant ...'

Ihaka spoke for the first time. 'That's two sugars.'

Ihaka's request seemed to startle Crouch and she dropped a teaspoon with a clatter. She put the three mugs, teapot, milk, sugar and teaspoons on a tray and carried it over to the table. When she'd served the tea, she took her mug and retreated to a bar-stool at the kitchen bench.

'Well, we have a genuine mystery on our hands,' said McGrail philosophically. 'Who or what led Balfour to Manacle Grange? We may never know.' He sipped his tea. 'There's an intriguing sidelight to all of this which may interest you. Balfour had a .22 rifle which we've traced back to a man named Al Grills. Does he ring a bell?'

Crouch was watching McGrail closely, even intently. She nodded.

'So here's another riddle. How did Balfour come by a rifle last seen in the possession of a man whom your ex-husband was assumed to've killed in a squabble over the cocaine. If you think about it,' – McGrail raised his eyebrows as if bemused at the direction this line of thought was taking him – 'there was a connection between you, Balfour and the drugs back in 1983 just as there is now.'

Crouch, who appeared to be thinking about it quite seriously, said nothing.

'October 1983 to be exact,' said McGrail. 'You were seeing Balfour in a counselling capacity at that time, I believe?'

'What other capacity is there, Inspector?' she said with a strange, almost coy smile. 'I'd have to check but it sounds right; it was round about then.'

McGrail studied her thoughtfully for a few seconds. 'Did you know Bart Clegg, Ms Crouch?'

The sudden change of tack took her by surprise. 'Well, yes,' she stammered. 'Vaguely. Only through Dale – he was Dale's lawyer. I didn't know him well.'

'Back in October 1983, did Clegg warn you that your ex-husband was sailing into an ambush?'

Crouch looked confused. 'I'm sorry, I … no, he didn't.'

'We have evidence that Clegg knew that Bryce Spurdle and his man Grills planned to double-cross Varty once the cocaine was landed,' said McGrail deliberately. 'Did Clegg pass that information on to you?'

Crouch sat utterly still, staring at McGrail. 'I told you,' she said in a low voice. 'No, he didn't.'

McGrail continued as if he hadn't heard her. 'I think what happened was this: Clegg told you that Varty was in for it as soon as the drugs were ashore. By then Varty was halfway across the Tasman where you couldn't get in touch with him.

So you talked Balfour into going down to Otama; I imagine he thought it'd be a great adventure – he seemed to have a taste for that sort of thing. Unfortunately he hit Grills a little harder than was necessary and Grills died. Isn't that what happened, Ms Crouch?'

'I'm a bit hazy on the law,' she said carefully, 'but it sounds like you're asking me to admit to being an accessory to manslaughter.'

'Maybe I am,' said McGrail as if the thought hadn't occurred to him. 'But even if we pursued it, you'd have to entrust your defence to a spectacularly incompetent lawyer to run any risk of being convicted.'

'I don't think that's quite as hard as you make it sound, Inspector. Anyway, it's certainly not a risk I'm inclined to take.'

McGrail smiled benignly. 'Fair enough. Let me ask you this, Ms Crouch: how did you feel when you discovered that what Balfour had brought back from Otama was icing sugar, not cocaine?'

Crouch's face went stiff. She took her mug over to the sink and rinsed it out. Without looking at McGrail she said, 'If you're going to ask questions like that, I think I should have a lawyer present – even a spectacularly incompetent one.'

McGrail finished his tea and stood up. 'Next time perhaps; the sergeant and I have to run along. Have you met Ricketts, by the way? You should – he tells an interesting story. I suppose retells would be more accurate, seeing it's what your ex-husband told him very shortly before he died. Varty told Ricketts that the fellow – let's call him Balfour – who popped up out of nowhere and donged Grills, made no bones about the fact that he'd come to get the cocaine.' McGrail paused. 'Or that his instructions were to allow Varty to be murdered.'

The hostile glow in Crouch's eyes eventually faded, giving way to a heavy-lidded indifference which McGrail admired but didn't believe. She got a bottle of Chivas Regal out of the cupboard above the sink and poured some into a tumbler. 'Balfour – if it was him – was mad,' she said coldly. 'He could – and did – say all sorts of things. Most of it was meaningless, deluded crap.'

'You're probably right.' McGrail's tone was as innocently conversational as if they were exchanging gardening stories. 'Still, it's hard to feel sorry for him after what he did to poor old Clegg. You know, after he'd drowned Clegg in his bubble bath, Balfour took a champagne glass away, obviously because it had fingerprints on it. For some bizarre reason – well, as you were just saying, the man wasn't all there – he kept the glass; we found it in the cellar under his house. So now we're running round taking people's fingerprints. I suppose we should take yours.'

Despite the Scotch, Crouch had gone quite pale. 'Why?'

'Oh I don't think for one moment that Balfour took it upon himself to kill Clegg. Why would he? I mean, if robbery was the motive, I think even a lunatic, having gone to the trouble of murdering the householder, would steal more than a glass. No, my guess is that Clegg liked sharing the tub and a bottle of champagne with his ladyfriends but this particular ladyfriend got Balfour to crash the party and perform that rather horrible deed.'

'This is fucking insane,' she hissed. 'Why the hell would I want to kill Clegg?'

'A very good question and one that had me stumped for a while, I don't mind telling you,' said McGrail imperturbably. 'Then, yesterday, when I was going through the file, I had the two newspaper clippings side by side and it suddenly hit me: Clegg was murdered on the night of Friday the 15th, by which time your ex-husband was dead. Except that as far as everybody knew, he was very much alive and on his way back here because that's what the story in

Friday morning's paper said. The follow-up story saying "as you were, Varty's actually dead," was in Saturday's paper.'

McGrail thrust his hands into his pockets and began to pace up and down. 'Now I can only speculate on what went through your mind when you read that Varty was coming back. Perhaps you had some sort of reconciliation in mind, the two of you and your daughter living happily ever after; perhaps not. Whatever, it all revolved around the cocaine. But first things first: you had to deal with Clegg double-quick because when he and Varty got together to compare notes, Clegg was bound to mention how he'd found out about the ambush and warned you. And at that moment, Varty would've realised that instead of using the information to save his life, you'd used it to try to get the cocaine for yourself and to hell with him. Bang would go any chance of a reconciliation – although I suspect that would've been purely tactical. Bang would go any chance of getting your hands on the drugs or sharing in the proceeds. So Clive Balfour, the faithful footsoldier, received another call to arms.'

McGrail stopped pacing; his eyes gleamed with sardonic humour. 'It must've well and truly put you off your Cornflakes, reading next morning that Varty was dead after all.'

There were beads of sweat on Rayleen Crouch's forehead and upper lip although her face was white and pinched. She about-turned, stalked down the corridor and held the front door open. As the two policemen walked to the door, Ihaka said, 'What about those notebooks from Balfour's cellar, sir? You had a look at them yet?'

'Just a glance,' said McGrail. 'They look like diaries to me. They'll take some deciphering, mind you – his writing's pretty well unreadable. We'll get there though; that's what we have handwriting experts for.' He paused at the door and stared impassively down at Crouch. 'Till next time then,' he said quietly. 'Somebody will be in touch about the fingerprints.'

Ihaka drove. As they cut across Ponsonby Road, he said: 'I'm glad to see someone's been using their head while I've been out there risking life and limb.'

McGrail nodded and tried to think of the last time he'd heard Ihaka pay anyone a compliment. He couldn't.

'We'll be pushing it uphill to nail the bitch, won't we?'

McGrail stared out the car window. 'We haven't got a prayer,' he said, 'which is a sobering thought because that's an evil little woman back there. I was in with the Crown prosecutor this morning. His advice, in a nutshell, was that we needed Balfour alive and sane to have a case. Whatever's in those notebooks, the fact of the matter, as Ms Crouch so bluntly observed, is that he was mad; madmen who kill have a long history of saying the devil made me do it. Hopefully we've put the wind up her a bit; she might do something silly, although I can't say I'm overly optimistic. Will you arrange surveillance?'

'Sure. What about if her print's on that glass?'

'If we had a compos mentis and co-operative Balfour, it would make first-rate circumstantial evidence. But the truth is there aren't any prints. It was a bluff. I wanted to be sure that I'd got it right about Clegg; I had, too – for a few seconds there, it was written all over her face.' McGrail sighed ruefully. 'Brother Balfour was tidy to a fault: all the lab technician found on the glass was a very faint residue of dishwashing liquid; his exact words were' – the Ulsterman put on a passable Kiwi-bloke accent – '"Tell you what, sir, I wish my missus got our glasses to sparkle like that."'

Neither spoke again until they were in the lift at Auckland Central police station.

'One thing I can't work out,' said Ihaka.

'What's that?'

'Why didn't Balfour let Grills bump Varty like she told him to?'

'Yes, I wondered about that,' said McGrail. 'I concluded that when it came to the crunch, Balfour couldn't simply stand back and let it happen. He wasn't a killer, not a cold-blooded one anyway. Now you're going to say, "What about Clegg?" I think Clegg was killed in hot blood. I'm sure Crouch and Balfour had a relationship – that's how she manipulated him. I think she knew he'd go berserk when he saw her in the bubble bath with Clegg. He wasn't wearing a swimsuit at the time and I suspect neither was she.'

Ihaka nodded slowly. 'That woman's wasted in social work,' he said.

Epilogue

A week and a half later Rayleen Crouch skipped the country. Accompanied by her daughter Electra and travelling on a one-way ticket, she flew out on an Air New Zealand 747 bound for London. She gave her employer, the Department of Social Welfare, a couple of days' notice and most of her friends and acquaintances none at all. She'd simply held a garage sale and given away what she couldn't sell, listed her house with a real estate agent, packed a couple of suitcases and gone. It was all done discreetly rather than surreptitiously and the police had soon realised what she was up to. They maintained surveillance right to the aircraft door but didn't try to stop her.

On Monday, 4 July, depositions hearings in the case of the Crown versus Bryce Spurdle began in the Auckland District Court. Spurdle had earlier entered a plea of not guilty to the charge of possession of cocaine for the purposes of supply and been remanded in custody without bail. The prosecution's star witness was Duane Ricketts, who was described as an undercover policeman. Giving evidence from behind an opaque screen, Ricketts told the court of an elaborate undercover operation designed to intercept a major consignment of cocaine before it reached the market. It had involved him going to Thailand and getting thrown into the Bombat Drug Rehabilitation Centre on a minor drugs charge. Once in jail he'd set about gaining the confidence of Dale Varty, a former member of the Mr Asia syndicate whose prison term was almost up; the police were certain that Varty would come straight back to New Zealand and put the ten kilos of cocaine he'd brought over from Australia in 1983 into circulation. When Varty was killed shortly before his release, Ricketts had returned to New Zealand to locate the cocaine, using the information he'd managed to glean from him. A sting operation was then mounted against Spurdle, Varty's original accomplice, which culminated in his arrest after he'd bought the drugs for $100,000.

When Ricketts mentioned this figure, the defendant Spurdle exclaimed loudly and incoherently and clutched at his chest prompting the magistrate to call a 15-minute halt to proceedings to enable him to regain his composure. A reporter trying to eavesdrop on the intense discussion between the defendant and his barrister outside the courtroom thought she heard the lawyer ask, 'What about the IRD?' For a moment she wondered what the Inland Revenue Department had to do with the price of fish, then she observed the instant tranquillising effect the question had on Spurdle and decided she must've misheard.

The media were getting quite excited over the prospect of Spurdle's trial, mainly because his legal team kept dropping off-the-record hints that they'd produce evidence which would be deeply embarrassing, not only for the police but also the government. The announcement at the commencement of the second day of depositions that Spurdle had changed his plea to guilty thus came as both a shock and a let-down. Ten days later Spurdle appeared in the High Court for sentencing and was given an eight-year jail term. The judge told the court that the period of imprisonment was half that which he'd normally impose for such a serious crime but he was mindful of Spurdle's co-operation with the authorities, co-operation which would significantly assist them in their efforts to combat the pernicious blight of narcotics. He did not specify what form the co-operation had taken.

That evening Jody Spurdle appeared on 'The Holmes Show'. She vowed to stand by her husband and to be there for him when he got out of jail; with parole, that was likely to be four or five years hence. She denied suggestions of a cover-up or that her husband had been pressured into changing his plea by people in high places. Most people who watched the interview found her deeply unconvincing, especially on the point of where she planned to be when the prison gates swung open and her 60-something husband walked free.

*

At 5.35 on the mild late-winter afternoon of Friday, 7 September, Duane Ricketts parked his Toyota Corolla outside his recently acquired Grey Lynn villa. Detective Sergeant Tito Ihaka, who was sitting on the steps leading up to the veranda and front door, said, 'About bloody time' and got to his feet. They went inside. Ricketts gave Ihaka a beer and a quick tour of his new house.

'Very nice,' said Ihaka when they were sitting down in the living room. 'How much?'

'Three hundred and ten.'

Ihaka whistled. 'Not that fucking nice, but what the hell? It's not as if it's your money.' He raised his bottle. 'To Bryce Spurdle, without whose generosity you'd still be in that dump in Mt Roskill.'

Ricketts toasted. 'Bryce, a true philanthropist.'

'What've been you up to?' asked Ihaka.

'Same old stuff. I've just been into Trubshaw Trimble to see one of the partners, the guy McGrail recommended me to. He reckons they'd have a couple of jobs a month for me. He's even talking about a retainer.'

'McGrail might regret that. He asked me the other day if I thought you'd be interested in coming back.'

'That yarn of mine put ideas in his head?'

'Must've. I told him you weren't suitable because you made it up as you went along; you can imagine what he said to that. Oh, I almost forgot.' Ihaka pulled a postcard out of the back pocket of his jeans. 'Your mail. It's from your little partner-in-crime.'

Ricketts rolled his eyes. 'Why don't you just give me the highlights? Save me the trouble of reading it.'

Ihaka flicked the card over to him. 'I had to occupy myself somehow. Highlights? I'd probably go for Mother Crouch getting her hooks into some rich old fart.' He shook his head. 'What an operator. Did I ever tell you McGrail reckoned she was blocking Balfour?'

'The nutter? You believe that?'

'McGrail's the biggest fucking prude I know but he can sniff a filthy secret at a hundred paces; if he says they were grunting, that's good enough for me.'

'Did she get a mention in his notebooks?'

'Christ knows. It was hard-core gibberish. The handwriting bloke said it was like a cross between *The Perfumed Garden* and *Cattle Breeders' Monthly*. He gave up on them in the end.'

While Ihaka went to the kitchen to get more beer, Ricketts read the postcard which had been redirected from his previous address. It said:

Ricketts,

Is this a shock to the system or what? You wondered why the swift exit, right? When I told Mum about the share of the you-know-what (you never know who reads your postcards) she said we're outa here, let's see the world. A case of all cashed up and no reason to stay I guess. Anyway, it's worked out really well – had some fab times travelling and London is excellent. I'm in a seriously cool band – when I told them about The Homo Dwarves, they adopted the name. Rayleen's a new woman partly because she's got a new man. He's a tad (!) older and loaded – I'm starting to see the attraction. The bottom line (as he always says) is I don't see us coming back for a while. Hope everything is OK and you had big fun spending your share.

XX

PS I'm even getting into Van M! What do you say we meet on the river of time one day?

Ihaka returned with the beers. 'What's this river of time crap?'

'It's from a Van Morrison song.'

'What's it mean?'

'It doesn't mean anything.'

'Bullfuck. She sent you a postcard – that means something for a start.'

'It means she's in London and I'm in Auckland. We're what's known as inseparable.'

After a pause Ihaka said: 'Maybe we should've told her about her old lady.'

'What's this "we", brown boy? You want to play God, go ahead but leave me out of it. On the subject of absent friends, what about pistol-packing Annie, whatever her name is?'

'C.C. Hellicar?' Ihaka thought about it for a while. 'Put it this way, I won't forget her in a hurry.'

Ricketts sat up straight 'Really? Exactly what did you crazy kids get up to?'

'We went up to the beach house and went fishing. Then we danced on the deck.'

'Get down, you dancing fool!' whooped Ricketts. Then, in a hushed, dramatic voice: 'I suppose one thing led to another, to sweet nothings whispered in the moonlight before …'

'Ricketts, shut your hole,' said Ihaka almost distractedly. 'One thing led to fuck-all. We'd just started dancing when McGrail rang to say they'd found the stiffs, the coke had been swiped by a couple of phoney cops and would I kindly get my black arse back to Auckland.' He looked bleakly at Ricketts. 'I don't think I ever got around to thanking you for that.'

There was a very long silence. A subdued Ricketts said, 'So I stuffed up what was going to be a night to remember?'

Ihaka shrugged. 'Who knows? Doesn't matter anyway. I danced with C.C. Hellicar. I saw the look on her face when the phone rang. I'll settle for that.'

There was another long silence. 'You really mean that?' asked Ricketts, surprised but respectful.

Ihaka threw him a pitying look. 'Course I fucking don't,' he said. 'What do you take me for?' His expression changed to his trademark sly, cocksure, ruthless grin. 'Anyway, enough of that shit. What's for tea?'

Just before the grin faded, Ricketts thought he saw a shadow descend on the brazen glitter in Ihaka's eyes. *Maybe he did mean it after all*, thought Ricketts. *Then again, maybe he's just hungry.*

The End